Elizabeth Armstrong Reed

Persian literature

Ancient and modern

Elizabeth Armstrong Reed

Persian literature
Ancient and modern

ISBN/EAN: 9783337203597

Printed in Europe, USA, Canada, Australia, Japan

Cover: Foto ©Andreas Hilbeck / pixelio.de

More available books at **www.hansebooks.com**

PERSIAN LITERATURE

ANCIENT AND MODERN

BY

ELIZABETH A. REED

MEMBER OF THE PHILOSOPHICAL SOCIETY OF GREAT BRITAIN
MEMBER OF THE INTERNATIONAL CONGRESS OF ORIENTALISTS
AUTHOR OF HINDU LITERATURE, ETC.

CHICAGO
S. C. GRIGGS AND COMPANY
1893

The Lakeside Press

R. R. DONNELLEY & SONS CO., CHICAGO

TABLE OF CONTENTS.

PERSIAN LITERATURE, ANCIENT AND MODERN.

DIVISION I.—EARLY TABLETS AND MYTHOLOGY.

CHAPTER I.

HISTORIC OUTLINE.

ORIGIN OF PERSIAN LITERATURE—ACCAD AND
SUMER—LITERATURE OF NINEVEH—BABY-
LON—ÌRÀN OR PERSIA—PHYSICAL FEA-
TURES—PERSIAN ART—MANUSCRIPTS—
EARLY LITERATURE—THE ARABIAN CON-
QUEST—LITERATURE OF MODERN PERSIA—
PERSIAN ROMANCE   1

CHAPTER II.

THE CUNEIFORM INSCRIPTIONS.

EARLY LITERATURE—HISTORIC TABLETS—THE
INSCRIPTIONS OF NEBUCHADNEZZAR—THE
FALL OF BABYLON—CYRUS, THE ACHÆME-
NIAN—BEHISTUN INSCRIPTIONS—DARIUS AT
PERSEPOLIS—INSCRIPTIONS OF XERXES—

ARTAXERXES — A LATER PERSIAN TABLET —
RÉSUMÉ   30

CHAPTER III.

THE POETRY AND MYTHOLOGY OF THE TABLETS.

PRIMITIVE MYTHOLOGY — ANŪ — SEVEN EVIL
SPIRITS — ACCADIAN POEM — ASSUR — HEA —
NIN-CI-GAL — SIN, THE MOON GOD — HEA-
BANI — NERGAL — MERODACH — NEBO — NINIP
— CHEMOSH — INCANTATIONS TO FIRE AND
WATER — IM — BAAL — TAMMUZ — ISHTAR — ISH-
TAR OF ARBELA — ISHTAR OF ERECH —
LEGEND OF ISHTAR AND IZDŪBAR — ISHTAR,
QUEEN OF LOVE AND BEAUTY — THE DESCENT
OF ISHTAR   53

CHAPTER IV.

PERSIAN MYTHOLOGY.

THE COMMON SOURCE OF MYTHOLOGY —
MYTHICAL MOUNTAINS — RIVERS — MYTHICAL
BIRDS — AHŪRA MAZDA — ATAR — THE STORM
GOD — YIMA — THE CHINVAT BRIDGE — MITHRA
— RÉSUMÉ   86

Division II.—Period of the Zend-Avesta.

CHAPTER V.

THE ZEND-AVESTA.

DERIVATION AND LANGUAGE — DIVISIONS — AGE
OF THE ZEND-AVESTA — MANUSCRIPTS — ZAR-

ATHUŚTRA—THE EARLY PARSĪS—THE MOD-
ERN PĀRSĪS 109

CHAPTER VI.

THE TEACHINGS OF THE ZEND-AVESTA.

THE GĀTHAS—THE WAIL OF THE KINE—THE
LAST GĀTHA — THE MARRIAGE SONG — THE
YASNA—COMMENTARY ON THE FORMULAS—
THE YASNA HAPTANG-HĀITI—THE SRAŌSHA
YAŚT—THE YASNA CONCLUDING . . . 127

CHAPTER VII.

TEACHINGS OF THE ZEND-AVESTA, CONCLUDED.

THE VENDĪDAD — FARGARD II — THE VARA OF
YIMA — THE LAWS OF PURIFICATION — DIS-
POSITION OF THE DEAD — PUNISHMENTS —
THE PLACE OF REWARD—THE VISPARAD—
TEACHING OF THE MODERN PĀRSĪS . . 146

DIVISION III.—THE TIME OF THE MOHAMMEDAN CONQUEST AND THE KORĀN.

CHAPTER VIII.

THE KORĀN.

THE SUCCESSOR OF THE ZEND-AVESTA—AUTHOR
OF THE KORĀN — FIRST REVELATIONS — THE
HIGRAH—CONTINUED WARFARE—DEATH OF
MOHAMMED — RECENSION OF THE TEXT —
TEACHING OF THE KORĀN — HEAVEN —

HELL — PREDESTINATION — POLYGAMY — LIT-
ERARY STYLE OF THE KORĀN . . 165

Division IV.—The Period Succeeding the Mohammedan Conquest.

CHAPTER IX.

THE ANWĀR-I-SUHALI.

HISTORY OF THE WORK—PREFACE—THE BEES
AND THEIR HABITS — THE TWO PIGEONS —
THE BLIND MAN AND HIS WHIP—AMICABLE
INSTRUCTION—THE PIGEONS AND THE RAT
—THE ANTELOPE AND THE CROW — THE
ELEPHANT AND THE JACKAL — GEMS FROM
THE HITOPADEŚA 189

CHAPTER X.

PERSIAN POETRY.

SEVEN ERAS—THE FIRST PERIOD—THE HOMER
OF ĪRĀN—THE SHĀH NĀMAH—HISTORY OF
THE PERSIAN EPIC—FIRDUSĪ—INVECTIVE—
MŪTESHIM — THE SHĀH'S REPENTANCE—
DEATH OF FIRDUSĪ—THE POEM . . . 214

CHAPTER XI.

STORY OF THE SHĀH NĀMAH.

SĀM SUWĀR — THE SĪMŪRGH'S NEST — THE
FATHER'S DREAM — RŪDABEH — THE MAR-
RIAGE—RUSTEM—THE TŪRĀNIAN INVASION
—THE WHITE DEMON 228

CHAPTER XII.

THE HEFT-KHĀN, OR SEVEN LABORS OF RUSTEM.

A LION SLAIN BY RAKUSH—ESCAPE FROM THE DESERT—THE DRAGON SLAIN—THE EN-CHANTRESS—CAPTURE OF AULĀD—VICTORY OVER DEMONS—SEVENTH LABOR, THE WHITE DEMON SLAIN—THE MARRIAGE OF RUSTEM—SOHRĀB 252

CHAPTER XIII.

ISFENDIYĀR.

THE HEFT-KHĀN OF ISFENDIYĀR—THE BRAZEN FORTRESS—THE CONFLICT WITH RUSTEM—THE FALL OF THE WARRIORS . . . 272

CHAPTER XIV.

SECOND PERIOD.

ANWĀRI—NIZĀMĪ—LAILĪ AND MAJNŪN—A FRIEND—THE WEDDING—DELIVERANCE—THE MEETING IN THE DESERT—DEATH OF THE LOVERS—VISION OF ZYD . . . 284

CHAPTER XV.

THIRD PERIOD.

GENGHIS KHĀN—JALAL-UDDIN RŪMI—SĀ'DĪ—WORKS OF SĀ'DĪ—THE BŪSTĀN—THE PEARL—KINDNESS TO THE UNWORTHY—SILENCE, THE SAFETY OF IGNORANCE—DARIUS AND HIS HORSE-KEEPER—STORIES FROM THE

GULISTÁN—THE WISE WRESTLER—DANGERS
OF PROSPERITY—BORES   309

CHAPTER XVI.

LATER PERIODS.

THE FOURTH PERIOD—LITERARY KINGS—HÁFIZ
PÍR-I-SEBZ—SHIRÁZ—THE FEAST OF SPRING
— MY BIRD — FIFTH PERIOD — JÁMI — THE
WORKS OF JÁMI — RECEPTION — THE SIXTH
PERIOD — THE SEVENTH PERIOD   .   .   321

CHAPTER XVII.

MEHER AND MŪSHTERI.

PERSIAN ROMANCE—THE TWO COMRADES—THE
SEPARATION—THE QUEEN—THE DEPARTURE
—THE ANNOUNCEMENT   338

CHAPTER XVIII.

MEHER AND MŪSHTERI—CONTINUED.

THE EXILES—THE DESERT—A SHIPWRECK—THE
RESCUE—THE CAPTURE   351

CHAPTER XIX.

MEHER AND MŪSHTERI—CONTINUED.

THE FUGITIVES — ROYAL INTERVIEWS — THE
CONFLICT—A GARDEN SCENE—AFTERWARDS
—THE DECISION   365

CHAPTER XX.

MEHER AND MŪSHTERI—CONTINUED.

THE CAPTIVES—ARREST AND TRIAL—ROYAL
FAVOR—THE SENTENCE 383

CHAPTER XXI.

MEHER AND MŪSHTERI—CONCLUDED.

THE WEDDING — A COUNCIL — ROYAL CAVAL-
CADE—THE MESSENGER—RECEPTION . . 392

CHAPTER XXII.

CONCLUSION.

SUMMARY—PRIESTLY RULE—RUSSIAN OPPRES-
SION 403

PREFACE.

THERE is a growing interest in the literatures of the Orient, but the difficulties in this field of investigation have been so great that few students have taken time to recover the gems from the worthless matter surrounding them. The author of the present volume, however, has chosen to devote years of persistent effort to the work of collecting and condensing the historic facts pertaining to this subject, and giving them to the public, together with the finest thoughts to be found upon the pages of these early manuscripts.

No labor has been spared to attain accuracy of statement, no difficulties have been ignored in these years of research, and the results, so far as completed, are now before the reader in two volumes: the one recently published on Hindū Literature, and the present work on Persian Literature.

Although this book was partially written long before the publication of its predecessor, still it might never have been completed, but for the kindly reception which a generous public gave to the preceding volume.

Cordial thanks are due to the American press, which not only gave to "Hindū Literature" hundreds of favorable notices, but in many instances devoted whole columns to able reviews of the work.

It is also a rare pleasure to acknowledge the courtesies of the British press, and especially the great kindness of leading European scholars, who have sent words of warm approval and congratulation to the author.

In the present volume the subject has been simplified as far as possible, by arranging the work in four chronological divisions; the epoch of Persian poetry being again divided into seven distinct periods, corresponding to the times of the leading poets, who have been called "The Persian Pleiades."

Not only does their literature present seven leading poets, but this number appears to have a peculiar charm for the Persian literati, and hence we find in this field of Eastern fable, the "Seven Evil Spirits" of Anū, the "Seven Labors of Rustem," the "Seven Great Feats of Isfendiyār," "The Seven Fair Faces" of Nizāmī, the "Seven Thrones" of Jāmi, and various other combinations of the same number.

In this as well as previous works, the author wishes to acknowledge the great value of the Chicago Public Library, where a wealth of Oriental lore is ever at the service of the student; here are valuable works which bear on the history and literature of the Sanskrit, Hebrew, Chaldaic, Persian, Arabic and other Asiatic tongues, besides many volumes in the modern languages.

Among the literati of Europe the author is indebted to such men as Prof. A. H. Sayce, Sir M. Monier-Williams, W. St. Chad Boscawen, Prof. F. Max Müller, Dr. Haug, Dr. L. H. Mills, and Ernest A. Budge; also Profs. Darmesteter, Eastwick, Atkinson, Davie and Owsley, the credits being given where the quotations are made.

Grateful acknowledgement is especially made to Prof. A. H. Sayce, of the Oxford University; to Sir M. Monier-Williams, and to Mr. Theo. G. Pinches, of the British Museum, each of these distinguished scholars having examined portions of the manuscript and affixed their valuable notes thereunto.

Cordial thanks are also due to Dr. R. Rost, of the India Office in London, who laid before the artist all the illuminated Persian manuscripts in that vast collection of Eastern lore, and to the honorable Council of the India Office, who placed these rare literary treasures at the author's service without the customary precaution of taking a bond therefor. The frontispiece is a section of the illuminated title-page of a Persian manuscript of priceless value. This is a copy of the Shâh Nâmah, which is a large folio, the pages being beautifully written in four columns. Each page is illuminated with delicate paintings, which are a triumph of art. This old manuscript, which is now invaluable, was purchased for the India House Collection at the celebrated Hastings sale about twenty-five years since. Our illustration gives only a portion of the page, and thus the full size of the figure has been

FAC SIMILE OF A PORTION OF A PAGE OF THE OLDEST ZEND MANUSCRIPT.
(See Page 117.)

PERSIAN LITERATURE.

DIVISION I.

The Early Tablets and Mythology.

CHAPTER I.

HISTORIC OUTLINE.

ORIGIN OF PERSIAN LITERATURE — ACCAD AND SUMER — LITERATURE OF NINEVEH — BABYLON — ÎRÂN OR PERSIA — PHYSICAL FEATURES — PERSIAN ART — MANUSCRIPTS — EARLY LITERATURE — THE ARABIAN CONQUEST — LITERATURE OF MODERN PERSIA — PERSIAN ROMANCE.

EVERY nation has a literature peculiarly her own, even though it may find its sources in foreign fields. As Persia was founded upon the ruins of more ancient monarchies, as she gathered into the halls of her kings the spoils of conquered nations, so also her literature was enriched by the philosophy and science, the poetry and mythology of her predecessors. The resistless horde, which poured down from the mountains and swept all of Western Asia into its current, formed the

1

kindred tribes into a single monarchy, and this monarchy gathered unto herself, not only the wealth and military glory, but also the culture and learning of the nations she had conquered. The whole civilized world was taxed to maintain the splendors of her court; the imperial purple was found in the city of Tyre, and her fleets also came from Phœnicia, for the experience of this maritime people was indispensable to their Persian masters. Indian groves furnished the costly woods of aloe and of sandal that burned upon her altars, while Syria and the islands of the sea filled her flagons with wine.

The richest fruits were brought from the sunny shores of Malay, and even the desert sent tributes of incense and gold. Herds of camels came from Yemen, and horses of the finest Arabian blood were found in the royal stables. What wonder, then, that the nation which rifled continents to supply her magnificence should appropriate also the wealth of the world of letters that came under her sway? In the background of Persian power there lies an historic past which is replete with the literary treasures of the Orient.

ACCAD AND SUMER.

There is the far away land of ancient Babylonia, with her territory divided into Accad[1] and Sumer or Shinar. These were the northern and southern divisions of the country.

According to Prof. Sayce, "the whole of Babylonia was originally inhabited by a non-Semitic race, but the

---

[1] Accad is first mentioned as one of the beginnings of the kingdom of Nimrod in Genesis x, 10.

Semites established their power in Accad, or North Babylouia, at an earlier date than they did in Sumer in the south; the non-Semitic dynasties and culture lingered longer therefore in Sumer." [1]

Their land was the home of the palm tree, and from the highlands, where their rivers found their source, down to the shores of the Persian Gulf, it presented a wealth of foliage and blossoms. Fields that were covered with ripening grain awaited the sickle of the reaper, while the fruit trees bent beneath their burdens, and the vines gleamed in the sunlight with clusters of gold and purple.

Although we know little of this primitive people, a few of their imperishable records have come down to us, and light is thus thrown upon the literary culture which prevailed from the Euphrates to the Nile long before the Exodus. We have the inscriptions [2] of Dungi, the king of "Ur of the Chaldees," and also "king of Sumer and Accad." We have, too, a portion of the clay tablets recounting the glory of Sargon I, who carried his conquests into the land of the Elamites, and even subdued the Hittites in northern Syria. The independent states of Babylonia also were brought under his sway, and he claimed to be "the sovereign of the four regions of the world," while his Accadian subjects gave him the name of "the king of justice and the deviser of prosperity." He was the patron of letters, and in the library [3] of this old Semitic king, in the city of

[1] Mr. Theo. G. Pinches, in his notes on this chapter, says: "The Sumerians are generally regarded as of the same race as of the Accadians. Sumerian is a dialect of Akkadian. Sumer and Akkad both contained Semitic and non-Semitic inhabitants."

[2] Decouvertes en Chaldee par E. de Sarzec, Plate No. 29.

[3] The catalogue of the astronomical works in the library of Sargon I

Accad, there was written on pages of clay a work on astronomy and astrology in seventy-two books.

Long before the poets of India, of Greece or of Persia began to weave their gorgeous web of mythology, the seers of Accad and of Shinar watched beside the great loom of Nature, as she wove out the curtains of the morning and the crimson draperies of the setting sun. They listened to the battle of the elements around their mountain peaks, and dreamt of the storm-king; they heard the musical murmurs of the wind, as it whispered to the closing flowers; they felt the benediction of the night, with its voices of peace, and the divine poem of earth's beauty found an echo in their hearts.

The bloom of Accadian poetry may be placed about four thousand years before our own times, when the primeval teachings of Nature had become the theme of the poet, and been voiced in the measures of song.

But the scientific impulse of ancient Accad remained an impulse only, the methods of science were undiscovered, and the student was led astray by his own fancies and misconceptions; still amidst all the false science of a primitive Chaldea there were germs of truth, which have been developed even in our own times. The classic writers said truly that Babylonia was the birthplace of astronomy. It was also the birthplace of mathematics; and although their figures were simple, the Chaldeans attained quite a proficiency in their calculations. The library at Larsa or Senkereh was famous

instructs the reader to write down the number of the book that he needs, and the librarian will thereupon give him the tablet required.—*Sayce, Bab. Lit., p. 9.*

for its mathematical works, and it formed a nucleus for students from various portions the country.

LITERATURE OF NINEVEH.

On the banks of the Tigris, a great city lifted her battlements and arches towards the skies, and became the home of Assyrian Kings. According to Diodorus[1] her walls were an hundred feet high, and so broad that four chariots could be driven abreast upon them, while fifteen hundred towers, apparently impregnable, arose from their massive foundations. Nineveh was the home of imperial splendor, and twenty-two kings were taxed to supply the materials for her costly palaces where the finest sculptures of the East were found. Assyrian art covered her angles with graceful curves, and built her temples with their gilded domes, while the interior walls were adorned with sculptured slabs of white alabaster. The germs of Greek art, as well as Greek mythology, were found in the valleys of the Tigris and the Euphrates, for here were Doric and Ionic columns; here were Corinthian capitals, with architrave, frieze and cornice, and yet the latest of these must have been carved before the earliest date which has been assigned to any work of Grecian art. Though her culture was confined to certain classes, and the great mass of her population could not discern between their right hands and their left, still, for centuries Nineveh[2] was the

[1] Diodorus, Sec. 23.

[2] The word Nineveh is made up of signs which mean city, couch and Nana respectively, all of which means the resting place of the chief god, Nana. (E. A. Budge.) The great commerce of Nineveh—the fact that her merchants were greatly "multiplied"—is illustrated by the large collection of contract tablets in the British Museum.

mistress of the East, even Babylon being subject to her power.

She reached the zenith of her glory under the rule of Assur-bani-pal (the Sardanapalus of the Greeks). He was the grand monarch of Assyria, and under his reign the treasures of the world flowed to this common centre, while the name of Nineveh was feared from the frontiers of India to the shores of the Ægean sea. Ambitious in his schemes of conquest, and luxurious in the splendors of his court, he nevertheless confided his military movements largely to the hands of his ablest generals, and devoted much attention to the accumulation of his strange library at the capital city. Here he gathered the literary treasures of the Orient, and scribes were kept busy copying and translating early works, or writing original books, either in the Assyrian or the Accadian tongue. The decaying literature of Babylonia was forwarded to Nineveh, where it was copied and edited by the Assyrians. A new text was the most valuable present that any city could send to this literary king, and it was received with the enthusiasm exhibited by a modern scholar on the reception of a rare manuscript. It is to the library of Assur-bani-pal, that we are indebted for much of our knowledge of Babylonian literature—stored away in those curious vaults, were thousands of books written upon pages of clay. There were historical and mythological works, legal records, geographical and astronomical documents, as well as poetical productions. There were lists of stones and trees, of birds and beasts, besides the official copies of treaties, petitions to the king, and the royal proclamations. Strangers came from the court of Egypt, from Lydia, and from Cyprus to this ancient seat of learning. But while the king was absorbed in his favorite pursuits, the spirit of revolution was abroad in the land,—Elam, Babylonia, Arabia, Palestine, Egypt and Lydia made a common cause against the reigning monarch, the insurrection being led by the king's own brother, the viceroy of Babylon. This great revolt shook the very foundations of the Assyrian monarchy, and ushered in the decline of an empire which extended from the borders of India to the Nubian mountains, and from the sands of Arabia to the snowy peaks of the Caucasus.

In a few years even Nineveh was captured and utterly destroyed, while her empire was shared between Media and Babylon.

BABYLON.

This was " the golden city " that gathered unto herself the wealth of conquered kingdoms and the dominion of many tribes. The multitude of gods in her pantheon represented the ideals of the various races of men who laid their offerings at her feet.

Babylon was the "hammer of the whole earth," and she forced the tributes of the nations into her treasury, and their legions into her armies. She was "the glory of kingdoms," and she gathered the culture of a thousand years into a great historic result that contained the arts and science, the literature, the wealth, and the commerce of half the world. The culmination of her power was in the days of Nebuchadnezzar, who was the Augustus of the Babylonian age.

He reconstructed the fallen temples of her idols and carried the hideous images in triumphal processions to their palatial courts.

Gold, silver and precious stones made bright the altars and temples of Baal, of Merodach, of Nebo, of Molech, and of Ashtaroth.

The choicest cedars were brought from the mountains of Lebanon. "The cedar of the roofing of the walls of Nebo, with gold I overlaid. . . . Strong bulls of copper, and dreadful serpents standing upright on their thresholds I erected. The cell of the lord of the gods—Merodach, I made to glisten like suns the walls thereof, with large gold like rubble stone. . . . I had them made brilliant as the sun." Nebuchadnezzar was the undisputed master of Western Asia, and the walls of his palace were hung with historic pictures of Chaldean thrones, and draped with the most gorgeous tapestries of the Eastern looms, while in his princely halls the cool air fell from glittering fountains, and the royal abode was filled with music, light, and costly perfume. He built the wondrous hanging gardens, where the almond trees waved their sprays of silvery blossoms, and the palms tossed their plumes in the sunlight,—there the pink fingers of the dawn opened the hearts of the roses, and white lilies nestled amid the green slopes and fragrant shades, while the breezes came up from the great river laden with the breath of lotus blossoms and the soft music of her waves. This haughty king was also the patron of letters, and his inscriptions throw a vivid light upon his pride of power, and magnificence—his constant devotion to his idols, and his never ceasing admiration of his capital city,—"this great Babylon which I have built." His books were written largely upon stone, and stored away beyond the reach of conquering kings.

The literary treasures, which may even yet lie buried beneath her soil, probably belong to the Babylon of Nebuchadnezzar, and owe their existence to him. In his days, too, there flourished the family of Egebi, who were tradesmen. This Jewish family is mentioned as early as the reign of Esar-haddon, and for five successive generations they deposited their legal documents in earthen jars which served the purpose of safes. These thrifty capitalists continued in prosperity even to the end of the reign of Darius the Great, and although coined money was then unknown and the precious metals[1] were reckoned by weight, they, like the Rothschilds of our own day, loaned money to the kings of their generation, and their well kept records are of great value as a chronological index of the times[2] in which they were written. The literature of the Babylonians, like that of the Hindūs, claims a fabulous antiquity. They enumerated ten kings who lived before the flood, whose reigns occupied four hundred and thirty-two thousand years, or more than forty-three centuries each, and during this immense cycle of time, there were strange creatures, half man and half fish, who ascended from the ocean and taught the tribes of Babylonia the rudiments of civilization. There were men with the bodies of birds and the tails of fishes,

[1] The problem of the relative value of gold and silver had been solved to a certain extent in this ancient kingdom, a silver shekel being one-tenth the value of a gold shekel, and the silver half shekel one twentieth of the value of the gold shekel. The drachma, or silver half shekel, is supposed to be the most ancient type of the English shilling, as one-twentieth of the English gold sovereign.

[2] For the empire of Nebuchadnezzar, the records of the Egebi family are invaluable—dated deeds extending, year by year, from the reign of Nebuchadnezzar to the close of that of Darius Hystaspes.—*Sayce, An. Emp.*, p. 105.

and men also with the beaks and faces of birds who in other respects wore the form of humanity.

But their literature was not all fable, though they really cared very little what the condition of their country had been before the deluge, for they were engaged in recounting the conquests of their own kings, and the power and splendor of their idols. Babylon, the Queen of the East, with her arts and sciences, with her painting and sculpture, was like other Asiatic cities, a hot-bed of moral corruption; even her religion was a craze of sorcery and enchantments—of witchcraft and horrible sensuality. Her high priests were astrologers and soothsayers, while her gods were the personification of evil. "Moloch demanded the best and dearest that the worshipper could grant him, and the parent was required to offer his eldest or only son as a sacrifice, while the victim's cries were drowned by the noise of drums and flutes. When Agathokles defeated the Carthaginians, the noblest of the citizens offered in expiation three hundred of their children to Baal-Moloch "[1]

The worship of Ishtar[2] demanded that every female devotee should begin her womanhood by public prostitution in the temple of the goddess, and young girls were often burned upon her altars, while young men were either burned or mutilated. Abominations even more revolting than these were practiced in connection with the worship of Bel, and the nations around her drank of her wine and were maddened with the frenzy of her corruption. What wonder, then, that even before the "Lady of Kingdoms" reached the zenith of her

[1] Sayce—An. Emp., p. 195.   [2] Astarte or Ashtaroth.

glory, the cry of the prophets had rung out in un-
measured denunciation of her crimes? "Therefore
I will execute judgment upon the graven images of
Babylon . . . and all her slain shall fall in the
midst of her . . . the treacherous dealeth treacher-
ously, and the spoiler spoileth. Go up, O Elam,
besiege, O Media. . . . Babylon is fallen, is fallen,
and all the graven images of her gods he hath broken
unto the ground."[1]

Elam and Media combined their forces, and set
their troops in battle array, while hundreds of banners
waved in the sunlight. "Elam bare the quiver with
chariots of men and horsemen," and they marched to
the "two leaved gates" of the city. Every sword in
the ranks was true to the young commander, and his
victory was easily won. Babylon was conquered, and
the story of her decay was written upon her forehead.
The seat of government was removed, the city was
left in desolation, and her gates were smitten with
destruction. Ruin fell upon her battlements, the owl
and the bittern dwelt amidst her prostrate columns,
while the wild beasts of the desert made their den in
her fallen palaces.

ĪRĀN OR PERSIA.

Persia is often called Īrān, this being the name which
the Persians themselves gave to their kingdom. Persepolis was for a long time the capital, but for almost
twelve centuries after the fall of that beautiful city,
the capital was located at Shīrāz. The oldest certain
use of the name Persia is found in the prophets,[2] and

---

[1] Jer. li, 47; Isa. xxi, 2-9.   [2] Ezekiel xxvii, 10; xxxviii, 5.

the kingdom was formed by the combination of the Medians with the Persians. These hardy mountaineers were brave and merciless, their troops of horsemen, armed with lance and quiver, swept down from the highlands with irresistible force, and drew the wandering tribes of the East into one great army. Frugal in their mode of life, strong in nerve and sinew, and severe in military discipline, even their kings believed that nothing was so servile as luxury and nothing so royal as toil.

The hardy tribes of Īrān which Cyrus led to victory were trained to manly exercise; they taught their children to endure hardship, to ride, to shoot and to tell the truth. They were strangers to dissipation, and so loyal to age that parricide was inconceivable to them. The royal edict was so inflexible that "the laws of the Medes and Persians" passed into a proverb. Their loyalty to their kings degenerated into servility, even legal injustice being considered a benefit to the victim, for which he should be duly grateful. No edict was too severe to be promptly obeyed, the very cruelty of their kings being considered a mark of greatness; they buried men alive in honor of the elements, they flayed their officials for bribery, while mutilation and stoning were legal punishments.

This hardy race of soldiers, that could rush into battle, almost without rations, was a terror to the pampered Lydian and the luxurious Babylonian, for the ideal life of the Persian was continual conquest, even his symbol of Ormazd being a winged warrior with bow and threatening hand. But when the contest was over, the conquerors irrigated the plains of Babylonia so faithfully that they were able to gather three harvests a year from the fertile soil. The roads of the kingdom were supplied with post-stations, and constantly traversed by government couriers, while a great commercial intercourse was carried even to the shores of Greece. It was not an enervated people that laid the wonderful masonry in the foundations of Persepolis, and reared the marble columns that still mock the changes of more than two thousand years. But luxury crept in with continued power, and after a time, it was said that the royal table was daily spread for fifteen thousand guests, even though the king dined alone. Their nobles were clothed in purple and decorated with jewels, while the person of the king was resplendent with diamonds and rubies. In the royal treasury pearls were piled up like the sands of the sea, and diamonds glittered amidst masses of amethyst and sapphire. The royal helmet and buckler flashed with the green light of emeralds and the crimson fire of the ruby.

But still they retained traces of the primitive simplicity which belonged to the early mountain tribes, and the constructive energy of their kings went on, building and planning, and forcing into their courts the splendors of rifled cities. Darius flung the floating bridge across the Bosphorus, that afterward furnished a highway for Alexander; their summer palaces rose upon the mountains of Media, while their winter homes, with marble pillars and graceful colonnades, were placed in sunny vales where fountains gleamed through the glossy leaves and the nightingale built her nest among thickets of roses. It is said of Artaxerxes that even

while he wore upon his person jewels to the value of
thousands of talents, he would still lead his army on
foot through mountain passes, carrying his own quiver
and shield, and forcing his way up the most rugged
heights.

The Persians were quick to learn, and gladly appropriated to themselves the civilization of Nineveh and
Babylon; but luxury and dissipation will unnerve the
strongest empire, and after a time the designing beauties of the harem became the rulers of weak and wicked
princes, and though Persian magnificence lasted from
Darius to the last Persian king, their final failure was
due to their own corruption as much as to the forces
of Alexander the Great. The Iránian mind seemed to
be the harbinger of progress, in the simplicity of its
beginnings, in its striving for the noble, the manly,
and the true, but the selfishness of the later Persian
kings developed not only into luxury, but also into
dissipation : reclining on couches with golden feet,
drinking the wines[1] of Helbon and Shíráz, they yielded
to no rule except their own pleasure—there was no precept of morality that they could not violate at will, no
law in their legal code that involved the recognition of
the rights of other nations; and this intense self-
worship prepared the way for the coming conqueror.
The government of Persia became what the government
of Turkey now is—a highly centralized bureancracy, the
members of which owed their offices to an irresponsible
despot ; the people of Persia therefore hailed Alexander
as their deliverer from disintegration and decay.

[1] The Persians called wine Zeher-e-kushon, or " delightful poison."

PHYSICAL FEATURES OF PERSIA.

"The Land of the Lion and the Sun," presents the
strongest physical contrasts; with the king of the forest
and the king of day emblazoned upon her banners, she
extended her dominion over rocky steppes and barren
sands, as well as fertile fields and stately forests. Persia
proper was a comparatively small province, but the tide
of conquest gathered many nations beneath her banners,
and the dominion of Cyrus extended from the Mediter-
ranean to the Indus, and from the snowy peaks of the
Caucasus, downward to the shores of the Persian Gulf
and the Arabian Sea. The court of Darius was enriched
by tributes from Egypt and Babylonia, from Assyria
and India, from Media, Lydia, Phœnicia and many
other lands.

Modern Persia occupies the larger portion of the
great Iranian plateau, which rises to the height of
from four to eight thousand feet, between the valleys
of the Indus and the Tigris, and covers more than a
million square miles. On the northwest the Persian
Empire is united to the mountains of Asia Minor by
the high lands of Armenia, while on the northeast the
Paropansius and the Hindū Kush connect it with the
Himālayas of ancient India. The eastern and western
boundaries are traced with more or less uncertainty,
amidst high ranges of mountains broken here and
there by deserts and valleys. The fertile lowlands are
found in the forest-clad regions south of the Caspian
Sea, and down toward the shore of the Persian Gulf.

Although she has of late exercised but little influence in the world's political councils, she retains a
fair position among the Asiatics, and the fact that a

portion of her territory is under Russian influence, while the rest is controlled to a greater or less extent by England, would indicate that in the near future her political position may become one of great importance. She still occupies a territory which is more than twice the area of France, and her climate varies according to the contrasting features of her formation, being rough and cold in the mountain ranges, and often severe on the great table-lands where the sand-storms rage across the desert, while other portions of the empire are luxuriant with tropical foliage.

Down by the shores of the gulf the rice fields lift their dainty plumes, farther away the acres of barley lie like golden billows in the sunlight, and the cots of the peasantry are nestled under groups of flowering trees. Beyond them rises the forest of almost primeval grandeur where the great trunks of the trees are clothed with velvet mosses and encircled with floral vines. Here the green shades of the wood are relieved by the vivid scarlet of the pomegranate blossoms, and streams that leap from snowy hills come dashing through the woodlands, laden with life and rippling with music. Far away in the distance, the barren table-lands arise, and beyond these the mountain ridges press upward, dim and silent against the fields of blue, and the white clouds drop their feathery snows upon peaks which are unsoiled by the foot of man.

PERSIAN ART.

The primitive cradle of art has been found on the banks of the Tigris, and in the valley of the Euphrates.

It has been shown that Greece was largely indebted
to the sculptured slabs and columns of Nineveh for
her first models, and perhaps also to the pictured
walls of Babylon for the inspiration that glowed upon
her canvas. But Asiatic art, like Oriental literature,
is tropical in its luxuriance and gorgeous in its decor-
rations. The classic taste of Greece subdued its more
extravagant features, and presented the simplicity of
chaste designs. The Persians, with their spirit of
monopoly, appropriated the sculptured forms of fallen
Nineveh, and absorbed also the love of painting, and
the passion for gorgeous draperies, which were characteristic of Babylon.

But the Irānian race had not the patience of fine
detail and elaboration which is found in the old
Assyrian sculptures, the military dash of the early
warring tribes showed itself even in their statuary.
The partial stiffness of their outlines was, however,
atoned for in the spirited poise of their figures. They
presented but few pictures of domestic life, but
there were hunting scenes and battle fields, terrific
struggles of their heroes with wild animals, and the
triumphant march of their conquerors—there were
gorgeous processions bearing tributes to the king, and
historic pictures of his victories. Darius the Great
was often represented in simple dress, but always in
the attitude of heroism or tragedy, sometimes grasp-
ing a monster by the horn, while he drives the dagger
into its vitals, and again, with the symbol of Ormazd
hovering in a winged circle above him, he conquers
the king of the forest.

In his Behistun inscriptions he is represented as the

"king of kings," standing with his right foot on the prostrate form of a conquered foe, while nine captive kings stand before him, with their hands in bonds and their heads uncrowned. The wondrous architecture of Persepolis, though laid with massive masonry, was made rich and graceful as that of a Greek temple, for the lofty marble pillars, more than sixty feet in height, were finished with capitals of sculptured animals reposing upon beds of lotus blossoms.

Their helmets and breastplates were often inlaid with silver and enameled with gold, and as the troops marched to the field of battle, the sun flashed upon shields where pictures of Zal and Rustem were inlaid with burnished gold [1] and the designs upon the royal armor were resplendent with rubies and diamonds.

Persian art has been essentially industrial, and it is claimed that what is known as Russia leather was first manufactured in Persia, while legend says, that the artisans achieved their success by carrying their work to the peak of Mount Elvend, where the lightnings imparted a peculiar value to the texture.

The arts of Nineveh, of Babylon, and of Egypt culminated in the ages past, but the rare porcelains, tiles, and mosaics—the vases and carved metals of Persia, are still the pride of Asia. Their carpets, tapestries and brocades are unrivaled in the markets of the world, while the richly embroidered shawls and portiéres of Kermān still present their delicate combinations of palm leaves with the soft coloring of the floral borders.

[1] Scarcely a century has elapsed since the burnished shields and helmets of ancient Persian royalty were laid aside for the lighter military accoutrements of modern Europe.

MANUSCRIPTS.

One of the important features of art is exhibited in their beautiful manuscripts, where the finest calligraphy is often combined with floral designs upon a golden background. The letters of their language run easily and gracefully into each other, and the Egyptian reeds with which they write, are fashioned for the finest touches of the penman.

Calligraphy is called "a golden profession," and a small but exquisite copy of the Korān has been valued at one hundred thousand dollars, while the artistic penman, who executed a copy of a popular poem, had his mouth stuffed with pearls, in addition to the promised reward.

Less fortunate, however, was Mīr Amar, a celebrated calligraphist of the fifteenth century. Being summoned to court to prepare an elaborate copy of the Shāh Nāmah, and his progress being too slow to satisfy the royal ambition, his beautiful manuscript was torn to pieces before his eyes, and Mīr Amar was then hastened to the executioner. Yet such was the extreme beauty of his work, that after the lapse of three hundred years, short screeds from his pen are set in gold and sold at fabulous prices.

Although the printing press is invading the domain of the Persian scribe, the art of calligraphy is still cultivated, and artistic penmen are held in great repute.

EARLY LITERATURE.

It is evident that the early kings of Persia possessed royal libraries, containing historical records and official decrees, for in the book of Ezra[1] it is said that "search was made in the house of rolls," in Babylon, for the imperial decree of Cyrus concerning the rebuilding of the temple. It was afterwards found at Ecbatana "in the palace that is in the province of the Medes," the decree having been made in the first year of King Cyrus. But aside from some of the inscriptions, the earliest literature we now have belonging to this people is the Zend-Avesta, our present version of which was possibly derived from texts which already existed in the time of the Achæmenian kings. Although there are no facts to prove that the text of the Avesta as we now possess it was committed to writing previous to the Sassanian dynasty[2] Prof. Darmesteter thinks it possible that "Herodotus may have heard the Magi sing, in the fifth century before Christ, the very same Gâthas which are sung now a days by the Mobeds of Bombay."[3]

As some of these early texts must have existed before the fifth century B. C. we place them chronologically before the inscriptions of Darius the Great.[4]

Historians claim that ancient Persian manuscripts were destroyed, when Alexander, in a condition of drunkenness, ordered the beautiful city of Persepolis to be set on fire, in order to please the courtesan Thais.

The modern worshippers of Alexander, however, have placed around his name all the possible glory of military achievement with a vast amount of rhetoric, concerning "the young hero" and "the thunder of

[1] Ezra vi, 1. [2] 226 A. D.
[3] Darmesteter, Sa. Bks. of the E., Vol. IV, Int., p. 3.
[4] These appear to have been written upon the face of the Behistun rock about 515 B. C.

his tread." They claim, indeed, that he had very few faults, except cruelty, drunkenness, and some worse forms of dissipation. Their defense of this barbarous act is that "only the palace and its environs were burned" at this particular time, and that this was an act of requital for the pillage of Athens, and also to impress the Persians with a due sense of his own importance. Whatever may have been the motive, or physical condition, of the incendiary, it is highly probable that when the palace, and its environs were burned, the royal libraries went down in the flames, and certain it is, that from the time of the Macedonian conquest to the foundation of the Sassanian dynasty, the history of the Persian language and literature is almost a blank page. The legends of the Sassanian coins, the inscriptions of their emperors, and the translation of the Avesta, by Sassanian scholars, represent another phase of the language and literature of Īrān.

The men who, at the rising of the new national dynasty, became the reformers, teachers, and prophets of Persia, formed their language and the whole train of their ideas upon a Semitic model. The grammar of the Sassanian dialect, however, was Persian, and "this was a period of religious and metaphysical delirium, when everything became everything, when Māyā and Sophia, Mitra and Christ, Virāf and Isaiah, Belus and Kronos were mixed up in one jumbled system of inane speculation, from which at last the East was delivered by the doctrines of Mohammed, and the West by the pure Christianity of the Teutonic nations."[1]

It was five hundred years after Alexander before

[1] Max Müller—Chips, Vol. I, p. 91.

Persian literature and religion were revived, and the books of the Zend-Avesta collected, either from scattered manuscripts or from oral tradition. The first collection of traditions, which finally resulted in the Shāh-Nāmah, was made also during the Sassanian dynasty. Firdusī tells us that there was a Pahlevan, of the family of the Dihkans,[1] who loved to study the traditions of antiquity. He therefore summoned from the provinces, all the old men who could remember portions of the ancient legends, and questioned them concerning the stories of the country. The Dihkan then wrote down the traditions of the kings and the changes in the empire as they had been recited to him. But this work, which was commenced under Nushirvan and finished under Yezdejird, the last of the Sassanians, was destroyed by the command of Omar, the Arabian chieftain.

The scanty literature of the Sassanian age was somewhat augmented by a notable collection of Sanskrit fables which was brought to the court of the Persian king, Koshrou,[2] and translated into the Persian, or Pahlavī tongue. This collection comprised the fables of the Panćatantra and the Hitopadeśa, and from it the later European fables of La Fontaine probably originated.

THE MOHAMMEDAN CONQUEST.

The warring tribes of the desert massed themselves together under the banner of the crescent. They were animated by Mohammed's doctrine of anarchy — the claim of a common right to their neighbors' goods, and trained to dash into the very jaws of death by his

---

[1] The Dihkans were the landed nobility of Persia. They kept up a certain independence, even under the sway of the Mohammedan Khalifs.

[2] About 570 A. D. See Quartremére.

promise of a sensual heaven to every man who fell upon the battle-field.

Therefore these fearless sons of the desert, stimulated by hunger and avarice, swept with irresistible force over the fair provinces around them. They raided the great cities of Central Asia, and gathered to themselves the treasures, which had been hoarded by the Aryan and the Turk. When in the seventh century they saw Persia weakened by internal dissensions and foreign wars, they gladly gathered under the standard of Omar to descend upon the wealth of her cities.

It was an old quarrel that they longed to settle with the Sassanian kings, reaching back through the history of their tribes to the time when they had raided northern Persia, and had been driven back by Ardeshir — they remembered, too, that Shapur had afterward ravaged Arabia to the very gates of Medina, and seized their territory down to the shores of Yemen, on the southern sea. All the force of traditional hatred and revenge was therefore added to their avarice, and lust for power, when these fearless warriors sprang to the saddle and rode to the conquest of Persia. Their terrible war-cry of Allah-il-Allah, rang through rifled cities, and seemed to rise from the very dust which was spurned from the feet of Arabian horses, until Persian nationality was crushed by the invaders. Her treasures of literature were again destroyed, so far as the conquerors could complete their work of devastation, and the altar fires of the Pārsis were quenched in the long night of Mohammedan rule, while the Korān supplanted the Avesta even upon its native soil.

LITERATURE OF MODERN PERSIA.

Modern Persian literature may be said to begin with the reconstruction of the National Epic.[1] This work marks an important era, in even the language of Persia, for it seems to close the biography of that peculiar tongue. There has been but little, of either growth or decay, in its structure since that period, although it becomes more and more encumbered with foreign words.

The Persian Epic could be reconstructed only when the national feeling began to reassert itself, and it was at this period that the patriotism of the people began to recover from the benumbing pressure of Mohammedan rule, and especially in the eastern portions of the empire, a distinctively Persian spirit was revived. It is true that Mohammedanism had taken root even in the national party, but the Arabic tongue was no longer favored by the governors of the eastern provinces. Persian again became the court language of these dignitaries, the native poets were encouraged and began to collect once more the traditions of the empire.

It is claimed that Jacob, the son of Leis,[2] the first prince of Persian blood, who declared himself independent of the Caliphs, procured fragments of the early National Epic, and had it rearranged and continued. Then followed the dynasty of the Samanians who claimed descent from the Sassanian kings, and they pursued the same popular policy. The later dynasty of the Gaznevides also encouraged the growth of the

[1] 1000 A. D.   [2] 870 A. D.

national spirit, and the great Persian Epic was written during the reign of Mahmūd the Great, who was the second king of the Gaznevide dynasty. By his command, collections of old books were made all over the empire, and men who knew the ancient poems were summoned to his court. It was from these materials that Firdusī composed his Shāh-Nāmah. "Traditions," says the poet, "have been given me; nothing of what is worth knowing has been forgotten; all that I shall say others have said before me."

Hence the heroes in the Shāh-Nāmah exhibit many of the traits of the Vedic deities—traits which have lived through the Zoroastrian period, the Achæmenian dynasty, the Macedonian rule, the Parthian wars, and even the Arabian conquest, to be reproduced in the poem of Firdusī.

The modern phase of their literature is emphatically an age of poetry; the Persians of these later centuries seem to have been born with a song on their lips, for their poets are numbered by thousands. Not only their books of polite literature, but their histories, ethics and science, nay, even their mathematics and grammar are written in rhyme. There are many volumes of these productions that cannot be dignified by the name of poetry, but their literature is tropical in its development and their annals bear the names of many illustrious poets. Firdusī, author of the great Epic, must always stand at the head of Persian poetry; but Sā'dī with his Būstān and Gūlistān, will ever be a favorite with his own people.

Nizāmī of the twelfth century has given us, perhaps, the best version of the beautiful Arabian tragedy of Lilī and Majnūn, and Hāfiz says of the author:

"Not all the treasured lore of ancient days
Can boast the sweetness of Nizāmī's lays."

The clear and harmonious style of Hāfiz, who belonged to the fourteenth century, has a fascination of its own, and it is claimed that the prophet Khizer carried to the waiting lips of the poet the water from the fountain of life, and therefore his words are immortal among the sons of men.

Jāmi is entitled to a goodly rank in the world of poetry, even though his Yūsuf and Zulaikhā, which has also been versified by many other Persian poets, seems to have been written for the express purpose of showing how an unprincipled woman may pursue a good man for a series of years, marry him at last, almost against his will, and make him wish himself in heaven the next day. The Persians may well be called the Italians of Asia, for, although they are burdened with sentiment and a certain exuberance of style, which meets with little favor in our colder clime, we accord them our sympathy in the beauty of their dreams and the tenderness of their thought.

PERSIAN ROMANCE.

The Arabic and even the Turkish tongue has intruded upon the classic Persian of Firdusī, but as the English has borrowed from all nations, and yet retains its own individuality, so also the Persian tongue, while absorbing and adapting the wealth of others, still retains its personal character, modified only by the changes of time.

In borrowing from the language of her neighbors,

Persia has not hesitated to adopt also portions of their literature. During the reign of the Moslem kings the choicest mental productions from India, and even from Greece, found the way to their courts. Alp Arslan, around whose throne stood twelve hundred princes, was a lover of letters, and from the banks of the Euphrates to the feet of the Himālayas a wealth of literature was called, to be wrought up by Persian scholars and poets under royal patronage. There was an active rivalry in literary culture, and much of the fire of Arabian poetry brightened the pages of Persian romance. There were the mystic lights and shadows of nomadic life, and desert voices mingled with the strains of native singers.

The terrible contrasts of life and death—the unyielding resentments and jealousies—passionate loves and hates, which are so distinctively Arabian, began to fill the pages of Īrānian romance with tragedy.

Even the vivid description of the Moslems could scarcely add to the gorgeousness of Persian fancy, where Oriental lovers wandered in the greenest of valleys, while around them floated the soft perfume of the orange blossoms. It could not add to the fabulous wealth of their nobles, where camels were burdened with the choicest of gems, and vines of gold were laden with grapes of amethyst. But it did add the element of fierce revenge and the tragedy of violent death, represented by the pitiless simoon and the shifting sand column, the hopeless wastes, the bitter waters, and the dry bones of perished caravans. It added the life-springs of the oasis, as well as the rushing whirlwind; it added the palm tree of the desert, with her feet in

the burning sand and her head in the morning light—
a symbol of the watch-fires of faith above the desert
places of life.   The best literature of Persia in our own
age is largely the reproduction in various forms of her
standard poets; her romances, however, still rival the
Arabian Nights in their startling combinations and
bewildering descriptions.   The imagination of her writers is not bound by the rules of our northern clime,
and there is nothing too wild or improbable to find a
place in Oriental story.   There are rayless caverns of
sorcery in a wilderness of mystery; there are mountains
of emerald[1] and hills of ruby[2]; there are enchanted
valleys, rich with fabulous treasure, and rivers gushing
from fairy fountains.   There is always the grand upris-
ing of the king of day and the endless cycle of the
stars—for this poetic people cannot forget the teaching
of the Pārsī and the Sabean.   In the literature found
on the banks of these southern seas there is also the
restfulness of night, with its coolness and dews, to be
followed by the glory of the morning and the fragrance from the hearts of the roses.

Persian literature rings with voices from ruined
cities, and mingles the story of the past with the
dreams of her future.   Her treasures are drawn from
the records of Chaldean kings; her historic pictures
have caught the light of early crowns and repeated
the story of their magnificence.   Her annals are filled
with the victories of her Cyrus, with the extended

[1] In Persian mythology the earth is surrounded by a mountain range
of pure emerald.

[2] "The Ausindom mountain is that which, being of ruby, of the sub-
stance of the sky, is in the midst of the sea Vouru-Kasha."—*Zend-Avesta*
—*Tir Yast, VI, 32, n.*

dominions of her great Darius, and the gorgeousness of her later sovereigns. Her poets have immortalized her myths as well as her heroes, and the Oriental world has contributed to the pages of her romance.

CHAPTER II.

THE CUNEIFORM INSCRIPTIONS.

EARLY LITERATURE—HISTORIC TABLETS—THE INSCRIPTIONS OF NEBUCHADNEZZAR—THE FALL OF BABYLON —CYRUS, THE ACHÆMENIAN — BEHISTUN INSCRIPTIONS — DARIUS AT PERSEPOLIS — INSCRIPTIONS OF XERXES—ARTAXERXES—A LATER PERSIAN TABLET— RÉSUMÉ.

THE early literature of Persia takes root in ancient soil, and the foundation of her world of letters must be sought for amidst the graven stones of forgotten tribes. The Persian heritage was not only the land of ancient Babylonia, but also the Chaldean and Semitic lore, which lay in the vaults of her kings, or lived upon the marble walls of her ruined palaces.

The story of a great civilization, and the poetry, as well as the prose of human history, were recorded upon the rocks or buried beneath the soil of Mesopotamia. It was even written in gold and alabaster, and placed in the corner-stones of temples that have lain beneath the tread of armies for three thousand years. When the stone is rolled away from the sepulchre of a buried literature, and the records of forgotten ages come with resurrection power into the living present, the heart of man must listen to the voice of these historic witnesses.

One of the greatest triumphs of modern science is the solution of the cuneiform inscriptions of antiquity. To the herculean labors of Grotofend, Bournouf, Lassen, Rawlinson, Layard, Oppert, Rassam, Sayce, Talbot, and others, the world owes a debt it can never pay. Their solution of these obscure alphabets, and the language, grammar and meaning of these old inscriptions rank with the grandest discoveries of modern science. They have not hesitated to devote their lives to the drudgery of cuneiform study, a score of years if necessary, being given to the solution of a single inscription. Without their long, unceasing labor many of the most valuable records of the past must have remained a sealed book. In vain would the spade of the explorer have exhumed the imperial libraries of Sennacherib and Nebuchadnezzar if no light could be thrown upon their strange inscriptions. In vain would the historic tablets of Karnak, or the cylinders of Babylon be brought before the bar of modern criticism, if no key could be found to their problems. It has been necessary to bring to this formidable task an understanding of the Chaldaic, and also of the old Accadian tongue. But even this did not suffice, and it would have been impossible to do more than to decipher a few proper names on the walls of Persian palaces without the aid of other ancient languages. As Lassen remarks: "It seems indeed providential that these inscriptions should be rescued from the dust of centuries at the very time when the discovery of Zend and Sanskrit had enabled Europeans to successfully grapple with their difficulties, for at any other period in the world's history they could only have been a strange combination of wedges[1] or arrow heads, even in the eyes of Oriental scholars." It is difficult to appreciate the long and tedious processes by which these men were compelled to shape their own intellectual tools, and test their own laborious methods; but even to those who have not time to follow their intricate path of research, the result of their labors is indeed marvelous. The accuracy of their work has been sufficiently verified. At the suggestion of the Royal Asiatic Society, four translations of several hundred lines of the inscription of Tiglath-Pileser I. were made independently by Sir Henry Rawlinson, Mr. Fox Talbot, Dr. Hincks and Dr. Oppert, and submitted under seal to the secretary of that society. When opened and compared, it was found that they exhibited a remarkable resemblance to each other, even in the transliteration of proper names, and the rendering of individual passages. This triumphant result abundantly proved the fact that their method was a sound one, and that they were working on a solid basis.

Absolute certainty, of course, is unattainable at present, but the decipherment of these inscriptions has reached a degree of accuracy sufficient for all practical purposes. Scholars, perhaps, will always dispute about the exact meaning of certain words or phrases, as they do in reference to the Hebrew and Greek Scriptures, but in either case it is seldom that any important point turns upon the particular shade of meaning. Still, it is evident that the Orientalists who have un-

---

[1] Cuneiform means "having the form of a wedge," and is especially applied to the wedge-shaped or arrow-headed characters of ancient inscriptions.

dertaken to restore the early chronology of Assyria and Babylonia have a difficult task in hand.

One of the points most surely settled by the deciphering of these inscriptions is, that so far as certain peoples are concerned the world of letters extends much farther back than has generally been supposed.

HISTORIC TABLETS.

There are philological tablets which are apparently designed, in some cases, to give the manner in which the names of Semitic kings were pronounced or written by their Accadian subjects.

An instance of this is found in the name of Sargon of Accad, the ancient hero of the Semitic population of Chaldea, who founded the first Semitic empire in the country and established a great library in his capital city, Accad, near Sippara. The seal of his librarian, which is of beautiful workmanship, is now in Paris, and has been published by M. de Clercq,[1] while a copy of his annals, together with those of his son Naram-Sin, may be found in Western Asia Inscriptions.[2]

Among these early records we also find tablets[3] which have been exhumed, placed in the British Museum and translated, bearing the old Assyrian record of the flood, which is marvelously like the account found in Genesis, even to the "building of the ship," which contained "the seed of all life," and the raven and the dove which were sent forth from its windows after the waters began to recede. Another tablet[4] describes the build-

[1] Collection de Clercq, Pl. 5. No. 46.
[2] 4-34.
[3] Deluge Tablets in British Museum, Records of the Past, 1-133.
[4] Marked K 3657 in British Museum. Trans. by Geo. Smith.

ing of some great tower or "stronghold," apparently
by command of the king, but the gods are represented
as being angry, for it is stated that " Babylon corruptly
to sin went, and small and great mingled on the mound.
. . . To their stronghold in the night he made án
end. In anger also the secret counsel he poured out—
to scatter (them abroad) his face he set. He gave a
command to make strange their speech. . . . Vio-
lently they wept—very much they wept."

There is a fragment of a tablet,[1] on which was written an Accadian poem; on being translated it was
found to contain a description of certain cities, of which
the names were not given. It was recorded, however,
that they were destroyed by a rain of fire, and the
legend gives an account of a person who escaped the
general destruction.

The inscriptions of ancient kings reveal to a certain
extent the times and the facts connected with their
reigns, but in discussing the tablets and monuments,
the pillars and palace walls of these royal historians, it
must be borne in mind that these heathen kings were
far from infallible, and whatever resulted in their own
aggrandizement was most eagerly recorded, while their
military defeats and political humiliations were either
passed over in silence or qualified to such an extent as
to virtually lose their force. This is especially true of
Sennacherib, who has the reputation among Assyriologists of being "the least trustworthy of the royal
historians of Assyria." Nevertheless, these records are
of inestimable value as giving an account of their own
wars and achievements by interested participants.

[1] Inscriptions of Western Asia, Vol. 19. Trans. by Prof. Sayce, Records
of Past, 11-119.

A hexagonal prism of clay, which was found at Nineveh and carried to the British Museum[1] contains an account of the first eight years of the reign of Sennacherib and of his siege of Jerusalem under the reign of King Hezekiah, when, according to the tablets, the king of Jerusalem "had given command to strengthen the bulwarks of the great gate of the city," when it was found to be so strong that the Assyrian king refrained from assaulting it.[2]

The strange libraries of Assyria and Babylon abounded also in astronomical and astrological reports, the records of lawsuits, contract tablets and other inscriptions, also a number of official dispatches sent by the king of Jerusalem and other potentates to foreign courts.

There are also Assyrian deeds of real estate,[3] bills of sale of Israelites for slaves, also a bill of sale of a woman to an Egyptian lady (Nitocris), who made the purchase in order to obtain a wife for her son, as well as the contract tablets of Belshazzar, and the "annals" of other kings.

Hundreds of these historic tablets have been brought to light, for the soil ruled over by Persian kings was indeed rich in this imperishable literature. Manuscripts may fade beneath the touch of time, or be burned by barbarian invaders, but these clay tablets have safely kept their records beneath the dust of centuries, and the germs of their thought lived, and were developed among other races, after they had lain for ages in the valley of the Euphrates.

[1] Brit. Mus. Ins., Plates 87-42. Trans. by Rawlinson.
[2] Annals, Col. 3, line 24. Also 2 Chron. xxxii, 5.
[3] These deeds are attested by the seal impressions, or in lieu thereof by the nail marks of the parties to whom they belonged. Many of them have been translated.— *W. St. Chad Boscawen.*

THE INSCRIPTIONS OF NEBUCHADNEZZAR.

These annals begin by declaring him to be "the King of Babylon, the exalted prince, the worshipper of the god Marduk, the prince supreme, the beloved of the god Nebo." This mighty king was the patron of all forms of idolatry, and one of the principal objects of his reign appears to have been the restoration of the idol temples, and the reconstruction of their images. The first or "lofty-headed," was the shrine of the god Bel. The celebrated golden image which Nebuchadnezzar set up represented this god.[1] There is but little genuine history[2] in his inscriptions, as he seemed to consider the account of the rebuilding of the city, and the restoration of the idol temples, of more importance than the record of his military triumphs. The work of rebuilding Babylon was surely a necessity, for the Babylonians having rebelled, Sennacherib had almost wholly destroyed it.[3] The vengeance of the Assyrian king must have been terrible, for in the Bavian inscription, he declares that he swept the city from end to end—that he destroyed the houses, threw down the wall and fortifications, and the ruins were, by his order, thrown into the river. It is true that he and Assur-bani-pal reconstructed many buildings, but Babylon[4] never re-

[1] Concerning the statue of Bel, see Daniel, chap. iii; Herodotus, bk. I; Strabo, XIV; Pliny, VI, chap. xxvi; Q. Curtius, lib. V; Arrianus, lib. VII.

[2] The mythology of Nebuchadnezzar's Inscriptions will be briefly treated in the following chapter.

[3] This devastation was accomplished during Sennacherib's campaign of 694 to 692 B. C.

[4] The city of Babylon was founded in very early times. It became the capital under Khammuragas (about 1700 B. C., who built a temple to Merodach there), and held this position for twelve hundred years. It was conquered by Tukulti-Ninip, 1271 B. C.; by Tiglath-Pileser II, 731 B. C.; by Merodach Baladan, 722 B. C.; by Sargon, 721 B. C. It was sacked and

gained her title of "the Glory of the East" until the time of Nebuchadnezzar, who was engaged throughout his long reign[1] in rebuilding the temples and cities of his kingdom.

There are in the British Museum some thirty or forty inscriptions of this king, which record the structure of great buildings. There are also a few fragments pertaining to his historical career, but the account thus given is so incomplete, that while it agrees with the Biblical record of his campaigns, it is far less definite in detail. Nebuchadnezzar III, son of Nabupolasser, came to the throne in the latter part of the seventh century B. C., having taken command of the Babylonian army during the war between his father and Necho, the king of Egypt. He routed the Egyptian troops at Carchemish, "and took all that pertained to the king of Egypt, from the river of Egypt unto the river Euphrates.[2]

No royal penman ever took greater delight in recording his achievements than did Nebuchadnezzar in describing the glories of his capital city: "Is not this great Babylon that I have built for the house of the kingdom, by the might of my power, and for the honor of my majesty?"[3] Upon the cylinders found at Senkereh in the ruins of the temple of the sun, upon tablets taken from the ruins of Birs Nimrud,[4] which

destroyed by Sennacherib, 692 B. C.; restored by Esarhaddon, 675 B. C.; captured by Assur-bani-pal, 648 B. C.; rebuilt in great splendor by Nebuchadnezzar during his long reign, and taken at last by the Medes and Persians about 539 B. C.—*Ernest A. Budge, Trans. Vic. Ins.,* V. 18, p. 147.

[1] Nebuchadnezzar reigned from about 605 to 562 B. C.

[2] 2 Kings xxiv, 7. In the tablets the river Euphrates is called "the river of Sippara."

[3] Dan. iv, 30.

[4] Translated by Fox Talbot, F. R. S., Records of the Past, I, 69–73.

still rise one hundred and fifty-three feet above the level of the plain, and elsewhere, we find the boastful records of this haughty monarch, and in one instance a single inscription consists of six hundred and nineteen lines. Thus writes the great king:

"The fanes of Babylon I built, I adorned. Four thousand cubits complete, the walls of Babylon, whose banner is invincible, as a high fortress by the ford of the rising sun, I carried around Babylon its fosse which I dug. With cement and brick I reared up a tall tower at its side like a mountain. I built the great gates, whose walls I constructed with pine woods and covering of copper. I overlaid them to keep off enemies from the front of the wall of unconquered Babylon. Those large gates for the admiration of multitudes of men, with wreathed work I filled—the invincible castle of Babylon, which no king had previously effected, the city of Babylon I fitted to be a treasure city,"[1] etc.

These few lines indicate the style and general character of the chronicles found upon many cylinders and slabs. During his reign Jerusalem was besieged, and captured[2] after a siege of a year and a half. King Zedekiah fled by night "by the way of the gate between the two walls which is in the king's garden," but was overtaken in the plains of Jericho, and brought before the king of Babylon at Riblah, where his sons were slain before him and his eyes were destroyed. A few years later Nebuchadnezzar besieged Tyre, with doubtful success. He had left Gedaliah in charge of Judah, but the new ruler was slain by Ishmael, the

[1] Translated by Fox Talbot, F. R. S., Records of the Past, 1-133.
[2] Jerusalem captured 587 B. C. See also Jer. xxxix, 1, 2 ; 2 Kings xxv.

son of Nethaniah. Again the king of Babylon came to take vengeance, and carried the Jews away to Babylon. He afterward turned his attention to the capture of Egypt, whose king had incited Palestine to rebellion. Nebuchadnezzar defeated and deposed him, swept over Egypt and installed a king who was tributary to Babylon.[1] After this he devoted himself to the rebuilding of his city, using thousands of captives as laborers and drawing upon all his provinces for his supplies.

All the writers of this period give their testimony to the glory of his city, his palaces, temples, hanging gardens, and the golden images of his gods. He builded the shrines of multitudes of gods at Babylon, and Jeremiah alludes to this fact when he says : " For it is a land of graven images, and they confide in their idols."[2] The prophets of Israel never stayed in their denunciation of this idolatrous king, even though they and their people were within the grasp of his mailed hand.

The land of Palestine has been called "the Piedmont of Western Asia ;" being situated midway between the two great empires of Egypt and Assyria, it became the battle-field of the Orient, and it was here that the fiercest conflict was waged. But during the reign of Nebuchadnezzar the Chaldean supremacy in Asia remained unshaken, for the active policy of that iron-handed ruler, with his mighty army kept all Western Asia under his control.

THE FALL OF BABYLON.

There are several tablets pertaining to the fall of Babylon which throw additional light upon that event.

[1] 572 B. C.   [2] Jer. l, 38.

It appears from these chronicles that Belshazzar reigned
in connection with his father Nabonidus, Belshazzar
being the grandson of Nebuchadnezzar on the maternal
side.   Under the date of the ninth year of Nabonidus,[1]
the record says: "Nabonidus, the king, was in the city
of Teva, the son of the king (Belshazzar), the chieftains, and the soldiers were in the land of Accad
(North Babylonia). . . .   The king until the month
Nisan (first month) to Babylon went not, Nebo to
Babylon came not, Bel went not forth. . . .   In the
month Nisan, Cyrus, king of Persia, his army gathered,
and below Arbela the river Tigris he crossed."   The
chronicle is here mutilated, and it can be seen only
that Cyrus, marching across the northern part of the
Euphratean valley, levied tribute upon some distant
king.   This may have been one of the campaigns in
the war against Crœsus, king of Lydia, and the rising
power of the now united Medes and Persians was
anxiously watched by the rulers of Babylonia.   Nabonidus appears from the record to have been a weak
ruler, leaving the government and command of the
army largely in the hands of his son.   Says Boscawen,
the eminent Assyriologist: "From the seventh year[2] of
his father's reign until the fall of the empire, Belshazzar appears to have been the leading spirit and
ruler of the kingdom, and this may account, in some
measure, for his prominence in the book of Daniel."[3]
In the cylinder inscription of Nabonidus, found in the
temple of the Moon-god at Ur, the king thus prays
for his son:

[1] 547 B. C.   [2] 549 B. C.
[3] W. St. Chad Boscawen, Trans. Vic. Ins., Vol. XVIII, No. 70, p. 117.

1. "As for me, Nabonidus, king of Babylon,
2. In the fullness of thy
3. Great divinity, (grant me)
4. Length of life
5. To remote days.
6. And for Belshazzar,
7. My first-born son,
8. The offspring of my heart,
9. Reverence for thy great divinity
10. Establish thou in his heart."[1]

Another tablet, by a contemporary scribe, gives a brief account of the fall of Babylon, which throws a most important light upon this great event, enabling historians to fix the year, month and day of the capture of the city, and as proving its agreement with the statements of classical writers, and the author of the book of Daniel. The ancient writers all agree, that the fall of Babylon took place by a surprise, the attack being made on the night of a great festival. Herodotus thus describes it: "The outer part of the city had already been taken, while those in the centre, who, as the Babylonians say, knew nothing of the matter, owing to the extent of the city, were dancing and making merry, for it so happened that a festival was being celebrated."

Xenophon claims that the attack was made "when Cyrus perceived that the Babylonians celebrated a festival at a fixed time, at which they feasted for the whole night." The Hebrew prophets,[2] also, were not unaware of this surprise upon the "Lady of King-

---

[1] Western Asia Inscriptions, Vol. I, pl. 68, col. lines 19.
[2] Jeremiah li, 89-57; also Daniel v, 1.

doms," and among the inscriptions taken from Babylon is a large tablet, containing, when complete, the calendar of the year, with notes appended to each day, specifying whether it was lucky or unlucky, whether it was a fast or a feast day. The calendar of the month Duza, or Tammuz, the month in which Babylon was taken, is fortunately complete, and contains a record of the festivals which were celebrated therein. The month opens with a festival of the Sun-god, or Tammuz, as the summer sun, restored in all his beauty (after his death in winter) to his bride, who is Ishtar, the moon. This festival is the same as that of Atys, the Phyrgian Adonis, which is celebrated at the same time. The festivals of Tammuz and Ishtar, his wife, extended over all the first half of the month, the second being the day of lamentation, and the sixth, the procession. On the fifteenth day of the month they celebrated the great marriage feast of Tammuz and his bride, and it consisted of wild orgies, such as can only be found in the lascivious East. It was this festival which Belshazzar was celebrating on the night in which Babylon was taken, and it was probably the only one in which not only the king, but also his "wives and concubines," would be present. There may have been an air of desperation imparted to the conduct of Belshazzar by the knowledge that, by the flight of his father and defeat of his army, the kingdom was virtually lost, and that this was probably his last festival as a Babylonian ruler. The gold and silver vessels which were brought forth at this reckless feast had been captured at the sacking of the temple at Jerusalem, and stored in the temple of Bel Merodach, and were brought from there in obedience to the command of Belshazzar, who was the last of the line of Nimrod. It is evident from the tablets and other authorities that the army of Cyrus, commanded by Gobyras,[1] entered the city "without fighting" on the night of the fifteenth of the month Tammuz, and the outposts were captured while the revelers were unconscious of the near approach of the foe. But within the walls and at the scene of festivity, surrounding the king, there was not only the tramp of armed men, but also the clash of swords and spears, a short but decisive combat, and Babylon, "the glory of kingdoms," became the victor's prize.[2]

The walls of the Chaldean palace were rich with gorgeous draperies on that fatal night. The golden cups were filled with costly wines, and long festoons of flowers were hung from wall and ceiling; there were beautiful faces, and the flashing of jewels, with music and mirth in the royal hall, but that festal scene was the background of the death of an empire. "Babylon the Great" had fallen in the midst of her splendor—had fallen with her temples and palaces, into the hand of the Persian king.

[1] The newly acquired evidence of the tablets seems to indicate that Gobyras, who commanded the armies of Cyrus, was Darius the Median, who acted as the viceroy of Cyrus on the throne of Babylon. Gobyras, the Ugbaru of the inscriptions, being formerly prefect of Gutium, or Kurdistan, was ruler of a district which embraced Ecbatana, the Median capital, and the province of the Medes, and was also, as his name indicates, a Proto-Mede, or Kassite, by birth. Xenophon states that the capture of Babylon was effected by Gobyras, and that his division was the first to reach the palace. Cyrus himself did not enter Babylon until later in the year, namely, on the third day of Marchesvan, four months after, when he "proclaimed peace, to all Babylon, and Gobyras his governor, and governors, he appointed."

[2] W. St. Chad Boscawen, Trans. Vic. Ins., Vol. XVIII, page 131.

CYRUS—THE ACHÆMENIAN.

The numerous inscriptions of Cyrus, Darius, Xerxes, and the three Artaxerxes found at Persepolis, at Mount Elvend, at Susa, and Suez, are the most important of the historical inscriptions of Persian kings, except that at Behistun. The Persian texts have been repeatedly and carefully edited. Following the preparatory labors of Grotofend, Rask, Beer and Jacquet, the documents have been carefully examined and explained by MM. Burnouf, Lassen, Sir H. Rawlinson, Benfey, Spiegel and Dr. Oppert.

The Median versions appeared afterward, coming from the competent hands of MM. Westergaard, De Saulcy, Holtzmann, Norris and Mardtmann, while the Assyrian translations have been examined by scholars whose work is equally careful, therefore, no doubt can be entertained concerning its general accuracy.

The supposed tomb of Cyrus merely bears in three languages—Persian, Median and Assyrian—the simple statement that "I am Cyrus, the King, the Achæmenian." There is, however, an Assyrian inscription on a Babylonian brick which was brought over to England by Loftus and translated by Sir Henry Rawlinson, which declares that "Cyrus, King of Babylon, Priest of the Pyramid and of the Tower (was) son of Cambyses, the Mighty Prince." This apparently simple legend is of great historical importance, as it proves that Herodotus[1] was right in calling Cyrus's father Cambyses, a name which was afterward borne also by the successor of Cyrus. The inscription also states, in harmony with

[1] Herodotus, I, 107, 122.

Herodotus, that the former Cambyses was not a king, but merely a private individual.

BEHISTUN INSCRIPTIONS.

Not only is the soil of Persia rich in historic lore, but even the cliffs of her mountains were "graven with an iron pen" where her records were "laid in the rock forever." At Behistun, far above the plain, is found an imperishable record of the reign of Darius Hystaspes.[1]

Major Rawlinson at last succeeded in scaling the heights and making casts of the mystic characters to be taken away and translated. The great inscription is written in three languages, and extends to nearly a thousand lines of cuneiform writing. It is at least four hundred feet above the plain, and this intrepid soldier, during the space of several years, made the perilous ascent a multitude of times, always bringing away, at the peril of his life, some portion of this 'great historic record. After thirteen years of persistent effort he succeeded in copying the whole inscription, and placing it in such a form that other scholars could assist him in the translation of it. The casts of the Sythic version were given into the care of Mr. E. Norris, the well-known Oriental scholar, who published from them an independent translation in the Journal of the Royal Asiatic Society. The Persian text was translated by Major Rawlinson, and Dr. Julius Oppert states that he devoted twenty years of his own life to the Median version.

In the subject-matter of this long inscription, King

[1] Darius Hystaspes reigned from 549 to 486 B. C.

Darius follows the custom of other potentates, and records only his triumphs, though he boastingly tells of
the barbarities he practiced upon would-be usurpers.
The record opens with a long line of genealogies, giving
the names of the kings who reigned before him. "And
Darius the king says, on that account we called ourselves
Achæmenian of race ; from ancient times we have been
mighty, from ancient times we have been kings."[1]

The royal historian then recites the countries over
which he reigned, including Assyria, Babylon, Persia,
Arabia, and Egypt, besides minor provinces, twenty-
three in all, and he says, "These are the provinces that
called themselves mine ; they brought tribute to me,
what was ordered by me unto them, in the night time
as well as in the day time, that they executed."[2]

The history is then given of various pretenders who
led revolts against him. The whole account of these
rebellions occupies many lines of cuneiform writing,
but victory was always gained by the crown, and the
usurpers were put to death in the most barbarous
manner. Their noses and ears and tongues were cut
off, their eyes were put out, and in this pitiable condition they were chained to the palace where "all
the people saw" them, and afterward they were carried away and placed upon crosses. The penalty inflicted upon each one is given in detail, but there is
a great uniformity in the accounts, although the punishment was sometimes varied by hanging the leader of

---

[1] Column I, line 3. Achæmenes was the last king independent of Persia,
and therefore the kings after Cyrus declared that they were his descendants.
It is supposed that he was superseded by Phraortes, the Median king (657-
635) as it was he who first subdued the Persians. Phraortes was the great
grandfather of Cyrus, who was born 599 B. C.
[2] Col. I, line 7.

the revolt, together with his principal followers. Often a decree of extermination was issued against all the people engaged in the rebellion. The great inscription is finished with a pictorial representation of the nine kings which Darius took in battle, one of whom claimed to be Bardes, the son of Cyrus. Another claimed to be the king of Susiana;[1] another led the revolt of the Babylonians; the fourth caused the rebellion of the Medians; the fifth, like the second, proclaimed himself the king of Susiana, while the sixth led the Sagartians in an attack upon their king. "The seventh was a Persian who lied and said, 'I am Smerdis, son of Cyrus, and he caused the revolt of Persia.'"[2] The eighth proclaimed himself king of Babylon, and the ninth claimed to exercise kingly power over the Margians. The first of these is represented by a prostrate figure, upon which the victorious king is trampling, the others are standing in the position of captives, and are branded as imposters by the inscriptions beneath them. The king also recorded the names of the warriors who assisted him in his campaigns, and requested those who might succeed him upon the Persian throne, to "remember to show favor to the descendants of these men."

DARIUS AT PERSEPOLIS.

Afar in the mountains of Persia stand the ruins of the capital city of her ancient kings. Porch and temple, hall and palace, lie together amidst the desolation wrought by the ages. The long stairway still leads to

---

[1] The name of this province appears to be derived from Susun, signifying a "lily."
[2] Col. III, line 41.

the great plateau, while the gray marble pillars stand like sentinels above the ruins at their feet, and the moonlight gleams upon sepulchres of Persian monarchs. But even here, on panel and column, we find symbols graven by a forgotten hand—the desert voice of the past, still boasting of the grandeur of her fallen kings.

An inscription on the door of a ruined palace, written in Persian, Median, and Assyrian, recounts the greatness of "Darius the great king,—the king of kings,—the king of the lands,—the son of Hystaspes, the Achæmenian (who) has built the palace." The "lands which are numerous" over which he holds sway are declared to be "Susiana, Media, Babylon, Arabia, Assyria, Egypt, Armenia, Cappadocia, Lycia, the Ionians, those of the continent and those of the sea, and the Eastern lands, Sagartia, Parthia, Sarangia, Aria, Bactria, Sogdiana, Chorasmia, Sattagydia, Arachotis, India, Gandaria, the Maxyans, Karka (Carthage), Sacians, and the Maka.[1]

Darius the king says "If thou say it may be so I shall not fear the other Ahriman.[2] Protect the Persian people. If the Persian people are protected by thee, Ormazd, the Good Principle, which has always destroyed the demon, will descend as ruler on this house. The great Ormazd, who is the greatest among all the gods, is he who created the heaven, and created

[1] This list of nations and provinces found at Persepolis is of great importance. It was executed after the first expedition of Darius to the Greek nations 496, B. C., or still later, and many Hellenic nations are enumerated as being subdued to the Persian power.

[2] If Dr. Oppert's version is correct this text gives us the first mention of the name of Ahriman to be found in the inscriptions, although the warring of the evil elements against the good is introduced in a Chaldean legend of the creation, which will be noticed in the following chapter.

the earth, who created the men and the Good Principle, and who made Darius king, and gave to Darius
the king, the royalty over this wide earth, which contains many lands; Persia and Media, and other lands
and other tongues, on the mountains, and in the
plains, of this side of the sea, and on the side beyond the sea; of this side of the desert, and on the
side beyond the desert." The inscriptions of Darius
at Mount Elvend, at Susa, and at Suez, are merely
repetitions of the greatness of Darius and of Ormazd.

INSCRIPTIONS OF XERXES.

These are engraved upon the staircase and columns
at Persepolis, and like the texts of Darius, they are
employed chiefly to represent the greatness of the king,
and the greatness of Ormazd. Says Dr. Oppert, "The
texts of Xerxes are very uniform, and not very important. The real resulting fact is the name of the
king, Khsayarsa, which proves to be identical with
Ahasuerus"[1] of the Book of Esther. There are also
legends on vases which were found in Egypt, at Susa
and Halicarnassus. The vase found at Halicarnassus is
now in the gold room of the British Museum, bearing
the inscription of "Xerxes the great king."

ARTAXERXES.

The texts of this monarch, which are written in
Persian, Median and Assyrian, are found on the bases
of columns at Susa, and also at Persepolis, as well as
upon vases. They comprise the records of three
kings—Artaxerxes I, II and III.

[1] Commentaire sur le livre d'Esther, p. 4.

We are indebted to the excavations of Loftus at Susa for the records of Artaxerxes II; these are far more important than the inscriptions of his prede- cessor, which merely illustrate the egotism of their author. The text which is borne upon these col- umns brings down to us a new historical statement, to the effect that the palace at Susa was burned under the reign of Artaxerxes I, and restored by his grandson. During this period the Persian monarchs resided principally at Babylon, and Darius II died there.

The great importance of these texts arises from the fact that they give the genealogy of the Achæmenidæ, and confirm the statements transmitted to us on this subject by the Greeks, which are in direct opposition to the traditions of the modern Persians. The text of Artaxerxes III contains the genealogy of that king up- ward to the names of Hystaspes and Arsames, who were the father and grandfather of Darius Hystaspes of the Achæmenian line.

A LATER PERSIAN TABLET.

A much later tablet is merely a note of hand given by a Persian king (Pacorus II), with a promise to pay "in the month of Iyar (April) in the Temple of the sun in Babylon," and it also bears the names of four witnesses. This little clay tablet was discovered by Dr. Oppert in the Museum of the Society of Antiqua- rians at Zurich, and has been carefully translated by him. It is interesting mostly from the fact of its comparatively modern origin, King Pacorus II having been contemporary with the Emperor Titus and Domitian. Some of the names mentioned upon it are Babylonish, and some of them Persian. All the witnesses, however, bear Persian names which may even be called modern. King Pacorus II commenced his reign A. D. 77, and hence this is the only tablet, so far as known, which belongs to the Christian era.

RÉSUMÉ.

These sculptured temples and graven stones have lain in the path of the ages with silent lips, but the questioning hand of the nineteenth century has broken the spell and wrested the story of the past even from the "heaps" of Nineveh and Babylon. From mountain cliff, from palace wall, from corner-stone and fallen pillar comes the same historic voice that speaks to us from the forgotten libraries of buried kings.

The literature of the tablets comes into our own age, leading a splendid retinue of historic figures— Sargon, the early king of Accad, with his imperishable library, with the monuments and tablets of Assyria, then Nineveh, "that great city," with her temples and palaces, where the gilded tiles of many a a dome flashed back the glory of the setting sun— Babylon, "the joy of the whole earth," and "the beauty of the Chaldee's excellency," who for centuries held her position as the queen of the world's commerce, and through whose hands the wealth of the Euphrates flowed down to the Persian Gulf. Babylon, with her maze of life and color, with her silver vases and golden vessels, with her princely halls and gorgeous hangings, with the breath of the myrtle and the bay, borne upward from her terraced gardens and moonlight meads.

Then the scene changes, and the kingly Cyrus is riding at the head of his Medo-Persian cohorts, and the crown of the Orient is within his grasp. "Bel boweth down—Nebo stoopeth," and the seat of government is removed, and "the daughter of the Chaldeans" sits in the dust beneath the foot of the invader.

Later still, Darius the Great is enthroned on Persian soil; haughtily he wears the imperial purple, and the crown of many kingdoms, while upon the face of Persia's mountains, he writes himself "The king of kings." But a reckless policy led the Persian host to a sure defeat upon the plains of Marathon, and prepared the way for the humiliation of Xerxes, and the later triumphs of Alexander. Then the sons of the desert poured like a mountain torrent over the plains of Irān, and the star and crescent flashed everywhere from banners on Persian soil, while to-day the Arab pitches his tent amidst the ruins of ancient cities, and only the spade of the explorer reveals their buried treasures.

CHAPTER III.

THE POETRY AND MYTHOLOGY OF THE TABLETS.

PRIMITIVE MYTHOLOGY—ANÛ—SEVEN EVIL SPIRITS—
ACCADIAN POEM — ASSUR — HEA— NIN-CI-GAL—SIN,
THE MOON GOD—HEA-BANI—NERGAL—MERODACH—
NEBO — NINIP — CHEMOSH — INCANTATIONS TO FIRE
AND WATER—IM—BAAL—TAMMUZ—ISHTAR—ISHTAR
OF ARBELA—ISHTAR OF ERECH—LEGEND OF ISHTAR
AND IZDÛBAR—ISHTAR, QUEEN OF LOVE AND BEAUTY
—THE DESCENT OF ISHTAR.

THE East was the home of poetry and the land of
mythology before the hundred gates of Palmyra
were swung upon their massive hinges, or the crown of
her beautiful queen had been set with its moonlight
pearls. A land which was rich with jewels and
radiant with flowers, held in her background a mythology so primitive that it appears to have been the
mother of them all. Tablet and palace walls have
alike been questioned concerning these early myths,
and behind the dust of the centuries, in the legends
that lie beneath them, we find stories of gods like
Indra, the storm-king of the Hindûs, and Jove of
Olympus — like Odin and Thor of the Northmen.
Even the gigantic symbols that guarded the portals of
ancient hall and palace are replete with wonder, for
their strange wings have sheltered the very beginnings

of mythology. Chaldea's cosmogonies comprehend the ideas of the Greek and Norseman—nay, even the wildest dreams of Hindū and Persian are apparently drawn from this common source.[1]

The intelligent study of Persian literature compels an examination of the early myths and legends where her poetry and romance found their sources—compels the study not only of the inscriptions of Persian kings, but of the tablets which have brought down to us the idols of a primitive people. Therefore, it is the province of this chapter to give a brief yet comprehensive outline of the principal deities and legends which seem to form the basis not only of Persian mythology, but of the luxuriant growth of myth and fable which has permeated India, Greece, and Rome, as well as Northern Europe.

A Chaldean legend of the creation is found upon a clay tablet which contains a description of the struggle between the evil powers of darkness and chaos, and the bright powers of light and order. This is doubtless the origin of the struggle between good and evil —the unceasing contest between Ormazd and Ahriman which forms the key-note of Persian thought so fully illustrated in the Avesta.

There are two contradictory tablets of the creation. The one coming from the library at Cutha and the other from the royal library at Nineveh. This latter consists of seven tablets, as the creation is described

[1] The Chaldean mythology represented by the worship of Baal and Ashtaroth appears to have been an organized system demanding the erection of a temple to Merodach, as early as the seventeenth century B. C., while the earliest songs of the Vedas are ascribed to the period between 1500 to 1000 B. C. and the greater portion of Hindu mythology appears only in much later works.

as consisting of seven successive acts. It presents a curious similarity to the account of the creation long before recorded in Genesis, the word Tiamat which is used to represent chaos seems to be the same as the biblical word *tehom*, the deep. A radical difference, however, is found in the fact that in the Assyrian story, Tiamat has become a mythological personage— the dragon mother of a chaotic brood. The legend in its present form is assigned by Prof. Sayce to about the time of Assur-bani-pal.[1] The oldest tablets are those which are written in the primitive Accadian tongue, and many of these have been found in the library of Assur-bani-pal,[2] having evidently been copied from the earlier text and supplied with interlinear translations in the Assyrian tongue.

The Assyrians counted no less than three hundred spirits of heaven and six hundred spirits of earth, all of which (as well as the rest of their mythology) appears to have been borrowed from the primitive population of that country. Indeed it would appear that ancient Babylonia was the birthplace of that common mythology[3] which in various forms afterward became the heritage of so many nations.

Elaborate and costly temples were built for these deities of an idolatrous people, and when the image of a god was brought into his newly built temple there were festivals and processions, and wild rejoicing among the worshippers.

The principal gods mentioned in these early tablets may be briefly sketched as follows:

1 Sayce, Rec. of P., Vol. I, pp. 123-130
2 Assur-bani-pal, king of Assyria, who reigned from 668 to 625 B. C.
3 Hindu Literature, Chaps. ii and iii.

ANŪ.

The sky god and ruler of the highest heaven, whose messengers are evil spirits. The Canaanite town of Beth-anath, mentioned in Joshua,[1] was named for Anat, the wife of Anū.

SEVEN EVIL SPIRITS.

These messengers of Anū are elsewhere described as the seven storm-clouds, or the winds, and their leader seems to have been the dragon Tiamat[2] (the deep), who was defeated by Bel-Merodach in the war of the gods. The tablets have preserved an Accadian poem on this subject, the author of which is represented as living in the Babylonian city of Eridu,[3] where his horizon was bounded by the mountains of Susiani, and the battle of the elements raging around their summit suggested to his poet-mind the warring of evil spirits.

It was these seven storm-spirits who were represented as attacking the moon when it was eclipsed, a description of which is given in an Accadian poem[4] translated by Prof. Talbot. Here they are regarded as the allies of the incubus, or nightmare, which is supposed to attack the moon.

ACCADIAN POEM ON THE SEVEN EVIL SPIRITS.

"O, Fire-god! those seven, how were they born? how
  grew they up?

[1] Joshua xix, 39.

[2] There is an Assyrian bas-relief now in the British Museum which represents Tiamat with horns and claws, tail and wings.

[3] Eridu—the Rata of Ptolemy, was near the junction of the Euphrates and Tigris, on the Arabian side of the river. It was one of the oldest cities of Chaldea.

[4] Cun. Ins. West Asia, Vol. IV, plate 15. Records of the Past.

Those seven in the mountain of the sunset were born.
Those seven in the mountain of the sunrise grew up.
In the hollows of the earth have they their dwelling;
On the high places of the earth are they proclaimed.
Among the gods their couch they have not;
Their name in heaven and earth exists not.
Seven are they; in the mountain of the sunset do
    they rise;
Seven are they; in the mountain of the sunrise do
    they set.
Let the Fire-god seize upon the incubus;
Those baleful seven may he remove, and their bodies
    may he bind.
Order and kindness know they not,
Prayer and supplication hear they not.
Unto Hea they are hostile;
Disturbing the lily in the torrents are they.
Baleful are they, baleful are they,
Seven are they, seven are they."

"They are the dark storms of heaven which unto fire
    unite themselves;
They are the destructive tempests which, on a fine
    day, sudden darkness cause;
With storms and meteors they rush,
Their rage ignites the thunderbolts of Im,
From the right hand of the thunder they dart forth.
They are seven, these evil spirits, and death they fear
    not;
They are seven, these evil spirits, who rush like a
    hurricane,
And fall like fire-brands on the earth."[1]

[1] This is one of the numerous bi-lingual texts, written in the original

Here we have more than a suggestion of the origin of some of the early songs of the Vedas, for these seven storm-spirits are represented by the Marūts of the Hindūs—"the shakers of the earth"—who dash through the heavens in chariots drawn by dappled deer. In this primitive mythology we find also

ASSUR.

The "god of judges" was the especial patron of Assyria, and afterward made to express the power of the later Assyrian empire by becoming "father of the gods" and the head of the pantheon.

The Assyrian kings claimed that their power was derived from this deity, and in one of the inscriptions it is said that

"The universal king,[1] king of Assyria, the king whom
    Assur,
King of the spirits of heaven, appointed with a king-
    dom,
Without rival has filled his hand.
From the great sea of the rising of the sun
To the great sea of the setting of the sun
His hand conquered and has subdued in all entirety."

In the inscriptions of Shalmanesar II, all honor is also ascribed to this god; he is invoked as ''Assur, the great lord, the king of all the great gods."

And it is said: "By the command of Assur, the great
    lord, my lord,
I approached the mountain of Shitamrat—

Accadian, with an interlinear Assyrian translation, which have been brought from the library of Assur-bani-pal at Nineveh.
[1] Rimmon-Nirari III. Records of Past, Vol. IV, p. 88.

The mountain I stormed.

Akhuni trusted to the multitude of his troops and came
forth to meet me;

He drew up in battle array.

I launched among them the weapons of Assur, my lord;

I utterly defeated them.

I cut off the heads of his soldiers and dyed the mountains with the blood of his fighting men.

Many of his troops flung themselves against the rocks
of the mountains."[1]

On his return, the victorious king purified his
weapons in the sea, and sacrificed victims to his gods.
He erected a statue of himself, overlooking the sea,
and inscribed it with the glory of Assur.

HEA.

Hea[2] was the god of choas or the deep; he was
"the king of the abyss who determines destinies."

In later times he was also called "the god of the
waters," and from him some of the attributes of Neptune may have been derived. It was said that Chaos
was his wife.

[1] Ins. of Shalmanesar II. Records of P., Vol. IV, p. 66.

[2] It is thought that the worship of Hea or Ea may have been a corruption of the worship of the God of Abraham, as Ea is another form of
El, and the early followers of Ea were evidently monotheists.

Mr. Hormuzd Rassam, the eminent archæologist, who is a native of
Assyria, claims that the early Assyrians worshipped the true God, but
under peculiar names and attributes, and that instead of practicing the
revolting sacrifices which were made by other gentile nations "they
imitated the sacrifices of the Jewish rites." He bases his proof largely
upon his discovery of the bronze gate of Shalmanesar II, with its sculptured presentation of the sacrifice of rams and bullocks, and he says
that "the same king, Shalmanesar, took tribute from Jehu, king of
Israel, as an act of homage."

Trans. Vic. Ins., Vol. XIII, pp. 190 and 214, also Vol. XXV, pp. 121.

NIN-CI-GAL.

In later mythology Nin-ci-gal, instead of Chaos, was the wife of Hea—she was the "lady of the mighty country" and "queen of the dead." This goddess may have been the prototype of Proserpine, who was carried away by Pluto in his golden chariot to be the "queen of hades."

SIN.

This name signifies brightness, and the moon-god was the father of Ishtar. Nannaru, "the brilliant one," was one of his titles.

A golden tablet[1] found in the "timmin," or corner-stone of a palace or temple at Khorsabed, contains an account of the splendid temples which King Sargon II built in a town near Nineveh (Dur Sărkin) and dedicated to Hea, Sin (the moon-god), Chemosh (the sun-god), and Ninip, the god of forces. The king's inscription[2] states that "I constructed palaces covered with skins, sandal wood, ebony, cedar, tamarisk, pine, cypress, and wood of pistachio tree." Among the gods presented on the tablets we find also

HEA-BANI.

This god was the companion of Izdübar, and on account of the peculiar circumstances attending his death was shut out of heaven. He is represented as a satyr, with the legs, head, and tail of an ox. This

---

[1] This tablet is almost three inches long and two inches wide. It weighs about three drams (Troy). The inscription was translated by Dr. Oppert.

[2] These inscriptions contain an account of a lunar eclipse mentioned by Ptolemy, which took place March 19th, 721 B. C. Sargon II probably ascended the throne about the year 722 B. C.

figure occurs very frequently on the gems, and may always be recognized by these characteristics. He is doubtless the original of Mendes, the goat-formed god of Egypt, and also of Pan, the goat-footed god of the Arcadian herdsman with his pipe of seven reeds. Heabani is represented as dwelling in a remote place three days' journey from Erech, and it was said that he lived in a cave and associated with the cattle and the creeping things of the field.

NERGAL,

the patron deity of Cutha, is identified with Nerra, the god of pestilence, and also with Ner, the mythical monarch of Babylonia, who it was claimed reigned before the flood. He was "the god of bows and arms." The cuneiform inscriptions show that the Lion-god, under the name of Nergal[1] was worshipped at Kuti or Cutha, where an elaborate temple was built in his honor, and an Assyrian copy of an old Babylonian text belonging to the library of Cutha, speaks of "the memorial stone which I wrote for thee, for the worship of Nergal which I left for thee." According to Dr. Oppert, Nergal represented the planet Mars, hence the Grecian god of war, "raging round the field," appears to have been merely a perpetuation of this early deity.

BEL MERODACH,

or Marduk, whose temple, according to the inscription, was built by Nebuchadnezzar, with its costly woods, "its silver and molten gold, and precious

[1] The fact that the " men of Cuth " worshipped Nergal is confirmed by 2 Kings xvii, 30.

stones" and "sea-clay" (amber), "with its seats of splendid gold, with lapis-lazuli and alabaster blocks," which are still found in the ruins of Babylon. And the king made the great festival Lilmuku, when the image of Merodach[1] was brought into the temple.[2] The inscription also speaks[3] of the temple as receiving "within itself the abundant tribute of the kings of nations, and of all peoples."[4]

NEBO.

From this god the name of Nebuchadnezzar was derived, and he was the favorite deity of that king. He was the eldest son of Merodach, and was "the bestower of thrones in heaven and earth." In a ten-column inscription of Nebuchadnezzar, which is engraved upon black basalt, and now forms part of the India House Collection, the king speaks of building a temple in Babylon "to Nebo of lofty intelligence, who hath bestowed on me the scepter of justice to preside over all peoples." He says, "The pine portico of the shrine of Nebo, with gold I caused to cover,"[5] etc. Nebo[6] or Nabo and Merodach are both used as the component parts of the names of certain kings of Babylon.

---

[1] An allusion to the destruction of the image of Merodach is found in Jeremiah: "Babylon is taken, Bel is confounded, Merodach is broken in pieces. Her idols are confounded, her images are broken in pieces." (Jeremiah l, 2.)

[2] 4th Col., lines 1-6.   [3] Col. 10.

[4] This portion of Nebuchadnezzar's inscription is confirmed by the following statement in the book of Daniel: "And the Lord gave the King of Judah into his (Nebuchadnezzar's) hand with part of the vessels of the house of God, which he carried into the land of Shinar to the house of his god." (Daniel i, 2.)

[5] Col. 3. lines 43-45.

[6] Nebo is alluded to as one of the heathen gods in Isaiah xlvi, 1, and kindred passages.

NINIP,

"the son of the zenith," and "the lord of strong actions," finds an echo in Grecian mythology as Her-cūles, who received his sword from Mercury, his bow from Apollo, his golden breastplate from Vulcan, his horses from Neptune, and his robe from Minerva, the goddess of wisdom.

Hercūles, who appears in Persian mythology as Mithras, the unconquered sun, is traced back to his Phœnician origin in the line of Baal. Therefore, the Persian Mithras represents Chemosh and Tammuz, both of whom are sun-gods as well as the "god of forces," for the sun is the most powerful influence in the planetary world. The mysteries of Mithras were celebrated with much pomp and splendor on the re-vival of the Persian religion under the Sassanidæ. The word appears in many ancient Persian names.

DAGON.

The Assyrian Dagon was usually associated with Anū, the sky-god, and the worship of both was car-ried as far west as Canaan.[1] He is spoken of in the tablets as "Dagon, the hero of the great gods, the beloved of thy heart, the prince, the favorite of Bel," etc. The name is a word of Accadian origin, mean-ing "exalted."

MOLECH.

Of Molech little is said in the tablets, except that "he took the children,"[2] but a curious fragment of

[1] Compare Judges xvi, 23; also 1 Samuel v.
[2] Tablets of Tel-El-Armana, "Dispatches from Palestine in the century before the Exodus," Rec. of P. Vol. I, p. 64.

an old Accadian hymn indicates that the children of these highlanders were offered, as burnt offerings, in very early times; and hence, says Prof. Sayce, "the bloody sacrifices offered to Molech were no Semitic invention, but handed on to them, with so much else, by the Turānian population of Chaldea."[1] The Mosaic law was especially severe upon this "abomination" of human sacrifices, the death penalty being ordered for every such offence.[2]

CHEMOSH.

This sun-god was worshipped as the Supreme, and in his honor, his early worshippers sang praises, offered sacrifices and performed incantations. The success of Mesha, king of Moab, in his revolt against the king of Israel, was commemorated by the erection of the celebrated Moabite stone[3] whereon was recorded the inscription ascribing his victory to Chemosh, his favorite deity. The principal title of Chemosh[4] was "Judge of heaven and earth," but he afterward held a less important position in the Chaldaic-Babylonian pantheon, which was adopted by the Assyrians, and

[1] Babylonian Literature, p. 64.

[2] Compare Lev. xx, 2; Deut. xii, 31, and kindred passages.

[3] The Moabite stone was about three feet and nine inches long, two feet and four inches in breadth and fourteen inches thick. The inscription contained many incidents concerning the wars of King Mesha with Israel; see also 2 Kings, 3d chap. The literature connected with this stone is very great, no less than forty-nine Orientalists having written in various languages upon this fascinating theme, and although many of these productions are merely papers or brochures, there are at least eight different volumes upon this subject.

The characters are Phœnician, and form a link between those of the Baal-Lebanon Inscription of the tenth century B. C. and those of the Siloam text.

[4] Chemosh, who is called "the abomination of the Moabites," is alluded to in Numb. xxi, 29; also Jer. xlviii, 7, and various other passages.

was considered inferior to Sin, the moon-god, who was sometimes said to be his father.   There are several tablets bearing magical incantations and songs to the sun-god.

But the hideous idols that occupied the palatial temples of Chemosh at Larsam, in Southern Chaldea, and at Sippara, in the north of Babylonia, became more refined in the poetry of the Vedas, and he appeared in the mythology of the Hindūs as Sūrya, the, god of day, who rode across the heavens in a car of flame drawn by milk-white horses.

INCANTATIONS TO FIRE AND WATER

There are also Assyrian incantations to fire and water, which represent the imagery of the primitive Babylonians, and these inscriptions also suggest a possible foundation for the hymns of the Ṛig-veda. There is a great similarity of style between the literature of the tablets and the early hymns of the Hindūs.   The tablets speak of "An incantation to the waters pure, the waters of the Euphrates—the water in which the abyss firmly is established, the noble mouth of Hea shines upon them.

Waters they are shining (clear), waters they are bright.   The god of the river puts him (the enchanter) to flight," etc.   In the incantation to fire, there are also many eloquent passages: "The Fire-god—the prince which is in the lofty country—the warrior, son of the abyss—the god of fire with thy holy fires—in the house of darkness, light thou art establishing.

Of Bronze and lead, the mixer of them thou (art).

Of silver and gold, the blesser of them thou (art)."[1]
This Fire-god of the Accadians was represented by the
Hindū Agni, from whose body issued seven streams of
glory, and by Loki, whose burning breath is poured
from the throbbing mountains of the Northmen.

IM.

In this pantheon of mythology, as defined by the
tablets, Im was the god of the sky, sometimes called
Rimmon, the god of lightning and storms, of rain and
thunder.   He is represented among the Hindūs as
Indra, who furiously drives his tawny steeds to the
battle of the elements.   With the Greek and Latins
he was personated by Zeus and Jupiter, "the cloud-
compelling Jove," while among the Northmen he
wears the form of Thor, whose frown is the gathering
of the storm-clouds, and whose angry voice echoes in
the thunder-bolt.

BAAL,

or Bel (plural Baalim), was also an important character, and indeed, according to Dr. Oppert, all of
the Phœnician gods were included under the general
name of Baal,[2] and human sacrifices were often made
upon their blood-stained altars.   He had a magnificent temple in Tyre, which was founded by Hiram,
where he had symbolic pillars, one of gold and one
of smaragdus.   An inscription[3] on the sarcophagus of

---

[1] Tablet K 4902 of the British Museum Collection, translated by Ernest
A. Budge.

[2] "They have builded also the high places of Baal, to burn their sons
with fire for burnt offerings unto Baal," etc. (Jeremiah xix. 5.   See
also many kindred passages.)

[3] This inscription was translated by Dr. Oppert, and Esmunazar is
supposed to have lived in the fourth century B. C.

Esmunazar, king of the two Sidons, claims that he, too, built a temple to Ashtaroth, and " placed there the images of Ashtaroth," and also "the temple of Baal-Sidon, and the temple of Astarte, who bears the name of this Baal ; " that is, the temple of Baal and tlfe temple of Astarte, or Ashtaroth, at Sidon.

The grossest sensuality characterized some forms of the worship of Baal and Ashtaroth. Indeed, it can only be compared to the unmentionable rites which two thousand years later pertained to the worship of Krishṇa and Śiva.

In the inscription of Tiglath Pilesar I, Baal is called "the King of Constellations," and the fact that he was thus worshipped is a peculiar explanation of the frequent condemnation in the book of Kings of the worship of "the host of Heaven," which is repeatedly spoken of in connection with the altars of Baal.[1]

TAMMUZ.

This is another form of the sun-god, who is represented as being slain by the boar's tusk of winter. June is the month of Tammuz, and his festival began with the cutting of the sacred fir tree in which the god had hidden himself. A tablet in the British Museum states that the sacred dark fir tree which grew in the city of Eridu, was the couch of the mother goddess.[2] The sacred tree having been cut and carried into the idol-temple, there came the search for Tammuz, when the devotees ran wildly about

---

[1] 2 Kings xvii. 16, and kindred passages.
[2] Western Asia Inscriptions, Vol. IV. p. 82.

weeping and wailing for the lost one,[1] and cutting themselves with knives. His wife, Ishtar, descended to the lower world to search for him, and the tablets furnish another poem which seems to celebrate a temple similar to that recorded by Maimonides, in which the Babylonian gods gathered around the image of the sun-god, to lament his death. The statue of Tammuz was placed on a bier and followed by bands of mourners, crying and singing a funeral dirge. He is also called Dûzi, "the son." Tammuz is the proper Syriac name for Adonis of the Greeks.

ISHTAR.

This goddess, who is sometimes called Astarte, was the most important female deity of this early pantheon. The Persian form of the word is Astara. In Phœnician it is Ashtaroth,[2] and according to Dr. Oppert all the Phœnician goddesses were included under this general name. Another form of the name afterward appeared in Greek mythology as Asteria, and it was applied to the beautiful goddess who fled from the suit of Jove, and, flinging herself down from heaven into the sea, became the island afterward named Delos.

The farther back we go in the world's history the nearer we approach to the original idea of monotheism, and originally there was only one goddess, Ishtar or Ashtaroth, personifying both love and war,

[1] The prophet Ezekiel speaks of the fact that "there sat women weeping for Tammuz," as even a "greater abomination" than burning incense to idols. (See Ezekiel viii. 13-14.)

[2] The worship of Ashtaroth, which represented the grossest licentiousness and demanded human sacrifices, is strongly condemned in Judges ii, 12-13, and many other passages.

but two such opposite characteristics could not long remain the leading attributes of the same deity, and hence after a time, there were mentioned three goddesses bearing the same name.

ISHTAR OF ARBELA

was the goddess of war, the "Lady of Battles." She was the daughter of Anū, whose messengers were the seven evil spirits, and the favorite goddess of King Assur-bani-pal, who claims that he received his bow from her, though he declares in his inscriptions that he worshipped also Bel or Baal, and Nebo; he frequently implores the protection of Ishtar.

"Oh, thou, goddess of goddesses, terrible in battle, goddess in war, queen of the gods! Teūman, king of Elam, he gathered his army and prepared for war; he urges his fighting men to go to Assyria. Oh, thou, archer of the gods, like a weight, in the midst of the battle, throw him down and crush him."[1] Ishtar of Arbela afterward became the Bellona of the Latins, and the Enyo of the Greeks. Under the name of Anatis, or Anāhid, she was worshipped in Armenia, and also in Cappadocia, where she had a splendid temple, served by a college of priests, and more than six thousand temple servants. Her image, according to Pliny,[2] was of solid gold, and her high priest was second only to the king himself. Strabo calls this goddess Enyo, and Berosus considers that she is identical with Venus. The inscriptions of Artaxerxes, discovered at Susa, call her Anāhid, which

1 Annals of Assur-bani-pal, Cylinder B, Column 5.
2 Pliny, Nat. Hist., Vol. II, p. 619.

was the Persian name of the planet Venus. The
characteristics of Venus, the queen of beauty, may
seem somewhat at variance with Ishtar of Arbela,
the goddess of war, but it will be remembered that
the Greeks of Cythera, one of the Ionian islands,
worshipped an armed Venus, and from this island
she took the name of Cythera; the fable that she
rose from the sea probably means that her worship
was introduced into the island by a maritime people, doubtless the Phœnicians.

ISHTAR OF ERECH,

the daughter of Anū and Annatu, is another form
of this popular goddess, and one of the Assyrian
tablets refers to the dedication of horses at the temple of Bit-ili at Erech, where the king of Elam
dedicated white horses with silver saddles to Ishtar,
the tutelar divinity of Erech.

In the sixth tablet of the Izdūbar series, we find
an Ishtar whose characteristics are so different from
either the goddess of love or the goddess of war, that
we are constrained to believe that it must refer to
Ishtar of Erech. She here appears as the queen of
witchcraft, resembling the Hecate of the Greeks in
her funereal abode. Indeed, Hecate was fabled to be
the daughter of Asteria, which is merely the Greek
form of the name Ishtar, and Pausanius[1] mentions an
Astrateia whose worship was brought to Greece from
the East.

[1] Pausanius, III, 25.

LEGEND OF ISHTAR AND IZDŪBAR.

COLUMN I.

"1. He had thrown off his tattered garments,
2. his pack of goods he had lain down from his back.
3. (he had flung off) his rags of poverty and clothed himself in dress of honor.
4. (With a royal robe) he covered himself,
5. and he bound a diadem on his brow.
6. Then Ishtar the queen lifted up her eyes to the throne of Izdūbar—
7. Kiss me, Izdūbar! she said, for I will marry thee !
8. Let us live together, I and thou, in one place ;
9. thou shalt be my husband, and I will be thy wife.
10. Thou shalt ride in a chariot of lapis-lazuli,[1]
11. whose wheels are golden and its pole resplendent.
12. Shining bracelets shalt thou wear every day.
13. By our house the cedar trees in green vigor shall grow,
14. and when thou shall enter it
15. (suppliant) crowds shall kiss thy feet !
16. Kings, Lords, and Princes shall bow down before thee !
17. The tribute of hills and plains they shall bring to thee as offerings,
18. thy flocks and thy herds shall all bear twins,
19. thy race of mules shall be magnificent,
20. thy triumphs in the chariot race shall be proclaimed without ceasing,

1 Literally "blue stone;" it was a brilliant dark blue.

21. and among the chiefs thou shalt never have an equal.

22. (Then Izdûbar) opened his mouth and spake,
23. (and said) to Ishtar the queen :
24. (Lady ! full well) I know thee by experience.
25. Sad and funereal (is thy dwelling place),
26. sickness and famine surround thy path,
27. (false and) treacherous is thy crown of divinity.
28. Poor and worthless is thy crown of royalty
29. (Yes ! I have said it) I know thee by experience.

COLUMN II.

1. Wailings thou didst make
2. for Tarzi thy husband,
3. (and yet) year after year with thy cups thou didst poison him.
4. Thou hadst a favorite and beautiful eagle,
5. thou didst strike him (with thy wand) and didst break his wings ;
6. then he stood fast in the forest (only) fluttering his wings.
7. Thou hadst a favorite lion full of vigor,
8. thou didst pull out his teeth, seven at a time.
9. Thou hadst a favorite horse, renowned in war,
10. he drank a draught and with fever thou didst poison him !
11. Twice seven hours without ceasing
12. with burning fever and thirst thou didst poison him.
13. His mother, the goddess Silili, with thy cups thou didst poison.
14. Thou didst love the king of the land

15. whom continually thou didst render ill with thy drugs,

16. though every day he offered libations and sacrifices.

17. Thou didst strike him (with thy wand) and didst change him into a leopard.

18. The people of his own city drove him from it,

19. and his own dogs bit him to pieces!

20. Thou didst love a workman,[1] a rude man of no instruction,

21. who constantly received his daily wages from thee,

22. and every day made bright thy vessels.

23. In thy pot a savory mess thou didst boil for him,

24. saying, Come, my servant and eat with us on the feast day

25. and give thy judgment on the goodness of our pot-herbs.

26. The workman replied to thee,

27. Why dost thou desire to destroy me?

28. Thou art not cooking! I will not eat!

29. For I should eat food bad and accursed,

30. and the thousand unclean things thou hast poisoned it with.

31. Thou didst hear that answer (and wert enraged),

32. Thou didst strike him (with thy wand) and didst change him into a pillar,

33. and didst place him in the midst of the desert!

34. I have not yet said a crowd of things! many more I have not added.

1 The eagle, the lion, the horse, the king and the workman are supposed to represent the numerous bridegrooms of this treacherous goddess.

35. Lady! thou wouldst love me as thou hast done
      the others.
36. Ishtar this speech listened to,
37. and Ishtar was enraged and flew up to heaven.
38. Ishtar came into the presence of Anû her father,
39. and into the presence of Annatu, her mother, she
      came.
40. Oh, my father, Izdûbar has cast insults upon
      me." [1]

The student of comparative mythology will recognize in the above legend the original idea of much of
the classic lore of Greece. Izdûbar's return, and the
throwing off of his disguise, suggest the adventures of
Ulysses as related by Homer, and his return to Ithaca
as a beggar.

"Next came Ulysses lowly at the door,
  A figure despicable, old and poor ;
  In squalid vests with many a gaping rent,
  Propped on a staff and trembling as he went."
                              Odyssey, Book xvii.

The character of Ishtar as presented in this tablet
is apparently a prototype not only of Hecate, but also
of Medea, whose chariot was drawn by winged serpents, and the cauldron or pot, which Ishtar filled
with her magic herbs, suggests the statement of Ovid
that Medea on one occasion spent no less than nine
days and nights in collecting herbs for her cauldron. [2]
The character of Ishtar may also have suggested that
of Circe, who

[1] Inscriptions Western Asia, Vol. IV, p. 48, published by the British Museum, and translated by H. Fox Talbot, F. R. S.
[2] Ovid's Metamorphoses, VII, 234.

"Mixed the potion, fraudulent of soul,
The poison mantled in a golden bowl,"

and she loved Ulysses as Ishtar loved Izdûbar, even though she had transformed all of his companions into swine.

In column II of the tablet under consideration, we find the story of the king whom Ishtar changed into a leopard, "and his own dogs bit him to pieces." No one can doubt that we see here the original of the Greek fable of Actæon, the hero who offended the goddess Diana, when she revenged herself by changing him into a deer, and his dogs no longer knowing their master, fell upon him and tore him to pieces.[1] The classic authors of Greece and Rome, however, attribute the fate of Actæon to the vengeance of the strong and graceful Diana, whom he offended by allowing his eyes to rest upon her rich beauty, while the tablet ascribes the fate of the king to the wanton cruelty of Ishtar.

Diana is sometimes identified with Hecate, the daughter of Asteria or Ishtar, and she retains the characteristics of her mother by appearing as the goddess of the moon. Her temple at Ephesus, with its hundred and twenty-seven columns of Parian marble, was one of the "Seven Wonders of the World," but the hideous idol within it was roughly carved of wood, not as a beautiful huntress, but as an Egyptian monster, whose deformity was hidden by a curtain.[2]

[1] The great celebrity of this fable is well illustrated by the fact that Ovid in his Metamorphoses (III, 206), has preserved the individual names of all the dogs, thirty-five in number.

[2] "Ye men of Ephesus, what man is there that knoweth not how that the city of the Ephesians is a worshipper of the great goddess Diana, and of the

The same Diana, however, in the hands of Grecian poets, becomes the strong and beautiful goddess of the chase, followed by her train of nymphs in pursuit of flying deer with golden horns.

Assyrian literature has evidently furnished the basis of several stories which are found in Ovid's Metamorphoses, besides that of Pyramus and Thisbe, which, as he expressly states, is a tale of Babylon.

ISHTAR, THE QUEEN OF LOVE AND BEAUTY.

Ishtar of Ninevch, who is identified with Beltis, the wife of Baal, became the goddess of love, "the divine queen" or "divine lady" of Kidmûri, which was the name of her temple at Nineveh. She was the daughter of Sin, the moon-god ; indeed, she is sometimes represented as the full moon, for which reason she is called the goddess Fifteen in Assyria, because the month consisting of thirty days, the moon was full on the fifteenth. She is the prototype of Freyja, the weeping goddess of love among the Northmen, and the Aphrodite of the Greeks — the beautiful nymph who sprang from the soft foam of the sea, and was received in a land of flowers, by the gold-filleted Seasons, who clothed her in garments immortal. Her chariot was drawn by milk-white swans, and her garlands were of rose and myrtle.

Ishtar of Nineveh appears as the imperious queen of love and beauty, and was undoubtedly the original of the Latin Venus. Indeed, Anthon says, "There

image which fell down from Jupiter ? (Acts xix, 35.) This question of the town clerk is strangely illustrated by an inscription found by Chandler near the aqueduct at Ephesus, which states that "It is notorious that not only among the Ephesians, but also everywhere among the Greek nations, temples are consecrated to her," etc.

is none of the Olympians of whom the foreign origin is so probable as this goddess, and she is generally regarded as being the same with the Astarte (Ashtaroth) of the Phœnicians."[1] We find upon the tablets a beautiful legend concerning her visit to Hades. She went in search of her husband Tammuz, as Orpheus was afterward represented as going to recover his wife, when the music from his golden shell stopped the wheel of Ixion, and made Tantalus forget his thirst. So also Hermöd, the son of Odin, in the mythology of the Northmen rode to Hel upon the fleet-footed Sleipnir in order to rescue his brother Balder.

It was doubtless through the Phœnicians that this legend reached the Greeks, and was there reproduced in a form almost identical with the fable of the tablets. Adonis, the sun-god, who was the hero, was killed by the tusk of a wild boar, even as Tammuz, the sun-god of Assyria, was slain by the boar's tusk of winter. Venus, the queen of love and beauty, was inconsolable at his loss, and at last obtained from Proserpina, the queen of hades, permission for Adonis to spend every alternate six months with her upon the earth, while the rest of the time should be passed in hades. Thus also the Osiris of the Egyptians was supposed to be dead or absent forty days in each year, during which time the people lamented his loss, as the Syrians did that of Tammuz, as the Greeks did that of Adonis, and as also the Northmen mourned for Frey.

Ishtar is represented as going down to the regions of darkness wearing rings and jewels, with a diadem

[1] Anthon's Class. Dict.

and girdle set with precious stones, and this fact would seem to indicate that the ancient city, which afterward came under the rule of Persian kings, was the home of the idea that whatever was buried with the dead would go with them to the other shore. Hence India, for ages, burned the favorite wives, with the dead bodies of her rajas, while other tribes placed living women in the graves of their chiefs, and our own Indians provide dogs and weapons for the use of their braves when they reach the "happy hunting grounds." We give the following legend complete, as it is found upon the tablets:

THE DESCENT OF ISHTAR.

COLUMN I.

"1. To the land of Hades, the region of her desire,

2. Ishtar, daughter of the moon-god Sin, turned her . mind.

3. And the daughter of Sin fixed her mind (to go there).

4. To the house where all meet, the dwelling of the god Irkalla,

5. to the house men enter but cannot depart from,

6. to the road men go but cannot return,

7. the abode of darkness and famine,

8. where the earth is their food; their nourishment clay;

9. light is not seen; in darkness they dwell;

10. ghosts like birds flutter their wings there,

11. on the door and gate-posts the dust lies undisturbed.

12. When Ishtar arrived at the gate of Hades,

13. to the keeper of the gate she spake:
14. Oh keeper of the entrance! open thy gate!
15. Open thy gate! I say again that I may enter.
16. If thou openest not thy gate and I enter not,
17. I will assault the door; I will break down the gate,
18. I will attack the entrance, I will split open the portals,
19. I will raise the dead to be the devourers of the living!
20. Upon the living the dead shall prey.

21. Then the porter opened his mouth and spake
22. and said to the great Ishtar,
23. Stay, Lady! do not shake down the door.
24. I will go and tell this to Queen Nin-ci-gal.
25. The porter entered and said to Nin-ci-gal
26. These curses thy sister Ishtar (utters)
27. blaspheming thee with great curses.

28. When Nin-ci-gal heard this
29. she grew pale like a flower that is cut off,
30. she trembled like the stem of a reed.
31. I will cure her of her rage, she said, I will cure her fury,
32. these curses will I repay her.
33. Light up consuming flames, light up blazing straw.
34. Let her groan with the husbands who deserted their wives.
35. Let her groan with the wives who from their husband's sides departed.
36. Let her groan with the youths who led dishonored lives.

37. Go, porter, open the gate for her,
38. but strip her, like others at other times.

39. The porter went and opened the gate.
40. Enter, Lady of Tiggaba[1] city. It is permitted.
41. The Sovereign of Hades will come to meet thee.

42. The first gate admitted her, and stopped her; there was taken off the great crown from her head.

43. Keeper! do not take off from me the great crown from my head.

44. Enter, Lady! for the queen of the land demands her jewels.

45. The second gate admitted her and stopped her; there were taken off the earrings of her ears.

46. Keeper! do not take off from me the earrings of my ears.

47. Enter, Lady! for the queen of the land demands her jewels.

48. The third gate admitted her and stopped her; there were taken off the precious stones from her head.

49. Keeper! do not take off from me the precious stones from my head.

50. Enter, Lady! for the queen of the land demands her jewels.

51. The fourth gate admitted her and stopped her; there were taken off the small lovely gems from her forehead.

---

[1] A principal seat of Ishtar's worship.

52. Keeper! do not take off from me the small lovely
    gems from my forehead

53. Enter, Lady! for the queen of the land demands
    her jewels.

54. The fifth gate admitted her and stopped her;
    there was taken off the emerald girdle of her
    waist.

55. Keeper! do not take off from me the emerald
    girdle from my waist.

56. Enter, Lady! for the queen of the land demands
    her jewels.

57. The sixth gate admitted her and stopped her;
    there was taken off the golden rings of her
    hands and feet.

58. Keeper! do not take off from me the golden
    rings of my hands and feet.

59. Enter, Lady! for the queen of the land demands
    her jewels.

60. The seventh gate admitted her and stopped her;
    there was taken off the last garment from
    her body.

61. Keeper! do not take off from me the last gar-
    ment from my body.

62. Enter, Lady! for the queen of the land demands
    her jewels.

63. After that mother Ishtar had descended into
    Hades.

64. Nin-ci-gal saw her and derided her to her face.

65. Ishtar lost her reason and heaped curses upon
    her.

66. Nin-ci-gal opened her mouth and spake
67. to Namtar, her messenger, a command she gave:
68. Go, Namtar
69. Bring her out for punishment.[1]

COLUMN II.

1. The divine messenger of the gods lacerated his face[2] before them.
2. He tore his vest (or vestments). Words he spake rapidly;
3. the Sun approached, he joined the Moon, his father.[3]
4. Weeping, they spake thus to Hea the king:
5. Ishtar descended into the earth and she did not rise again.

(Here follow a few lines which are unworthy of repetition, as they very coarsely describe the pitiable condition of the world when forsaken by the goddess of love.)

11. Then the god Hea in the depth of his mind laid a plan;
12. he formed for her escape a figure of a man of clay.
13. Go to save her, Phantom! present thyself at the portal of Hades:
14. the seven gates of Hades will open before thee;
15. Nin-ci-gal will see thee and will come to thee.

[1] The end of this line, and all the remaining lines of Column I, are lost, but some mutilated fragments indicate that Namtar is commanded to afflict Ishtar with dire diseases of the eyes, the feet, the heart, the head, etc.

[2] A sign of violent grief in the East, forbidden in Deut. xiv, 1; also Lev. xix, 28.

[3] Nabonidus says in his inscription (Col. II, 17) Oh, sun, protect this temple, together with the moon, thy father.

16. When her mind shall be grown calm and her anger shall be worn off

17. name her with the names of the great gods!

18. Prepare thy frauds! On deceitful tricks fix thy mind!

19. The chiefest deceitful trick! Bring forth fishes of the waters out of an empty vessel.

20. This thing will astonish Nin-ci-gal,

21. Then to Ishtar she will restore her clothing.

22. A great reward for these things shall not fail.

23. Go save her, Phantom! and the great assembly of the people shall crown thee!

24. Meats the first in the city shall be thy food.

25. Wine the most delicious in the city shall be thy drink.

26. A royal palace shall be thy dwelling.

27. A throne of state shall be thy seat.

28. Magician and conjurer shall kiss the hem of thy garment.

29. Nin-ci-gal opened her mouth and spake

30. to Namtar her messenger, a command she gave:

31. Go Namtar! clothe the Temple of Justice!

32. Adorn the images and the altars.

33. Bring out Anunnaka.[1] Seat him on a golden throne.

34. Pour out for Ishtar the waters of life and let her depart from my dominions.

35. Namtar went; and clothed the Temple of Justice;

36. he adorned the images and the altars;

---

[1] A genius often mentioned, who here acts the part of a judge, pronouncing the absolution of Ishtar.

37. he brought out Anunnaka; on a golden throne he seated him;

38. he poured out for Ishtar the waters of life.

39. Then the first gate let her forth, and restored to her the first garment of her body.

40. The second gate let her forth and restored to her the diamonds of her hands and feet.

41. The third gate let her forth and restored to her the emerald girdle of her waist.

42. The fourth gate let her forth and restored to her the small lovely gems of her forehead.

43. The fifth gate let her forth and restored to her the precious stones of her head.

44. The sixth gate let her forth and restored to her the earrings of her ears.

45. The seventh gate let her forth and restored to her the crown of her head." [1]

Surely here is poetry—the haughty queen of love and beauty imperiously demands an entrance into the land of shadows that she may recover her beloved. She threatens to break down the very gates of hades and raise the dead to devour the living if her wish is refused. She shrinks at no sacrifice which her love-lighted mission may cost. A great crown is taken from her head, but she stays not. Her jewels and precious stones—her girdle of priceless gems—is taken from her, and still she presses forward in quest of her love.

But when at last the seven gates of hades have closed upon her luxurious form, the world misses her

[1] Tablet K, 162, British Museum, translated by H. Fox Talbot, F. R. S. Records of the Past, Vol. I, 1st Series.

joyous presence—the splendor is stolen from Beauty's eyes—the crimson touch of life has faded from her lips—the doves and sun-birds no longer chant their love songs in the crowns of the palm trees, and the sorrowing night bird trills the plaintive tale to the closed and weeping roses. Nay, even the sky seems to forget to light up the couch of the dying sun with draperies of crimson and gold, and all the world is shrouded in darkness and cold despair. But Hea, in his ocean home, hears the wail of the gods who mourn the absence of Ishtar, and he comes to the rescue. The seven gates of hades swing again upon their hinges, and with crowns and jewels and girdle restored, the imperial goddess comes forth to resume her sway amid the flowers of a love-lighted earth.

CHAPTER IV.

PERSIAN MYTHOLOGY.

THE COMMON SOURCE OF MYTHOLOGY — MYTHICAL
MOUNTAINS — RIVERS — MYTHICAL BIRDS — AHÛRA
MAZDA—ATAR—THE STORM GOD—YIMA—THE CHIN-
VAT BRIDGE—MITHRA—RÉSUMÉ.

WE have briefly sketched in the preceding chapter the more tolerable features of a mythology which is evidently the common source of the later pantheons. The picture of human sacrifices, and practices which are still more revolting, have been avoided, as unnecessary to the general purpose, while the poetic figures of these ancient myths are dwelt upon with peculiar pleasure.

Persian civilization was to a great extent the product of Babylonian elements, and her mythology was born of that type of sensual idolatry too gross for description. But the Persians were a poetic people, and in their hands these ancient myths were refined and somewhat elevated. The hideous idols called sun-images, which were used in the worship of Chemosh, gave place to the adoration of the sun itself, as the great source of all physical light. It was by the hand of Persia that the sacred bull of Egypt was smitten down, and also the golden couch of Baal, with all its attendant horrors. But even Persia is accused of hav-

ing at times practiced the horrible rite of human sacrifice, and the Babylonian Venus found admission, even
among the people whose king had stabbed the Egyptian Apis, and overturned his shrine.[1]

Persia was a land of extremes, and the richest part
of her dominions was fated to lie beneath the early
snows, and feel the severity of winter, while the
central portion of the country was one vast desert,
whose scorching simoons were as much to be dreaded
as the snows of her northern table-lands. The early
settlers of Īrān, therefore, were forced to win their
bread and develop their resources by the most ardu-
ous labor, and the dreamy mythology of the Hindūs
gave way in their minds to the sterner conflict between good and evil.

The opposition between light and darkness became
a prominent feature of their mythology, for the battles which raged in Hindū skies between Indra, the
storm king, and his constant enemy, Vṛitra, became
to the sons of Īrān a personal strife with the powers of nature, and instead of dreaming of a contest
in the clouds, they sang of the daily battle in lives
which were crowded with hardship. Hence it is
that Ormazd and Ahriman, in their continual strife,
form the background of the national mythology,
although Persia took the sun for her emblem, and
called her kings by his royal name ; a flashing globe

---

[1] The statement of Herodotus concerning the attack upon the sacred bull
is probably correct, even though the Egyptian monuments claim that Cambyses, and also the Roman emperors, bowed down to the Egyptian gods.
We may conclude that Cambyses, in doing reverence to the gods of Egypt,
was following in the footsteps of his cool and politic father (Cyrus), and
was guided in these acts by the precedent which his father had set in reference to the gods of Babylonia.

was the signal light above the imperial tent, and the golden eagle was perched upon the ensign that led the Persian troops to victory.

MYTHICAL MOUNTAINS.

The silent mountains standing calmly beneath the skies of blue, while the ages come and go, always command the reverence of the human heart. With forests around their feet, the gray peaks reach upward to dim and ashen heights, where the white snow lies unpolluted by the foot of man. Their frost-crowns gleam in the sunlight of noon, or change to tints of opal and crimson light beneath the farewell fires of the setting sun. No wonder, then, that in the fables of all people the gods are enthroned on wondrous heights. The old Assyrian kings wrote upon their strange tablets of "the world mountain," which, although rooted in hades, still supported the heavens with all their starry hosts. The world was bound to it with a rope, like that with which the sea was churned in the later Hindū legend, for the lost ambrosia of the gods,[1] or like the golden cord of Homer with which Zeus proposed to suspend the nether earth, after binding the cord about Olympus.[2] This mythical mountain was the abode of the gods, and it was this of which the Babylonian king said :

" I will exalt my throne above the stars of God ;

[1] Hindu Literature, p. 59.
[2] "Let down our golden everlasting chain,
  Whose strong embrace holds heaven and earth and men;
  I fix the chain to great Olympus height,
  And the vast world hangs trembling in my sight."—Il. viii, 19-26.

I will sit upon the mount of the congregation in
the sides of the north;
I will ascend above the heights of the clouds;
I will be like the Most High."[1]

It was between the "Twin Mountains" that the
sun passed in its rising and setting, and the rocky
gates were guarded by the "scorpion men," whose
heads were at the portals of heaven, and their feet
in hell beneath.[2]

In the mythology of the Hĭndŭs, Mount Meru rises
in her solitary grandeur in the very centre of the
earth to the height of sixty-four thousand miles; and
there on her sun-kissed crown, amidst gardens of fabulous beauty, and flowers that never of winter hear—
where the skies are of rose and pearl, and the dream-
like harmonies of far-off voices are borne upon the air,
we find the heaven of Indra, the abode of the gods.[3]

Among the Greeks the gates of Olympus open to
receive the imperial throng, when

"The gods with Jove assume their thrones of gold."

When the chambers of the east were opened, and
floods of light were poured upon the peak, the Greek
poet dreamt that:

"The sounding hinges ring on either side,
The gloomy volumes pierced with light divide,
The chariot mounts, where deep in ambient skies
Confused Olympus' hundred heads arise—
Where far apart the Thunderer fills his throne
O'er all the gods, superior and alone."

[1] Isa. xiv, 13.
[2] Ninth tablet of the Epic of Gisdhubar.
[3] Hindu Literature, pp. 126-148.

But even the storm-swept heights of Olympus, where the chariots of the gods were crushed to fragments beneath the lightnings of Jove, were not lofty enough for the spirit of the Norseman. Odin's Valhal, with its roof of shields and walls of gleaming spears, lies in heaven itself, and higher still is Gimle, the gold-roofed hall of the higher gods. Far away to the northward, on the heights of the Nida mountains, stands a hall of shining gold which is the home of the Sindre race.[1] These are they who smelt earth's gold from her rough brown stone, and flashing through her crystals, the tints which are hidden in the hearts of the roses, they are changed to rubies and garnets. These are they who make the sapphires blue with the fresh lips of the violet, and mould earth's tears into her purest pearls.

In Persian mythology we find a trace of "the world mountain" of the old Assyrian kings, as well as a thought which is akin to the vine-clad bowers of Meru, the shining gates of Olympus, and the Nida mountains of the Norsemen, for here the Qāf mountains surround the world after the manner of the annular system described in the Mahā-Bhārata.[2] This mythical range is pure emerald, and although it surrounds the world, it is placed between two of the horns of a white ox, named Kornit or Kajūta. He has four thousand horns, and the distance from one horn to another could not be traversed in five hundred years. These mountains are the abode of giants, fairies and peris, while their life-giving foun-

[1] Anderson—Norse Mythology, pp. 104-434.
[2] Hindu Literature, p. 126.

tains confer immortality upon those who taste of their waters.

The highest portion of the emerald range is the Alborz,[1] where the fabled Sīmūrgh builds her colossal nest of sandal wood, and the woven branches of aloe and myrtle trees. Mount Alborz is represented as standing upon the earth, while her crown of light reposes in the region far beyond the stars. It is Hara-Berezaita (the lofty mountain)—the sphere of endless light, where the supreme god of Persian mythology dwells in his own temple which is the "abode of song." This is the "Mother of Mountains" and from it have grown all the heights that stand upon the earth; it is the fabled center of the world, and around it the sun, moon and stars revolve. Hence, in the Vendīdad[2] we find the following hymn:

"Up, rise and roll along, thou swift horsed sun,
Above Hara-Berezaita and produce light for the world.
Up, rise up, thou moon—
Rise up, ye stars, rise up above Hara-Berezaita
And produce light for the world,
And mayest thou, O man, rise up along the path
          made by Mazda—
Along the way made by the gods,
The watery way they opened."

RIVERS.

In the mythology of every people we find mystic rivers in connection with the worship of their divini-

---

[1] Alborz, being changed into Elburz, became the name of a mountain range on the southern shore of the Caspian sea, and Mount Demavend, its highest peak, is looked upon as the home of the Simurgh, and it is also the scene of many mythical adventures.

[2] XXI.

ties. They are winding everywhere through the enchanted land of fable. Often born in the high-lands of the celestial mountains, they are represented as coming down to earth with the glint of the sun-light on their waves. The great river of Egypt, which is supposed to give life to the gods as well as men, is thus fabled to have sprung from the mountains of the sky, and a "Hymn to the Nile," recorded on a clay tablet, begins with the words:

"Adoration to the Nile!
Hail to thee, O Nile!
Who comest to give life to Egypt!
Thou givest the earth to drink, inexhaustible one!
Thou descendest from the sky." [1]

In Greek mythology, we find the river ocean flowing around the earth, with its calm current un-broken by storm, and unswerved by the angry tem-pest. The sea, with her sun-kissed billows, received her waters from this unfailing fountain, and far be-yond the northern mountains, where the "golden gardens" gleamed in the sunlight and the winds were rocked to sleep, there lived a happy people, where sorrow could not enter and death would never come.

Among the Hindūs, the sacred Ganges flowed at first only through the blue fields of heaven, and fell to the earth from the divine feet of Vishnū:

"And white foam clouds and silver spray
    Were wildly tossed on high,
Like swans that urge their homeward way
    · Across the autumn sky."

[1] Trans. by Paul Guieysse. Rec. of P., Vol. III, p. 48. The belief in

The Norseman also sings of heavenly rivers, as well as· the Ifing, which flows in a never-freezing current between the world of men and the world of gods ; he sings, too, of the river Gyöll, which flows nearest to the gates of Hel,[1] and over whose golden bridge the countless bands of the dead are passing.

In Persian mythology there is a crystal stream which gushes from a golden precipice of the mythical mountain and descends to the earth from the heavens, as does the celestial Gangä of the Hindūs. This is the heavenly spring from which all the waters of the earth come down. . . . It is the Ardvi Sūra Anāhita which ever flows in a life-giving current, bringing blessings unto man and receiving in return the sacrifices of the material world.

This river has a thousand cells and a thousand channels, and each of these extend as far as a swiftly mounted horseman can ride in forty days ; in each channel there stands a palace gleaming with an hundred windows and a thousand columns ; these palaces are surrounded with ten thousand balconies founded in the distant channels of the river, and within their courts are luxurious beds, " well scented and covered with pillows." In the golden ravines around these palace halls are the wondrous fountains of the Ardvi Sūra Anāhita, and the stream rushes down from the summit of the mountain with a volume greater than all the rivers of earth, and falls into the bosom of the celestial sea that lies at the foot of the Hara-Berezaita. When the waters of

the celestial origin of the Nile survived in Egypt as lately as the time of Joinville. (Histoire de Saint Louis, Chap. II.)

[1] Hel, the world of the dead, irrespective of character.

the river fall into the Vourū-Kasha, the waves of the sea boil over the shores, and the billows chant a song of welcome.

This celestial spring, with its mighty torrent of waters, is personified as a beautiful goddess [1]—a maiden tall and shapely, who is born of a glorious race. She is stately and noble, strong as the current of a mighty river, and pure as the snows that lie on the mountain's crown. Her beautiful arms are white and thick, her hair is long and luxuriant, for she is large and comely, radiant with the glory of a perfect womanhood.

This glorious maid of the mountain has four white horses, which were made for her by Ahūra Mazda; one is the snow, and one is the wind, while the others are the rain and the cloud; thus it happens that ever upon the earth it is snowing, or the rain is somewhere coming down to gladden the flowers with refreshing touch.

The beautiful goddess springs from a golden fissure in the highest peak, and mounting her chariot draws the reins above her white steeds and drives them down the steep incline, which is a thousand times the height of a man, and continual sacrifice is offered to her brightness and glory.

Clothed with a golden mantle and wearing a crown radiant with the light of an hundred gems, she comes

[1] The first record of the worship of Ardvi Sura is in a cuneiform inscription by Artaxerxes Mnemon (404–361), in which her name is corrupted into Anahata. Artaxerxes Mnemon appears to have been an eager promoter of her worship, as he is said to have first erected the statues of Venus-Anahita in Babylon, Suza, and Ecbatana, and to have taught her worship to the Persians, the Bactrians, and the people of Damas and Sardes (Clemens Alexandrians, Protrept. 5, on the authority of Berosus; about 260 B. C.).

dashing down the mountain side, thinking in her heart: "Who will praise me? Who will offer me a sacrifice with libations?"

The cloud-sea represents the "dewy treasures" of the Hindūs—the rains which are held in the reluctant cloud, and only drawn therefrom by the lightning bolts of Indra, who is assisted in the battle by the Maruts when they "harness their deer for victory."[1] The Persian Vendīdad represents a continual interchange between the waters of the earth and sky.

"As the Vourū-Kasha is the gathering place of the waters
Rise up, go up the aerial way and go down upon the earth . . .
The large river that is known afar
That is as large as all the waters of earth
Runs from the height down to the sea, Vourū-Kasha."[2]

MYTHICAL BIRDS.

Birds have always held a prominent place in the various mythologies. Among the Assyrians, the *zu* or vulture was the symbol of the "god of the storm-cloud," who was believed to have stolen the laws and attributes of Bel for the benefit of mankind, and to have been punished for the theft by transformation into a vulture.[3]

In Egyptian mythology, the tablets represent Isis as a bird. "For she is Isis, the charmer, the avenger of her brother, who seeks him without failing, who traverses the earth with lamentations, without resting

[1] Hindu Literature. p. 39.   [2] Vendīdad, xxi.
[3] Sayce, Lec. Rel. Babylonians, pp. 293-299.

before she has found him—creating the light with her feathers, producing the wind with her wings, celebrating the sacred dances, and depositing her brother in the tomb . . . raising the remains of the god, with immovable heart . . . she makes him grow, his arm becomes strong in the great dwelling."[1]

In the Hindŭ poem of the Rāmāyaṇa, during the banishment of the innocent and beautiful Sīta, the pitying birds dipped their pinions in the sacred waters of the Ganges, and fanned her feverish face, that she might not faint with the heat.[2] In the same poem we have also descriptions of Garuḍa, the eagle-steed of Vishṇu, and Sampati, the sacred vulture, who gave information concerning the demon king that carried away the beautiful princess. Hindŭ mythology also contains "the celestial birds," who were acquainted with right and wrong, and who, in one of the Purāṇas answered the questions of the sages, and also gave an account of the creation.

In northern Europe we find a wondrous eagle, who sits amongst the branches of the Ygdrasil—that beautiful tree of Norse mythology, whose three great roots strike downward among the Anglo-Saxons, Scandinavians, and Germans. This great ash tree spreads its life-giving arms through the heavens, and on the topmost bough is the eagle "who knows many things," and between his eyes sits the keen-eyed hawk, Vedfolner.[3]

We have also the Griffin of chivalry, the fabulous

[1] Hymn to Osiris on the stele of Amon-em-ha. Translated by D. Mallet. Rec. of P., IV, 21.
[2] Hindu Literature, p. 267.
[3] Anderson—Norse Mythology, pp. 75-190.

monster, half bird and half lion, that protected the gold of the Hyperborean regions from the one-eyed Arimaspians, and the Phœnix of Egyptian fable—the bird of gold and crimson plumage, that is burned upon her nest of spices every thousand years, and as often springs to life from her ashes. The Turks have their Kerkes, and the Japanese their Kirni, while China exhibits a nondescript dragon, which is a combination of bird and reptile. In the Greek Iliad we have the imperial bird of Jove—"Strong sovereign of the plumy race" bearing a signal from the god. Among the Persian myths we find the Karmak, a gigantic bird "which overshadowed the earth, and kept off the rain until the rivers were dried up." And the law was brought to the Var of Yima by the bird Karśipta who recites the Avesta in the language of birds.

The raven was sacred to Apollo, and in Persia the priests of the sun were named ravens. In the Avesta this bird is called "the swiftest of all—the highest of the flying creatures . . . he alone of all living things—he or none—overtakes the flight of an arrow, however well it has been shot; he grazes in the hidden ways of the mountains, he grazes in the depths of the vales, he grazes on the summit of the trees listening to the voices of the birds."[1] Again it is said of the Vūrengaṇa or raven: "Take thou a feather of that bird, with that feather thou shalt rub thine own body—with that feather thou shalt curse thine, enemies; if a man holds a bone of that strong bird, no one can smite or turn to flight that fortu-

[1] Bahram Yast, vii.

nate man. The feather of that bird of birds brings him help, it brings unto him the homage of men, it maintains him in glory."[1] It is said that the glory departed from Yima three times in the shape of a raven, and the raven is also one of the incarnations of the genius of Victory.

The Saēna, which, in later literature, is the Sīnamrū or Sīmūrgh, occupies an important place in Persian mythology. His resting place is on the Jaḍ-bēsh, or the tree of the eagle; this tree is the bearer of all seeds, and when the Sīmūrgh leaves it in his flight, a thousand twigs will shoot from the tree, and when he returns and alights thereon, he breaks off the thousand twigs, and sheds the seed from them. Then the bird Chaṇmrōsh who always sits near, watching the tree, will collect the seed which falls from the Jaḍ-bēsh, or tree of all seeds, and carry it to the fountain where Tishtar (or Tiśtrya) receives the waters, so that Tishtar may gather the seed of all kinds with the waters, and may shower it down upon the world with the rain.[2]

The Sīmūrgh was the son of Ahūm-stut, who was perhaps "the holy falcon—praiser of the lord." He builds his nest amidst the cliffs of Mount Alborz, and the gigantic structure is woven with the branches of the aloe and the fragrant sandal-wood. Around it gleam the white cliffs in the sunlight, and precious stones lie beneath it, for it is far beyond the reach of man. The Sīmūrgh became, in later literature, a mythical incarnation of supreme wisdom.

---

[1] Bahram Yast, xiii.
[2] Minokhirad—62 and 87. Trans. by West.

AHŬRA-MAZDA.

This deity is represented as the supreme god of the Persians, the creator of the other gods, and the ruler of them all.

The word Ahūra appears to have much kinship with Asūra, of the Hindū mythology. In the early portions of the Ṛig-veda this word has a good meaning, but in the latter part of the same work the Asura is represented as a black demon, who committed fearful devastation until he was defeated by Indra. Among the Persians, Asūra, or Ahūra is pictured as the sky-god, who is represented among the Hindūs as Varuṇa, who looks down from heaven with his countless starry eyes and "wields the universe as the gamesters handle dice." [1]

The heaven of Ahūra-Mazda surrounds the highest peaks of the "Lofty Mountain" in the upper air, and it is called the "Abode of Song." It is said "the maker Ahūra-Mazda has built a dwelling on the Hara-Berezaita, the bright mountain around which the daily stars revolve. . . . With his arms lifted up towards immortality, Mithra, the lord of wide pastures, drives forward a beautiful chariot, wrought by Ahūra-Mazda and inlaid with stars." [2]

The attributes of Ahriman, the serpent, or evil principle, became personified, and the various forms of falsehood, darkness and death became abstract demons. So, also, Ahūra-Mazda was afterward worshipped as a multitude of deities, and thus it happened that victory, benevolence, sovereignty, and even

---

[1] Rig-veda Sanhita—Wilson's Trans., Vol. V, p. 102
[2] Yast, x.

health were each worshipped as a separate divinity, and gathered together in the heavenly councils as a band of Yazatas or angels. These are numbered by thousands, but the one demanding the greatest reverence is

ATAR.

This is the god of fire. He was called the "most great Yazata," and as such he commanded the undying worship of the Persian devotee.

The first duty of each Pārsī householder was to cherish the sacred fire upon his own hearth, feeding it only with delicate bits of fragrant sandal wood, while the fires in the temples were committed to the care of the priests. Atar is the Persian form of the Hindū Agni, the guardian of the home, and the symbol of social union.

The cypress tree was planted in front of their fire temples, and when it had reached a towering height, it was surrounded by a gilded palace like a sheath of flame,[1] while more simple altars arose from their mountain tops and blazed with the sacred symbol.

THE STORM GOD.

The Persian myth of the struggle of Tistrya with Apaosha, the drouth fiend, in order to obtain rain, is merely another form of the battle of the elements in the Ṛig-veda, when Indra rides forth to the conflict and shoots his arrows into the gathering clouds.

The early idolaters worshipped the host of heaven, and from this doubtless arose the worship of the star Sirius as the storm god—Tistrya. The rising of

---

[1] See the Bundehesh.

this star to a prominent position marks the period of the ever welcome rains, when the parched earth drinks in the refreshing flood, and the flowers spring from the soil.

The dog-days are supposed to represent the time of Tištrya's great conflict with Apaosha, and the battle is long and closely contested before he conquers his foe.

The storm god comes into the arena in three different forms; he first attacks the foe in the form of a beautiful youth, then as a bull with golden horns, and at last as a white horse with golden caparison and golden ears. The drouth fiend is represented as a black horse, and "They meet together hoof against hoof, they fight for three days and three nights, and then the Deva[1] proves too strong for bright and glorious Tištrya; he overcomes him." Tištrya then flees from the sea and cries out: "Oh Ahûra-Mazda, men do not worship me with sacrifice and praise, invoking me by my own name; should they worship me with sacrifice and praise, invoking me by my own name as the other Yazatas are invoked, they would bring me the strength of ten horses, of ten camels, ten bulls, ten mountains and ten rivers."

Ahûra then offers him a sacrifice, in which he is invoked by his own name, and which gives him the strength of ten horses, of ten camels, ten bulls, ten mountains and ten rivers, whereupon Tištrya returns to the conflict, and Apaosha flies before him. The white horse being victorious, the copious rains come

[1] This word is frequently spelled Daeva.

down, glad brooks spring from the rocky hillsides—
they come with pearly sandaled feet, laden with love
and mercy to the sun-parched plain; hence the following hymn:

" We sacrifice unto Tištyra, the bright and glorious
    star,
  For whom the longing flocks and herds and men
    are looking forward
  When shall we see him rise up, the bright and
    glorious star Tištrya . . . . .:
  For whom long the standing waters and the run-
    ning spring waters,
  The stream waters and the rain waters?
  When will the springs with a flow run to the beau-
    tiful places and fields?[1]
  And to the roots of the plants that they may grow
    with a powerful growth?"

YIMA.

The Persian god of death is scarcely changed
from the Hindū Yama, who is "the king of death
and the judge of the dead." Among the Hindūs,
however, he appears as the first of men who died,
while among the Persians he has many ancestors.
He offered sacrifices upon the summit of "the beautiful mountain," and prayed the gods to grant him
power and dominion. Thus he became a king over
men and even over the Devas. As the regions of
Pluto were guarded by the three-headed dog Cerberus,
and the path of Yama was watched by two terrible
dogs of the "four-eyed tawny breed of Sarama,"

[1] Yast, viii.

so also the souls of good men are defended from the howling and pursuing demons, by the dogs that guard

THE CHINVAT BRIDGE.

The Chinvat[1] or *K*invaḍ bridge reaches to Mount Alborz, and it is also called the "Bridge of the Gatherer," over which the souls of the righteous pass easily into the abodes of bliss, while the wicked fall from it into the den of falsehood and iniquity.

The Mohammedans call it the Al-Sirat, and it is represented in the Korān as being finer than the thread of a famished spider and sharper than a two-edged sword.

More beautiful by far is the Bi-frost, or rainbow arch of the Norseman—the bridge between heaven and earth, which was also borrowed from Chaldea:

"A link that binds us to the skies
A bridge of rainbows thrown across
The gulf of tears and sighs."

And every day the gods come down to the judgment hall, of the Udar fountain, at the roots of the great ash tree and ride back on heavenly steeds across the bridge of many hues.

MITHRA.

As fire is the favorite symbol of the Persian, so the sun-gods are their most important deities, and of these Mithra stands at the head. One of the Sanskṛit names for the sun is Mitra, and the Persian

---

[1] Chinvat, the popular orthography of this word, is adopted as it represents the pronunciation.

form of the word retains its full significance, as the pure light of day. The sun is never without his shrine, and he is also represented in the human form. His terrible power, especially in tropical climes, could not fail to be recognized, and hence the Persian swore by the sun, while the temples and images consecrated to this god of day arose in every part of the land. Persian decrees of the fourth and fifth centuries demanded the highest worship for the sun itself, while fire and water should receive inferior service. Christians were persecuted for refusing to perform these services in Armenia[1] and the Roman Emperor Julian centered his apostasy in the philosophy which permitted him to call the sun the living image of God and even God himself.[2]

Mithra is represented in the Avesta as riding across the broad arch of heaven, his chariot drawn by milk-white steeds whose feet are shod with gold and silver, while the god himself wears a golden helmet and a silver breastplate. He is represented as "The first of the heavenly gods who reaches over Hara, who, foremost in battle array, takes hold of the summits, and from thence looks with a beneficent eye over the abodes of the Āryans, where the valiant chiefs draw up their many troops in array; where the high mountains, rich in pastures and waters, yield plenty to the cattle; where the deep lakes with salt water stands; where the wide flowing rivers swell and hurry. . . . Four stallions draw that chariot, all of the same white color, living on heav-

[1] History of Vartan by Elisaeus (Newman's trans.), p. 9.
[2] Gibbon, Chap. 23.

enly food and undying. . . . The hoofs of their fore feet are shod with gold, the hoofs of their hind feet are shod with silver."[1]

This is the Persian picture of the Hindū myth, where the god of day is represented as coming out of the crimson chambers of the east, in his fiery car, while his white steeds are led by the fair goddess of the morning, wearing her garments of silver and changeful opal fire.[2]

The mythology of Mazdeism is very rich with demons, many classes of which belong to the Indo-Irānian period. The Vedic Yātus are found unchanged in the Avesta, and these are demons who can assume any form they choose. The Pairikas in the oldest Avesta are the fiendish females, who rob the gods and men of the heavenly waters. They hover between heaven and earth in the midst of the sea Vourū-Kasha, to keep off the rain floods, working in harmony with Apaosha, the drouth fiend. There are many other female demons, which it is unnecessary to describe, as their characteristics are most revolting.

There is also a host of storm fiends, called "the running ones" on account of the headlong course of the fiends in a storm—"the onsets of the wounding crew." The Devas represent demons which belong to the Indo-European mythology, and the term originally meant "the gods in heaven." When they were converted into evil spirits they became "the fiends in the heavens" or the fiends who assail the sky, but they afterwards became the demons of lust and doubt. Death gave rise to several abstractions, such as Saurū,

which was identical in meaning as well as name with
the Vedic Sarū, "the arrow," a personification of the
arrow of death, as a god-like being. The same idea
is conveyed by Iśus, the self-moving arrow, a designa-
tion which is perhaps accounted for from the fact
that Sarū, in India, before becoming the arrow of
death, was the arrow of lightning, with which the
god killed his foe. The god of death in another form
becomes "the bone divider" who, like the Yama of
the Mahā-bhārata, holds a noose around the neck of
all living creatures. In the conflict between gods and
fiends he takes an active part through the sacrifice.
The sacrifice is more than an act of worship, it is an
act of assistance to the gods. Gods, like men, need
drink and food to be strong; like men, they need
praise and encouragement in order to be brave; when
not strengthened by the sacrifice they fly before their
foes.

Sraosha is the priest-god, he first tied the sticks
into bundles and offered up sacrifice to Ahūra;
he first sang the holy hymns and thrice each day
and night he smites the demon crew with his up-
lifted club, and thus protects the world of the living from the terrors of the night, when the fiends
rush upon the earth; it is he who protects the dead
from the terrors of death, from the assault of Ahriman. It will be through a sacrifice performed by
Ormazd and Sraosha that Ahriman will finally be
vanquished. A number of divinities sprang from the
hearth of the altar, most of them having existed
during the Indo-Īrānian period. Piety, who every day
brings her offerings and prayers to the altar, was

worshipped in the Vedas as Aramati, the goddess who every morning and evening, being anointed with sacred butter, offers herself up to Agni. She was praised in the Avesta as an abstract genius, but there are yet a few practices which preserve the evident traces of the old myths in relation to her union with Atar, the fire-god. The riches that go up to heaven in the offerings of man, and come down to earth in the gifts of the gods, were deified as Rāta, the gift, Ashi, the felicity, and more vividly in Parendi, the keeper of treasures, who comes on a sounding chariot, a sister to the Vedic Puramdhi.

Thus we have seen the fabulous "world mountain" of early Babylonia pervading the mythologies of Europe and Asia, taking the form of the star-crowned Olympus on the Ægean sea, and of Meru, with her fadeless flowers, in the valleys of India. In northern Europe it is represented by the Nida mountains with their golden palaces, and in Persia by the beautiful Hara with her crown of living light.

The Chaldean river of death, Datilla, flows also through the realms of Grecia under the name of Styx, and in the regions of the north it becomes the Ifing, and also the Gyöll. Again the mythical river seems to mount upward, and like the heavenly Nile, the Ganges springs from celestial heights and flows through the starry highlands of heaven, while the silvery torrents of the Persian stream come pouring down from the white summit of the Hara-Berezaita.

The early Baal, with all the unspeakable abominations attending his worship, becomes refined in the form of Zeus or Jove, who hurls his lightnings from the brow of Olympus, and in the Ahūra-Mazda of the Persians, whose throne is "the lofty mountain." Tammuz and Chemosh, whose hideous images called forth the contempt of the prophets, appear in the Persian pantheon as Mithra with his glittering steeds; Ashtaroth of Sidon, and Diana of Ephesus, lay aside their revolting sensuality, and come forth as the chaste and strong Diana of Grecian poetry, or the fair goddess of the dawn among the Hindūs and Persians. The germs of European and Asiatic mythology are therefore found in that cradle of idolatry, where the image-worship of Babylonia received the rebuke of the prophets, and where the red altars of Baal and Moloch were stained with human blood even amidst the highest forms of early art and culture.

DIVISION II.

THE PERIOD OF THE ZEND-AVESTA.

CHAPTER V.

THE ZEND-AVESTA.

DERIVATION AND LANGUAGE—DIVISIONS—AGE OF THE
ZEND-AVESTA — MANUSCRIPTS — ZARATHUŚTRA — THE
EARLY PÁRSÍS—THE MODERN PÁRSÍS.

WE use the ordinary form of the word, Zend-Avesta, for though some Orientalists claim that it should be called the Avesta-Zend, it is an open question whether this is the original and only correct term. According to the Pārsīs, Avesta means the sacred text, and Zend its Pahlavī translation, but in the Pahlavī translations themselves, the original work is called the Avesta-Zend, although there is no reason given for this course. Neither the word Avesta nor Zend occurs in the original Zend texts. The word Avesta, however, seems to be the Sanskrit *avastha*, meaning "authorized text," while Max Müller[1] claims that the name Zend was originally a corruption of the Sanskrit word *Khandas*, or "metrical language," which

---

[1] Chips, Vol. I, p. 82.

is a name given by the Brāhmans to the hymns of the Veda. The word Zend, or Zand, is also used to designate the language[1] in which the greater part of the Avesta is written.

In relation to its antiquity, the Zend ranks next to the Sanskṛit, and such authorities as Westergaard and Spiegel, while differing upon many points, agree in considering the Veda the safest key to an understanding of the Avesta. Many of the gods which are unknown to any of the Indo-European nations are worshipped under the same name in Sanskṛit and in Zend, and indeed many of the gods of the Zoroastrians seem to be mere reflections of the more primitive gods of the Veda, but at times the tendency to monotheism in the Zoroastrian religions would appear to be a solemn protest against the worship of all the powers of nature which is found in the Veda. Although there is much kinship between the two tongues, and many striking similarities between the gods of the two mythologies, it does not necessarily prove that portions of the Zend-Avesta were borrowed from the Veda. It does prove, however, that the two works proceeded from a common source of Āryan tradition, and it also proves that the Sanskṛit and the Zend continued to live side by side long after they were separated from the common stock of the Indo-European tongues.

There are decided differences between the themes of the Veda and the Avesta, but the link which binds them to a common source is never broken. Some Orientalists claim that there was a schism between the two

[1] Prof. Darmesteter and M. de Harlez claim that the Zend was the language of Aryan Media.

and that the differences are the result of a religious
revolution, while others argue that there was only a
long and slow movement which led, by insensible degrees, the vague dualism of the Indo-Iränians onward
to the sharply defined dualism of the Magi. It has
been clearly shown that the mythologies of Europe
and Asia have a common origin in the idolatry found
the valley of the Euphrates; so also the Veda and the
Zend-Avesta are two great literary productions flowing
from the same fountain head, which is found in the
Indo-Irânian period.

DIVISIONS.

The Zend-Avesta, or sacred books of the Pârsîs, is
really a collection of various fragments. The first
part, which may be called the Avesta proper, contains
the Vendîdad, the Visparad and the Yasna. The
Vendîdad is a compilation of religious lore and mythological tales, the Visparad is a collection of litanies
for the sacrifice, while the Yasna, too, is composed of
litanies, but it also contains five hymns or Gâthas
written in a different dialect, which is older than the
language of the greater part of the Avesta.

These three books are found in manuscripts in two
different forms. Sometimes either of them is found
alone or accompanied by a Pahlavî translation, or the
three are mingled together according to the require-
ments of the liturgy.

The second portion of this work is generally known
as the Khorda-Avesta, and is composed of short prayers, which are recited not only by the priests but by all
the faithful, at certain moments of the day, month or

year, and in the presence of the different elements. It is also customary to include in the Khorda or small Avesta, the Yaśts or hymns of praise to the several Izads or Yazatas.

The sacredness of the Avesta is to a certain extent reflected upon a work called the Bundehesh, which was written in Pahlavī, or mediæval Persian, during the Sassanian age. According to the Pārsī traditions the bulk of Zoroastrian literature was formerly much greater than now. It is claimed that the Vendīdad is the only survivor of the twenty-one Nosks or books which formed the primitive Avesta revealed by Ormazd to Zoroaster, and also that the eighteen Yaśts were originally thirty in number, there having been one for each of the Izads who preside over the thirty days of the month. The classic authors agree with the Pārsīs in the statement that the early books of the Zend-Avesta were much more extensive than at present, the sacred literature of the Zoroastrians having suffered heavy losses in consequence of the ravages of the Persian empire by Greeks and Arabians. It appears from the third book of the Dīnkard that at the time of Alexander's invasion there were only two complete copies of the sacred books, one of which was traced upon skins in golden letters and deposited in the royal archives at Persepolis, where it was burned by Alexander[1] while the other having been placed in another treasury fell into the hands of the Greeks, and was translated into their language. The Arḍā-Vīrāf-nāmak mentions only one copy of the Avesta, which was de-

1 See page 20.

posited in the archives at Persepolis and burned by
Alexander; it also mentions the fact that he killed
many of the priests and nobles. Both of these accounts were written, it is true, long after the events
they describe, so they merely represent the tradition
which had been handed down from one generation to
the next, but as they were written before the Arabian
conquest[1] they cannot have confounded the ravages
of Alexander with those of the Mohammedans, and
their accounts are freely confirmed by classic writers.[2]

AGE OF THE ZEND-AVESTA.

There is no data by which the age of the Zend-
Avesta may be definitely determined. It is certain,
however, that as the Zend is later than the Sanskrit,
so also the Avesta is later than the Vedas. It is also
certain that this work is not the product of any one
generation, as several centuries have intervened between the dates of the earliest and latest portions.
The Gāthas which form the earliest portion of the
work, are writen in the old Āryan metre, but the
favorite deities of the Hindūs are absent from the
Gāthas, although they reappear in various forms in
the later portions of the Avesta. It is evident that
the migrating tribes, in consequence of their separation from their brethren in Īrān, soon became es-
tranged from them, and their most favored gods fell
slowly into neglect or disfavor. Considerable time

---

[1] Haug's Rel. of Parsis, p. 123.

[2] Diodorus (xvii, 72) and Curtius (v. 7) declare that Alexander burned
the citadel and royal palace at Persepolis in a drunken frenzy at the in-
stigation of the Athenian courtezan Thais, and in revenge for the destruction of the Greek temple by Xerxes. Arrian (Exped. Alex., iii, 18) also
speaks of his burning the royal palace of the Persians.

must have been required for the accomplishment of so
great a change. The oldest portions of the Avesta may
therefore fall a few centuries this side of the hymns
of the Ṛig-veda, while the oldest portions of the later
Avesta may be placed at a period somewhat later than
Darius.[1] We have a right to suppose that the hymns
and other portions of the Avesta which were then in
existence were gathered together and committed to
writing about the time of Darius, and according to
Dr. Oppert's rendering of the Behistun inscription,
the Persian king says: "By the grace of Ormazd, I
have made the writings for others in the Āryan language, which was not done before; and the *text* of
the law and the *collection*. . . . I made and wrote,
and I sent abroad; then the old writings among all
countries I restored for *the sake* of the people."[2]
Thus Darius claims to have restored the writings that
had been destroyed or injured by the Magian revolt,
but the word Avesta had not yet become a technical
term;[3] it was the care of Darius that gave it a fixed
and restricted sense. Five centuries afterwards, during the Sassanian period, these books were again
gathered, either from scattered manuscripts or from
oral traditions, and the later Avesta took a definite
form in the hands of Adarbad under King Shapur II,[4]
who, like another Diocletian, aimed at the extirpa-
tion of the Christian faith. Mazdeism having been
shaken by the Manichean heresy, a definite form was

---

[1] Sacred Books of the East, Vol. IV, Int., p. 89.

[2] This is a literal rendering of the passage, the meaning of all the
words being certain, except the four which are written in *italics*.

[3] In the Elamite and Babylonian versions Avesta is simply rendered
"law" or "laws."

[4] Shapur II ascended the throne about A. D. 809.

thus given to the religious code of Īrān, and it was then promulgated as the sacred law of the nation. We may conclude, therefore, that even the most modern portions of the Avesta cannot belong to a later date than the fourth century of the Christian era.

As the Pārsīs are the ruins of a people, so also their sacred books represent the ruins of a religion. There has been no other great belief in the world that left such poor monuments of its fallen splendor. Yet great is the value of the Avesta, and the belief of the few surviving Pārsīs, in the eyes of the historian, as they present to us the last reflex of the ideas which prevailed in Īrān during the five centuries which preceded and the seven which followed the birth of Christ. By the help of the Pārsī religion and the Avesta, we are enabled to go back to that momentous period in the history of literature which saw the blending of the Āryan mind with the Semitic, and thus opened the second stage of Āryan thought.[1]

MANUSCRIPTS.

The recovery of the manuscripts of the Zend-Avesta, and the translation of them proved to be a herculean task for Orientalists, and more than one valuable life has been given largely to this work. For an hundred years this great problem has cost tireless effort, for its solution demanded as much pioneer work as the deciphering of the cuneiform inscriptions of the ancient kings.

We are largely indebted to Anquetil Duperron, the young Frenchman who was so fearless in his enthusi-

[1] Sa. Books of East, Vol. IV. Int., p. 2.

asm that he enlisted [1] as a private soldier in order to secure a passage to India, and spent six years in that country collecting the manuscripts of the Avesta, and in trying to obtain from the Dastūrs a knowledge of their contents. But his was pioneer work, and his translation of the Avesta, which was made with the assistance of Dastūr Dārāb, was by no means trustworthy; it was in fact a French translation of a Persian rendering which had itself been made from a Pahlavī version of the Zend original. [2]

Afterward Dr. Rask went to Bombay in the interests of the Danish government and after collecting many valuable manuscripts, wrote his essay " On the Age and Genuineness of the Zend Language."

About the middle of the present century, Westergaard, who is also a Dane, and one of the most accomplished Zend scholars of Europe, published an edition of the sacred books of the Zoroastrians.

Burnouf, Spiegel and Bopp were also enthusastic students of these books of the Magian literature, and after a time Dr. Haug, a young and enthusiastic German, was appointed to a professorship of Sanskrit in the Poona College; while here he availed himself of his opportunity to make a thorough study of the literature of the Pārsīs. He contributed a valuable collection of "Essays" on the subject.

There are at present five editions, more or less complete, of the Zend-Avesta. The first was lithographed and published [3] under Burnouf's direction in Paris, and the second was transcribed into Roman characters and published [4] at Leipsic by Prof Brock-

1 About 1754.
2 Chips, Vol. I, p. 119.

3 1829–1843.
4 1850.

haus. The third edition was presented in Zend characters, and was prepared[1] by Prof. Spiegel, and the
fourth was published at Copenhagen,[2] by Westergaard;
there are also one or two editions of the Zend-Avesta
published in India with Gujerātī translations, which are
sometimes quoted by native scholars.

The Yasna, being that portion of the Zend-Avesta
containing the Gāthas, which are supposed to be the
original hymns of Zoroaster, is the oldest and most
important part of the Magian literature. Early in the
present century,[3] Dr. Rask succeeded in bringing to
Europe a celebrated manuscript of the Yasna with
Pahlavī translation which is now in the University
Library of Copenhagen,[4] and this is the only document
of the kind upon the continent of Europe.

Another priceless manuscript has for centuries been
hereditary property in the family of a High Priest of
the Pārsīs,[5] who has now presented it to the University at Oxford, and through the courtesy of Prof. F.
Max Müller we are enabled to give our readers a fac
simile representation[6] of this famous Yasna manuscript
which constitutes one of the fundamental documents of
Zend philology. It contains nearly eight hundred
pages,[7] and was written by Mihirāpān Kaī-Khūsrō, the
same copyist who transcribed the Copenhagen manuscript, but it is from a different original.

---

[1] 1851. [2] 1852–1854.
[3] About 1826. [4] Codex numbered 5.
[5] Dastur Jamaspjī Minocheherjī Jamasp Asana, Ph. D. of Tübingen,
Hon. D. C. L. Oxon. Dr. L. H. Mills applied to the Dastur for the loan
of his manuscript to enable him to complete a critical edition of the
Zend and Pahlavī texts of the Gathas, and Dastur Jamaspjī not only
loaned it to Dr. Mills, but most generously presented it to the University
of Oxford.
[6] See page xx. [7] 382 folios.

ZARATHUŚTRA.

Zarathuśtra or Zoroaster[1] is supposed to have been the prophet of Irān, and the author of the earliest hymns or Gāthas, but the fact that the composition of the books of the Zend-Avesta, extended over a period of several centuries, precludes the possibility of their authorship by any one individual. There is no historic record of the birth, the life or the death of Zarathuśtra, and this fact, together with the vast amount of myth and legend which has grown up around his name, has led some Orientalists to question whether or not such a man ever lived at all.

Firdusī teaches in a mythical way that he belonged to the time of Darius. Hyde, Prideaux and several others claim that Zarathuśtra was the same as the Persian Zerdūsht, the great patriarch of the Magi, who lived between the beginning of the reign of Cyrus and the end of that of Darius Hystaspes, while others still claim that the prophet of Irān belonged to an earlier date.[2] It seems probable that he was a veritable personage, who, although not necessarily the author of any considerable portion of the Zend-Avesta, may have led the departure in this direction from the mythology of the Vedas, toward the simpler forms of Mazdeism, but whether he lived and first taught

[1] Clement, who is supposed to have written in the first century of the Christian era, claims that the original name was Nebrod, but that "the magician being destroyed by lightning, his name was changed to Zoroaster by the Greeks on account of the living ($Z\omega\sigma\alpha\nu$) stream of the star ($\dot{\alpha}\sigma\tau\dot{\epsilon}\rho\sigma\varsigma$) being poured upon him."—*Clementine Homilies, IX, Chap. 5.*

[2] Masudi, the noted Arabian historian and traveler who wrote about A. D. 950, remarks that "according to the Magi, Zoroaster lived two hundred and eighty years before Alexander the Great," or about 610 B. C., in the time of the Median king Cyaxares.

among the mountains of Media, or in the land of Baktriana, is an open question.

Indeed, the controversy which prevails among scholars upon the exegesis of the Zend-Avesta is one of unusual severity, and while the storm seems to center upon the value of the Asiatic translations, there are other questions which are involved; the personality of Zarathuśtra[1] is not only questioned, but even amongst those who admit that he was an historical personage, the field of his early labors, the exact time to which he belonged, and many other points are subjects of spirited discussion.

In the Gāthas, or earlier hymns, Zarathuśtra appears as a toiling prophet, and his sphere does not seem to have been greatly restricted. The objects of his concern were provinces as well as villages, and the masses as well as individuals. His circle was largely composed of the reigning prince and prominent chieftains—and these, together with a priesthood comparatively pure, were the greater part of his public. The king, the people, and the peers were all portions of it.

It is claimed that Zarathuśtra had three sons, and these were respectively the fathers and chiefs of the three classes, priests, warriors and herdsmen ; they played little part, however, in the Mazdean system, and are possibly only three subdivisions of Zarathuśtra, who was "the first priest, the first warrior and the first husbandman."

But when the student leaves the Gāthas and turns to the Yaśts or the Vendīdad, he goes from ground

---

[1] Dr. Haug, while maintaining the personality of Zarathustra Spitama, claims that after his death, and possibly during his life, the name of Zarathustra was adopted by a successive priesthood. (Essays, p. 297).

which is apparently historic into a land of fable. He
leaves behind him the toiling prophet, who is apparently real, and meets the Zarathuśtra of these latter
productions in the form of a fantastic demi-god. He
is no longer described as one who brings new truth
and drives away error, but as one who overthrows demons—the valiant smiter of fiends, like Tiśtrya and
Vāyu. He smites them chiefly, it is true, with spiritual weapons, but he also repels the assaults of Ahriman with the stones which Ahura gave him—stones
which are as large as a house[1]—missiles like those
that were hurled at their foes by Indra, by Agni
and by Thor. These are "the flames wherewith, as
with a stone,[2] the storm-god smites the fiend." A
singular incident of Zarathuśtra's birth, according to
Pliny, and later Pārsī tradition, is that he alone of
all mortals laughed while being born. This tradition
would indicate that his nativity was in the region
which was the birthplace of the Vedic Marūts—those
storm genii which are "born of the laughter of the
lightnings."

Zarathuśtra is not the only lawgiver and prophet
which the Avesta recognizes. Gayo Maratan, Yima
and even the bird Karśipta,[3] appear under different
names, forms and functions, as god-like champions in
the struggle for light, and they knew the law as well

[1] Vendidad, Farg. xix, 4.

[2] Rig-veda, ii, 30, 40.

[3] The bird Karśipta dwells in the heavens. Were he living on the earth
he would be the king of birds. He brought the law into the Var of Yima,
and recites the Avesta in the language of birds (Bund. xix and xxiv). As
a bird, because of the swiftness of his flight, was often considered an incarnation of lightning, and as the thunder was supposed to be the voice of a
god speaking from above, so the song of a bird was often thought to be the
utterance of a god.

as Zarathuśtra. Many of the features of Zarathuśtra point to a god, but the mythology has probably grown up around a man, and the existing mythic elements have been woven into a halo to surround a human face. There has been much of individual genius in the formation of Mazdeism, but the system as a whole was probably produced by the elaboration of successive generations of the priesthood.

THE EARLY PĀRSĪS.

It is evident to the historian that the Zend-Avesta should be carefully studied by all who value the records of the human race, but its influence for good or evil cannot be determined without understanding something of the character and habits of the people to whom it peculiarly belonged. There have been periods in the world's history when the religion of the Pārsīs threatened to dominate over all others. If Persia had won the battles of Marathon and Salamis, and thus succeeded in the final conquest of Greece, the worship of Ormazd might have become the religion of the whole civilized world. Persia already ruled over the Assyrian and Babylonian empires; the Jews were under her power, and the sacred monuments of Egypt had been mutilated by the Persian soldiery.

Again, during the Sassanian dynasty, the national faith had revived to such an extent that Shapur II gathered the sacred books and issued their code of law to the people, while the sufferings of the persecuted Christians in the east were as terrible as they had ever been in the west—Rome herself being rivaled in the work of cruelty. But the power of Persia was broken by the Mohammedan conquest, and the war-cry of the Moslem was the herald of defeated tyranny; hence it is that Mazdeism, although once the fear of the world, has for a thousand years had but little interest except for the historian. It was once the state religion of a powerful empire, but it was virtually driven away from its native soil by the sons of the desert, and the star and crescent waved in triumph above its broken altars. Deprived of political influence, and without even the prestige of an enlightened priesthood, many of its votaries became exiles in a foreign land, while the few that remained on Persian soil almost disappeared under the iron hand of Mohammedan rule. In less than a century after their defeat, nearly all the conquered people who remained upon their native soil were brought over to the faith of their new rulers, either by persecution or policy, or by the attractive power of a simpler creed, while those who clung to the faith of their fathers sought a new home in the land of the Hindūs, and found a refuge on the western coast of India and the peninsula of Gujarāt. Here they could worship their old gods, repeat their old prayers, and perform their old rites; and here they still live, and thrive to a certain extent, while their co-religionists in Persia are daily becoming fewer in numbers.

The Pārsīs of the old school used mats for seats, and ate with their fingers from platters, but these and similar practices were cleanly and refined when compared to some of their revolting and loathsome ceremonies. Anthon says, "If the religion of Zoroaster was originally pure and sublime, it speedily degenerated and allied itself to many very gross and hideous forms of superstition; if we were to judge of its tendency by the practice of its votaries, we should be led to think of it more harshly than it may have deserved. The court manners were equally marked by luxury and cruelty—by luxury refined until it had killed all natural enjoyment, and by cruelty carried to the most loathsome excess that perverted ingenuity could suggest. It is above all the barbarity of the women that fills the Persian chronicles with their most horrible stories, and we learn from the same sources the dreadful depravity of their character, and the vast extent of their influence."[2] It is a well known fact in the world's history that the influence of an unprincipled woman is much stronger over a man who yields to her power than is the influence of kindness and truth to win him to higher associations, and therefore we find that at a certain period, the men of Persia, cramped by the rigid power of ceremonials, and surrounded by the ministers to their artificial wants, became the slaves of their priests and concubines. It is probably true that even after the people had lost much of the original purity and simplicity of their manners, the noble youth of Persia were still educated in the severe discipline of their ancestors, which is represented as nearly resembling that of the Spartan, but gradually the ancient discipline became either wholly obsolete or degenerated into empty forms.

THE MODERN PĀRSĪS.

The religion of the Pārsīs is sometimes called Dualism, on account of its main tenet; it is called Maz-

[1] Chips, Vol. I, p. 167.   [2] Class. Dict., p. 1015.

deism, because Ahūra Mazda is its supreme god ; it is called Magism, because its priesthood are the Magi ; it is called Zoroastrianism, as representing the doctrines of its supposed founder, and it is also called Fire Worship, because fire has for centuries apparently received the adoration[1] of the people.

At present the number of the Pārsīs in western India is estimated at about one hundred thousand, while Yezd and Kermān together can claim only about fifty-five thousand. Hence, while the colonies upon the soil of India have retained their strength much better than the others, the grand total is very small, being only about one-tenth of one per cent. of the population of the world. They are still known as Fire-Worshippers, although they protest against the name, as indicating that they are mere idolators. It is doubtless true that at one time fire itself was worshipped, and Atar, the fire-god, held high rank among the Zoroastrians. The primitive Āryan hearth, upon which the sacred element blazed, was also an object of adoration, and the Pārsīs still admit that in their youth they are taught to face some luminous object while worshipping God, although they claim that they look upon fire as merely an emblem of divine power. There is certainly the existence of a strong national instinct—an indescribable one—which is felt by every

[1] Clement says: "The Persians, first taking coals from the lightning which fell from heaven, preserved them by ordinary fuel, and honoring the heavenly fire as a god, were honored by the fire itself, with the first kingdom, as its first worshippers. After them the Babylonians, stealing coals from the fire that was there, and conveying it safely to their own home and worshipping it, they themselves also reigned in order. And the Egyptians, acting in like manner, and calling the fire in their own dialect *Phthaï*, which is translated *Hephaistus* or *Osiris*, he who first reigned amongst them is called by its name."—*Clementine Homilies, IX*, Chap. vi.

Pārsī in regard to both light and fire. They are the only Eastern people who abstain entirely from smoking, and they will not even blow out a candle unless compelled to do so.

The modern Pārsīs believe in monotheism, and use a table, as well as knives and forks at their meals. Their prayers are recited in the old Zend language, although neither he who repeats, nor they who listen can understand a word that is said. Every one goes to the fire temple when he chooses and recites his prayers himself, or pays the priest to recite them for him. Among the whole body of priests, there are perhaps not more than twenty who can lay any claim to a knowledge of the Zend-Avesta, and even these have only learned the meaning of the words they are taught, without knowing the language either philosophically or grammatically.

The modern Pārsīs are monogamists, and hence the manifold evils of the harem are abolished from among the people. They do not eat anything which is prepared by a cook belonging to another creed. They also object to beef and pork. Their priesthood is hereditary. None but the son of a priest can take the orders, and it is not obligatory upon him to do so. The high priest is called Dastūr, while the others are called Mobed. They are greatly attached to their religion on account of its former glory, and it is felt that the relinquishment of it would be the giving up of all that was most sacred and precious to their forefathers. Still they have, in many essential points, unconsciously approached the doctrines of Christianity, and if they could but read

the Zend-Avesta they would find that their faith is
no longer the faith of the Yasna or the Vendīdad.[1]
As historical relics these works will always be of
value, but as the oracles of faith they lack the
vitality of principle necessary for the building of
human character.

[1] Chips, Vol. I, pp. 162-177.

CHAPTER VI.

THE TEACHINGS OF THE ZEND-AVESTA.

THE GĀTHAS—THE WAIL OF THE KINE—THE LAST GĀTHA—THE MARRIAGE SONG—THE YASNA—COMMENTARY ON THE FORMULAS—THE YASNA HAPTANG-HĀITI—THE SROSH YAŚT—THE YASNA CONCLUDING.

THE teachings of the Zend-Avesta have been partially treated in the chapter devoted to Persian mythology, but other features of the work seem to demand attention here. Briefly presented, the present world is two-fold, being the work of two hostile beings—Ahŭra-Mazda, the good principle, and Angra Mainyu, or Ahriman, the evil principle. All that is good in the present state of things comes from the former, and all that is evil from the latter. The history of the world is the history of the conflict between these two powers, as Angra Mainyu invaded the world of Ahŭra Mazda, and marred its beauty and truth. Man is active in the conflict, his duty being revealed to him in the law which was given by Ahŭra Mazda to Zarathuśtra.

Although of later date, it is evident that the religion of the Pārsīs is derived from the same source as that of the Hindŭs—derived from the faith of the Āryan forefathers of the Hindŭs and the Īrānians.

We therefore find two strata in the mythology which is under discussion; the one comprises all the gods and myths which were already in existence during the Indo-Īrānian period, and the other comprises the gods and myths which were only developed after the separation of the two mythologies.

There are two principal points in the Indo-Īrānian religion. First, that there is a law in nature; and second, that there is also war in nature. There is law in nature, because day returns with its golden splendor and night with its eloquent mystery; seed-time and harvest, the planting and the fruiting, succeed each other with unfailing regularity. There is war in nature, because it contains powers that work for evil, as well as those that work for good. Hence the unceasing struggle goes on, and it is never more apparent to the human eye than in a storm, where a fiend seems to bear away the waters which the earth so sadly needs, and fights with the god who at last brings them to the thirsting plants. Amidst all the various myths of the Indo-Īrānian system there is a monotheism and an unconscious dualism. But both of these disappeared in the further development of Hindū mythology. Mazdeism, however, lost neither of these two ideas; it clung strongly to them both.

Hence we have the Ahūra-Mazda, "the lord of high knowledge," "the all-embracing sky." He was the Varuṇa of the Hindūs, but this name was lost in Īrān, or remained only as the name of a mythical region—the Varena, which was the scene of a mythical fight between a storm-fiend and a storm-god.

Ahûra, the heaven-god, is white, and his body is the fairest and greatest of bodies. He is wedded to the rivers, and the sun is his eye, while the lightnings are his children, and he wears the heavens as a star-spangled garment.

In the time of Herodotus, the Persians, while invoking Ahûra-Mazda as the creator of heaven and earth, still called the whole vault of the sky the supreme god. This deity slowly brought everything under his sway, and the other gods finally became, not only his subjects, but also his creatures.

While the single elements of Mazdeism do not differ essentially from those of the Vedic and the Indo-European mythology generally, still the grouping of these elements in a new order presents them in a new form. Thus we find that in Mazdeism everything is referred either to Ahûra Mazda or to Angra Mainyu as its source, and hence the world is divided into two parts, in each of which a strong unity prevails, representing the dualism of this system. Ahûra is all light, truth, goodness and knowledge, while Angra Mainyu, or Ahriman, is all darkness, falsehood, wickedness and ignorance.

Man, according to his deeds, belongs to Ormazd or to Ahriman. He belongs to Ormazd if he sacrifices to him, and helps him by good thoughts, words and deeds; if he enlarges his dominion and makes the realm of Ahriman smaller by destroying his creatures; while the man who is a friend of Ahriman and represents evil thoughts and evil deeds, who slays the creatures of Ormazd, is classed as a demon. Even animals are classified as belonging to one spirit or the other, in accordance with the idea that they had been incarnations of either the god or the fiend.

Killing the Ahriman creatures is killing Ahriman himself, and many sins can thus be atoned for, while killing Ormazdean animals is an abomination like the killing of the god. The struggle between the good and evil, however, is limited, for the world is not to last forever, and Ahriman will be defeated at last.

There had been an old myth that the world would end in a fearful winter like that of the Eddic Fimbul, which would be succeeded by an eternal spring, but as a storm is the ordinary symbol of strife, the view which finally obtained in their mythology, is the prediction that the world will finally end in a battle of the elements.

The Pārsīs came at last to a pure monotheism, and to a certain extent this change may have been influenced by the creed of the Moslem that "there is one God, and Mohammed is his prophet," but the difference in sentiment cannot be ascribed to any one generation, for it is really deeper and wider than the movement which, in earlier times, brought the Magi from an imperfect form of dualism to one which was much more decided in its presentations.[1]

THE GĀTHAS.

The five Gāthas which have been attributed to Zarathuśtra are doubtless the earliest portions of the Zend-Avesta. They comprise seventeen sections of poetical matter, equal in extent to twenty-five or thirty hymns of the Ṛig-veda. They are composed in the

[1] Sa. Bks. of the East, Vol. IV, Int., pp. 56, 83.

ancient Āryan metre, and ascribe supreme power to Ahūra Mazda, who is opposed constantly by the spirit of evil.

In these early songs, the kine, as the representative of the people, laments the burden which is laid upon Irānian life. The effort to win their bread by honest labor is opposed, although not entirely frustrated, by the Deva-worshipping tribes, who still struggle with the Zarathuśtrians for the control of the territory. The kine, therefore, lifts her wail to Ahūra, who responds by the appointment of Zarathuśtra as the being who is entrusted with her redemption; and he, accepting his commission, begins his labors. We then have a series of lamentations and praises addressed by Zarathuśtra and his immediate associates to Ahūra; also exhortations which are addressed to the people.

These hymns were composed amidst an agricultural people, many of whom were also herdsmen. Their land and their cattle being their most valuable property, the raids of the Deva-worshippers were looked upon as most terrible visitations. In the course of these invasions, we have also intimations of an organized effort on the part of the foe to overwhelm the Zarathuśtrians, and it appears that at times they very nearly accomplished their object, sanguinary conflicts being repeatedly alluded to. It may be inferred by the prevalence of the thankful tone in the Gāthas, that the Zarathuśtrians were not conquered during the Gāthic period, although at the time that the last hymns of the series were written, the struggle was by no means over.

There is an historical tone in the Gāthas, which

should be carefully observed. Their doctrines and exhortations concern an actual religious movement,
which was taking place at the time of their composition, and that movement was apparently pure and earnest. Their tone is always serious, and nearly all the
myths are dropped; even the old Āryan gods, who reappear in the later Avesta, being ignored with a single
exception.

In the first Gātha, the soul of the kine, as representing the herds of the Īrānian people, raises her
voice in lamentation. She asks why and for whom
she was made, since afflictions compass her and her
life is constantly threatened by the incursions of pred-
atory tribes. She also beseeches the Bountiful Immortals to instruct her as to the benefits of agriculture,
and confirm her protectors in the science, as the only
remedy for her sufferings.

THE WAIL OF THE KINE.

"Unto you, O Ahūra and Asha, the soul of the
        kine cried aloud,
    'For whom did ye create me ?
    And for whom did ye fashion me ?
    On me comes the assault of wrath and of violent
        power ;
    The blow of desolation and thievish might.
    None other pasture given have I than you;
    Therefore do ye teach me good tillage
    For the fields, mine only hope of welfare.'"

Ahūra speaks:

    "Upon this the Creator of the kine asked of Right-
        eousness,

'How was thy guardian for the kine appointed
    by thee,
When having power over all her fate ye made her?
In what manner did ye secure for her, together
    with pasture
A cattle-chief who was both skilled and energetic?
Whom did ye select as her life's master
Who might hurl back the fury of the wicked?'"

Asha answers:

To him the Divine Righteousness answered:

"Great was our perplexity;
    A chieftain who was capable of smiting back
        their fury
    And who was himself without hate
    Was not to be obtained by us."

Zarathuśtra intercedes:

"The Great Creator is himself most mindful
    Of the uttered indications which have been ful-
        filled beforehand
    In the deeds of demon gods.
    The Ahūra is the discerning arbiter;
    So shall it be to us as he shall will.
    Therefore it is that we both,
    My soul and the soul of the mother kine,
    Are working our supplications for the two worlds
    To Ahūra, and he will answer,
    'Not for the righteous—
    Not for the thrifty tiller of the earth,
    Shall there be destruction together with the
        wicked?'"

Ahúra speaks :

Upon this the Lord spake thus:

"Not in this manner is a spiritual master found;
Therefore *thee* have I named
For such a head to the tiller of the ground.
. . . This man is found
Who alone has hearkened to our enunciations:
Zarathústra Spitama
I will give him the good abode
And authoritative place."

Voice of the Kine:

Upon this the soul of the kine lamented:

"Woe is upon me
Since I have obtained for myself in my wounding
A lord who is powerless to effect his wish,
The voice of a feeble and pusillanimous man;
Whereas I desire one who is lord over his will,
And able as one of royal state,—
Who is able to accomplish what he desires to
effect."

Zarathústra:

"Do ye, O Ahúra, and thou, O Righteousness,
Grant gladness unto these:
Bestow upon them the peaceful amenities of
home
And quiet happiness . . .
Do ye now therefore assign unto us your aid in
abundance
For our great cause.
May we be partakers of the bountiful grace of
these your equals,
Your counsellors and servants."

Zarathuśtra, having entered upon the duties of his office, composes a liturgy for the benefit of his colleagues, which is given in the second hymn. The doctrine of dualism is next taught. The progress and struggles of the cause are presented. There is a song of thankfulness offered in gratitude· for improved fortunes.

In the third Gātha, salvation is announced as universal for believers, and also contains the reflections of Zarathuśtra upon the sublimity and bountifulness of Ahūra. There are also personal hopes and appeals.

THE LAST GĀTHA.

While the matter of this hymn is homogeneous with that of the other Gāthas, it bears some evidence of having been composed in the latter portion of Zarathuśtra's life. The subject is a marriage song of a political and religious character. The freshness and vigor of the style may indicate Zarathuśtrian influence, if not authorship. The marriage festival of the prophet's daughter must have been a semi-political occasion, and the author would naturally express himself in reference to the struggle which was still going on.

THE MARRIAGE SONG.

"That best prayer has been answered,
The prayer of Zarathuśtra Spitama
That Ahūra Mazda
Might grant him those boons
Which flow from the Good Order;
Even a life that is prospered for eternal duration;
And also those who deceived him;

May he also grant him,
As the good faith's disciples in word and in
deed."

The master of the feast then speaks as follows:

"And him will they give thee,
Oh Pouroukista,
Young as thou art of the daughters of
Zarathustra,
Him will they give thee
As a help in the true service Asha and Mazda,
As a chief and a guardian.
Counsel well then together,
And act in just action."

The bride answers:

"I will love him,
Since from my father he gained me.
For the master and toilers,
And for the lord-kinsman,
He, the Good Mind's bright blessing.
The pure to the pure ones.
And to me be the insight which I gain from his
counsel.
Mazda grant it for good conscience forever."

Priestly master of the feast:

"Monitions for the marrying,
I speak to you, maidens,
And heed ye my saying:
By these laws of the faith which I utter
Obtain ye the life of the good mind
On earth and in heaven.

And to you, bride and bridegroom,
Let each one the other in righteousness cherish,
Thus alone unto each shall the home life be
    happy.
Thus real are these things, ye men and ye women
From the lie-demon protecting
A guard o'er my faithful
And so I grant progress and goodness
And the hate of the lie with the hate of her
    bondsmen
I would expel from the body—
Where is then the righteous lord that will smite
    them from life
And beguile them of license?
Mazda! there is the power which will banish and
    conquer."[1]

THE YASNA.

The word Yasna means worship including sacrifice.
This was the principal liturgy of the Zarathuśtrians,
in which confession, invocation, prayer, exhortation
and praise are all combined.   The Gāthas are sung
in the middle of it and in the Vendīdad Sadah; the
Visparad is interpolated within it.   Like other compositions of its kind, it is largely made up of the
fragments of different ages and modes of composition.
We have no reason to suppose that the Yasna existed
in its present form in the earlier periods of Zara-
thuśtranism, but the fragments of which it is composed, may, some of them, reach back to that era, and
even its present arrangement is comparatively early in

the history of Mazdean literature. The following extracts have been chosen as representing the finest
specimens of poetic fervor to be found in the Yasna :

COMMENCEMENT OF THE SACRIFICE.

" I will announce and I will complete my Yasna
  to Ahūra Mazda,
The radiant and glorious, the greatest and best,
The one whose body is the most perfect,
Who has fashioned us,
And who has nourished and protected us,
Who is the most bounteous spirit. . . .

" I will announce and I will complete my Yasna
  to the Good Mind,
And to Righteousness the best,
To the Universal Weal and Immortality,
To the body of the Kine and to the Kine's soul,
And to the fire of Ahūra Mazda,
Who, more than all the Bountiful Immortals
Has made the effort for our success. . . .

" I will announce and I will complete my Yasna
  to Mithra of the wide pastures,
Of the thousand ears, and of the myriad eyes
The Izad of the spoken name.[1]

" I celebrate and complete my Yasna to the Fravishas[2] of the saints,
And to those women who have many sons,

---

[1] Having an especial Yast.

[2] The first month is called Fravisha, and indicates the particular time of
this celebration. Fravisha also means the departed souls of ancestors, and
these angels or protectors are numberless. Every being of the good creation, whether living, dead or still unborn, has its own Fravisha or guardian
angel, who has existed from the beginning.

And to a prosperous home life
Which continues without reverse throughout the
    year,
And to that might which strikes victoriously. . .

" I announce and complete my Yasna to the Māhya,
The monthly festivals, lords of the ritual order,
To the new and the later moon, and to the full
    moon which scatters night. . . .

" I announce and complete my Yasna to the yearly
    feasts. . . .
Yea, I celebrate and complete my Yasna
To the seasons, lords of the ritual order. . . .

" I announce and complete my Yasna
To all those who are the thirty and three,[1]
Lords of the ritual order. . . .

" To Ahūra and to Mithra, to the star Tištrya,
The resplendent and glorious,
To the moon and the resplendent sun,
Him of the rapid steeds, the eye of Ahūra
    Mazda."

The sacrifice is long continued, and the gods are
again approached with interminable ritual, and the
naming of the objects of propitiation; the offerings
are then made to each of the gods, the fire of
earth receiving especial attention, as well as the stars
of heaven and all the Bountiful Immortals.

At each presentation of the offering by the priest,
the object of propitiation is named. There are invo-

---

[1] Haug was the first to call attention to this striking coincidence with
Hindu mythology; in the Aitareya, and Satapatha Brahmanas, in the
Atharva-veda, and in the Ramayana, the gods are numbered at thirty-three.

cations and dedications almost without number, Zarathuśtra being also mentioned as an object of worship.

> " And we worship Zarathuśtra Spitama in our sacrifice,
> The holy lord of the ritual order,
> And we worship every Izad as we worship him;
> And we worship also the Fravisha of Zarathuśtra Spitama, the saint.
> And we worship the utterances of Zarathuśtra and his religion,
> His faith and his love.
> And we worship the former religions of the world devoted to Righteousness,
> Which were instituted at the creation,
> The holy religion of Ahūra Mazda,
> The resplendent and glorious. . . .
> And we worship the milk offering and the libation,
> The two which cause the waters to flow forth,
> And we worship all waters and all plants,
> And all good men and all good women." [1]

COMMENTARY ON THE FORMULAS.

This commentary is written in the Zend language, and is valuable as a specimen of early exegesis. Zarathuśtra is here represented as holding a conversation with Ahūra Mazda, and in reply to his questions Ahūra says: " Whoever in this world of mine shall mentally recall a portion of the Ahuna-vairya (formulas), and having thus recalled it, shall undertone it, and then utter it aloud; whoever shall worship thus,

[1] Yasna, xvi.

then even with threefold safety and speed I will
bring his soul over the bridge of *K*invaḍ (Chinvat).
I who am Ahūra Mazda will help him to pass over
it to heaven, the best life, and to the lights of heaven."

"And whoever, O Zarathuśtra, while undertoning
the parts of the Ahuna-vairya, takes aught therefrom,
I who am Ahūra Mazda will draw his soul off from
the better world; yea, so far will I withdraw it as
the earth is large and wide.

"And this word is the most emphatic of the words
which have ever been pronounced, or which are now
spoken, or which shall be spoken in the future, for
this utterance is of such a nature that if all the living world should learn it, and learning, hold fast by
it, they would be redeemed from their mortality."[1]

THE YASNA HAPTANG-HĀITA.

This Yasna of the "Seven Chapters" appears to
rank next in antiquity to the Gāthas, but the tone
is considerably changed, although the dialect remains
the same. We have here a stronger personification
of the Bountiful Immortals, while fire is still worshipped; also the earth and grass. We find here praise
to Ahūra and the Immortals, to fire, to the creation, to
the earth and to sacred waters. The sacrifice to the
"Soul of the Kine" is also given, and the sacrifices to
both earth and heaven, to the stormy wind that
Mazda made, also to the peaks of the beautiful
mountain.

"And we worship the Good Mind and the spirits
of the saints. And we sacrifice to the fish of fifty-

[1] See Yasna, xlix.

five fins, and to the Unicorn which stands in Vourū-
kasha, and to the sea where he stands, and to the
Haoma, golden flowered, growing on the heights.
We sacrifice to Haoma, that driveth death afar, and
to the flood streams of the waters, and to the great
flight of the birds, and to the approach of the Fire-
priests as they approach us from afar,[1] and seek to
gain the provinces and spread the ritual law."[2]

The Yasna also includes several Yaśts, or hymns of
praise, some of which contain poetry as well as
praise. As Sraosha is the only divinity of the later
groups mentioned in the first four Gāthas, the Yaśt
which is dedicated to him appears to rank in antiquity
next to those fragments which are found in the
Gāthic dialect. The name of Sraosha appears still to
retain its meaning as the abstract quality of obedience
although it is personified.

THE SRAŌSHA YAŚT.

"Propitiation be to Sraosha, Obedience the blessed,
    the Mighty,
  The incarnate mind of reason,
  Whose body is the Mithra,—
  Him of the daring spear devoted to the Lord
  For his worship, homage, propitiation and praise.

"We worship Sraosha, the blessed, the stately,
  Him who smites with the blow of victory,
  For his splendor and his glory,
  For his might and the blow which smites with
    victory.

[1] This expression probably points to an immigration of Zarathustranism.
[2] Yasna, xlii.

"I will worship him with the Yasna of the Izads.
And we worship all the words of Zarathustra
And all the deeds well done for him. . .

"We worship Sraosha, the blessed,
Whom four racers draw in harness,
White and shining, beautiful and powerful
Quick to learn and fleet,
Obeying before speech,
Heeding orders from the mind,
With their hoofs of horn, gold-covered,
Fleeter than our horses, swifter than the winds;
More rapid than the rain-drops as they fall,
Yea, fleeter than the clouds or well-winged birds,
Or the well-shot arrow as it flies
Which overtake not these swift ones
As they fly after them pursuing,
But which are never overtaken when they flee,
Which plunge away from all the weapons
And draw Sraosha with them,
The good Sraosha and the blessed.

"We worship Obedience, the blessed,
Who, though so lofty and so high, yea, so stately,
Yet stoops to Mazda's creatures, even to the
    girdle . . . .
For his splendor and his glory,
For his might which smites to victory.
I will worship him with the Yasna of the Izads,
And may he come to aid us,
He who smites with victory.
Obedience the blessed."[1]

[1] Yasna, lvii.

THE YASNA CONCLUDING.

This Yasna, having been composed long after the supposed time of Zarathuśtra, can hardly be genuine in its present shape. It may, however, be an elaboration of an earlier document.

"Frashaośtra the holy, asked the saintly Zarathuśtra, 'What is, in very truth, the memorized recital of the rites? What is the completed delivery of the Gāthas?'"

"Zarathuśtra said, 'We worship Ahūra Mazda with our sacrifice as the holy lord of the ritual order, and we sacrifice to Zarathuśtra likewise as the holy lord of the ritual order, and we sacrifice to the Fravisha of Zarathuśtra, the saint.

'And we sacrifice to the Bountiful Immortals, the guardians of the saints, and we sacrifice to all the good, heroic and bounteous Fravishas of the saints. . . . And we worship all the five Gāthas, the holy ones and the entire Yasna, and the sounding of its chants.

'And we sacrifice to all the springs of water and to the water streams as well, and to growing plants and forest trees, and to the entire land and heaven, and to all the stars, and to the moon and sun, even to all the lights without beginning. . . .

'We sacrifice to the active man and to the man of good intent, for the hindrance of darkness, of wasting of the strength and life, and to health and healing.

'We sacrifice to the Yasna's ending words, and to them which end the Gāthas, and we sacrifice to the bounteous hymns themselves, which rule in the ritual course, the holy ones. . . .

'And we sacrifice to the souls of the dead which are the Fravishas of the saints, and we sacrifice to that lofty Lord who is Ahūra Mazda himself.'"

CHAPTER VII.

TEACHINGS OF THE ZEND-AVESTA, CONCLUDED.

THE VENDĪDAD—FARGARD II—THE VARA OF YIMA—
THE LAWS OF PURIFICATION—DISPOSITION OF THE
DEAD—PUNISHMENTS—THE PLACE OF REWARD—THE
VISPARAD—TEACHING OF THE MODERN PĀRSĪS.

THIS portion of the Zend-Avesta is also a collection of fragments, although the Pārsī tradition
claims that it has been preserved entire. The Vendīdad
has often been called the book of the laws of the
Pārsīs, but the greater portion of the rules here given
pertain to the laws of purification. The first two
chapters deal largely with mythical matter, and are
remnants of an old epic and cosmogonic literature—
the first dealing with the creation of Ahūra and the
marring of his work by the evil principle, and the
second treating of Yima as the founder of civilization.
Three chapters of a mythical nature about the origin
of medicine are placed at the end of the book, and
the nineteenth Fargard or section treats of the revelation of the law by Ahūra to Zarathuśtra. The other
seventeen chapters deal largely with observances and
ceremonies, although mythical fragments are occasionally met with, which have more or less connection
with the text, many of them, perhaps, being interpo-
lations of a later date. About eight chapters[1] are

[1] From the fifth to the twelfth.

devoted to the impurity of the dead and the method of dispelling it; this subject is also treated in other Fargards, while two long sections are devoted to the care of the dog, the food which is due him and the penalties for offenses against him.[1] The apparent lack of order is, perhaps, largely due to the form of expression which was adopted by the first composers of the Vendīdād. The law is revealed by Ahūra in a series of answers, which are given in reply to the questions of Zarathuśtra, and as these queries are not of a general character, but refer to details, the matter is presented in fragments, each of which (consisting of a question with its answer) appears as an independent passage.

FARGARD II.

This is the most poetical chapter in the work, and is devoted to Yima. Ahūra here proposes that Yima, the son of Vīvanghat, shall receive the law from him and carry it to men. Yima, however, refuses to do so, whereupon Ahūra gives him a commission, bidding him to keep his creatures and make them prosper. Yima, therefore, makes the creatures of Ahūra to thrive and increase, keeps death and disease away from them, and three times enlarges the earth, which had become too small for its inhabitants. On the approach of a dreadful winter, which was to destroy every living thing, Yima, being advised by Ahūra, built a Vara to preserve the seed of all animal and vegetable life. and there the blessed still live happily under his rule.

[1] When a dog dies his spirit passes to Ardvī Sura, the goddess of the living waters that pour into the celestial sea. The penalty for frightening a pregnant dog was from ten to two hundred stripes.

The world, after lasting a long year of twelve millenniums, was to end in a dire winter, to be followed by an everlasting spring, when men, being sent back to earth from the heavens, should enjoy upon the earth the same happiness which they had found after death in the realms of Yima. But when a more definite form was taken by the Mazdean cosmology the world was made to end by fire, and therefore the Vara of Yima, instead of remaining the paradise from which the inhabitants of earth return, came to be a comparatively modern representative of Noah's Ark. In the Vedas, Yama is the first man, the first priest and "the first of all who died"; he brought worship here below, as well as life, and "first he stretched out the thread of sacrifice."

Yima had at first the same right as his Hindū prototype to the title of a founder of religion, but he lost it, as in the course of the development of Mazdeism, Zarathuśtra became the law-giver. Zarathuśtra asked of Ahūra Mazda:

" Who was the first mortal before myself, Zarathuś-
    tra,
With whom thou, Ahūra Mazda, did'st converse?
To whom did'st thou teach the law of Ahūra?"

Ahūra answered:

" The fair Yima, the great shepherd,
O holy Zarathuśtra!
He was the first mortal before thee
With whom I, Ahūra Mazda, did converse—
Whom I taught the law of Ahūra—
The law of Zarathuśtra.

"Unto him, O Zarathuśtra,
I, Ahûra Mazda, spake, saying :
'Fair Yima, son of Vîvanghat,
Be thou the bearer of my law.'
But the fair Yima replied,
'I was not born, I was not taught
To be the preacher and the bearer of thy law.'
Then I, Ahûra Mazda, said thus unto him :
'Since thou wantest not to be my preacher
And the bearer of my law,
Then make thou my worlds to thrive—
Make my worlds increase ;
Undertake thou to nourish, to rule
And to watch over my world.'
And the fair Yima replied unto me :
'Yes, I will make thy worlds thrive—
I will make thy worlds increase—
Yes, I will nourish and rule
And watch over thy world.'
Then I, Ahûra Mazda,
Brought the implements unto him,
A golden ring and a poniard
Inlaid with gold,[1]
Behold here Yima bears the royal sway."

Thus, under the sway of Yima, three hundred
    winters passed away,
And the earth was replenished with flocks and
    herds,
With men, and dogs and birds, and with red
    blazing fires,

---

[1] As the symbol and instrument of sovereignty. He reigned supreme
by the strength of the ring and of the poniard.

'Till there was no more room for flocks and herds
    and men.
Then Yima stepped forward toward the luminous
    space
To meet the sun, and he pressed the earth with
    the golden ring
And bored it with the poniard, saying, thus:
" O Spenta Ārmaiti,[1] kindly open asunder, and
    stretch thyself afar
To bear flocks and herds and men."

And Yima made the earth grow larger by one-third
than it was before, and there came flocks and herds
and men, at his will, as many as he wished.

THE VARA OF YIMA.

Ahûra Mazda then called a council of the gods,
and here he spake to Yima saying, "Upon the ma-

---

[1] Spenta Armaiti is a general name for heavenly counsellors, and they
represent also the genii of the earth and waters. Under Ahura were six
Amesha Spentas, which were at first mere personifications of virtues and
moral powers, but as their lord and father ruled over the whole world, in
later times they took each a part of the world under especial care. The
dominion of the trees and waters was vested in Haurvatad and Ameretad,
or Health and Immortality; here we find the influence of the old Indo-
Iranian formulæ, in which waters and trees were invoked as the springs
of health and life. Perfect Sovereignty had molten brass for his emblem,
as the god in the storm established his empire by means of that "molten
brass," the fire of lightning, and he thus became the king of metals in
general. Asha Vahista, the holy order of the world, as maintained chiefly
by the sacrificial fire, became the genius of fire. Armaiti seems to have
become a goddess of the earth as early as the Indo-Iranian period, and
Vohu-mano, or Good Thought, had the living creation left to his superin-
tendence. These Amesha Spentas projected, as it were, out of themselves
as many demons who were hardly more than inverted images of the gods
they were to oppose; for instance, Health and Immortality were opposed
by Sickness and Decay, but these very demons were changed into the
rulers of hunger and thirst when they came in contact with the genii of
the waters and the trees. Vohu-mano, or Good Thought, was reflected in
Evil Thought, and after these came the symmetrical armies of numberless
gods and fiends.—*Darmesteter in Sa. Bks. E.*

terial earth the fatal winters are going to fall that shall make the snow-flakes thick and deep on the peaks of the highest mountains, and all the beasts shall perish that live in the wilderness, and those that live on the mountains, and those that live in the bosom of the vale. Therefore make thee a Vara, long as a riding-ground on every side of the square, to be an abode for men and a fold for flocks. There thou shalt make the waters flow, there thou shalt settle birds by the evergreen banks that bear the never-failing food. There shalt thou establish dwelling places and bring the greatest, the best and the finest of the earth, both men and women; thou shalt bring the animals, and the seeds of the trees, two of every kind to be kept there, so long as men shall stay in the Vara."

And Yima made a Vara, and brought into it all the varieties of cattle and of plants, and the men in the Vara which Yima made, live the happiest life,[1] and he who brought the law of Ahûra into the Vara was the bird Karśipta. And Yima sealed up the Vara with the golden ring, and he made a door and a window which was self-shining within. And Ahûra Mazda said "There the stars, the moon and the sun, only once a year seem to rise and set, and the year seems only a day."

THE LAWS OF PURIFICATION.

The larger portion of the Vendîdad is devoted to a description, with numberless repetitions, of the Mazdean

---

[1] According to the hymns of the Rig-veda, "Yama the king, the gatherer of the people, has descried a path for many which leads from the

laws of purification and the long ceremonies pertaining
to them. Impurity or uncleanness may be described
as the condition of a person or thing that is possessed
of a demon, and the process of purification is for the
purpose of expelling the evil presence. Death is the
triumph of the demon, and therefore it is the principal
cause of uncleanness; when a man dies, as soon as the
soul has left the body, the Drūj Nasu, or Corpse-
Drūj, comes from the regions of hell, and falls upon
the body, and whoever thereafter touches the corpse is
not only unclean himself, but every one whom he
touches is also unclean.

The Drūj is expelled from the dead by the Sag-
dīd, or "the look of the dog;" "a four-eyed dog," or
"a white one with yellow ears," must be brought
near the body, and made to look upon the dead, and
as soon as he has done so the Drūj hastens back to
hell. [1] The Drūj is expelled from the living by a process which is too revolting for description. The ceremonies are accompanied by the constant repetition of
spells like the following: "Perish, O fiendish Drūj!
Perish, O brood of the fiend! Rush away, O Drūj!
Perish away to the regions of the north, never more
to give unto death the living world."

The feeling out of which these ceremonies grew
was not original with Mazdeism; the Hindū also considered himself in danger while burning the corpse,

depths to the heights; he first found out a resting place from which no-
body can turn out the occupants; on the way the forefathers have gone,
the sons will follow them."—Rig-veda, X, 14, 1, 2.

[1] The Drūj went back to hell in the shape of a fly. The fly that came
to smell of a dead body was thought to be a corpse-spirit that came to
take possession of the dead in the name of Ahriman.

and he cried aloud, "Away, go away, O Death! injure not our sons and our men."[1]

The Pārsīs, not being able to find a four-eyed dog, interpreted the law to mean a dog with two spots above the eyes, while in practice they are still less particular, and the Sag-dīd may be performed by a house-dog, or by a dog four months old. As birds of prey are fiend-smiters as well as the dog, the devotee may claim their services when there is no dog at hand. The four-eyed dog, which the ceremony originally called for, is doubtless a reproduction of "the four-eyed dogs of the tawny breed of Saramā," belonging to Yama,[2] which guard the realms of death in Hindū mythology. The identity of the four-eyed dog of the Pārsīs with the dogs of Yama is confirmed by the tradition that the yellow-eared dog watches at the head of the Chinvat bridge, and, as the souls of the faithful pass over, he barks to drive away the fiend who would drag them down to hell. Wherever a corpse is carried, death walks beside it all the way, from the house to the last resting-place, and the fatal presence constantly threatens the living who are near the pathway.

DISPOSITION OF THE DEAD.

As the centre of contagion is in the corpse, it must be disposed of in such a way that death may not be spread abroad. The old Indo-European customs have in this respect been completely changed by Mazdeism. The corpse was formerly either burned or buried; both of these customs, however, are held to be sacreligious

---

1 Rig-veda, X, 18, 1.　　　2 Hindu Literature, p. 35..

in the Avesta. The elements, fire, earth, and water, are
holy, and even during the Indo-Īrānian period they
were already so considered, being represented in the
Vedas as objects of worship.   But this did not prevent
the Hindūs from burning their dead, and the dead man
was really considered as a traveler to the other world,
while the kindly fire was supposed to carry him on
flashing pinions to his heavenly abode.   The funeral
fire, like that of the sacrifice, was the god that goes
from earth to heaven, the mediator most friendly to
man.

In Persia, however, it remained more distant from
him and represented the purest offspring of the good
spirit; therefore no uncleanness could be allowed to
enter it.   Its only function appears to be the repelling
of the fiends by its blaze.   In every place where the
Pārsīs are settled, an everlasting fire is still kept,
which is always fed by perfumes and costly woods, and
wherever its flames are carried by the wind, it kills
thousand of fiends.   No degradation must be inflicted
upon this sacred element, even blowing it with the
human breath is a crime, because the outgoing breath
is unclean ; burning the dead is therefore the most
criminal act ; in the time of Strabo [1] it was a capital
crime, and the Avesta places it in the list of sins for
which there is no atonement.

Water was looked upon in the same light, and throwing dead matter into it was as unpardonable as to
pollute the sacred flame with its presence.   The Magi
are said to have overthrown a king for having built
bath-houses, and the Jews were forbidden to practice

[1] Strabo XV, 14; Herod. I, 138.

their ablutions; in some cases the sick were even forbidden to drink it, unless it was decided that death
would be caused by longer abstinence. The earth was
equally holy, for in her bosom there dwelt Spenta
Ārmaiti, the goddess of the earth, and to defile her
sacred dwelling by burying the dead was also a deed for
which there was no atonement.

In earlier times the Persians practiced burial even
after burning had been forbidden. Cambyses aroused
the national indignation by cremating the body of
Amasis, and years later the Persians were still burying
their dead. Afterward, however, when the Mazdean
law became dominant, the worship of the earth was included, although it was sometime before it was considered as sacred as fire and water. In later times the
Persians builded Dakhmas, or "Towers of Silence" for
the bodies of their dead; these towers were about
twenty feet high, and they enclosed an annular stone
pavement on which the bodies were placed. These
towers were usually built on the summit of a mountain
far from the haunts of men. A barren cliff was chosen,
free from trees or water, and the tower was even
separated from the earth herself, for it was isolated by
a layer of stones and bricks, while it was claimed that
a golden thread ran between the tower and the earth.
Here, afar from the world of men, the dead were left
to lie "beholding the sun." The Avesta and commentary are especially emphatic upon this point, for
"it is as if the dead man's life were thus prolonged,
since he can still behold the sun."

PUNISHMENTS.

The penalties for the violation of the Persian law were very severe, and human life was considered of very little value, capital punishment being inflicted even for the killing of a dog. Their laws were far more barbarous than those of England in Sir William Blackstone's time, when one hundred and sixty offenses[1] were declared by act of Parliament to be worthy of instant death;[2] and death was the most humane of the Persian punishments, when it was promptly inflicted, for their methods were too terrible for description. Two hundred stripes were awarded if one tilled land in which a corpse had been buried within a year, or if the mother of a very young child drank water. Four hundred stripes were the penalty if one covered with a cloth a dead man's feet, and eight hundred if he covered the whole body. The penalty for killing a puppy was five hundred stripes, six hundred for killing a stray dog, eight hundred for a shepherd's dog, and ten thousand stripes for killing a water-dog.[3]

In the old Āryan legislation there were many crimes which were considered more criminal than murder, and Persians who defiled the earth were not more severely punished than were the Greeks who defiled the ground of Delos, nor would the Athenians, who put Atarbes

[1] The Mosaic law mentions only seventeen crimes as being worthy of capital punishment.

[2] Blackstone's Commentaries, IV, 4. 15, 18.

[3] Says Prof. Darmesteter: "It may be doubted whether the murder of a water-dog could actually have been punished with ten thousand stripes unless we suppose that human endurance was different in ancient Persia from what it is elsewhere; in the time of Chardin the number of stripes inflicted on the guilty never exceeded three hundred ; in the old German law, two hundred ; in the Mosaic law, forty."—*Sa. Bks. E.*, *Vol. IV*, *p. 99*, *Int.*

to death, have wondered at the awful punishment inflicted for the killing of the Persian water-dog. There
are but few laws in the Vendîdad, however absurd,
that may not find a counterpart in the legislation of
the Greeks or Latins.

Every crime, according to the Persian law, makes the
guilty man[1] liable to two penalties, one here on earth
and another in the next world, but in ancient Persia,
as in modern legislation, there was a money value
attached to many crimes, and the rich criminal escaped by paying his fine, so far as this present world
was concerned. In the next, however, his money is of
no value to him; when he comes to the head of Chinvat bridge, his conscience becomes a maiden, either
of divine beauty, or of fiendish deformity, according
to his merits. The bridge itself, which reaches over
the awful chasm of hell to the heavenly shore on the
other side, widens, if he be a good man, to the width
of nine javelins; but for the souls of the wicked it
narrows to a thread and they fall down into hell.

THE PLACE OF REWARD.

"O, Maker of the material world! where are the
rewards given? where does the rewarding take place?"

Ahûra Mazda answered: "When the man is dead,
when his time is over, then the hellish evil-doing

---

[1] The penalties for uncleanness in men were far more severe upon
woman; after giving birth to a child she was forbidden to taste of water,
as her touch would defile the element, and at times her food was handed
to her upon a long-handled spoon. Woman was made a creature of contract, and disposed of by a bill of sale; like land or cattle, she was classed
under "the fifth contract," being considered more valuable than cattle,
but far cheaper than real estate. They were sometimes sold in the cradle
and often when only two or three years of age.— *See Donabhoy Framjee's*
work on The Parsis, p. 77.

Daevas assail him; and when the third night is gone—
when the dawn appears and brightens up, and makes
Mithra, the god with the beautiful weapons, reach the
all-happy mountains, and the sun is rising. Then the
fiend carries off in bonds[1] the souls of the wicked, who
live in sin. The soul enters the way made by Time,
and open both to the wicked and the righteous. At
the head of the Chinvat bridge, the holy bridge made
by Mazda, they ask for the reward for the goods
which they have given away here below. Then comes
the well-shapen, strong and noble maiden, with the
dogs (that keep the Chinvat bridge) at her side—she
is graceful and of high understanding.

She makes the soul of the righteous one to go up
above the Hara-berezaita; above the Chinvat bridge she
places it in the presence of the heavenly gods themselves; Vohu-manō from his golden seat exclaims,
'How hast thou come to us, thou holy one, from
that decaying world into this undecaying one? Gladly
pass the souls of the righteous to the golden seat of
Ahūra Mazda—to the abode of all the other holy
beings."[2]

THE VISPARAD.

The word Visparad means "all the chiefs," referring to "the lords of the ritual," therefore the various chapters are merely used in the course of the sacrifice. The following extracts will give the reader a
definite idea concerning the literary merit of this portion of the Zend-Avesta:

---

[1] Every one has a noose cast around his neck; when a man dies, if he
is righteous, the noose falls from his neck ; but if wicked, they drag him
with that noose down to hell.—(*Farg.*, *V, 8.*)

[2] Fargard, xix, 27-32.

In this Zaothra, with this Baresman,
I desire to approach the lords of the ritual
Which are spiritual with my praise;
And I desire to approach the earthly lords as well.

And I desire to approach the lords of the water with
    my praise
And the lords of the land;
And I desire to approach with my praise,
Those chiefs which strike the wing,
And those that wander wild at large,
And those of the cloven hoof, who are chiefs of the
    ritual.

And in this Zaothra with this Baresman,
I desire to approach thee, Zarathuśtra Spitama, . .
I desire to approach the man who recites the ritual
    rites
Who is maintaining thus the thought, well thought,
And the word well spoken, and the deed well done.
I desire to approach the seasons with my praise
The holy lords of the ritual order, ...
And I desire to approach those mountains with my
    praise,

Which shine with holiness, abundantly glorious,
And Mithra of the wide pastures,
And I desire to approach the question,
Asked of Ahúra, and the lore of the lord—
And the farm-house of the man possessed of pastures,
And the pasture produced for the kine of blessed gift,
And the holy cattle-breeding man.

    *   *   *   *   *   *   *   *   *

And we worship the fire here, Ahūra Mazda's son,
And the Izads, having the seed of fire in them;
And we worship the Fravishas of the saints
And we worship Sraosha who smites to victory
And the holy man, and the entire creation of the clean.

    *   *   *   *   *   *   *   *   *

And we sacrifice to the fields and the waters.   .   .
We take up our homage to the good waters,
And to the fertile fruit-trees,
And the Fravishas of the saints, and to the kine.

And we sacrifice to that listening, that hears our
    prayers,
And to that mercy, and to the hearing of our homage,
And to that mercy shown in response to our praise,
And we sacrifice to that good praise which is without
    hypocrisy.
And which has no malice as its end.

    *   *   *   *   *   *   *   *   *

With this chant fully chanted,
And which is for the Bountiful Immortals
And by means of these ceremonial actions,
We desire to utter our supplications for the kine.
It is that chant which the saint has recognized
As good and fruitful of blessed gifts,
And which the sinner does not know.
May we never reach that misfortune
That the sinner may outstrip us in our chanting.
Nor in the matter of the plan thought out,
Or in words delivered, or ceremonies done,
Nor yet in any offering whatever, when he approaches
    us for harm.[1]

[1] Visparad, II, V, XVI, XXII.

TEACHING OF THE MODERN PÁRSÍS.

This résumé of the ancient books will be closed by a brief explanation of their faith in Dualism, as given by some learned Indian Pārsīs of Bombay to Sir M. Monier-Williams during his stay in India. In speaking of the Dualism of Zoroaster, as understood in modern times, Prof. Williams says:

"The explanation given to me was that Zoroaster, although a believer in one Supreme Being, and a teacher of Monotheism, set himself to account for the existence of evil, which could not have its source in an all-wise Creator.

He therefore taught that two opposite—but not opposing, forces, which he calls 'twins,' were inherent in the nature of the Supreme Being, called by him Ahūra Mazda (or in Persian Ormazd), and emanated from that Being, just as in Hindūism, Vishṇu and Śiva emanate from the Supreme Brahmā. These two forces were set in motion by Ahūra Mazda, as his appointed mode of maintaining the continuity of the Universe.

The one was constructive, the other destructive.

One created and composed. The other disintegrated and decomposed, but only to co-operate with the creative principle by providing fresh material for the work of re-composition.

Hence there could be no new life without death, no existence without non-existence.

Hence, also, according to Zoroaster, there was originally no really antagonistic force of evil opposed to good.

The creative energy was called Ahūra Mazda's beneficent spirit (Spento-Mainyus), and the destructive force was called his maleficent spirit (Angro-Mainyus, afterwards corrupted into Ahriman), but only because the idea of evil is connected with dissolution.

The two spirits were merely antagonistic in name.

They were in reality co-operative and mutually helpful.

They were essential to the alternating processes of construction and dissolution, through which the cosmical being was perpetuated.

The only real antagonism was that alternately brought about by the free agent, man, who could hasten the work of destruction, or retard the work of construction by his own acts.

It is therefore held, that the so-called dualistic doctrines of Zoroaster were compatible with the absolute unity of the one God (symbolized especially by fire).

Ultimately, however, Zoroastrianism crystallized into a hard and uncompromising dualism. That is to say, in process of time, Spento-Mainyus became merely another name for Ahūra Mazda, as the eternal principle of good, while Angro-Mainyus or Ahriman became altogether dissociated from Ahūra Mazda, and converted into an eternal principle of evil.

These two principles are believed to be the sources of two opposite creations which were incessantly at war.

On the one side is a celestial hierarchy, at the head of which is Ormazd; on the other side, a demoniacal, at the head of which is Ahriman. They are opposed to each other as light to darkness—as falsehood to truth.

The whole energy of a religious Indian Pārsī is

concentrated on the endeavor to make himself—so to speak—demon-proof, and this can only be accomplished by absolute purity (in thought, word and deed), symbolized by whiteness. He is ever on his guard against bodily defilement, and never goes out to his daily occupation, without first putting on a sacred white shirt and a sacred white girdle. Even the most highly educated and Anglicized Pārsīs are most rigorous observers of this custom, though it is probable that their real creed has little in common with the old and superstitious belief in demons and evil spirits, but rather consists in a kind of cold and monotheistic pantheism.

How far Zoroastrian dualism had affected the religion of the Babylonians at the time of the Jewish captivity is doubtful, but that the Hebrew prophets of those days had to contend with dualistic ideas seems probable from these words : ' I am the Lord, and there is none else. I form the light and create darkness ; I make peace and create evil. I the Lord do all these things.' [1] The New Testament, on the other hand, might be thought by a superficial reader to lend some support to dualistic doctrines. . . . I need scarcely point out, however, that the Bible account of the origin, nature, and destiny of Satan and his angels differs, *toto cœlo* from the Zoroastrian description of Ahriman and his host. Nor need I add that the various monistic, pantheistic, and dualistic theories, briefly alluded to in this paper, are utterly at variance with the Christian doctrine of a Personal, Eternal and Infinite Being, existing and working outside man, and

[1] Isaiah xlv, 6.

outside the material universe, which He has Himself created, and controlling both, and in the case of human beings, working not only outside man, but in and through him." [1]

[1] Sir M. Monier-Williams, Trans. Vic. Ins., Vol. XXV, p. 10.

DIVISION III.

The Time of the Mohammedan Conquest and the Korān.

CHAPTER VIII.

THE KORĀN.

SUCCESSOR OF THE ZEND-AVESTA — AUTHOR OF THE
KORĀN — FIRST REVELATIONS — THE HIGRAH — CON-
TINUED WARFARE — DEATH OF MOHAMMED — RECEN-
SION OF THE TEXT — TEACHING OF THE KORĀN —
HEAVEN — HELL — PREDESTINATION — POLYGAMY —
LITERARY STYLE OF THE KORĀN.

THE Korān or Qur'ân [1] was the immediate successor of the Zend-Avesta upon Persian soil. When
the star and crescent of the Arabian banners floated
in triumph over the land of Īrān, and the altars of
the Pārsīs were stricken down, when the people themselves were either driven from their native land or humiliated by their conquerors, then the new creed supplanted the old, and the war-cry of Islām became the

---

[1] The word Qur'an, a reading, comes from the verb qara'a, "to read."
It is also called El Forqān, "the discrimination," a word borrowed from
the Hebrew. It is also designated by the words El Mus-haf, volume, or
El Kitāb, the book.

watchword of the new faith.[1] By methods peculiarly their own, the invaders set up the standard of their prophet, and his law became the law of the land.

The Arabian peninsula extends southward from Babylonia and Syria down to the Indian Ocean ; its eastern coast is washed by the waves of the Persian Gulf, while the western boundary forms the shore of the Red Sea.   The low lands on these shores lie at the feet of barren ranges of hills, which lead upward from the coast of the Red Sea to the highlands beyond them.   This rugged frontier was the barrier from whence the desert tribes had effectually resisted the attacks of the nations who fought around them for the dominion of the Orient.   Persia, Egypt and Rome had each unsuccessfully tried to penetrate this rocky fortress of Arabia and conquer its hardy defenders. Although the Arabs were mostly a nomadic race, whose wealth consisted largely of camels and horses, still their country contained cities and towns, and of these the most important were Mecca and Medîna, where the creed of Islâm found its early home.

The religion of the Arabs was Sabænism, or the worship of the host of heaven, but in the time of Mohammed the comparatively simple star-worship had been greatly corrupted, and countless superstitious rites and practices had been introduced.   The wandering Arabs had peopled the desert wastes with imaginary beings, and they fancied that every rock and cavern —every stream in the oasis—and every palm tree had its presiding genius.

[1] The chronology of this conquest is in many points uncertain, as the accounts differ. The most important event, however, in the long war was the battle of Nehâwend, which took place probably about A. D. 641.

The vast solitudes, with their terrible stillness—the simoon and the sand column—the breaking of a storm on a distant mountain, and the change of a dry ravine into a rushing torrent—these and other surroundings produced a strong effect upon the vivid imaginations of the children of the desert; and at last their pantheon contained three hundred and sixty-five idols.

When, therefore, the voice of Mohammed rang out upon the startled air, with the cry "There is one God, and Mohammed is his prophet," it came as an omen of strife and bloodshed. Devotion to his tribe and to his gods being one of the strongest characteristics of the Arab, innovations were fought against, with all the fierceness of a vindictive race. A few followers gathered around the new prophet, and then began that series of conflicts, which, after years of fraternal strife, resulted in the triumphant rule of the new creed.

Christianity had long been partially established in Arabia, and some of the more important tribes had embraced it, but neither Christianity nor Judaism was generally accepted by these restless sons of the desert; the logic of the sword, however, is an argument that every man can appreciate, and Mohammed proved to be a successful military leader, giving the spoils of war to his followers in this world as well as promises of reward in the next. Knowing the value of unity of action among his followers, he never abandoned his designs upon Syria, and thus the turbulent tribes of the desert found ample scope for their warlike propensities, while a successful raid was always rewarded with rich booty. The triumphs of Islām were largely due to the love of exciting raids, and the desire for the spoils of conquest.

THE AUTHOR OF THE KORĀN.

However fiercely the contest may be waged around the origin of the Zend Avesta, there is no question among scholars in relation to the authorship of its successor. The individual portions of the Korān were not always written down immediately, as Mohammed often repeated them several times, sometimes forgetting the original statement, and sometimes changing it; he says, however: "Whatever verse we may annul or cause thee to forget, we will bring a better one than it or one like it."[1] It is seriously questioned among the Arabs whether he could read or write—one party claiming that he could and the other maintaining that he could not. On some occasions he certainly employed an amanuensis, and tradition claims that he would frequently direct in which sūrah the passage dictated should be placed. The arrangement of the Korān, however, was left to those who came after him.

The exact date of Mohammed's birth is uncertain,[2] but he began life in the shadow of poverty; all that he inherited from his father being five camels and a slave girl. The boy having lost his mother when he was only six years old was obliged, in his youth, to attend the sheep and goats of the Meccans in order to obtain a livelihood, and this position is still considered by the Bedawīn to be very degrading to any one except a woman. At the age of twenty-four he married a rich widow, who was fifteen years his senior, and it

[1] Chap. II, v. 100.
[2] It was probably about A. D. 571.

is said that this marriage was eminently a happy one.
Three years after her death he married Āyesha, who
was in the habit of saying that she never was jealous
of any of his wives except the first. Six children were
born of this marriage, two of whom were sons, but
they died at an early age.

FIRST REVELATIONS.

Mohammed had reached his fortieth year when he
claimed to receive the first revelations. Perhaps they
might be considered the natural result of his mode of
life, his habits of thought and especially of his physical condition. For many years he had suffered from
nervous troubles, and tradition claims that the disease
was epilepsy. Medical men of to-day would, perhaps,
be more likely to diagnose the case as one of the forms
of hysteria, which is often accompanied with halluci-
nation, and also with a certain amount of deception,
both voluntary and otherwise. Persons who were thus
afflicted were supposed by the Arab to be possessed by
an evil spirit, and the complaint is made in various
places in the Korān that he was regarded in this light
by his own people. His faithful wife Hadiḡah, however, believed in him from the first. The earlier chapters of the Korān are full of enthusiasm, and they
indicate that the author at that time believed in the
reality of his revelations. His daughters soon became
converts to his teachings, and they were followed by
other relatives and friends. Although his first converts were mostly women and slaves, he afterward secured the adhesion of influential chiefs. But the new
faith incurred the open hostility of the great majority

of the Meccans, and the position of its converts became critical. While the more powerful were comparatively secure, the weaker ones, especially the slaves and women, were severely persecuted, and in some cases they suffered martyrdom.

The surroundings became so dangerous that Mohammed advised his little band of followers to seek safety in flight, and they emigrated to the Christian country of Abyssinia until the colony there numbered about one hundred souls. The Quráiś were much annoyed by the escape of the Muslims, and sent a deputation to the king of Abyssinia demanding the return of the fugitives. The request was refused, and the failure of their attempt increased the hostility of the Quráiś toward those who still remained in Mecca.

Being left almost alone, and exposed to constant danger, Mohammed conceived the idea of a compromise. The Quráiś promised that if he would recognize the divinity of their three principal idols—Allát, Al 'Huzzá and Manát, they would acknowledge him to be the apostle of Allâh. He, therefore, recited one day before a public assembly, the following words from the Korán:[1] "Have ye considered Allát and Al 'Huzza and Manát the other third?" He then added: "They are the two high-soaring cranes, and verily their intercession may be hoped for." When, therefore, he came to the last words of the chapter, "Adore God, then, and worship," the Meccans, true to their promise, prostrated themselves to the ground and worshipped as they were bidden.

A great political victory was thus gained, at the

[1] Chap. liii, v. 19–20.

sacrifice, however, of the very principle that many of his followers had given their lives to maintain. He keenly felt his own humiliation in the matter, and on the morrow he hastened to recant from his new position, and condemned his own cowardice in a manly way, declaring what he undoubtedly believed, that the words had been put into his mouth by Satan. The recantation brought upon him redoubled hatred, and at last his whole family were placed under a ban to such an extent, that they could not join the Meccan caravans, and being unable to equip one of their own, they lost their means of livelihood. At last they took refuge, with what few provisions they could collect, in a ravine in the mountains, being able to sally forth for food only during the sacred months, when every man's person and property were safe. After two years of privation their foes became tired of the restriction which they had placed upon the clan, and voluntarily allowed the prisoners to mingle with the rest of the world.

Mohammed, however, again incurred the contempt of the public by adding another wife to the three he already possessed. It was not the number of his household that created the Arabian scandal, but the fact that the new candidate for his favor had been divorced from her husband with this object in view— having been surrendered by him when he learned that Mohammed admired her.

The prophet claimed, however, that he had a revelation sanctioning his conduct in this matter.

THE HIGRAH.

Between the inhabitants of Yaṭhrib and those of Mecca there existed a strong feeling of animosity, and therefore the former tribe were inclined to favor the claims of the new prophet. After some careful negotiations, the leaders espoused his cause, and the persecution of the Qurāiś then became so violent that the followers of Mohammed at Mecca fled from the city. At last there were only three members of the new faith left in the community, and these were Abū Bekr, Alī and Mohammed himself.

His enemies now held a council of war, and decided that eleven men, each belonging to one of the most influential families in the city, should simultaneously attack and murder Mohammed, and by thus dividing the responsibility, avoid the deserved penalty, as the clan of the prophet would not be sufficiently powerful to avenge themselves upon so many families. Mohammed, however, received a warning of their designs; and giving Alī his mantle, ordered him to pretend to be asleep on the couch usually occupied by himself, and thus divert the attention of his enemies. In the meantime Mohammed and Abū Bekr escaped from a back window in the house of the latter, and hid themselves in a cavern of a mountain more than a mile from Mecca, before their absence was discovered. A vigorous search was at once instituted, and for three days they lay concealed, while tradition claims that a spider wove a web across the mouth of the cave and the pursuers, thinking that no one had entered it, passed by in their search.

At length they ventured out once more, and succeeded in reaching Yaṭhrib in safety. Here they were soon joined by Alī, who had been allowed to leave after a few hours' imprisonment. This was the celebrated Hiǧrah or "flight," from which the Mohammedan era is dated.[1]

As soon as possible after he was established at Medīna, Mohammed built a mosque and proceeded to institute regular rites. He also appointed Bilāl, an Abyssinian slave, to call the believers to five daily prayers. He tried to conciliate the Jews of Medīna by adapting his religion as far as possible to their own, but when it became evident that they would never accept him as their prophet, he withdrew his concessions, and instead of turning his face toward Jerusalem while in prayer, he turned toward the Kaābah at Mecca.

As soon as he felt sufficiently strong, he began to agitate the idea of a crusade against the city of his birth, which had compelled him to fly from her borders, in order to save his life. After some petty raids upon their property he decided to attack a rich caravan which was ·returning from Syria laden with valuable merchandise. The returning Arabians were, many of them, influential men of Mecca, and they sent a swift messenger to the city for aid. Their call was responded to by nearly a thousand men, but although the contest was long and bitter, the Muslims won the victory; some of Mohammed's bitterest foes were slain, many prisoners were captured and rich booty was taken. Of the captives six were executed by Moham-

1 It took place on June 16, A. D. 622.

med's order, some embraced his views and others were
ransomed by their friends.

This victory [1] gave Mohammed so much military
prestige that he lost no time in following up the advantage thus gained. The Jews were the first people
upon whom his vengeance was visited, and his first
victim amongst them was a woman, who was put to
death, and soon afterward a whole Jewish tribe was
attacked, their property confiscated and the people sent
into exile.

CONTINUED WARFARE.

Years of bloodshed followed the early military triumphs of Islāmism, and the contest between Mecca
and Medīna was continued, with varied results, until a
truce of ten years was agreed upon; [2] any of the Meccans who chose to do so were allowed to join the ranks
of Mohammed, by the conditions of the treaty, while
upon the other hand those who preferred to leave him
and espouse the cause of the Meccans were permitted
to do so.

This was a political triumph for Mohammed, as it
recognized his position as an independent chief, and he
availed himself of the opportunity thus given him to
reduce the neighboring tribes to submission. He also
wrote letters to the king of Persia, to the Byzantine
Emperor and the ruler of Abyssinia, ordering them to
embrace his faith and submit to his rule. One favorable reply only was received, which came from a
governor of Egypt, and he sent in addition to other
presents two female slaves, one of whom was a Coptic

1 A. D. 624.   2 About A. D. 629.

girl, whom Mohammed added to his already numerous family of wives. The Muslim troops afterward experienced a terrible defeat on the Syrian frontier,[1] but the prestige of the leader was soon re-established by new victories and the accession of various tribes. Two years after the conclusion of the treaty, a tribe which was under the protection of Mohammed was attacked by a tribe which was an ally of the Meccans. This was a violation of the compact, and Mohammed gladly availed himself of the opportunity thus offered him for the renewal of hostilities. Explanations and apologies were alike useless, and he prepared for an expedition against Mecca.

On becoming master of the capital of Arabia, his first act was to repair the Kaābah, or ancient shrine of Arabian worship, and then proclaiming a general amnesty, the Meccans readily embraced the creed of Islām, and flocked to his standard, hoping for the rewards which the prophet promised in Paradise, as well as the rich spoils from the conquered tribes around them. In his first victories he gave the Meccan chiefs more than their share of the booty, for the purpose of kindling their enthusiasm, but in so doing he incurred the displeasure of his old adherents, and he only appeased their wrath by promising never again to make his residence at Mecca or to desert their own city.

DEATH OF MOHAMMED.

The ninth year after the flight is called "the year of deputations," as it marked the adhesion of numerous tribes to his cause; it was also the last year

[1] A. D. 629.

in which Mohammed was able to conduct military expeditions in person. The Arabs, with characteristic fickleness, were not always loyal to their chief, even during his lifetime. Tribe after tribe raised the standard of revolt, and required the close attention of the chieftain during the last years of his life.

He controlled them largely by keeping them occupied with new conquests, and animated by the constant hope of still greater booty, and this became the bond of unity, which, perhaps more than anything else, saved his newly established government from disruption.

At the time of his last pilgrimage to Mecca he stood upon an elevation and addressed the assembled thousands of his followers, admonishing them to stand firmly by the faith which he had taught them. Soon afterward his health failed, but he rallied a little and went to the mosque at Medina, where a large congregation had gathered to hear the latest news from their leader. Mounting the lower steps of the pulpit, he said a few parting words to the people, and then gave some careful injunctions to the general whom he had entrusted with the command of an army to Syria; having finished his admonitions he went to the rooms of his favorite wife, Āyesha, and here he breathed his last.[1] That his successors were able military leaders, is abundantly proven by the later story of Persia and other conquered lands.

RECENSION OF THE TEXT.

At the time of Mohammed's death, no collected edition of the Korān was in existence. Many frag-

[1] June 8, A. D. 632.

ments were in possession of his followers, which had
been written down at different times, and upon various materials, but by far the greater portion was preserved only in the memories of men, and liable at any
moment to be carried away by death. Abū-Bekr, or
Omar, had a collection made during his reign, and he
employed a native of Medīna to collect and arrange
the text from the best available material. This he
did, collecting the texts which were written on palm-
leaves, skins, blade-bones, and other material, besides
recording what could be gathered from the memories
of men. He then presented the Caliph with a copy,
which was, perhaps very much like the one we now
have. It was compiled without reference to any chronological order, and with very little regard to the logical connection of the various portions. The longer
chapters were placed at the beginning, and the shorter
ones at the end, without regard to the order in which
they were written, and there were many odd verses
inserted, apparently for no other reason, than because
they were in harmony with the rhythm. There were
very few vowel points, and these often make a great
difference in the meaning of words. The wording of
many passages which were copied from memory, was
disputed, for the reason that the persons who remembered them did not agree in their statements.

In the present recension of the text there are comparatively few different versions recognized, but it is
evident that great variations have existed from the
time when the first copy was collected, as even then
the various wordings were hotly contested.

Some twenty years later, the Caliph Othmân appointed a commission. consisting of Zäid, the original editor, and three men of Mohammed's own tribe, to decide more definitely upon the proper text.

When this edition was completed, Othmän sent copies to all the principal cities in the empire, and his recension has remained the authorized text, having been adopted by all schools of Mohammedan theologians from the time of its completion [1] to the present.

No attempt was made in this work to present any chronological arrangement, although the chapters have prefixed to them the name of the place where they were supposed to be revealed. Attempts have been made by both Arabic and European scholars to prepare an intelligible chronological .arrangement, but it will be seen that the work is one of great difficulty. The most critical effort upon this subject, and the most successful, has been made by Nöldeke, whose arrangement is the best which Arabic tradition, combined with European criticism, can furnish.

TEACHING OF THE KORÄN.

The Korän is largely composed of fanciful stories, which have been woven around the characters and incidents of Biblical narration. There are however some cardinal points of doctrine which are freely taught, and the great central creed of Mohammedanism is that "There is no god but God, and Mohammed is his prophet."

The confession of this Kelimah, or creed, is the first duty of every convert, and after this he is required to pray, fast, give alms, and make pilgrimages.

[1] A. D. 660.

The name of God in Arabic is Allah, being composed of the article al, "the," and ilâh, "a god." It is a very old Semitic word and is evidently connected with, or derived from the El and Elohím of the Hebrews. According to Muslim theology, Allâh is eternal, and everlasting—comprehending all things, but comprehended of nothing. His attributes are expressed by ninety-nine epithets which are used in the Korân, and which in Arabic are single words, and generally participial forms, but in the translation they are sometimes rendered by verbs as "He creates" for "He is the creator."

Besides a belief in God, the Korân requires a belief in angels; it is claimed that they are pure, without distinction of sex; are created of fire, and neither eat nor drink. Two angels are appointed for each human being, and one stands at his right hand, and the other at his left; the one recording his good deeds, and the other his transgressions of the law. Munkîr and Nakîr are the two angels who preside at the "examination of the tomb." They visit a man in his grave immediately after his burial, and examine him concerning the soundness of his faith. If he acknowledge that there is but one God, and that Mohammed is his prophet, they allow him to rest in. peace, otherwise they beat him with iron maces until he roars so loud that he is heard by all the beings in the universe, except men and ginns. They then press the earth down upon him, and leave him to be torn by dragons and serpents until the resurrection.

The ginns (collectively gâhn) represent a class of beings who are inferior to the angels, but they are also created out of fire, and are both good and evil. Their abode is Mount Qâf, the mountain of emerald which, in Persian mythology, surrounds the world.

HEAVEN.

Heaven, according to the Korân and the traditions, consists of seven divisions, as follows: The Garden of Eternity—The Abode of Peace—The Abode of Rest—The Garden of Eden—The Garden of Resort—The Garden of Pleasure—The Garden of the Most High, and The Garden of Paradise. "Who created seven heavens in stories? . . . Why, look again! canst thou see a flaw? . . . And we have adorned the lower heaven with lamps; and set them to pelt the devils with; and we have prepared them for the torment of the blaze."

"And the fellows of the right hand—what right lucky fellows!
These are they who are brought nigh in gardens of pleasure!
And gold-weft couches, reclining on them!
Around them shall go eternal youths, with goblets and ewers and a cup of flowing wine; no head-ache shall they feel therefrom, nor shall their wits be dimmed!
And fruits such as they deem the best;
And flesh of fowls as they desire;
And bright and large-eyed maids like hidden pearls;
And the fellows of the right—what right lucky fellows!
Amid thornless lote trees
And trees with piles of fruit;

And outspread shade,

And water outpoured ;

And fruit in abundance, neither bitter nor forbidden ;

 * * * * * * * * *

And God will guard them from the evil of that day
  and will cast on them brightness and joy;

And their reward for their patience shall be Paradise
  and silk !

Reclining thereon upon couches, they shall neither see
  therein the sun nor piercing cold;

And close down upon them shall be its shadows ;

And lowered over them its fruits to cull ;

And they shall be served round with vessels of silver
  and goblets that are as flagons—

Flagons of silver shall they mete out ! . . . .

And there shall go round them eternal boys ;

When thou seest them thou wilt think them scattered
  pearls;

And when thou seest them thou shalt see pleasure and
  a great estate !

On them shall be garments of green embroidered satin
  and brocade;

And they shall be adorned with bracelets of silver." [1]

HELL.

Hell also has seven divisions, which are arranged in
the following order: Gehenna—The Flaming Fire—The
Raging Fire that splits everything to pieces—The
Blaze—The Scorching Fire—The Fierce Fire—The
Abyss.

---

[1] Koran, Chaps. 56, 67, 76, Palmer's Trans. The more sensuous portions
of these descriptions are necessarily omitted.

"It is thus that we reward sinners; for them is the couch of hell-fire with an awning above them! Thus do we reward the unjust! . . .

The fellows of the fire shall call out to the fellows of Paradise, 'Pour out upon us water, or something God has provided you with.' They will say 'God has prohibited them both to those that misbelieve.' . . .

Faces on that day shall be humble, laboring, toiling—shall broil upon a burning fire; shall be given to drink from a boiling spring!

No food shall they have save from the foul thorn, which shall not fatten nor avail against hunger!

And the fellows of the left—what unlucky fellows!

In hot blasts and boiling water;

And a shade of pitchy smoke,

Neither cool nor generous!

Verily, they were affluent ere this, and did persist in mighty crime and say 'What, when we die and have become dust and bones, shall we then indeed be raised?'

Then ye, Oh ye who err! who say it is a lie!

Shall eat of the Zaqqûm tree!

And fill yourselves with it!

And drink thereon of boiling water!

And drink as drinks the thirsty camel.

This is their entertainment on the judgment day!

Whenever a new troop is brought forward to be thrown into hell they shall hear its brayings as it boils, for it shall well nigh burst for rage, and the treasures of hell shall come forward and shall ask them, 'Did not a warner come to you?' They shall stay, 'Yea! a warner came to us, and we called him a liar,'

And they shall say, 'Had we but listened or had sense we had not been among the fellows of the blaze!'" [1]

PREDESTINATION.

The Korān teaches the doctrine of predestination in its most radical form; every act of every living being having been written down from all eternity in "the preserved tablet." This predestination is called taqdīr "meeting out," or quismeh, "apportioning."

It is said in the Korān that "God leads astray whom he will, and guides whom he will." [2]

The Arabians were glad to argue that they were not responsible for their deeds, but every act of theirs being foreordained it was therefore justified. They were forbidden to turn back in battle, for he who turns back "save turning to fight or rallying to a troop, brings down upon himself wrath from God, and his resort is hell, and an ill journey shall it be."

They were exonerated from all charge of killing unbelievers, even in battle, for it is said, "Ye did not slay them, but it was God who slew them; nor didst thou shoot, when thou didst shoot, but God did shoot." [3] When the Abyssinian, Abrahat el Aśram, marched upon Mecca with a large body of troops and elephants, he was suddenly defeated, and when the Korān was written it was said, "Hast thou not seen what thy Lord did with the fellows of the elephant? Did he not make their strategem lead them astray, and

[1] Chap. vii, v. 88, 56, 67. [2] Chap. xiv, v. 95.
[3] Chap. viii, v. 15.

send down on them birds in flocks, to throw down on them stones of baked clay, and make them like blades of herbage eaten down?"[1] This legend of the destruction of an army by flocks of birds who carried stones in their beaks has been repeated in various forms in Oriental story. The object of the invader was supposed to be the destruction of the Kaäbah, a shrine to which devotion had been paid from time immemorial. This was the one thing which the scattered Arabian people had in common, and which gave to them a national feeling. Mohammed, therefore, did not abolish it, but cleared it of its idols and dedicated it to the new faith. As it was predestinated that the Kaäbah should stand throughout the ages, it was readily supposed that even the birds of heaven would repulse the forces of the infidel invader.

POLYGAMY.

One of the most fatal blots upon the creed of Islâm is the open countenance which it gives to polygamy. We have not here the case of a prophet placed in the midst of an ignorant and barbarous people, who confronted and modified institutions which he could not at once suppress, but we have Mohammed inculcating the doctrine of polygamy, by both precept and example. It is repeatedly taught in the Korän, and men are commanded to "Marry what seems good to you of women, by twos, or threes, or by fours."[2] When his other wives objected to the introduction of the Coptic slave girl, Mary, into the harem of Mohammed, he claimed to receive a revelation from heaven jus-

[1] Chap. xv.   [2] Chap. iv, v. 1.

tifying his conduct. He also divorced the woman who gave the information to the others, and banished them all (except the Coptic girl) from his presence for the space of a month. He enjoined his followers to treat their wives and slaves more kindly, but they could marry and divorce them at pleasure; the Korān, however, states that "If he divorce her a third time, he cannot marry her after that until she marry another husband:" if the new husband divorces her, however, the first may marry her again.

They were also allowed to exchange wives, but it is said: "If ye wish to exchange one wife for another, and have given one of them a talent, then do not take from it anything."[1]

They required the most careful conduct and seclusion in their wives, and the penalty for adultery was imprisonment for life, but of their partners in guilt it was said, "if they turn again and amend, leave them alone."[2] Again it is said, "Men stand superior to women. . . . But those wives whose perverseness ye fear, admonish them and remove them into a bedchamber and beat them; but if they submit to you, do not seek a way against them."[3]

The Mohammedans of Persia have by no means forgotten their early training, and they still fill their Anderoons with as many women as they can afford. Every Persian house is constructed on the plan of secrecy. No windows are visible from the street, but the interior is built around courts or gardens, with beautiful fountains and fragrant flowers; indeed, there may be groves of fruit trees which cannot be seen

---

[1] Chap. iv, v. 24. [2] Koran, iv, v. 15-20. [3] Koran, iv, v. 38.

from the street. In the main portion of the house
the lord of the mansion lives and transacts his busi-
ness during the day, while the inmates of his Ande-
roon are kept in the most rigid seclusion, passing
their time as best they may, in doing fine embroidery,
and possibly acquiring some proficiency in music or
painting. They cannot go out at all without a
mantle or veil which covers them from head to foot ;
and when the wives of the Shah go upon the street
they are not only followed by the royal guards, but
the event is announced by a herald, the shops are
closed and the streets must be deserted.

Still, it is claimed that with all their seclusion and
ignorance, the women of Persia have a certain amount
of influence, and if one man wishes the assistance of
another, he confides the matter to one or all of his
wives, and they visit the wives of the man whose aid
is needed, and by solicitation and costly presents the
object is often accomplished. It is said that many
important transactions in Persia are conducted in this
way.

LITERARY STYLE OF THE KORĀN.

The language of the Korān is generally considered
the most perfect form of Arabian speech. It must
be remembered, however, that the acknowledged position of the book, as a work of divine authorship,
made it impossible for any Muslim to criticize the
Korān, either in regard to its mode of expression or
its doctrinal teaching. On the contrary, it became the
standard by which other Arabian compositions must be
judged. All literary critics assumed that the Korān

must be right, and therefore other works only approached merit in proportion as they more or less successfully imitated its style.

The language of this literary model of Arabia is surely rugged and forcible, even though it is not elegant or refined. Mohammed often spoke with a rude and startling eloquence; there was no mistaking the language of his fierce denunciations, for instance: "Verily, those who disbelieve in our signs, we will broil them with fire; whenever their skins are well done, then we will change them for other skins, that they may taste the torment."[1]

Each chapter of the Korān is called a Sūrah—an Arabic word which signifies a course of bricks in a wall. These Sūrahs resolve themselves into two different classes; the one claiming to have been given at Mecca, the other including only the revelations which were supposed to be received at Medīna after the flight. The earlier Sūrahs have a tone of enthusiasm and impassioned eloquence, which is not found in the later productions. The style of these earlier chapters is often poetic, and sometimes almost sublime; the principal doctrine found in them is monotheism, and the author seeks to impress his followers by his eloquence rather than by his logic; by appealing to their emotions rather than to their reason. He called upon nature to witness the presence of God, and proclaimed vengeance against those who still clung to their idols. He also gave the most glowing pictures of the future reward of believers, and the

[1] Chap. iv, v. 59.

most revolting descriptions of the unending tortures designed for those who refused to accept his message.

In the Sûrahs of the later portion of the Meccan period, we find long stories which are woven in a fanciful way around the characters of Biblical narrative, still showing, however, more or less of the poetic fire and eloquence of Mohammed's earliest productions.

At a later period he appears in Medîna, as a military leader of great ability and influence. He is now surrounded, not only by the loyal friends who have shared his persecutions, and accompanied him in his flight, but also by a large class who have been forced to adhere to his cause, and whose sincerity is so questionable that they are openly called "hypocrites."

The style of the Sûrahs which were given amidst these surroundings, and during the later years of the author's life, varies greatly from that of the earlier chapters. We find here incidents which are scarcely embellished, and which are often expressed in the most prosaic language. Instead of the impassioned appeal of an orator, we have the more authoritative language of an acknowledged chief, giving his people whatever instruction they may require. He still follows, however, the rhythmical style of expression, which has so long been characteristic of the Arabians. The Arabs of the desert still employ it to a great extent in their formal orations, while the peculiar style of the Korân remains their standard of literary excellence.

DIVISION IV.

The Period Succeeding the Mohammedan Conquest.

CHAPTER IX.

THE ANWĀR-I-SUHALI.

HISTORY OF THE WORK — PREFACE — THE BEES AND THEIR HABITS — THE TWO PIGEONS — THE BLIND MAN AND HIS WHIP—AMICABLE INSTRUCTION—THE PIGEONS AND THE RAT—THE ANTELOPE AND THE CROW — THE ELEPHANT AND THE JACKAL — GEMS FROM THE HITOPADEŚA.

THERE were two collections of early fables in Sanskrit literature, called the Pançatantra and the Hitopadeśa, and during the reign of the Sassanian kings a quaint old book containing these stories was brought to the Persian court and translated into the Pahlaví tongue. This was a notable event in the history of Āryan literature, and since that time[1] this rare collection of simple stories has passed through more mutations than has the Roman Empire; it is now extant, under various names, in more than twenty languages,

[1] About A. D. 570.

the Persian version being known as the Anwâr-i-Suhali, or "The Lights of Canopus."[1]   It is recorded that King Nūshirvan commissioned an officer of state to procure a translation of this work, and, being obtained after years of difficulty, it was deposited in the cabinet of the king's most precious treasures, and was regarded as a model of wisdom and didactic philosophy. But at the time of the Arabian conquest, this work, with many others, was destroyed by the vandals of the desert. More than a hundred years later the book was discovered and translated into Arabic by Almokaffa,[2] it then passed through the hands of several Arabic poets, and was afterward retranslated into Persian, first into verse, by Rudāki in the tenth century, and into prose in the twelfth century by Nasrāllah.   As early as the eleventh century the Arabic work of Almokaffa was translated into Greek by Simeon, and then passed into the Italian.   Again the Arabic text was translated into Hebrew by Rabbi Joel, and this Hebrew version became the principal source of the European books of fable.   Before the end of the fifteenth century, John of Capua had published a Latin version, and a more elegant Persian rendering was made in the beginning of the fifteenth century by Husain Va'iz.   A Turkish translation had been made early in the tenth century, but there was no Hindūstānī version until much later.   The number of translations indicated the extreme popularity of the

[1] Canopus was a star which stood at the right in the heavens when the observer was looking from Hirat, and consequently it lay in the direction of Arabia, which the prophet claimed as the home of wisdom, and therefore wisdom was represented by Canopus.

[2] Translated by Almokaffa about A. D. 770.

work in Europe, and in the sixteenth century it was read in German, Italian, Spanish and French. The English has not so many versions, although both Sir William Jones and Prof. Max Müller have translated the Hitapodeśa, and Prof. Eastwick has given us a faithful reproduction of Husain Va'iz's work, the Anwār-i-Suhali.

The Persian version is the book which candidates for the position of interpreter are required to read after the Gūlistān, as the great number of words and the variety of its style make it the best book in the language to be studied by one who wishes to make rapid progress in Persian. In the present century Major Stewart, professor of Persian at the East India College at Haileyburg, published a translation of the seventh book of this work, and dedicated it to the civil and military employés of the East India Company. The repetition of metaphor and highly florid style of composition is often offensive to the English reader, but these very characteristics form its greatest attraction in the eye of Persian *litterateurs,* and many stories are delightful to them which are wearisome or repulsive to the simpler taste of the western student. In this fanciful work kings are represented as sitting on thrones as stable as the firmament, while they touch the stars with their foreheads, and have all other kings to serve them. Royalty is always just, wise, valiant and most beneficent—ministers are invariably gifted with intellects which are an ornament to the world, and they can solve all problems with a single thought. Mountains rival the planets in their height, and all gardens are fair as dreams of paradise, while the heroes conquer animals so furious that even their appearance frightens the constellations out of the heavens. These absurdities are so prominent that they tempt the student to turn away in disgust, but those who patiently peruse the book will discover many beautiful thoughts, many striking and practical ideas, which are forcibly and often beautifully expressed.

The preface is similar to that of many other Persian works, being composed very largely of a eulogy upon Mohammed, and especially upon the royal dignitary to whom the work is dedicated.

A brief extract from this literary curiosity will give the reader an example of the fulsome praise which Persian authors thought best to bestow upon the kings or court officials who encouraged their pursuits.

"And he is the great Amîr, the place where all excellences and high qualities centre, through the sublimity of his spirit, . . . who, without compliment, is the star Canopus shining from the right hand of Yaman, and a sun diffusing radiance, from the dawning place of affection and fidelity.

Where Canopus falls thy ray, and where
Thou risest, fortune's marks are surely there.

With a view to the universal diffusion of what is advantageous to mankind, and the multiplying of what is beneficial to the high and low, he condescended to favor me with an intimation of his high will, that this humble individual, devoid of ability, and this insignificant person of small capital, should be bold enough to clothe the said book in a new dress, and bestow fresh ornament upon the beauty of its tales of esoteric meaning, which were veiled and concealed by the curtain of obscure words and difficult expressions, by presenting on the stages of lucid style and the chambers of becoming metaphors after a fashion that the eye of every examiner, without a glance of penetration, may enjoy a share of the loveliness of these beauties, of the ornamented bridal chamber of narrative, and the heart of every wise person, without the trouble of imagining, may obtain the fruition of union with those delicately reared ones of the closet of the mind." [1]

A preface of this kind is surely calculated to deter the student from seeking further for the beauties of this peculiar work, but when divested of the cumbersome verbiage these stories will be found both quaint and pleasing. A few of the best of them are here given in simple phrase :

THE BEES AND THEIR HABITS.

There stood in the garden an old tree, whose leaves had fallen, and there was no vitality with which to replace them. The hatchet of the peasant Time had mutilated its limbs, and the saw of the carpenter Fortune had sharpened its teeth in making shreds of its warp and woof. The centre of the tree had become hollow, and a busy swarm of bees had made it their fortress. When the king heard the buzzing of the little workers, he inquired of his sage why these little insects gathered in the tree, and at whose command they resorted to the meadow. Then the minister replied:

---

[1] See preface, Eastwick's version, p. 10.

"O, fortunate prince, they are a tribe doing much good and little harm. They have a queen larger in bulk than themselves, and have placed their heads on the line of obedience to her majesty; she is seated upon a square throne of wax, and she has appointed to their several offices her vizier and chamberlain, her porter and guard, her spy and deputy. The ingenuity of her attendants is such that each one prepares hexagonal chambers of wax, having no inequality in their partitions, and the best geometricians would be unable to do such work without instruments. When this work approaches completion they come forth from their abode at the queen's command, and a noble bee explains to them that they must not exchange their cleanliness for grossness, nor pollute their purity by evil associations. They therefore sit only beside the fair lily or fragrant rose, in order to draw therefrom the purest honey. When they come to the home the warders try them by smelling, and if they have kept their sacred trust and avoided all impure associations, permission is given them to re-enter the immaculate chambers of white wax. But there are many blossoms which, though beautiful to the eye, will poison those who touch them, and the foolish bee who is attracted by their deceitful loveliness is also polluted by their fatal breath; when he comes to the portals of the hive the quick scent of the warders detect the fact if he has been polluted by evil surroundings, and the offender is quickly punished by decapitation. If, however, the warders should be negligent enough to allow the culprit to enter, and the queen of this spotless palace should detect the offensive taint, both the culprit and the careless warders will be conducted to the place of punishment and the warders will be executed first. It is recorded that Jamshid, 'Emperor of the World,' borrowed from these wise disciplinarians the regulations respecting warders and guards, the appointment of chamberlains and door-keepers, and also the arrangement of thrones and regal cushions, which, in the course of time, perfected our customs."

Upon hearing this wonderful illustration of the effects of bad company upon the unfortunate bee, and learning that every man carries with him a portion of the vileness of his evil companions, the king exclaimed: "I have been convinced to-day that the society of some persons is more hurtful than the poison of a viper, and the association with them more dangerous than a position which involves the peril of one's life, and I reason therefrom that it may be better to live in seclusion." But the sage replied: "Great leaders have preferred the companionship of the good and true, but when a sincere friend is not to be found, then indeed solitude is better than society."

THE TWO PIGEONS.

There were two faithful pigeons who at one time consorted together in one nest, with their loyal hearts undisturbed by treachery, and free from misfortune. One was named Bázindah (playful), and the other was called Nawázindah (caressing), while every morning and evening their voices were mingled in the soft notes of love. But some were envious of the happy pair, and evil counsellors attempted to "sever love, and friend from friend divide."

An anxious desire for travel was carefully instilled into the ambitious heart of Bāzindah, and he said to his loving mate, "How long shall we continue in one nest, and spend our time in one abode? I feel a desire to wander through different parts of the world, for, in a few days of travel, many marvelous things are seen, and many experiences are gained. There is no honor awarded until the sword comes forth from the scabbard upon the field of the brave; the sky is ever journeying, and it is the highest of all things, while the earth which is ever still is always trampled down, and kicked by all things, both high and low:

'View the earth's sphere and the revolving skies,
This sinks by rest, and those by motion rise;
Travel, man's tutor is, and glory's gate,
On travel, treasure and instruction wait,
From place to place had trees the power to move,
No saw nor ax could wrong the stately grove.'"

To this his gentle mate replied, "My beloved, when thou removest thy heart from the society of thine own, thou dost sever the cord of unity; thou mayest unite with new comrades, but never wilt thou find them so loyal, as those which long years of trial have shown to be true. Remember the precept of the wise man, and

'Do not an old and well tried friend forego
For new allies, for this will end in woe,'

Thou mayest transgress, and what impression will my word have upon thee then? Remember that

'He shall his foeman's fondest wish fulfill,
Who to well wishing friends bends not his will.'"

Bāzindah, however, tore his heart away from his loving mate, and set forth upon the wing, exulting in his liberty and freedom from her gentle admonitions. With great curiosity, and perfect pleasure, he traveled for a while through the blue air, and passed over the bright hills and gardens of roses and lilies. After a time he came to a mountain, and at its feet lay a beautiful meadow; its green surface was delightful as the gardens of heaven, and the northern breeze swept down from the cool hills, laden with the perfume of a thousand flowers.

"There countless roses their pavilions kept,
  The grass moved wakeful, while the waters slept,
  The roses painted with a thousand hues,
  Their heavenly fragrance each a league diffuse."

The setting sun was bathing the hills with its glory when the weary pigeon reached the lovely spot, and he nestled gratefully down amidst the green grass and fragrant flowers to spend the night in peace and happiness; with his head tucked under his wing, he did not see that a shadow had darkened the fair sunset; he did not see that its glory was shaded by an angry storm-cloud. But soon the restless wind was tossing the canopy of clouds into the high court of the air, and Bāzindah's heart was quaking with terror as the fiery lightnings flashed around him, consuming the hearts of the tulips beside him; the pitiless hail dashed the bright narcissus to the earth, while the thunderbolts seemed to tear the very heart of the mountain.

"In pieces was the mountain's breast, by the light-
    ning's arrows riven,
And earth to its foundations shook, at the fearful
    voice of heaven."

Bāzindah had no shelter from the storm—no refuge
from the pitiless hail and searching wind ; in vain he
tried to hide beneath some friendly branch or amidst
the leaves and grass, still the cruel hail pelted him
like some remorseless foe, and the cold rain still
poured upon him.

" Night ! gloomy night !—Heaven's awful voice—
    What tempest shower so fierce as this ?
    What care the gay in banquet halls ?
    Our perils do not mar their bliss."

In terror and peril, the traveler passed the night
thinking of the home-nest, and the gentle mate who
would so gladly shield him from the storm with her
own pinions, and who was even now grieving her life
away in loneliness, because he came not.

But whatever feelings of penitence may have been
cherished during the perils of the night, were quickly
dissipated by the beauty of the morning light.

" From the east then drew the sun,
    His golden poniard bright,
    And through the earth's dark regions
    Spread a flood of yellow light."

Bāzindah again arose upon his faithful wings, and
pursued his journey; but a royal white falcon was
abroad looking for prey,—a falcon which descends upon
the head of its quarry, swifter than the rays of the

sun, and when soaring on high he reaches heaven quicker than the sight of man.

"Attacking now, it left the thunderbolt behind,
And soared more swiftly than the chilling wind."

For the pitiless bird had marked the pigeon for his prey, and the victim's heart began to flutter, while his wings, paralyzed with fear, seemed to lose all power of motion.

"When on the dove the rapid falcon swoops,
The helpless quarry unresisting droops."

In that moment of helpless terror, Bāzindah thought again of his faithful mate, and quickly resolved that could he but escape this deadly peril, he would be content at home in her downy nest. He was already beneath the claw of the falcon, when the flashing eye of an eagle fell upon them,—an eagle whose talons were so sharp that the sign of Aquila was not safe in the nest of the sky, and who, when hungry, carried off from the meadows of heaven the signs of Aries and Capricorn.

"Aries itself, through fear of him
Would gaze not on the sky,
Save that Bāhram,[1] the blood drinker
Each day stood watchful by."

This fearful bird was on the wing searching for food, and seeing the falcon and the pigeon, he said to himself, "Although this pigeon is only a mouthful, nevertheless one may break one's fast upon it," and quickly he dashed at the falcon:

---

[1] The planet Mars.

"The feathered rivals then to fight began,
The quarry, dodging, from between them ran."

While the fight went fiercely on, Bázindah threw himself under a stone, and crowded himself into a hole hardly large enough for a sparrow, and here he passed the day and another night, quivering with terror and distress. But the morning light again illumined the mountain peaks, for the white-pinioned dove of the dawn began to fly from the nest of heaven, and the black raven of night went to his rest like the Símûrgh, behind the shades of the distant mountains. Bázindah began to flutter his weary wings, and look hungrily around him, when he gladly spied another pigeon, with a little grain scattered before him. Rejoicing to see one of his own species, he fluttered eagerly to the grain, but alas! his foot was caught in a snare.

"Satan's the net, the world's the grain,
Our lusts the enticements are,
Our hearts, the fowl which greediness
Soon lures within the snare."

With bitter reproaches upon the captive pigeon who had thus lured him to destruction, he trembled and struggled, until he broke the decayed net, and turned his tired face toward the home-nest, and flew as rapidly as his forlorn condition would permit. Fearing to attempt again to satisfy his hunger, he was nevertheless compelled to rest, at last, on a wall near a field of corn. A thoughtless boy sent an arrow toward him, and wounded he fell, but he lay so quietly that the young hunter failed to find his game, and at last, weak and wounded, hungry and discouraged, he fluttered by short flights homeward. Nawâzindah heard the flutter of his wings, and flew joyously out to meet him saying:

"'Tis I whose eyes expand, my love to find—
How shall I thank thee—thou so true and kind."

But when she had caressed him, she saw that he was weak and thin, and she exclaimed, "Oh, beloved, where hast thou been?"
Bâzindah replied:

"Ask me not what woes, my love,—
What pangs have been my lot,
All the grief that parting brings,
I've tasted—ask me not.
For travel's conflict I'll not lust again,
With home and friends perpetual pleasures reign."

The truth of the matter is, that I have had much experience, and as long as I live, I will not make another journey, nor go forth until compelled from the corner of our nest." Then the gentle wife flew out and brought him the daintiest food she could find, and tenderly she caressed the wounded wing with her loving bill, and no thought of reproaches entered her grateful heart. Gently she nursed him back to health and strength, and together they cooed and nestled in their quiet home.

THE BLIND MAN AND HIS WHIP.

A sage, who was discoursing to a king upon lessons of wisdom and morality, gave him the following illustration of an important principle: "Once upon a time a blind man and his friend were making a journey together, and they halted in a wild place for the night; the morning found them cold and little rested, for the weather had suddenly grown severe. In searching for his whip the blind man picked up a frozen snake, which he found smoother and more nicely polished than his whip, and greatly pleased he mounted his horse, forgetting the faithful old whip which he had lost. His friend, however, could see, and when he beheld the snake in the hand of the blind man, he cried out: ' Oh, my friend! what thou takest for a whip is a poisonous snake, fling it away before it makes a wound upon thy hand.' But the blind man fancied that his friend was jealous of his great success in finding so beautiful a whip, and he answered: ' Oh, friend! it is owing to my good luck, that I have found a better one, and I am not going to be wheedled out of my good fortune by idle tales.' His friend continued to plead, but the man was obstinate and conceited, as well as blind, and he became angry and frowned upon his faithful friend, while he clung closely to what he believed to be a beautiful thing. After a time the sun rose higher in the heavens, and the air grew more balmy, the snake was also comforted by the warmth of the blind man's body, and recovering from her torpor, she turned backward, and bit the poor fool who had clung to her because he fancied she was beautiful; he died of the venom given in the wound." Then said the sage, "I have adduced this story that thou mayst not be deceived by appearances or fascinated with outward charms, which are as deceitful as the beauties of a snake. Be not attracted by the softness and delicacy of flattery and hypocrisy, for their poison is deadly and their wound is fatal; it is far better to listen to the admonitions of a faithful friend, even though his advice may not always be agreeable, than to be led into the snare of the flatterer, by the poison of her honeyed words.

'Think not sweet sherbert from the world to drink,
Honey with poison is mingled there,
That which thou, fondly, dost sweet honey think,
Is but the deadly potion of despair.'"

AMICABLE INSTRUCTION.[1]

It is said that there lived a wise and virtuous prince, who was greatly afflicted with the conduct of his sons. The young princes "knew no books and were continually working in evil ways," therefore the râja asked himself, "Of what use is it that a son should be born who has neither learning nor virtue? Of what use is a blind eye except to give pain? Of a child unborn, dead or ignorant, the two first are preferable, since they make us unhappy but once, and the last by continual degrees. A numerous family under such circumstances is poison, as is a young wife to an old man."

Considering these things, the king gave orders for a council of learned men to be called, in order that they might study the solution of his problem, and devise, if possible, some method by which his sons might be taught the lessons of morality and wisdom.

Among the wise men who were thus called together, there was a great philosopher named Vishnu-sârman[2] who understood the principles of ethics. He

[1] From Sir Wm. Jones' revision of the Hitopadesa.
[2] Sometimes called Pilpay.

declared that as these young princes were born of good family there was still a hope of their reformation, and he offered to give them the necessary instruction.

His proposition was gladly accepted by the anxious father, and soon the class was called together on the roof of the palace to receive the instruction of the sage. The teacher decided to interest his listeners, and also to convey the lessons of morality by repeating fables. Therefore, with many wise admonitions, and carefully pointing the moral of each lesson, he told them the following stories:

THE PIGEONS AND THE RAT.

Near the Godāvarī river there stood a large Salmali tree, on which the birds found their nightly rest. One morning, when the darkness had just departed, leaving the moon—friend of the night flowers—still in his mansion, a raven who sat in the tree saw a fowler approaching like the genius of death, and he said to himself, "This morning an enemy appears, and I know not what poisonous fruit is ripening." The fowler went on, however, fixing his net and scattering grains of rice. Soon a flock of pigeons, led by their prince Citāgriva, or *painted neck*, came flying that way. They saw the rice and were eagerly descending, when the leader counseled caution, for he feared a snare; but led away by their appetites, they all flew downward upon the rice, being followed, even by the leader, who was unwilling to desert the flock. In a moment more they were snared. But although covetousness had brought them into trouble, the leader counseled that a wise unity of action might even yet deliver them from it. He ordered that they should all fly together, and doing so, they raised the net and carried it along with them. They were followed by the fowler, who expected to see them soon fall into his power.

In a wood near by dwelt a rat, who was a friend of Ćitágriva's, and to him they directed their flight, coming down near his hole. The prisoned birds then besought him to gnaw the strings that held them. The rat replied that "to abandon our own is not the conduct of moralists. Let a man for the sake of relieving his distresses preserve his wealth ; by his wealth let him preserve his wife, and by both wife and riches let him preserve himself." "I am but weak," said he, "and my teeth are small, but as long as they remain unbroken will I continue to cut thy strings." And gnawing dilligently away, he severed their bonds and received them as guests.

Thus the sage taught the princes that "covetousness leads to lust, to anger, to fraud and illusion." He taught also that the union, even of the small and the weak, is beneficial, and also that the humble friend who stands by us faithfully, in the hour of adversity, is of more value than the flatterers, who are watching for our prosperity, in order that they may absorb our gain.

THE ANTELOPE AND THE CROW.

In the country of Magádha there was a forest, in which an antelope and crow had long dwelt in friendship. The antelope was fat, and his flesh was greatly desired by a jackal, who sought to obtain it by gaining his confidence. Going to him, therefore, she pleaded for his friendship, saying, "I am friendless and alone like a dead creature, but having gained thy friendship I shall live again, and I will ever be thy servant," and saying this, she slipped into his home under the branches of a tree, where dwelt the friendly crow. Then the crow inquired of the antelope, "Who is this comrade of thine?" And the antelope replied, "It is a jackal who is my chosen friend." "O my beloved," said the crow, "it is not right to place thy confidence with too much celerity." But in vain the faithful bird pleaded with the infatuated antelope, who still listened eagerly to the flatteries of the jackal, until the aggrieved and disgusted friend flew away to another part of the wood.

"My beloved antelope," said the jackal one day in her softest and sweetest tones, "at one side of the wood is a field of corn, I will take thee there." The antelope found the corn rich and tender, and going there he fed freely. The owner of the corn perceived his loss as the wily jackal had anticipated, and he spread a strong net there, wherein the antelope was captured. The jackal crept softly near, saying to herself, "It has befallen as I wished, and soon I shall satisfy my appetite on his tender flesh." As soon as the antelope perceived his false friend he was glad, for he anticipated deliverance by the gnawing of his bonds. The jackal examined the net, and congratulating herself that it was strong, she said, "Oh, my beloved, I cannot do it to-day, but to-morrow I will come and deliver thee," and going away a short distance she awaited for him to die in order that she might regale herself upon his flesh. The crow, however, in flying over the wood, saw the condition of his imprudent friend, and hastened to his side. "This," said the antelope "is the consequence of rejecting friendly counsel. The man who listens not to the words of affectionate friends, will give joy in the moment of distress to his enemies."

"Where is the jackal?" inquired the crow. "She is near by," answered the antelope, "waiting to feed upon my flesh." "This I predicted," said the crow. "I escape such calamities because I place no such trust; the wise are continually in dread of wicked associations. A pretended friend who flatters thee should be shunned as a dish of milk with poison at its brim. Contract no friendship with flatterers; at first they fall at your feet in their anxiety to drink your blood; they hum strange tunes in your ears with soft murmurs, and, having found an opening, they will ruin you without remorse."

The faithful crow watched until he saw the farmer approaching, then he said to the antelope, "Feign to be dead and remain motionless until thou hearest me make a noise, then run swiftly away."

The owner of the corn, with his eyes flooded with joy, saw the antelope who pretended to be dead, so he took away the snare, and was busily engaged in taking care of his net, when the crow cried out, and the antelope hearing the signal, bounded to his feet and ran away with great speed. The disappointed farmer threw a club after him, and struck the deceitful jackal, who was hidden in a bush, for thus it is written: "In three years, in three months, in three days, the fruit of great vices may be reaped, even in this world."

THE BRĀHMAN AND THE ICHNEUMON.

There was a Brāhman named Modeva, who lived alone with his wife and their infant daughter. One day the mother went away to perform her ablutions and acts of adoration. She therefore left the child in the father's care. Soon after the mother left home a great rāja sent for the Brāhman to perform a religious ceremony called the Srāddha, or offerings to the ghosts of his ancestors. It is customary upon these occasions to bestow rich presents upon the officiating Brāhman or priest, and this was an opportunity that ought not to be lost. Knowing that if he did not go promptly another would be called in his place, he committed the care of his child to a faithful ichneumon, which he had long cherished, and having done so, he hastened away to obey the call of the rāja. Soon after he went away a terrible serpent crawled into the little home and approached the child. He was attacked, however, by the faithful ichneumon, who killed him and cut him in pieces; then seeing his master returning the animal ran to meet him, even while his mouth and paws were still wet with the blood of the serpent. Seeing him thus, the Brāhman promptly decided that he had killed the child, and in his rage he slew the ichneumon. Then going to his house he found the babe sleeping peacefully with the mangled body of the snake beside it. Then, indeed, he knew that, in his haste and unreasonable anger, he had slain the faithful protector of his child. Therefore, he who knows not the first principle, and the first cause, and who is in subjection to his wrath, is tormented like a fool. Let not a man perform an act hastily. Want of circumspection is a great cause of danger.

THE ELEPHANT AND THE JACKAL.

In a forest there lived an elephant in quietness and in peace, but there were hungry jackals around him who thirsted for his blood. They conferred among themselves, and decided to accomplish by stratagem that which they could not hope to effect by force. Then a wily old jackal approached the elephant, and saluting him most humbly he thus addressed him, "Royal sir, wilt thou grant me an interview?" "Who art thou," said the elephant, "and why dost thou come hither?" "I am a jackal," he replied, "and my name is Little and Wise. I am sent into thine august presence by the assembled inhabitants of these woods. Since this vast forest ought not to be compelled to exist without a king, it is therefore determined to perform the ceremony of washing thee, and thus installing thee as the sovereign of the forest. It is said that he who is eminent in birth, in virtue and justice—he who is perfect in words, is fit to be the ruler of the world. Therefore, we salute thee as our king. Now I beseech thee to come quickly, lest the fortunate time for thine inauguration should slip away." So saying he walked hastily away, and the conceited elephant elated with the hope of royalty, followed the jackal until he came into a little pool, wherein his immense weight caused him to slowly sink in the mud at the bottom.

"Friend Jackal," said he "what can be done for me? I have fallen into the mire so deeply that I cannot rise out of it." Thereupon the jackal laughed loudly and rushed away to find those who were to feast with him upon the flesh of the elephant.

Then said the elephant sadly, "Such is the fruit of my confidence in your deceitful speeches. It is, indeed, true that if thou enjoyest the company of the good, then wilt thou thyself be happy and virtuous, but if thou fallest into the company of the wicked, then thou wilt fall indeed."

So saying he resigned himself to his fate, and soon became the food of his flatterers. It is safe to contract no friendship—not even acquaintance with the deceitful, for the hypocrite resembles a coal, which when hot burneth the hand, and when cold blackens it.

GEMS FROM THE HITOPADEŚA.

As there are many gems in this quaint old volume of fables which are well worthy of preservation, the best of them are here presented :.

1. "Always avoid flatterers and hypocrites; their tongues claim to be covered with honey, while their hearts are filled with poison, and a desire to suck the blood of their victim."

2. "The learned man may fix his thoughts on science and wealth, as if he were never to grow old or to die; but when death seizes him by the locks he must practice virtue."

3. "Knowledge produces mildness of speech; mildness of speech a good character; a good character

wealth, and wealth, if virtuous actions attend it, produces happiness."

4. "Among all possessions, knowledge appears eminent; the wise call it supreme riches, because it never can be lost, has no price, and can at no time be destroyed."

5. "Knowledge acquired by a man of low degree places him on a level with the prince, as a small river at last attains the ocean, and his fortune is then exalted."

6. "The science of arms and the science of books are both causes of celebrity, but the first is ridiculous in an old man, and the second is in all ages respectable."

7. "Learning dissipates many doubts, causes things otherwise invisible to be seen, and is the eye of every one that is not absolutely blind."

8. "Knowledge forgotten is poison, food is poison to him who cannot digest it; a numerous family is poison to the indigent, and a young wife is poison to an old mate."

9. "Life, action, property, knowledge, and death, these five were formed for all."

10. "The potter forms what he pleases with moulded clay, so a man accomplishes his own works."

11. "Prosperity is acquired by exertion, and there is no fruit for him who doth not exert himself; the fawns go not into the mouth of a sleeping lion."

12. "Knowledge is destroyed by associating with the base, with equals equality is gained, and with the distinguished, distinction."

13. "Virtues to those who know their value are

virtues, but even these, when they come in the way of the vicious, are vices; as rivers of sweet water are excellent, but when they reach the sea are not fit to be tasted."

14. "He who restrains his appetite, a dutiful son, a prudent and good wife, and he who acts considerately, give birth to no misfortune."

15. "In perils we prove a friend; in battle a hero; in contracted fortunes a wise man, and in calamity our kinsmen."

16. "Thus may the character of treacherous persons be described; at first they fall at your feet, and then drink your blood; thus the false friends and black gnats practice alike every mode of treachery."

17. "Make no league with an avowed enemy, or with a flatterer. Water, though well warmed, would quench, nevertheless, the fire that warmed it."

18. "If the friendship of the good be interrupted their minds admit of no long change; as when the stalks of the lotus are broken, the filaments within them are more visibly connected."

19. "Charity, forbearance, participation in pains and pleasures, goodness of heart, and truth; these are the sciences of friendship."

20. "Goodness and truth are discerned by a man's discourse, but cowardice and a variable mind are easily discerned by his conduct."

21. "It is one thing to hear the words of a friend whose heart is pure as water, and another to hear the words of a base dissembler."

22. "A wise man walks slowly and circumspectly,

and lives in one place, nor having seen another station should he desert his former abode."

23. "It is easy for all men to display learning in instructing others, but it is the part of one endued with a great mind to form himself by the rules of justice."

24. "As those who have caught cold, take no pleasure in moonshine, or those who have fever, in the heat of the sun, so the mind of a woman delights not a husband where there is great disparity of years."

25. "It is better to pull up by the roots a loose tooth, and a wicked counsellor."

26. "He is a friend whom favors have not purchased, and he is a man who is not subdued by his senses."

27. "The seed of good advice must be cherished with extreme care, it must not be broken ever so little, if it be, it will not grow."

28. "A hundred good words are lost upon the wicked; a hundred wise words are lost upon a fool; a hundred good precepts are lost upon the obstinate, and a hundred sciences upon those who never reflect."

29. "A serpent drinking milk only increases his venom, thus a fool being admonished is provoked, but not benefitted. A sensible man may be admonished, but not a fool."

30. "He who knows not his own weakness must be routed by flatterers and enemies."

31. "A great man becomes little, and his virtue is diminished by associating with an unprincipled person."

CHAPTER X.

PERSIAN POETRY.

SEVEN ERAS—THE FIRST PERIOD—THE HOMER OF ĪRĀN
—THE SHĀH NĀMAH—HISTORY OF THE PERSIAN EPIC
—FIRDUSĪ—INVECTIVE—MŪTESHIM—THE SHĀH'S RE-
PENTANCE—DEATH OF FIRDUSĪ—THE POEM.

THE history of Persian poetry may be divided into
seven distinct periods of from one to two centuries each.

The first period reaches from the beginning of the
tenth century to the close of the eleventh, and it may
be said to represent the national poetry in its original
purity. Previous to this time, there had been fragments
of verse, which had been composed by Bāhram Gor, a
Sassanian king, and a few other authors, but this early
literature had perished at the hands of the Moslem invaders. The conquerors not only destroyed, as far as
possible, the literature of Īrān, but even discarded the
language, using Arabic in all official documents. The
vitality of the Persian tongue, however, was so great
that the patriotic people finally founded another national
literature, under the patronage of the Samanian kings.

To this period belonged, Rūdāki, who has been
called "The father of Persian poetry," and who was
said to be the author of one hundred volumes of verse,
besides his metrical version of the work which has been

discussed in the previous chapter under the Persian
name of Anwār-i-Suhali. To this period also belonged
Omar Khayyām, who was a mathematician as well as a
poet. His beautiful quatrains are a great improvement
upon the rubā'ī of Abu Sa'īd, who was his predecessor
in this peculiar style of verse, and his rhapsodies upon
love and wine resemble those of Ḥāfiz.

The position of "King of Poets," which was established by Mahmūd the Ghaznevide, is still maintained
at the court of Persia, as well as in England, where
Tennyson so long filled the office of Poet Laureate.
Firdusī was the great literary light of the first period
of Persian poetry, indeed he was the Homer of Irān,
and his great epic will always command the first position among the poetical productions of his native land.

THE SHĀH NĀMAH.

During the reigns of the Sassanian and Ashkanian
princes over Persia, extensive researches were made to
collect the most authentic materials[1] for a general
history of that country. This work having been accomplished during the reign of Yezdejird, that monarch
called upon the priests of the Fire worship to write
out the annals of Persia from the reign of Keiūmers
down to the end of that of Khosru Parviz. Their
work was completed, but this and other valuable
manuscripts were carried away with the spoil of the

[1] That there were historic materials of great antiquity, we have the
testimony of Herodotus and Ctesius, and also of the book of Esther—"On
that night the king could not sleep and he commanded to bring the
books of records of the chronicles, and they were read before the king."
—Esther vi, 1. Also it is written, "And all the acts of his power and
his might and the declaration of the greatness of Mordecai, are they not
written in the books of the chronicles of the kings of Media and Persia?"
—Esther x, 2.

conquerors after the great victory of Saad Vekas over
Yezdejird.[1] It was brought before Omar, and he sent
it, with other portions of the spoils to the king of
Abyssinia, who had several copies made, and distrib-
uted them among his friends in different portions of
the East. In this way the valuable work was preserved, and in the course of years reached Khorasân.
In the ninth century[2] the Persian king, Yakub bin
Leith called a council of the most learned Fire-
worshippers, and with their assistance selected the best
materials for continuing the history of Persia down to
the final defeat of Yezdejird, and they also added to
it the ancient history by Danishber Dehkan, which in
the meantime had been translated into modern Persian.

When Shâh Mahmûd Sabuktugîn came to the
throne, he conceived the idea of having the history of
Persia versified in such a form that it would be appre-
ciated by his poetry-loving people, and after many
tests of the poetic ability of his literary subjects, he
finally confided the works to the hands of

FIRDUSÎ.

This celebrated poet, whose true name was Abul
Kâsin,[3] was a native of Tus, a city of Khorasân, and
many happy hours of his boyhood were spent on the
banks of the beautiful river that swept along its
course near his home. But the rebellious waters occasionally flooded their banks, leaving ruin in their

[1] A. D. 636.   [2] A. D. 837.
[3] The name of Firdusi is said to have been given him by the Governor of Tus, because his garden, which was called Ferdus (Paradise),
was looked after by the father and brother of the poet, and it was in this
delightful spot that he began the versification of the great national epic,
the Shah Namah.

path, and the dream of the young poet's life was the
hope that some day he might command the means to
build a suitable bridge over this turbulent stream, and
also to confine its rising waters within banks of solid
masonry. When, therefore, he received the royal commission to write the long Persian epic, he felt that
this great public improvement was within his reach,
and he gladly undertook the task. After several sam-
ples of his poem had been presented to the Shāh, the
prime minister was ordered to pay the poet a thousand drachms of gold for every thousand couplets
which he produced until the work was completed.

A magnificent residence was erected for Firdusī
near the palace of the king, and the best painters of
the age were employed to cover the walls with the
portraits of kings and heroes, with paintings of battles
and sieges, with the most imposing military scenes,
and everything that could excite the martial valor and
fire the imagination of the writer.

The only member of the court with whom the poet
was not upon friendly terms was the conceited prime
minister, who expected, and generally received, almost
as much adulation from the court poets as the king
himself. Firdusī refused to render him this servile
homage, and not only so, but finally ignored him to
such an extent that he would not go to his house to
receive the payment of gold coin which became due
upon the completion of each thousand couplets. The
only reason he gave for this was that he preferred to
receive the whole amount at once, and thereby be
enabled to carry out his favorite project and build a
bridge in his native city.

All of these little exhibitions of animosity on the part of the poet combined to make him offensive to the vizier, and gave opportunities to other envious courtiers to cultivate the favor of the prime minister by flatteries of himself, and curses upon the head of Firdusī.

At the end of thirty years of hard work the Shāh Nāmah was completed, consisting of sixty thousand couplets. The vizier then revenged himself upon the poet by misrepresenting the condition of the treasury to the king, and, urging upon him the absurdity of paying such an enormous price for a poem, he finally induced him to send to the poet sixty thousand drachms of silver instead of the gold which he had promised.

Firdusī was coming out of his bath when the bags of silver arrived from the treasury, and learning the value of their contents he contemptuously gave them away, giving recklessly, and without judgment, until the sum was exhausted.

This insult to the Shāh was duly reported and exaggerated by the prime minister, and while the monarch was furious with rage, the poet, at the suggestion of the vizier, was condemned to be trampled to death by elephants. His apartments, however, being close to the royal residence, he took advantage of that fact and threw himself at the king's feet, suing for pardon, and this was granted upon the condition of his immediate departure from the city. Sick at heart, and burning with indignation, he sought the apartment of the king's favorite attendant, Ayaz, who had always been a faithful friend to the bard. To him Firdusī related his story, and from him received the fullest sympathy. Here he wrote a bitter poetic invective against the Shāh, and having sealed it up, requested Ayaz to deliver it to him after the poet's departure, and also to choose the time for doing so when some defeat had rendered the Shāh more low-spirited than usual.

INVECTIVE.

" In Mahmūd shall we hope to find
  One virtue to redeem his mind?
  A mind no generous transports fill,
  To truth, to faith, to justice chill.

" Son of a slave. His diadem
  In vain may glow with many a gem.
  Exalted high in power and place,
  Outbursts the meanness of his race.

" Place thou within the spicy nest,
  Where the bright phœnix loves to rest
  A raven's egg—and mark it well,
  When the vile bird has chipped its shell,
  Though fed with grains from trees that grow
  Where Salesbel's [1] sweetest waters flow—
  Though airs from Gabriel's wings may rise
  To fan the cradle where he lies;
  Though long these patient cares endure,
  It proves at last a bird impure.

" A viper nurtured in a bed
  Where roses all their beauties spread,
  Though nourished with the drops alone
  Of waves that spring from Allah's throne,

[1] The sacred well at Mecca, the waters of which are claimed to have wondrous healing power.

Is still a poisonous reptile found,
And with its venom taints the ground.

" This truth our holy prophet sung—
All things return from whence they sprung.
Pass near the merchant's fragrant wares,
Thy robe the scent of amber bears ;
Go where the smith his trade pursues,
Thy mantle's folds have dusky hues.

" Let not those deeds thy mind amaze
A mean and worthless man displays.
An Ethiop's skin becomes not white,
Thou canst not change the clouds of night.
What poet shall attempt to sing
The praises of a vicious king ?

" Hadst thou, degenerate prince, but shown
One single virtue as thy own,
Had honor, faith, adorned thy brow,
My fortunes had not sunk as now ;
But thou hadst gloried in my fame,
And built thyself a deathless name.

" Oh Mahmūd, though thou fear'st me not,
Heaven's vengeance will not be forgot.
Shrink, tyrant, from my words of fire,
And tremble at a poet's ire."

The indignant and unfortunate bard escaped from
Ghizni by night, on foot and alone, for his friends
dared not incur the enmity of the king by rendering him any assistance. Ayaz alone had the generous courage to brave the Shāh's displeasure by aiding
the refugee. He sent a trusty slave after him, who

soon overtook him, and giving him the horse and a sum of money and other little comforts for his journey, besought him in the name of Ayaz to hasten out of the territory of Sháh Mahmúd if he valued his life.

MŪHTESHIM.

In the meantime reports of the vizier's animosity and of the sultan's cowardice were spread all over the country, exciting universal detestation of the king and his minister. The accounts of the poet's misfortunes and the king's injustice reached Mūhteshim, the prince of Kohistan, about the time the fugitive approached his seat of government. This prince was the dear friend of Shāh Mahmūd, and bound to him by ties of gratitude for countless favors, but he hesitated not to show his respect for genius, and he sent a deputation of learned and distinguished men to meet Firdusī and invite him to the royal presence. In the midst of this flattering and honorable reception Mūhteshim learned that the offended poet intended to publish a satirical work, holding up to the detestation of the world the treachery of Mahmūd, and he endeavored to dissuade him from this act of revenge, which he considered unworthy of the greatest literary genius of the age. The poet afterward sent him an hundred indignant couplets, that the prince might destroy them himself. Firdusī stated in a letter sent with the lines that, although he dreaded not the anger of Mahmūd, still, out of grateful friendship for the generous Mūhteshim, he gave up the cutting rebuke. The closing paragraph states that—

"On thy account, most amiable prince, do I now con-

sent to transfer my just revenge from this vain world
to a higher court."

Mûhteshim presented Firdusī with a goodly sum of
money and forwarded him on his journey, fearful lest
the sultan's rage or the vizier's malice might overtake
and ruin him.

This proved to be a wise precaution, for the king
had discovered a sarcastic epigram which Firdusī had
written on the wall of the great mosque the night of
his departure, and on the next day Ayaz delivered to
the furious monarch the insulting letter which the poet
had left with him for that purpose, and a large reward was offered for the apprehension of the fugitive.
At length, however, the sultan received a. long letter
from his friend Mûhteshim, who related his meeting
with Firdusī, now, in his old age, a penniless wanderer, after having devoted the best years of his life in
the constant exercise of his great talents for the execution of his king's wishes, and gently reproached the
Shāh for allowing himself to be imposed upon by the
evil advice of malicious courtiers; he also informed
him of the forgiving spirit the poet had manifested in
destroying his own brilliant satire which was composed
at the monarch's expense, and closed the letter by
quoting the couplet which Firdusī had used in the
letter to himself.

The complaints from his subjects also began to come
to the royal ears, and all of this, together with the
reproaches of his own conscience, produced in his mind
a strange combination of grief and rage, of indignation and regret.   He disgraced the malicious vizier,
and fined him sixty thousand drachms of gold, the

same amount which he had prevented him from paying to Firdusī, and deeply regretted his own injustice to the gifted bard; but still, he could not forgive the cutting satire of the letter which had been brought him by Ayaz, in which the poet had taunted him with his low birth as being one of the causes of his cowardice and meanness.

DEATH OF FIRDUSĪ.

Firdusī was protected by the Arabian government, and after some years returned and lived with his family at Tus, but he was old, grieved and broken down, and at last he died in his quiet home, at the age of eighty-three. In the meantime Shāh Mahmūd, hearing of his return to Tus, and anxious to render justice, though tardily, to the man he had wronged, sent an envoy with sixty thousand drachms of gold, together with quantities of silks, brocades, velvets, and other costly presents, to Firdusī as a peace offering. But as the royal train of loaded camels entered one gate of the city a mournful procession went out of another, and followed the dead poet to the place of his burial.

The Shāh's ambassadors offered the presents intended for Firdusī to his only daughter, but she possessed her father's spirit, and haughtily dismissed the courtiers, rejecting their gifts with proud disdain.

The Shāh, wishing to make some offering to the memory of the departed poet, ordered the sum which had been intended for him to be expended in erecting a caravansera and bridge in Tus, in accordance with Firdusī's life-long ambition. These monuments of the poet's fame and of the king's tardy justice existed for many years, until destroyed by an invading army of Ousbegs under Obeid Khan.

THE POEM.

This great epic, which was written under royal favor, though its author afterward suffered from royal scorn, is a valuable Persian classic. In the Persian tongue it exists only in manuscript form, and its text was corrupted by ignorant transcribers to such an extent that it excited the indignation of the sultan (a grandson of Timur, who reigned in the fifteenth century), and he collected a vast number of copies of the work; from these he had a transcript made, which was, perhaps, tolerably correct.

But since that time copies have been so greatly multiplied and their contents differ so widely, that it is only by a careful collation and comparison of manuscripts that scholars can hope to arrive at a reasonable degree of correctness. These manuscripts are finely executed and highly ornamental, having the frontispiece and titles beautifully illuminated and sprinkled with gold; the volumes are often profusely illustrated by colored drawings of exquisite finish. They cost about one hundred guineas, or about five hundred and twenty-five dollars each. But although these manuscripts can only be multiplied at such great expense, the original work has lived through eight centuries, and is still the most popular epic in the Persian tongue.

The author of the Shāh Nāmah [1] has often been

---

[1] In addition to the Shah Namah, Firdusi composed a poem of nine thousand couplets on the loves of Yusuf and Zulaikha, that abounds in elegant

called the Homer of the East, Firdusī occupying the same position in relation to other Persian poets that Homer has so long held in the West. Like Homer, too, he describes a rude age, where muscular strength and animal courage were chiefly valued. The correspondence is very striking between the old heroic times which were described by Firdusī and Homer, and the pictures which are sometimes given us of the age of European chivalry. It is well known that the Moors carried into Spain the poetry and romance of Arabia and Persia, and some of our best fiction is supposed to be derived from that source.

Although Firdusī wrote in the beginning of the eleventh century, it was not until the twelfth that the romances of chivalry began to amuse the Western world. The "Orlando Innamorato," a poem by Bayardo, which was afterward improved and paraphrased by Berni, gave life and character to a great number of the stories of chivalry. In a similar way the Shāh Nāmah was largely indebted to the Būstān-Nāmah, which comprised the chronicles, histories, and traditions of the Persians, collected under the patronage of Yezdjird, the last king of the Sassanian race. Like the beautiful Rāmāyaṇa and the martial Mahā-bhārata of the Hindūs, the Shāh Nāmah claims to be a history in rhyme. It is supposed to comprise the annals and achievements of the ancient kings of Persia from Kaiūmers[1] down to the Saracenic invasion and con-

and spirited diction, but it is inferior to the greater epic, partly in consequence of his adoption of the same metre which he used in the Shah Namah, and which was well adapted to that martial poem, but not at all appropriate for the expression of the gentle strains of a love song.

[1] Kaiumers is represented as the grandson of Noah.

quest of that empire,[1] an estimated period of more than three thousand six hundred years. But this bold lyric can lay but little more claim to historic accuracy than can the Hindū epics whose gorgeous colorings mock the very name of history. The Shāh Nāmah, like the other Oriental poems, abounds in adventures of the wildest description, in fabulous feats of strength and valor, and the heroines of the Persian bard are as intrepid and beautiful as the maidens who conquered the heroes of Western poetry.

The legends of all nations are rich with terrible dragons, which are vanquished by unconquerable knights. Even England has her St. George, and other countries boast of cavaliers who were equally valiant.

The hero of the Shāh Nāmah is Rustem, the Persian Hercules, and the strong similarity between the myths pertaining to them is another argument in favor of the common origin of various mythologies.[2] The labors of Rustem, however, were only seven, while those of Hercules were twelve. In the Shāh Nāmah, Isfendiyār has his seven labors as well as Rustem, and both succeeded in the overthrow of devouring monsters, and the destruction of talismans and works of enchantment. Isfendiyār is always accompanied, however, by a troop of horsemen, while Rustem performs his exploits alone, being mounted upon his magnificent horse Rakush. This splendid animal will often remind the reader of the horses of Indra, the Hindū "Lord of the Thunderbolt," or Jove with his "steeds of light,"

"Adorned with manes of gold, and heavenly bright."

Indeed, the boldest heroes of all people rode to battle upon gallant chargers like those of Rhesus, which were "swift as the wind, and white as winter snow."

The splendid picture of the Northern god would have lost its force without the presence of the fleet-footed Sleipnir, and Neptune were scarcely the king of ocean without his celestial steeds,

> " Fed with ambrosial herbage from his hand,
> And their fetlocks linked with golden band."

Achilles, too, drew the reins over

> " Xanthus and Balius, of immortal breed,
> Sprung from the wind, and like the wind in speed.
>
> *   *   *   *   *   *   *   *   *
>
> From their high manes they shake the dust, and bear
> The kindling chariot through the parted war."

Būddha is represented, too, as deserting his wife and child, riding upon his coal-black steed, Kanthāka, which was said to be thirty feet in length, and able to clear the high gates of the palace, or the broad rivers that flowed across his pathway, at a single bound.

The Persian poem, like the colossal epics of India, is of such interminable length that the readers of modern times would not be willing to scan the many pages of endless description and hyperbole. We therefore give, in simple phrase, the best incidents of this heroic legend.

CHAPTER XI.

STORY OF THE SHĀH NĀMAH.

SĀM SUWĀR—THE SĪMŪRGH'S NEST—THE FATHER'S
DREAM—RŪDABEH—THE MARRIAGE—RUSTEM—THE
TŪRĀNIAN INVASION—THE WHITE DEMON.

IN the golden age of Persian chivalry there lived a
famous warrior by the name of Sām Suwār. He
was the son of the great chieftain Narimān, and he
was the commander-in-chief of the Persian armies, and
not only a valiant hero upon the battlefield, but more
than once he had warred against the allied hosts of
demons, and come off victorious. He had conquered
the furious monster Soham, which was of the color
and nature of fire, and, bringing it beneath the obedient rein, he made it his war horse in all his later
battles with the demons.

Suwār had an heir born to him, and knowing that
a son would inherit his own power and fame, his
heart was filled with exultation. But when the child
was placed in his arms, this dark-haired Persian warrior was appalled, for the babe, otherwise perfect, had
a head of silvery white hair.

> " His hair was white as a goose's wing,
> His cheek was like the rose of spring,
> His form was straight as a cypress tree,
> But when the sire was brought to see

> That child with hair so silvery white,
> His heart revolted at the sight."[1]

The gentle mother gave the child the name of Zāl, but the superstitious people began to whisper that this white-haired child was an evil omen to the house of Suwār. Surely it could bring only calamity into the family. It must be that in some way the child belonged to the demon race, or,

> " If not a demon, he, at least,
> Appears a parti-colored beast."

The father bore the sneers and reproaches of the people for a time, and then resolved to abandon the boy upon the mountain crags to be destroyed by beasts of prey. In vain the faithful mother pleaded to be allowed to retain her babe; in vain she promised to keep him in seclusion so sacred that the sight of him should never again offend the father's eye; her child was torn from her arms, and carried to a distant mountain in the depths of the night, and there deserted by the cruel and superstitious father.

THE SĪMŪRGH'S NEST.

An inaccessible cliff of the Alborz mountains is said to be the home of the Sīmūrgh,[2] a mammoth bird with golden plumage, who carries elephants to her nest for her birdlings to feed upon. Far beyond the reach of man, this wondrous nest is hidden amidst the white cliffs, which are threaded thickly with veins of golden quartz, while around the base of the structure

---

[1] Unless otherwise indicated, the poetical quotations in this legend will be from Atkinson's Translation.
[2] The Anka of the Arabians.

there gleam the stones of fire—the amethyst, the
topaz and ruby, and in the rocks not far away the
sunset fires have left their glow in the heart of the
opal. The bird of golden plumage loves these precious stones, for they flash back the fire of her eye,
and seem to warm her heart with their gleaming
beauty. The night was dark, for even the stars were
hidden behind the floating clouds that told of a coming storm, then

> " A voice not earthly thus addressed
> 　The Sīmūrgh in her mountain nest—
> To thee this mortal I resign,
> Protected by the power divine.
> Let him thy fostering kindness share,
> Nourish him with maternal care ;
> For, from his loins in time will spring
> The champion of the world, and bring
> Honor on earth, and make thy name
> The heir of everlasting fame."

The bird listened to the voice, and peering down
between the mountain crags and rocky cliffs, she saw
a man with coward heart leaving a tender babe upon
one of the foot-hills. Her mother-heart beat faster
while she waited a moment listening to the coming
storm, and then the strong wings moved upward
through the darkness, and circling round in stately
flight, she swept nearer and nearer to the desolate
babe. Down she came at last, and the little one
looked up with wondering eyes upon the great mass of
plumage that seemed to have been borne to him upon
the wings of the coming storm, and the boy smiled

and reached out his baby hands toward his new-found friend. The tender mother-bird fastened her talons carefully in his little dress, and floated away past mountain stream and rocky crags, beyond the foot-hills and the higher peaks, until she reached the won-drous nest hidden amidst the stones of fire. A sweet, familiar note caused the nestlings to cling more closely together, and here, in the newly made space, the ban-ished child was laid, and his shelter from the cruel storm that night was the golden feathers of the Sīmūrgh.

When the sunlight touched the white cliffs and lighted up the fires in ruby and opal, the great bird was awakened by a strange cry beneath her wing, and she remembered the human nestling within her habita-tion. Then, like the sacred bird of Jove, she rises from her nest, and

> " Wide as appears some palace gate displayed,
>   So broad the pinions stretched their ample shade,
>   As stooping dexter with resounding wings,
>   The imperial bird descends in airy rings." [1]

Not as a guide to the tent of Achilles does the Sīmūrgh wheel her lofty flight, but to find food for the helpless babe within her walls. With dainty bits within her bill she comes again to her mountain home, and the stranger babe is fed before her own young have broken their fast. The Sīmūrgh's nest-lings learned from the mother-bird the lessons of mercy and love, and soon on tender wing they too brought dainties to the banished child, and year after

[1] Iliad, B. 24.

year he lived in the Sīmūrgh's home, or played amidst the rough jewels in the crags around her nest.

THE FATHER'S DREAM.

The years went by with muffled feet, bringing no balm to the heart of the bereaved mother. The cruel way in which her child had been torn from her arms by the unnatural father, to suffer a still more cruel fate, had left a wound in her heart that her husband's later kindness had no power to heal. The father, too, was ashamed of his own brutality, but too cowardly to confess his fault, no word of repentance had ever passed his lips. The only sign of remorse was seen upon his head, for the dark locks of the Persian chieftain had grown as silvery white as the hair of the banished child. His sleep was disturbed, and he was haunted night after night by strange and troubled dreams. One night there flashed before his vision a gallant youth of martial bearing, who rode at the head of a troop of horsemen, with banners flying before him, and coming into the warrior's presence, he cried:

" Unfeeling mortal, hast thou from thine eyes
Washed out all sense of shame ? Dost thou believe
That to have silvery tresses is a crime ?
See thine own head is covered with white hair,
And were not both spontaneous gifts from heaven?"

Suwār awoke with a scream and called the astrologers around him. They declared that the boy was still alive, and in the early morning the father went to the lonely mountain, and climbing into its cliffs as far as possible, he bemoaned his child and prayed

for his return. His cry went up to the wondrous nest
amidst the stones of fire, and the Sîmûrgh shook her
golden plumage as she looked lovingly down upon the
white-haired child that played with unpolished gems
upon the cliffs beneath her.

Rising from her nest, she nestled down beside him,
and while he stroked her feathers, she caressed him
with her beak, and said: "I have fed and protected
thee, but now the Persian warrior has come for his
boy, and I must give thee up." The child wept and
flung his arms around the soft neck of his foster
mother, but the Sîmûrgh told him it were better so,
and taking from her wing one golden plume, she
gave it to him with the promise that she would not
desert him. "Take this," said she, "and when thou
art in danger put the feather upon the fire, and I
will instantly come to thine aid."

Then the Sîmûrgh took the boy carefully in her
talons and in graceful circles she slowly swept down
toward the wondering father. "Receive thy son," said
the wondrous bird. "He is worthy of a throne and
diadem." Then the repentant father gladly caught his
rescued boy in his arms, and bore him exultingly
homeward, where he placed him in the glad arms of
his mother, who wept tears of joy over the white-
haired child. The beautiful plume was laid carefully
away as one of the treasures of the household, to be
used by the boy only in times of greatest need.

When the Persian king Minûchir heard the story,
he sent to Suwâr a splendid troop of horsemen, led
by the heir to the throne, and they conveyed the

royal congratulations to the warrior and his son, and escorted them into the royal presence. Here

"Zāl humbly kissed the earth before the king,
And from the hands of Minūchir received
A golden mace and helmet. Then those who knew
The stars and planetary signs were told
To calculate the stripling's destiny;
And all proclaimed him of exalted fortune,
That he would be prodigious in his might,
Outshining every warrior of the age."

The delighted king then presented the boy with Arabian horses and gorgeous armor, with gold and rich garments, and appointed the father to be the ruler of Kabūl, Zabūl, and Ind. Zāl accompanied his father upon the return homeward, and then he was placed under the care of renowned instructors at Zabūlistān.

RŪDABEH.

While the Persian youth was reaching the age of manhood, in the delightful pursuits of art and science, he was also occasionally intrusted with the care of the province during the father's absence. Kabūl, one of the provinces which the Persian king had assigned to Suwār, had been ruled over by a chieftain named Mihrāb, who was descended from Zohāk, and this chieftain still retained a subordinate position in the government by paying an annual tribute to Suwār.

Mihrāb had a beautiful daughter named Rūdabeh, and although she was kept in the most careful seclusion, still the fame of her great loveliness was spread among the neighboring princes.

"If thou wouldst make her charms appear,
Think of the sun so bright and clear,
And brighter far with softer light,
The maiden strikes the dazzled sight.
Think of her skin, with what compare?
Ivory was never half so fair!
Her stature like the sabin tree,
Her eyes! so full of witchery,
Glow like the Nigris[1] tenderly,
Her arching brows their magic fling,
Dark as the raven's glossy wing.
Soft o'er her blooming cheek is spread
The rich pomegranate's vivid red;
Her musky ringlets unconfined
In clustering meshes roll behind.
Possessed of every sportive wile,
'Tis heaven, 'tis bliss, to see her smile."

Zāl was not insensible to the charms he had heard so vividly described, but he remembered that Mihrāb was descended from Zohāk, the Serpent King,[2] and he knew that if he made any advances toward the fair daughter of the fatal line he should provoke the rage

[1] The Narcissus, to which the beautiful eyes of Eastern women are often compared.

[2] Called the "Serpent King" because he at one time allowed an evil creature to kiss his shoulder, and from the spot two fearful serpents sprang that required human brains for their food. The king used to select the victims by lot, and when the blacksmith Kaveh found his name upon the fatal register he tore the document in pieces, and

"On his javelin's point
He fixed his leathern apron for a banner,
And lifting it high he went abroad
To call the people to a task of vengeance."

The multitude of rebels joined a foreign foe, and the hated Zohak was destroyed, and then the leathern banner was splendidly adorned with gold and jewels, and it is said that this legend gave rise to the blacksmith's apron as the royal ensign of Persia.

of his father, and also of the Persian monarch Minûchir.

Mihrâb had occasion to communicate with Zâl, and
on his return homeward his wife, Sindokht, inquired
after the white-haired youth, asking what he was like
in form and feature, and what account he gave of
his stay with the Sîmûrgh.

Mihrâb described his host in the warmest terms of
admiration, telling of his valor, his accomplishments,
and his manly beauty, his only defect being the
strange crown of silvery hair.

The beautiful princess was present, and, with her
dark eyes fixed upon her father's face, she drank in
every word of his eulogy, and her heart warmed
toward the stranger. When she retired to her own
apartments, she confided to her maid the fact that
she was deeply impressed with the description she had
heard, and a few days later she declared to the attendant that she was deeply in love with the stranger,
and besought the maid's assistance.

The servant was startled and frightened by this confession, and remonstrated with her beautiful mistress
upon the absurdity of her position:

"What, hast thou lost all sense of shame,
　　All value for thy honored name!
　　That thou in loveliness supreme,
　　Of every tongue the constant theme,
　　Should choose, and on another's word,
　　The nursling of a mountain bird!
　　A being never seen before,
　　Which human mother never bore!

And can the hoary locks of age
A youthful heart like thine engage ? ”

But her remonstrance was in vain, the willful Persian beauty had set her heart upon a man whom she had never seen,[1] and she quietly answered:

“My attachment is fixed, my election is made,
And when hearts are enchained 'tis vain to upbraid.
Neither Kizar nor Faghfūr I wish to behold,
Nor the monarch of Persia with jewels and gold;
All, all I despise, save the choice of my heart,
And from his beloved image I never can part.”

When the attendants learned that the princess was so deeply in earnest they loyally entered into her feelings far enough to aid her in every possible way in bringing about a meeting with the man she loved.

It was springtime in the beautiful vales of Persia, and the earth was rich with many colored flowers,

---

[1] It appears to have been not unusual amongst the secluded women of the East to fall deeply in love with men of whom they knew very little. Josephus claims that the king's daughter betrayed the city of Sava in Ethiopia into the hands of Moses, having fallen in love with his valor and bravery as she saw him from the walls of the city gallantly leading the Egyptian host. Dido was won merely by the fame of Æneas, and Kotzebue has pictured Elvira as enamored of the glory of Pizarro; but when at last she discovered the savage and merciless disposition of the conqueror, she taunted him with being a fraud. The lovely Desdemona affords another instance:

> OTH.—“ Her father loved me; oft invited me;
>   Still questioned me the story of my life.
>   *   *   *   *   *   *
>   “ I ran it through, even from my boyish days,
>   Wherein I spoke of most disastrous chances.
>   *   *   *   *   *   *
>   “ She loved me for the dangers I had passed,
>   And I loved her that she did pity them.”
>   (*Othello, Act. I, Sc. 3*)

while the breath of hyacinths and lilies of the valley
floated upon the air. The glittering pheasant moved
through the undergrowth, and the bulbul sang his love
song in the lofty trees.

A party of maidens strayed near the tent of Zál in
their earnest quest for the most beautiful roses to be
found in that sunny vale. Already their baskets were
laden with fragrance, but still they lingered, until the
prince asked his attendants why these girls presumed
to invade his territory. He was told that the damsels were sent by the beautiful princess of Kabúlistán
from the palace of Mihráb to gather roses for her
boudoir. His eyes brightened, and calling a servant
to bear his bow and arrows, he rose carelessly and started
for a ramble along the winding river. He was not far
from the maidens, when he sent an arrow through a
beautiful bird sailing above them. The bird fell at
their very feet, and his servant was sent to bring it.

When he approached them they inquired who this
skillful archer was. He answered, "Know you not
that this is Zál, the greatest warrior ever known."
The maidens then told him that they belonged to a
beautiful princess, the star in the palace at Mihráb, and
cautiously inquired why, as these young people were of
equal rank, a marriage might not be arranged between
them. The servant reported the question to his
master, and was sent back with royal presents for
Rúdabeh.

> " They who to gather roses came—went back
> With precious gems and honorary robes,
> And two bright finger-rings were secretly
> Sent to the princess."

The maids returned exultant, but still the way was full of peril, and political difficulties seemed to forbid even an interview between the lovers. There was, however, a beautiful summer retreat seldom visited in the absence of the Persian king, which was luxuriously furnished and adorned with paintings of Persia's most illustrious chieftains. It stood midway between the two territories, and to this resort the princess and her maids retired while on a pleasure excursion, and Zāl was duly invited by the attendants to visit them as soon as the stars came out.

The shadows of evening had fallen upon the rose gardens, and the air was heavy with their fragrance, when the young warrior cautiously approached the balcony from which he heard a sweet voice singing. Soon the low musical tones of a manly voice were borne upon the breeze as he softly chanted—

> " How often have I hoped that heaven
> Would in some secret place display
> Thy charms to me, and thou hast given
> My heart the wish of many a day. "

And soon the singer stood by the woman he sought. They passed hand in hand within the gorgeous chambers, where the porphyry pillars upheld the rich fretwork of gold in the roof, and the vast illuminated halls were silent and bright, save the gentle music of the waters that were rippling from many a jasper fountain. The royal abode was glowing with softly colored lights, which reflected the rare beauty of painting and statuary, but Zāl could scarcely see what art had done, for his eyes and thoughts were

absorbed with the witching radiance of his love.
Long they remained rapt in admiration of each
other. At length the warrior rose and exclaimed:
"It becomes us not to be forgetful of the path of
prudence. How will my father rave with anger when
he hears of this adventure? How will King Min-
úchir indignantly reproach me for this dream?—
this waking dream of rapture! But I call high heaven
to witness that whoever may oppose my sacred vows,
still I am thine, affianced thine, forever." And Rúdabeh answered, "Thou hast won my heart, and kings
may sue in vain; thou art alone my warrior and my
love." Then Zāl, with fond adieus, softly descended
from the balcony and hastened to his tent.

The loyal son wrote a letter to his father, frankly telling him the story of his love, and asking his sympathy
and co-operation. To his great joy, these were promptly
accorded, and he wrote an exultant letter to the princess,
informing her of the fact. But the girl was detected by
the queen in carrying messages and presents to the
princess, and the queen approached her daughter, who
frankly told the story, and it was thus communicated
to Mihrāb, whose rage knew no bounds. The infuriated
king drew his sword, and would have rushed to his
daughter's room and slain her upon the spot, if his
wife had not thrown herself at his feet and pleaded that
time at least might be given her.

The daughter was then summoned to her father's
presence, but she disdained to come as a culprit or
a suppliant, therefore she fearlessly appeared in the
royal presence, and proudly told him of the valor of
her betrothed. She retired from his presence without

harm, but when Minūchir, king of Persia, was apprised of the loves of Zāl and Rūdabeh, another storm broke over the heads of the royal lovers, for he anticipated only the ruin of his kingdom if so valiant a warrior as Zāl joined his fortunes with a member of the house of the Serpent King.

When Suwār returned, however, from his successfu﹘ expedition against the demons, he ingeniously pleaded his son's cause before the king:

"I am thy servant, and twice sixty years
 Have seen my prowess. Mounted on my steed,
 Wielding my battle-ax, o'erthrowing heroes,
 Who equals Suwār the warrior? I destroyed
 The mighty monster[1] whose devouring jaws
 Unpeopled half the land, and spread dismay
 From town to town. The world was full of horror;
 No bird was seen in air, no beast of prey
 In plain or forest: from the stream he drew
 The crocodile: the eagle from the sky.
 Armed for the strife, I saw him towering rise
 Huge as a mountain, with his hideous hair
 Dragging upon the ground: his long black tongue
 Shut up the path; his eyes two lakes of blood.
 Forward I sprang, and in a moment drove
 A diamond-pointed arrow through his tongue,
 Fixing him to the ground. Another went
 Down his deep throat, and dreadfully he writhed
 And deluged all around with blood and poison.
 There lay the monster dead, and soon the world
 Regained its peace and comfort. Now I'm old,

---

[1] This picture is highly suggestive of the Demon King of Ceylon, who is so prominent in Hindu mythology, especially in the Ramayana.

The vigor of my youth is past and gone,
And it becomes me to resign my station
To Zāl, my gallant son."

But while approving cordially of the work already
done, he gave the warrior a new commission, which
was no less than the destruction of Kabūl by fire and
sword, especially the house of Mihrāb, and declared that
the ruler of the serpent-race and all of his adherents
were to be put to death. In vain the horror-stricken
warrior pleaded the cause of mercy, the king's vindictive intentions were well known, and the greatest consternation reigned at Kabūl, especially in the family of
Mihrāb.

Mihrāb himself a tyrant, and consequently a coward,
could see no way of avoiding the king's wrath except
by putting his wife and daughter to death.

At last in his desperation, Suwār sent an earnest
letter to the king, and sent it by the hand of Zāl,
who thus obtained permission to plead his own cause.
The king finally consulted the astrologers, who informed him that the marriage was most propitious,
and from it would be born a hero of matchless
strength and valor—the champion of Persia. So at
last the faithful lover bore back to Rūdabeh the joyous tidings that the greatest obstacle was removed,
after which it was an easy matter to pacify Mihrāb,
and the approbation of all parties was finally secured.

THE MARRIAGE.

The marriage was celebrated at the beautiful royal
retreat where the lovers first met, and it was a scene
of unequaled magnificence. There were splendid horses

with gold and silver housings, and multitudes of richly attired damsels bearing golden trays of jewels and perfumes. There were camels laden with the richest brocades and velvets of the East; there were Indian swords and elephants; there were bowers of roses and orange blossoms, and garlands of fragrant lilies, and finally there was a golden crown and throne. Having consented to the union, the Persian king taxed the treasury to the utmost to make it the grandest wedding in the land.

After several days had been devoted to the festivities, the newly married pair settled down amid the roses and fruits of their vine-wreathed home. From the white crown of a distant mountain down to the river that flowed by their garden temples, the very air seemed tinted with a golden haze, while every breeze was laden with rich perfume.

The time passed blithely and rapidly to the young chieftain and his beautiful wife; but one night there was darkness in the garden temples, and gloom in the thickets of roses where the night-bird trilled his sorrowful song to the drooping flowers. There was darkness upon the inner room, for the shadow of death was falling upon court and hall—the fair young wife lay in terrible peril, from which there seemed to be no rescue. The court physicians held council in the adjoining room, while the agonized husband bent over his suffering wife.

At last he bethought him of the Sīmūrgh's plume, and, hastily unlocking the casket, the golden feather was laid upon the fire. His heart stood still while he waited and listened, and lo, there came the rushing sound of a tempest, as the wing of the Sīmūrgh gleamed through the darkness, and she stood beside her foster child. Zāl's eyes lighted up with hope and gladness as he threw his arms around her soft golden neck, and leaned upon the gorgeous plumage. Then she bent her head caressingly toward his face and whispered a few directions into his ear. Immediately her command was obeyed and the court physicians were interrupted in their solemn conclave, for the cry of a newly-born babe was wafted to their ears, and the young wife was shedding happy tears in the arms of her joyous husband.

RUSTEM.

The boy who was born that night was a herculean babe, and he became the champion of Persia.[1] As the years went by his marvelous strength became the wonder of the nation, and the especial pride of his father and the old chieftain Suwār.

> " In beauty of form and vigor of limb,
> No mortal was ever equal to him."

Before Rustem reached the age of manhood the king of Persia died, and the kingdom fell into the hands of weaker princes. The Tartar chieftain, Afrāsiyāb,

---

1 Firdusi thought proper to bestow upon his hero a gigantic stature and marvelous physical powers, but other classic writers have done the same. It will be remembered that Hercules had but completed his eighth month before he strangled the serpents that Juno sent to devour him, and Homer says of Otus and Ephialtes:

> " The wondrous youths had scarce nine winters told,
> When high in air, tremendous to behold,
> Nine ells aloft they reared their towering heads,
> And full nine cubits broad their shoulders spread.
> Proud of their strength and more than mortal size,
> The gods they challenge and affect the skies."

Odyssey XI, 310.

improved the opportunity which he long had sought, of making an invasion upon the rich provinces of Persia, and collecting an immense army he marched to the front, under the pretext of avenging old wrongs.

> " Afrāsiyāb a mighty army raised,
> And passing plain and river, mountain high,
> And desert wild, filled all the Persian realm
> With consternation and universal dread."

The Persian hosts were in confusion, for the Tartar chief was continually threatening the border. The people looked to Zāl as their natural preserver, but Zāl decided to place his boy at the head of the army, for although very young, Rustem had been carefully trained in warlike exercises, and the long line of warrior blood from whence he came, thrilled his veins with martial valor.

All the horses of the imperial stables were brought forth, that the young commander might take from them a steed to bear him through the campaign. But Rustem was not content to choose from these, for his eye fell upon a wild horse of wondrous strength and beauty which was the offspring of a demon. After a fearful struggle the magnificent animal was conquered, and placed beneath saddle and rein, when the young warrior rode into the conflict.

THE TŪRĀNIAN INVASION.

Mihrāb, the ruler of Kabūl, was the leader of one wing of the Persian army, and Gustāhem of the other, while Rustem led the front, and the glorious banner of Kāvah[1] was flung to the breeze. The Tūrānian

---

[1] The blacksmith's apron.

king rode in black armor at the head of his dark legions, while his ablest generals led the wings and protected the rear of his vast army.

There was one terrific onslaught in which it seemed as if heaven and earth had closed in deadly conflict. The clattering of hoofs, the shrill roar of the trumpets and the rattle of brazen drums were mingled with the cries of dying men, while the glittering spear hastened to the deadly work, and the Tartar king believed that the imperial crown of Persia was just within his reach.

When the tide of battle ebbed for a moment, Rustem shouted to his father that he intended to engage the hostile monarch in single combat, but Zāl endeavored to dissuade him from so hopeless a task.

> "My son, be wise and peril not thyself;
> Black is his banner, and his cuirass black—
> His limbs are cased in iron—on his head
> He wears an iron helm—and high before him
> Floats the black ensign; equal in his might
> To ten strong men. . . .
> Then beware of him.
> Rustem replied: 'Be not alarmed for me—
> My heart, my arm, my dagger, are my castle.'"

He bravely urged his splendid horse toward the foe, and the warriors closed in a long and doubtful struggle. At last, however, Rustem caught him by the belt and dragged him from his horse. He intended to drive his captive thus to the Persian king, but the belt gave way and the Tartar fell upon the ground, and was quickly borne off by his own warriors, but not before Rustem had snatched off the monarch's crown, which he carried away as a trophy with the broken girdle.

The fight now became general again, and the earth shook with the trampling of the steeds; the drums rattled; loud clamors from the troops echoed around, and by the mailed hands of contending warriors many a life was sacrificed. With his huge mace, cow-headed, Rustem flooded the ground with the crimson blood of his foes, and wherever seen he was impatiently urging forward his fiery horse. Severed heads fell like the withered leaves in autumn when he brandished his sword, horseman and steed falling together. On that dreadful day, with sword and dagger, battle-ax and noose,[1] he cut and tore, and broke and bound the brave, slaying and making captive. The Tartar hordes fled in dismay, and their black banner trailed upon the earth until captured by the Persian troops.

Day after day the conquered legions pursued their noiseless retreat, for neither drum nor trumpet told their foes which way they took. The Persian host, burdened with a multitude of prisoners, fell slowly back to the capital, where Rustem was received with the wildest demonstrations of joy. Soon there came from Tûrân a messenger bearing proposals of peace. To this the Persian king replied that the war had not been of his seeking, but he would accept the overtures of peace upon condition that Afrâsiyâb take his solemn oath never to cross the boundary line formed by the river Jihun, or disturb the Persian throne

[1] Herodotus speaks of a people confederated with the army of Xerxes who employed the noose.

again.　Peace was accordingly concluded, and the highest honors were conferred upon Rustem and Zāl.　Rustem was appointed captain general of the armies, under the title of the "champion of the world."　He was also given a golden crown, and the privilege was granted him of giving audience while seated upon a golden throne.

THE WHITE DEMON.

After many years a new king, Kai-kaus,[1] ascended the Persian throne.　Lacking the wisdom of his father, he sought the fascinations of the wine cup, and while under this influence he astonished and mortified his people by his intense self-admiration and pride.　One day, when he was half-crazed with his favorite beverage, a demon, disguised as a musician, waited upon him and sang a song extolling the beauties of Mazinderān:

"And thus he warbled to the king,
Mazinderān is the bower of spring,
My native home; the balmy air
Diffuses health and fragrance there.
So tempered is the genial glow
Nor heat, nor cold, we ever know;
Tulips and hyacinths abound
On every lawn; and all around
Blooms like a garden in its prime,
Fostered by that delicious clime.
The bulbul sits on every spray,
And pours his soft melodious lay;

[1] Kai-kaus, the second Persian king belonging to the dynasty of Kainanides.

Each rural spot its sweets discloses,
Each streamlet is the dew of roses.
And mark me, that untraveled man
Who never saw Mazinderān
And all the charms its powers possess,
Has never tasted happiness."

No sooner had the king heard the minstrel's lay concerning the unknown land than he began to foster the desire for conquest, and he declared to his warriors that the glory of his reign should exceed that of his most illustrious predecessors. The warriors, more cautious, protested against their monorch's insane idea of making war upon the demons, and Zāl was chosen as the most influential of their number to bear their protests to the king. But the conceited king announced that he was superior in might and influence to any of his predecessors—that he had a bolder heart, a larger army, and a fuller treasury than any of them. He haughtily announced that he needed neither Zāl nor Rustem, that they might stay at home and care for the kingdom, while he himself conducted the campaign in person. The keys of the treasury and the jewel chamber were left in the hands of Milād, with instructions to act under the advice of Zāl and Rustem. Then the great army was put in motion, while at its head rode the conceited king, with his magnificent retinue of richly caparisoned horses and camels.

When the columns came near to Mazinderan, the king ordered his favorite general, Gīw, to select two thousand of his bravest men, the boldest wielders of the battle-ax, and proceed rapidly toward the city. In accordance with the king's command, this was a vandal march, marked by fire, sword, and the pitiless murder even of women and children.

While the terrible work of slaughter and destruction was going on under the hands of his chosen men, the Persian king was encamped in splendid state on a plain near the city, indulging in the wildest dreams of complete victory, and intending to follow his advance guard with the main body of his army the next day.

But when the insulted king of Mazinderān saw this ruthless invasion of his beautiful realm, he called the White Demon[1] to his aid, and that night the dark storm-clouds rolled over the Persian host, and pitiless hailstones fell upon the panic-stricken army. The morning light found the troops dismayed and scattered, while many of them were killed outright, and the conceited king with his leading warriors were smitten with blindness.

There were selected from the demon army twelve thousand chosen warriors to hold in custody the Irānian captives, which were easily taken, together with the treasures and horses of Kai-kaus. Arzang, one of the demon leaders, having taken possession of the wealth, the crown, and jewels of the audacious invaders, escorted the captive king and his troops to Mazinderān, where they were placed in the custody of the guards.

The blind king, however, succeeded in sending information concerning his condition to Zāl, and that

[1] In the Shah Namah, where so much fiction is founded upon so little historic fact, we find, as in Hindu literature, an active race of demons. These are generally defined as being in human shape, with horns, long ears, and sometimes with tails, like the monkeys in the Ramayana. Again, they assume the characteristics of the Rakshasas in Hindu mythology, and appear as enchanters, sorcerers, etc.—(*Compare Hindu Literature, pp. 189-232.*)

warrior, though furious over the conduct of the royal
imbecile, was still loyal enough to attempt his rescue,
and turning to Rustem, he said, "The sword must be
unsheathed since Kai-kaus is bound a captive in the
dragon's den. Rakush must be saddled for the field,
and thou must bear the weight of this campaign."

Rustem replied that it was a long journey to Mazinderân, and the king was six months upon the road.
But Zāl replied that there were two roads, one of them
being very short, but filled with dangers, lions and
demons haunting the pathway. Still, if he could overcome these foes, he might reach the capital city of
demon-land in seven days.

The gallant warrior promptly chose the shorter road,
saying:

> "It is not wise, they say,
> With willing feet to track the way
> To hell: Though only men who've lost
> All love of life by misery crossed,
> Would rush into the tiger's lair,
> And die, poor reckless victims there;
> I gird my loins whate'er may be,
> And work and wait for victory."

He then donned his armor and walked toward the
richly caparisoned Rakush, who stood impatiently waiting for his master. The young warrior took his beautiful mother in his arms and kissed her tenderly, then
mounting his gallant steed he rode away into the unknown dangers of his perilous campaign.

CHAPTER XII.

THE HEFT-KHĀN, OR SEVEN LABORS OF RUSTEM.

A LION SLAIN BY RAKUSH—ESCAPE FROM THE DESERT—THE DRAGON SLAIN—THE ENCHANTRESS—CAPTURE OF AULĀD—VICTORY OVER DEMONS—SEVENTH LABOR, THE WHITE DEMON SLAIN—THE MARRIAGE OF RUSTEM—SOHRĀB.

WITH only his faithful horse for company, the young chieftain set out upon his perilous attempt to rescue the infatuated monarch from the foe in whose hands he was so justly suffering. The generous steed pushed rapidly forward, making two days' journey in one, and after a time they entered a gloomy forest, which was filled with herds of gor.[1] Oppressed with hunger, Rustem saw not the dangers of the chase, and at last captured one of the animals, which was quickly slain.

A fire was built, and a portion of the meat was roasted upon the point of his spear, while Rakush grazed near his master. His hunger appeased, the young warrior lay down upon the wild herbage with his faithful sword under his head, and fell asleep. The odor of the gor's flesh had attracted another enemy, and a pair of fiery eyeballs moved stealthily around the

[1] The gor is the onager, or wild ass of the East, and in its native wilds is a very dangerous foe to encounter. Its flesh is often used for food when the hunter is driven to extremity.

252

dying fire. The watchful horse scented the foe and
stepped a little closer to his unconscious master. Here
he waited for the attack, and soon a huge lion
bounded from the underbrush, and would have struck
the sleeping man, but he was received with a terrific
and well-aimed kick that sent the astonished assailant
back into the bushes from whence he came, and before
he had time to recover from his amazement the furious horse was upon him, and was still stamping, in
his rage, the now lifeless carcass when Rustem awoke.

"Ah Rakush,[1] why so thoughtless grown,
   To fight a lion thus alone?
   For had it been thy fate to bleed,
   And not thy foe, Oh gallant steed!
   How could thy master have conveyed
   His helm, and battle-ax, and blade?"

Then Rustem again composed himself to sleep, and
rested until the morning light tinted the distant
mountain peaks with rose and amber, then rising, he
saddled his faithful horse, and pursued his perilous
journey.

---

[1] It was evidently the custom, even among the Greeks also, to harangue
their horses. for Homer repeatedly puts these speeches into the mouths of
his heroes. Hector addresses his horses in the Eighth Book:
     " Be fleet, be fearless, this important day,
     And all your master's well-spent care repay.
     Now swift pursue, now thunder uncontroll'd,
     Give me to seize rich Nestor's shield of gold."
And in the Nineteenth Book, Achilles reproaches his horses with the death
of Patrocles, when
     " The generous Xanthus as the words he said
     Seemed sensible of woe and drooped his head;
     Trembling he stood before the golden wain,
     And bowed to dust the honors of his mane,"
before he makes a spirited reply foretelling his master's death.

ESCAPE FROM THE DESERT.

The morning hours passed quickly to both man and horse, but when the noontide sun poured its heat upon the heads of the travelers it found them in a desert, where the burning sand seemed to possess the elements of fire. Horse and rider were tortured with the most maddening thirst. At last, unable to endure it longer, Rustem alighted and vainly wandered around in search of relief until his eye fell upon a desolate sheep, which he followed, and came to a fountain of water. He afterward killed a gor, and lighting a fire he again roasted the savory flesh and satisfied his hunger. By this time the shades of night were coming on, and he gladly sought for a resting place in the desert, while Rakush fed upon the stunted herbage around him. Before lying down, however, he gave his horse a parting injunction:

> "Beware, my steed, of future strife,
> Again thou must not risk thy life;
> But should an enemy appear,
> Ring loud thy warning in my ear."

THE DRAGON SLAIN.

The bright constellations in the tropical sky pointed to the hour of midnight, when the horse was again startled. A colossal dragon-serpent eighty yards in length moved slowly toward them. It was the terror of the desert, and neither elephant, lion, nor demon dared to venture near its lair. Rakush stepped nearer to his unconscious master and neighed loudly, but the noise so startled the dragon that when Rustem awoke and looked around he could see nothing, and lying

down he went to sleep again. The darkness became
thicker and more impenetrable, but in its midst the
watchful horse again saw the gleaming of the snaky
eyes, and again he roused his master, who rose up in
alarm but tried in vain to penetrate the darkness
around him. Then annoyed by these apparently
needless alarms, he spoke sharply to Rakush:

> " Why thus again disturb my rest,
>   When sleep had softly soothed my breast ?
>   I told thee if thou chanced to see
>   Another dangerous enemy
>   To sound the alarm ; but not to keep
>   Depriving me of needful sleep."

Rustem again went to sleep, while the tireless
watcher stood undaunted by his side, even though
grieved and wounded by unjust reproaches. The
dragon appeared, and the faithful horse tore up the
earth with his feet in trying to arouse his master.
Rustem again awoke, and sprang angrily to his feet,
but in that moment he caught a gleam of the snaky
eyes of the foe, then quickly he drew his sword and
closed in strife with the huge monster. Dreadful was
the shock, and perilous to Rustem ; but when Rakush
saw that the contest was doubtful, with his keen
teeth he furiously bit and tore away the dragon's
scaly hide, when quick as thought the champion severed the ghastly head, and deluged all the plain with
horrid blood.

THE ENCHANTRESS.

When Rustem again resumed the saddle, his way
lay through a land of enchantment. The feathered

palm trees along his way whispered to the listening gods, and the softly breathing pīpal boughs told to the south wind the story of their lives. Citrons and rose-apples lay in rich profusion upon the ground, and the broad bananas flaunted their silken flags around the ripening fruit. A crystal stream flowed along between verdant banks of luxurious foliage, and the bulbuls chanted in the depths of the wood. And lo, in this beautiful wilderness was a daintily spread table awaiting the hungry traveler, where the richest tropical fruits lay beside a roast of venison, and the cups were filled with purple wine, while the sweet voice of an invisible singer was borne upon his ear. As he alighted and approached the table, the voice of the singer came nearer, and soon there stood revealed upon the other side of the tempting table, a woman of peerless beauty.

Her complexion was like shell-tinted ivory, and ner dark, love-lighted eyes were curtained with long, sweeping lashes. Her cheeks were tinted with rose color, like the pearly tints of morning, and her beautiful figure was scarcely concealed by the misty Oriental robes that she wore. Rustem gazed upon her rich beauty in a dazed and helpless way, while she came nearer, and nearer—singing as she came, and holding out her little hands to him. At last she stood almost within his arms, and turning her beautiful face up towards his, she chanted a low love song, pleading with the warrior for a place in his heart. A moment —one perilous moment—he wavered, and nearly became her victim, but his conscience and his manliness came to his rescue. "Away," he cried, "thou

beautiful sorceress," and as he drew his sword the figure vanished, and the low, mocking laugh of a fiend
was heard in the distance.   Gone the dainty table
with its tempting viands and poisoned wine—gone
the beautiful enchantress—and the brave warrior was
again the victor.

CAPTURE OF AULĀD.

Then, proceeding on his way, he approached a region destitute of light, a void of utter darkness.   Neither moon nor star shone through the gloom ; no
choice of path remained.   Therefore throwing loose the
rein, he gave Rakush liberty to travel on unguided.
At length the darkness was dispersed, the earth became a scene of light, and the soil was covered with
waving grain.   There Rustem paused, and dismounting from his steed, he laid himself down and slept,
with his shield beneath his head and his sword before
him.

While he slept his faithful horse grazed upon the
growing corn, and the keeper of the grounds came
and saw, and, hastening away, told his master, Aulād,
that a black demon and his horse were destroying the
growing grain.   Then Aulād hastily gathered his troops
to take the warrior prisoner, but their leader was
killed by Rustem, and great numbers of his men were
scattered lifeless over the plain.   Aulād himself was
taken prisoner, for the warrior needed a guide, and
thus he spoke to his captive :

" If thou wilt speak the truth, and faithfully point
out to me the caves of the White Demon and his warrior chiefs, where Kai-kaus is prisoned, thy reward

shall be the kingdom of Mazinderän, for I myself will place thee on that throne. But if thou play'st me false, thy worthless blood shall answer for the foul deception."

"Stay! Be not wroth," Auläd at once replied. "Thy wish shall be fulfilled, and thou shalt know where Kai-kaus is prisoned, and also where the White Demon reigns. Between two dark and lofty mountains, in two hundred caves, immeasurably deep, his people dwell. Twelve hundred demons keep the watch by night upon the mountain's brow, and like a reed the hills tremble whenever the White Demon moves. But dangerous is the way. A stormy desert lies full before thee, which the nimble deer has never passed. Then a broad stream two farsangs wide obstructs thy path, whose banks are covered with a host of warrior demons guarding the passage to Mazinderän. Canst thou o'ercome such fearful obstacles as these?" The champion simply said, "Show me but the way."

Auläd proceeded, Rustem following fast, mounted upon Rakush. Neither night nor day they rested—on they went until they reached the fatal field where Kai-kaus was overcome. At the midnight hour a piercing clamor echoed through the woodland, and blazing fires were seen, while numerous lamps gleamed brightly on every side. Rustem inquired what this might be. "It is Mazinderän," Auläd rejoined, "and the White Demon's chiefs are gathered there." Then Rustem bound to a tree his obedient guide—to keep him safe—and, to recruit his strength, laid down awhile and soundly slept. When morning dawned he rose, and mounting Rakush put his helmet on. The

tiger skin [1] defended his broad chest, and sallying forth
he sought the Demon chief, Arzang, and summoned
him to battle with such a call that stream and mountain shook.   Arzang sprang up on hearing a human
voice, and from his tent hastily issued. The champion
met him, and tearing off the gory head, he cast it far
into the ranks of the shuddering demons, who fell
back and fled, lest they should likewise feel that
,dreadful punishment.

VICTORY OVER DEMONS.

The principal chieftain of the White Demon having
met this fearful death at the hands of the Persian
warrior, he released Aulâd from his bonds, and commanded the guide to show him the way to the place
where Kai-kaus was confined. Entering Mazinderân
by night, the guide led the way to Kai-kaus and his
fellow captives, the blind and helpless warriors. Great
rejoicing heralded his arrival, for the prisoners looked
to Rustem for a deliverance from their sorrows. The
blind king told the Persian hero where to find the
stronghold of the demons, away in the caverns of the
Seven Mountains, where, within a deep and horrible
recess, lived the White Demon.

" Conquer him, destroy that fell magician, and re-

[1] This "tiger skin" is supposed to be a magic garment which had the
power of resisting the impression of every weapon. It was proof against
fire, and would not sink in water. According to some classic authorities, he
received it from his father, Zal; others say it was made from the skin of an
animal which Rustem killed on the mountain of Sham. It will be remembered that the heroes of ancient poets frequently wore the skins of animals.
Hercules wore the skin of the Nemæan lion. The skins of panthers and
leopards were worn by the Greek and Trojan chiefs, and Virgil says of Alcestes:
  " Rough in appearance, with darts, and a Libyan bearskin around him,
  Whom once a Trojan mother had borne to the river Cremisus."
                                        (*Æn., Book V, 36.*)

store to sight thy suffering king and all his warrior train. The wise in cures declare that the warm blood from the White Demon's heart dropped in the eye cures all blindness. It is then my hope that thou wilt slay the fiend, and save us from the misery of darkness without end."

Rustem therefore hurried on toward the enchanted heights of the Heft-khān, or Seven Mountains. He found every cave guarded by companies of demons, and, consulting with his guide, he determined to make the attack at noonday, when the demons were overpowered by the heat, and were accustomed to sleep. He therefore waited the auspicious hour, and binding Aulād again to a tree, he drew his sword and rushed into the horde of demons, slaying first the few sentinels who were awake, and then rapidly destroying the slumbering fiends. When one awoke he received his death blow so suddenly that he had no time to give the alarm. The mountain ravines received the slaughtered demons, and the few that escaped fled screaming into the deepest caves, and left the Persian victorious upon his chosen field.

SEVENTH LABOR—THE WHITE DEMON SLAIN.

In this preliminary carnage Rustem had discovered the stronghold of the White Demon, and he determined to give battle to this king of fiends. Advancing to the cavern, he looked down, down into its gloomy recesses—dismal as hell itself—but not one of the sorcerers could be seen. Awhile he stood and waited, holding his faithful falchion in his grasp, until there slowly came in sight a mountain form, with flaming eyes, and covered over with long white hair. The colossal shape filled the mouth of the huge cavern as forth he came, bearing a great stone in one mammoth hand. His fiery breath came quickly, and his eyes flashed with ire, as he haughtily asked:

> "Art thou so tired of life that reckless thus
> Thou dost invade the precincts of demons?
> Tell me thy name, that I may not destroy
> A nameless thing."

The warrior then replied, "My name is Rustem, sent by Zāl, my father, who was descended from Sām Suwār, to be revenged on thee; the king of Persia being now a prisoner at Mazinderān."

When the demon heard the name of Suwār he cringed with fear. Then springing forward he hurled the huge stone against his adversary who fell back, and thus avoided the fearful blow.

The demon frowned more darkly, and Rustem wielding high his sword, severed one dreadful limb. Then they grappled in a death struggle, and the mountain trembled beneath the shock. The flesh of both was torn, and the streaming blood crimsoned the earth. As the fearful strife went on, Rustem said in his heart, "If I survive this dreadful day I am surely immortal," and the White Demon muttered to himself, "I now despair of life—sweet life—nevermore shall I be welcomed at Mazinderān."

And still they struggled on, while sweat and blood were mingled at every strain of muscle, until Rustem, gathering all his power for one last effort, raised up the gasping demon in his arms and threw him over

the face of the cliff into a yawning chasm below.
The monster fell, and the life-blood oozed from the
crushed and mangled form. Then rushing down the
steep incline, beside the mountain, he tore out the heart
of the conquered demon, and releasing his fettered
guide he hastened away to restore the sight of the king
and his helpless warriors.

> " The Champion brought the demon's heart
> And squeezed the blood from every part,
> Which, dropped upon the injured sight,
> Made all things visible and bright."

The restored monarch immediately returned to his
throne, and the return march of his warriors was a
triumphal one ; but Rustem stayed until he conquered the whole demon host, and placed Aulād upon
the throne of Mazinderān, according to the promise he
had made.   Then he returned to receive the highest
honors the Persian king could lavish upon him.

THE MARRIAGE OF RUSTEM.

Weary at last of the luxuries and honors pertaining to the court, Rustem set out upon a hunting expedition.   Mounted upon his splendid steed he soon
passed the confines of the Persian domain and reached
the beautiful wilds of Tūrān ; here the herds of onager roamed at will from the sullen grandeur of the
uplands to the fairer vales below them.   He urged the
gallant Rakush on through wood and glen, while the
swift-footed gor dashed through the thickets or sported
over the plain ; his quivering darts were often sent
through the glossy skin of the dangerous game, and

when he wearied of the sport the hunter sought the shade of a thicket, and far above his head the palm trees waved their plumes, while doves and sunbirds fluttered through their swinging crowns. A little stream near by, flashed in the sunbeams and rippled away midst the flowers. The gallant horse was allowed to graze while the master slept, and tempted by the rich herbage he wandered away from the sleeper. A band of Tartar horsemen saw his perfect form and marked his splendid chest and well-poised head. Slowly they approached and quickly flung a noose over the noble head, then coming near to make the capture sure the animal charged upon his foes, and two of them bit the dust beneath his steel-clad hoofs.

The others had grown more cautious, and another noose was thrown. Then another horseman ventured near, only to be torn in pieces by the quick feet of the horse. Another was thrown, and this time no approach was made, but with long lines on either side the victim was led between the Tartar chiefs until they reached their own encampment.

Rustem awoke and called his steed, but no answering neigh rang out the glad reply. Long he searched, but searched in vain. He knew that Rakush had not willingly strayed away, and indignantly he traced his steps to Samenegān, the capital of Tūrān, for the broad track of his horse led that way.

As he approached the shining turrets of the city he met the king with all his court, anxious to do honor to the distinguished guest. But Rustem haughtily refused the proffered friendship until his horse should be restored.

" I've traced his footsteps to your royal town.
    Here must he be, protected by your crown.
    But if retained—if not from fetters freed,
    My vengeance shall o'ertake the felon deed."
" My honored guest," the wondering king replied,
" Shall Rustem's wants or wishes be denied ?
    If still within the limits of my reign,
    The well-known courser shall be thine again.
    For Rakush never can remain concealed
    No more than Rustem on the battle-field."

Then again he urged his royal hospitality upon the
Persian hero, as he sent out men to look for the horse.
Pacified with the royal promise of restoration, Rustem
accepted the hospitality of the king.   Soon

" The ready herald by the king's command,
    Convened the chiefs and warriors of the land,
    And soon the banquet social glee restored,
    And china wine cups glittered on the board ;
    And cheerful song, and music's matchless power,
    And sparkling wine beguiled the festive hour."

When the royal banquet was over a magnificent
couch was prepared for the great chieftain, and in the
perfumed bed the weary traveler slept soundly.   One
watch of the night had already passed when Rustem
was awakened by a light in his room, and there before
his astonished eyes stood the peerless daughter of the
Tartar king in all her wondrous beauty.   She stood
with frightened look, the rich color flushing her olive
cheeks, her dark eyes beaming beneath the splendid
lashes, and her mouth, flower-soft and sensitive, seemed
moulded for an expectant kiss.   Her black ringlets were

snares[1] for a warrior's heart. Her graceful hands were
perfectly formed and stained with henna upon the
dainty palms. But she was fully robed, and she, the
daughter of the king, had not come alone into the
room of this stranger guest—her faithful maid stood
beside her, and bore the taper from which a soft
radiance filled all the room.

The astonished warrior asked what stranger this,
and why she had broken upon his rest. " What is
thy name ? " he said. " Fair vision, speak ! "   Then
from the mouth of rose and pearl there fell the
accents of sweetest music :

" No curious eye has yet these features seen,
  My voice unheard beyond the sacred screen.
  But often have I listened with amaze
  To thy great deeds, enamoured of thy praise.
  How oft from every tongue I've heard the strain,
  And thought of thee, and sighed, and sighed in
        vain.
  The ravenous eagle hovering o'er his prey,
  Starts at thy gleaming sword and flies away !
  Thou art the slayer of the demon brood
  And the fierce monsters of the echoing wood.
  Enchanted with the stories of thy fame,
  My fluttering heart responded to thy name.
  Oh, claim my hand, and grant my soul's desire,
  Ask me in marriage of my royal sire ! "

[1] Compare Shakespeare—
            " Here in her hairs
       The painter plays the spider—and hath woven
       A golden mesh to entrap the hearts of men
       Faster than gnats in cobwebs : but her eyes."
                        —*Merchant of Venice*, iii, 2.

Not a word was lost upon Rustem, whose heart beat out a glad response to her plea, and before another day had passed his suit had been duly presented to the king.

" O'erjoyed the king the honoring suit approves,
    O'erjoyed to bless the doting child he loves,
    And happier still in showering smiles around,
    To be allied to warrior so renowned. "

The nuptials were not long delayed, and the marriage bower were crowned with roses and decked with white lilies, while the royal abode was flooded with music and light. It seemed to Rustem that all the world, like some vast tidal wave, had rolled away and left him on a golden shore—alone with his beloved.

SOHRĀB.

Not long could the Persian warrior remain with his Tartar bride, for his king claimed his allegiance, and summoned him to lead important campaigns. Before their son was born he was called away, but he left a radiant bracelet set with rare and peculiar gems as a heritage for his child, and mounted upon his faithful Rakush he was borne away to the field of conflict.

The wife Tamīneh was later blessed with a wondrous boy—the image of his noble sire. But when the father's fond inquiry came, the coward-heart of the mother betrayed her into falsehood. Fearing that the boy might be taken away and educated at the Persian court, and thus alienated from his Tartar blood, she sent her husband word that it was a daughter that had been born unto them, and the fact

was carefully hidden from the father that he had a
son. So little were daughters prized in the East, that
he never asked to see the child, and the boy came to
manhood with very little knowledge of his father.
Sohrāb bore the splendid physique of his noble race;
as a hunter or wrestler he had no equal in all the
realms of Tūrān. The Tartar king placed him at the
head of his armies, and mounted on his splendid
horse—the son of Rakush—the gallant youth took his
place at the head of the glittering host.

" His grandsire pleased beheld the warrior train
  Successive throng and darken all the plain.
  And bounteously his treasures he supplied,
  Camels and steeds and gold. In martial pride
  Sohrāb was seen—a Grecian helmet graced
  His brow—and costliest mail his limbs embraced.
  The insidious king sees well, the tempting hour
  Favoring his arms against the Persian power,
  But treacherous, first his martial chiefs he prest
  To keep the secret fast within their breast ;
  For this bold youth shall not his father know,
  Each must confront the other as his foe.
  Unknown, the youth shall Rustem's force withstand,
  And soon o'erwhelm the bulwark of the land.
  Rustem removed, the Persian throne is ours,
  An easy conquest to confederate powers."

By the careful intrigues of the king, the Tartar
host was soon arrayed against Persia, and all unknown
to each, the father and son were drawn up in battle
array against each other. When the eye of Rustem
fell upon the magnificent figure of the young Tartar

prince, he was astonished at his martial bearing, for
he seemed to wear the manly form of his own race.
He marked the strong shoulders, so much resembling
Zāl, and knew that this strong warrior knight sat his
splendid horse like Rustem's self.   He thought:

> " He cannot be my son unknown to me;
> Reason forbids the thought—it cannot be.
> At Samenegān, where once affection smiled,
> To me Tahmīneh bore her only child.
> That was a daughter. "

Then the trumpets' clang announced the attack of
the invader, as the Tartar horde sprang into the
fight. The troops of horse and foot were blended in
the wild disorder of Oriental battle, and the very
earth seemed to shake beneath the shock, while the
dust driven in dark eddies whirled high in air, ob-
scuring the very face of heaven.

The bright steel armor glittered over all the plain,
but alas, it covered the forms of fallen heroes as
often as it shielded the daring hearts of living riders.
The light flashed from the gold emblazoned shields
as the glittering spears struck the bright surface,
until it seemed as if the clouds were pouring showers
of sparkling amber upon the plain.

Thus the tide of battle ebbed and flowed, while
thousands were falling on either side, until the shades
of night came down upon the fearful scene.   Then a
council of the chiefs on either side was called, and
it was decreed that the next day the question of
victory should be decided by single combat between the leaders of the forces. Thus was Rustem

brought into close conflict with his only child. Father and son, unknown to each other, struggled in awful strife, while the treacherous Tartar chiefs looked gladly on, glorying in the thought that they would be rid of either a dangerous foe or a still more dangerous rival—possibly both. The younger blood and stronger sinews of Sohrāb won the first victories, but Rustem sprang again upon him and inflicted a fatal blow. As Sohrāb fell he felt that his wound was fatal, and he cried out, " I came here hoping to find my father, but have found only death instead." " Who is thy father?" demanded the Persian champion. " My father is Rustem, and my mother is the daughter of the King of Samenegān."

The words went through the father's heart like a poisoned spear, and he fell almost unconscious beside his murdered boy. " Ungird my mail," faltered the dying warrior, " and behold the bracelet my mother bound upon my arm. An instinct was ever at my heart that thou wert Rustem, but the Tartar chiefs ever and always told me nay—that thou wast not in the fight—that only thy servant led thy troops."

The sight of the amulet was a fearful blow to Rustem, for it proved at once the identity of his murdered son, and the falsehood of his treacherous wife.

" Prostrate he falls. ' By my unnatural hand
My son, my son is slain—and from the land
Uprooted.' Frantic in the dust, his hair
He rends in agony and deep despair.
The western sun had disappeared in gloom,
And still the Champion wept his cruel doom.

His wondering legions marked the long delay,
And seeing Rakush riderless astray,
The rumor quick to Persia's monarch sped,
And there described the mighty Rustem dead."

The king's chosen men were sent to find the warrior, whether he be slain or wounded. They found him
in his terrible grief, and the war-spirit seemed dead in
his bosom.

"Go," said he, "to the Tartar chiefs, and say to
them, 'No more shall war between us stain the earth
with blood.'" A moment more, and the young warrior
was dead, and on a Persian bier his lifeless form was
laid, while Rustem, sick of martial pomp and show,
ordered the gorgeous pageantry of war to be consigned
to the flames,[1] for all the warrior's pride lay in dust
and ashes as he followed the bier to the imperial resting place which was provided for Sohráb. But to the
mother was carried the most fearful blow, when the
Tartar chiefs led back the splendid steed all riderless,
and laid at her feet the coat of mail her son had
worn, while they told the story of his fall beneath his
father's hand. What a terrible penalty her falsehood
had brought upon her head and heart!

" Distracted, wild, she sprang from place to place,
With frenzied hands deformed her beauteous face.
The strong emotion choked her panting breath,
Her veins seemed withered by the cold of death.
Then gazing up, distraught, she wept again,
And frantic, seeing midst her pitying train

---

[1] In Virgil there is a similar scene, where Dido bids her sister erect a
pile to burn the arms and the presents of Æneas.

The favorite steed—now more than ever dear—
The hoofs she kissed and bathed with many a tear ;
Clasping the mail Sohrāb in battle wore,
With burning lips she kissed it o'er and o'er.
His martial robes she in her arms comprest,
And like an infant strained them to her breast."

Day after day, night after night, she gave way to
her helpless grief. Unceasingly she raved and wept
by turns for one long year, then nature gave way,
and she found rest in the arms of Death—"the great
Consoler."

CHAPTER XIII.

ISFENDIYĀR.

THE HEFT-KHĀN OF ISFENDIYĀR—THE BRAZEN FORT-
RESS—THE CONFLICT WITH RUSTEM—THE FALL OF
THE WARRIORS.

" R USTEM had seven great labors — wondrous
power
Nerved his strong arm in danger's needful hour.
And now Firdusī's legend strains declare
The seven great labors of Isfendiyār."

When the old Persian king, Kai-Khosrou, abdicated
in favor of his successor, he gave to Rustem the dominions of Zabūl, and Kabūl and Nimruz, and in
course of time Gushtāsp,[1] the Constantine of the Fire-
worshippers, came to the throne of Persia. This
monarch had two sons. One of them was Bashūtān,
and the other was Isfendiyār, a knight whose valor
was only second to that of Rustem. He had led his
father's armies in many a long campaign—had invaded
Hindūstān and Arabia, and several other countries,
and had, to a greater or less extent, established the
religion of the Fire-worshippers in them all. But Arjasp, a demon king, had invaded the Persian empire,
and carried captive two daughters of Gushtāsp. The

---

[1] There is a tradition that Gushtasp was Darius Hystaspes, and that his
son Isfendiyar was Xerxes.

fair prisoners were confined in a brazen fortress on the top of an almost inaccessible mountain, which was also the palace home of Arjasp, and he required the most servile labor from the Persian maidens.

were therefore undertaken in order to conquer Arjasp, and restore the sisters of the warrior. Like Rustem, he chose the shortest and most perilous passage to the stronghold of the enemy, and in the first stage of his journey he slew two monstrous wolves who disputed his advance. In the second stage he conquered an immense lion and his ferocious mate. In the third he slew a dragon, whose roar made the very mountains tremble with fear, while the poisonous foam dropped from his hideous jaws. Upon the fourth day he withstood the wiles of a beauteous woman, who appealed to him most piteously to rescue her from the power of a demon, whom she claimed had stolen her from her home and friends. She expressed the strongest admiration for Isfendiyár, and pleaded with him

> "To free me from his loathed embrace,
> And bear me to a fitter place,
> Where in thy circling arms more softly pressed,
> I may at last be truly loved and blest."

Isfendiyár called the beautiful tempter to him, and she came beaming with smiles, and dropping words of sweetest flattery from her crimson lips. Then he threw his noose around her, and writhing in the bonds she could not break, the enchantress became first a cat, then a wolf, and at last appeared in her true character of a black demon, with flames issuing from her mouth, whereupon she was slain by Isfendiyār.

On the fifth day he had the misfortune to offend a Sīmūrgh, who attacked him intending to bear him away to her mountain nest, but he succeeded in slaying the angry bird with his trenchant sword.

The sixth labor consisted in bringing his troops safely through a furious storm of wind and snow, when all the earth was covered with whiteness, while "keenly blew the blast and pinching was the cold." But the seventh trial of his fortitude was found in the passage of a desert waste, of which it was said

> "Along these plains of burning sand
> No bird can move, nor ant, nor fly,
> No water slakes the fiery land,
> Intensely glows the flaming sky.
> No tiger fierce, or lion ever
> Could breathe that pestilential air,
> Even the unsparing vulture never
> Ventures on blood-stained pinions there."

But a rain had fallen and partially cooled the scorched earth, so that this danger was safely passed.

THE BRAZEN FORTRESS.

When the darkness of night had fallen upon the landscape, Isfendiyār and a few chosen men advanced rapidly and carefully up the long, precipitous path, and examined the bulwarks of the brazen fortress that crowned the summit of the cliff. They found its iron bulwarks and brazen gates impregnable on every side, and returned to the command discouraged and dismayed. It had been a difficult undertaking, and they came into camp just as the tints of morning were lighting up the eastern sky.

It was indeed useless to attempt to storm this metallic fort, where neither sword nor spear nor battle-ax could be wielded to advantage, therefore Isfendiyár collected a hundred camels, and loaded a few of them with embroidered cloths, and others with pearls and precious jewels, while upon each of the others two chests were placed, and one warrior was hidden in each chest.[1] Other warriors were disguised as camel drivers and servants, so that altogether this caravan, which carried apparently only merchandise, was quite a warlike host.

Then Isfendiyár arranged with his brother to lead the rest of the troops to the attack as soon as he saw signal fires upon the summit, and set out with his caravan of merchandise for the fortress. He was received as a Persian merchant bringing valuable goods, and the avaricious demons exulted in the thought that a rich caravan had unsuspiciously fallen into their very hands. Isfendiyár carried rich presents to the king, and besought permission to sell Persian goods to his subjects. The liberality of the newcomer won the heart of the king, and the rich Persian wines that he brought proved especially attractive. Soon the king and his court, and also his leading warriors, were helpless under its influence. Then the signal fires were lighted, and the warriors were released from the chests, while the brazen gates were opened to

1 Compare the wooden horse that caused the fall of Troy, also the fall of Arzestan, which the Saracen general conquered by smuggling into the city a portion of his troops in chests, having obtained leave of the governor to deposit there some old lumber which impeded his march.

admit the invaders. Soon the Persian banner floated from the walls, for the demon king and his leading warriors were slain, and the sisters of Isfendiyār were rejoicing in the arms of their brother. The conqueror issued a proclamation offering pardon to all who would swear allegiance to the Persian king, then with his camels laden with the richest treasures of Arjasp he returned in triumph to his native city. The royal banners were flung to the breeze when the prince returned with his recovered sisters and heavy spoils. A great banquet was given, and the wine flowed freely. Isfendiyār was placed in a golden chair to receive the adulations of the multitude, while he gave them the thrilling story of his great Heft-khān and the capture of the demon fortress.

THE CONFLICT WITH RUSTEM.

Partially crazed by prosperity, and also instigated by jealousy against his own son, Gushtāsp demanded of Isfendiyār that he should lead a campaign against the provinces over which Rustem reigned, and either slay that chieftain or bring him in irons to the Persian king. In vain the son pleaded the loyalty and nobility of the warrior, the father answered that by the foolishness of his predecessor nearly half of Persia had been given into Rustem's hands, and he demanded a restitution of the territory, and the captivity of their ruler. "Take with thee," said the king, "my whole army and all my treasure. What wouldst thou have more? He who has conquered the terrific obstacles of the Heft-khān, and has slain Arjasp, and subdued his kingdom, can have no cause to fear any other chief." Isfendiyár replied that he was not prompted to decline the campaign from cowardice, but that Rustem had been the monitor and friend of their ancestors, enriched their minds and taught them to be brave, and he was ever faithful to their cause. "Besides," said he, "thou wert the honored guest of Rustem two long years; and at Sistan enjoyed his hospitality and friendship—his festive social board; and canst thou now, forgetting that delightful intercourse, become his bitterest foe ?"

Gushtásp replied : "'Tis true he may have served my ancestors, but what is that to me ? His spirit is proud, and he refused to yield me needful aid when danger pressed ; that is enough, and thou canst not divert me from my settled purpose." Kitabún, the mother of Isfendiyár, begged him to disobey the king rather than to undertake so dangerous and dishonorable a campaign. She claimed that curses must fall upon the throne, and ruin seize the country which returned evil for good and spurned its benefactor, and pleaded with him to restrain his steps, and engage not in a war which could do him no honor.

But Isfendiyár replied that his word was pledged to his royal father, and taking a tender leave of his mother and bidding the king a formal farewell, he placed himself at the head of the Persian host, and set out upon the campaign in which he had so little heart. When he arrived in Rustem's province, that chieftain rode out to welcome him, and cordially invited him to accept their hospitality. Isfendiyár was obliged to refuse the kindly offer and explain the unpleasant nature of his mission, whereupon Rustem

promptly declined to be bound and carried in fetters
to the Persian king. In order to save unnecessary
bloodshed, it was decided to settle the matter by
single combat, and the next morning Rustem rode
out to meet his unwilling foe, and both were clad in
shining mail.

Rustem sat upon Rakush, while Isfendiyār rode a
night-black charger, swift as the driving cloud, and in
his stride he scattered the desert stones as if a hail-
storm reveled around his master's head. The chieftains closed in the long and useless fight, while many
javelins whizzed upon the air, and helm and mail were
bruised. Spear fractured spear, and then with gleaming swords the strife went on until they too snapped
short. The battle-ax was next wielded in furious wrath;
each bending forward struck the bewildering blows—
each tried in vain to hurl the other from his fiery
horse. Wearied at length, they stood apart to breathe,
their chargers covered with foam and blood, and the
strong armor of steed and rider both were rent. So
severely was Rakush wounded that Rustem dismounted
and impelled his arrows from the ground, while the
gallant horse pursued his way painfully homeward.

When Zūara saw the noble animal riderless crossing
the plain he gasped for breath, and in an agony of
grief he hastened to the fatal spot, where he found
his gallant brother fighting still, even while the blood
was flowing copiously from every wound. Isfendiyār
had escaped with fewer wounds, and Zūara placed
Rustem upon his own steed and offered himself as a
substitute; but Rustem refused, saying that to-morrow
he would continue the fight.

Isfendiyār retired sadly to his tent and wrote a letter to his father, saying: "Thy commands must be obeyed, and Heaven only knows what may befall tomorrow." When Rustem arrived at his court Zāl discovered that he, as well as his gallant steed, was terribly wounded. The old chieftain carefully dressed the wounds of his son, and Rustem said to his father: "I never met with any foe, be he warrior or demon, with such amazing strength and bravery as this. He seems to have a brazen body, for my arrows, which I can drive through an anvil, cannot penetrate his chest. If I had applied the strength which I have exerted to a mountain it would have been moved from its base, but he sat firmly in his saddle and scorned my efforts."

"Let us not despair," replied the father. "Did not the Sīmūrgh promise her assistance in the time of greatest need." So saying, Zāl took the precious feather, which had been only slightly burned before, and going out upon the cliff he burned it in a censer. The darkness grew deeper for a moment, and then there was the rush of mighty wings, as the mountain bird circled slowly down out of the darkness and stood in her rich and massive beauty beside her foster child, now an old and retired warrior. Zāl's eye lighted up with hope and love as he gently laid his hand upon her golden plumage and told her of his sad affliction.

The faithful Rakush stood near by with drooping head and bleeding form, and he first caught the eye of the loving mother-bird. Going to him she pulled out the cruel arrows with her beak, and gently passed the feathers of her wing over the wounds; they quickly healed, and the old war horse raised his gallant head and stamped his feet impatiently as if he longed again to hear the trumpet call to battle. The Sīmūrgh then went to Rustem and soothed him with the gentle caresses of her head and beak, and drawing forth the hidden darts from his body she sucked the poisoned blood from out the gaping wounds, and then they closed and healed; so the champion was soon restored to life and strength. Being thus invigorated under her magic care, he sought her aid in the battle of the coming day. But the bird replied: "There never appeared a more brave and perfect hero than Isfendiyār, for in his Heft-khān he succeeded in killing a Sīmūrgh, and the further thou art removed from his invincible arrow the greater will be thy safety."

But Zāl interposed, saying: "If Rustem retires from the contest his family will be enslaved—we shall be in bondage and affliction." Then she told Rustem to mount Rakush and follow her. He obeyed, and she led him far away across a broad river, and on the other side she came to a low marsh filled with reeds, where the moonlight flashed on the white wings of the pelicans and the night bird sang his lowest notes to the pale and drooping lilies. Then from the stems that bloom on the banks of Īrān's rivers she chose the Kazū[1] tree, and directed Rustem to take from it a straight shaft and form it into an arrow and shoot it into the eye of his enemy. "The arrow," said she, "will make him blind, and I would that it were only so, for he who spills the blood of Isfendiyār will never again in life be free from calamity." Then she es-

---

[1] Pichula, used anciently for Persian arrows. During the rainy season it blooms profusely on the banks of the rivers, where it is interwoven with twining Asclepias.—*Sir W. Jones in " Botanical Observations."*

corted Rustem, who carried the charmed arrow, back
to his tent, and caressing his face with her beak and
soft feathers she spread her golden pinions and soared
away into darkness.

THE FALL OF THE WARRIORS.

Isfendiyár was amazed to see Rustem bearing gallantly down upon him, clad in full armor, and riding
the self-same steed that seemed wounded to the death
the day before. "How is this?" he cried.

"But thy father Zál is a sorcerer,
  And he by charm and spell
  Has cured all the wounds of the warrior,
  And now he is safe and well.
  For the wounds I gave could never be
  Closed up except by sorcery."

Rustem replied, "If a thousand arrows were shot
at me they would fail to kill, and in the end thou
wilt fall at my hands. Therefore come at once and
be my guest, and I swear by the Zend-Avesta that I
will go with thee, but unfettered, to thy father."

"That is not enough," returned Isfendiyár.
"Thou must be fettered, I will not disobey the commands of the king," and he seized his bow to com-
mence the combat. Rustem did the same, and as he
placed the Símúrgh's arrow in the bowstring, he exclaimed, "I have wished for a reconciliation, and I
would now give all my treasures and wealth to go
with you to Írán and avoid this conflict, but my offers are disdained, for you are determined to consign me to bondage and disgrace."

An arrow from Isfendiyár came quickly against his armor, but by turning himself he eluded its point, and in return he quickly lodged the Símúrgh's arrow in the eyes of his antagonist.

> " And darkness overspread his sight,
>   The world to him was hid in night,
>   The bow dropped from his slackened hand,
>   And down he sunk upon the ground."

Báhman, the son of Isfendiyár, seeing his father fall, uttered loud lamentations, and all the Persian troops drew near in sorrow and mourning, The stricken man was carried to his tent, and the next day both Zál and Rustem came to offer their sympathy and condolence.

The wounded prince replied, " I do not ascribe my misfortunes to thee; fate would have it so, and thus it is. But I consign my son Báhman to thy care and guardianship ; instruct him in the science of government, the custom of kings, and the rules of the warrior, for thou art perfect in all things." Rustem readily promised, saying that it should be his duty to see that the young prince was firmly seated upon the throne of his fathers.

Then Isfendiyár sent a message to his father, and with a few tender, loving words for his mother, he lay back and died. Then Rustem returned home, carrying with him as a sacred trust the son of the slain prince, who was carefully instructed in all the arts of war and the accomplishments of peace, and finally placed upon the throne that should have been his father's.

But the blood of the gallant Isfendiyãr carried with it a curse, as the Sīmūrgh had said, and Rustem himself fell a victim to the treachery of his half-brother. He and his gallant horse fell together in a pit which had been prepared for them while on a hunting excursion, and although Rakush bounded gallantly out of the first, it was only to fall into another, and they struggled on, until mounting up the edge of the seventh pit, and covered with deep wounds, both horse and rider lay exhausted. With one supreme effort, Rustem sent an arrow through the man who had betrayed him, and then Persia's gallant son was dead, and not a kingly follower remained. Zūara and other followers had fallen and perished in other pits dug by the traitor king and traitor brother. All were lost save one, who escaped and carried the sad tidings to Sistan, where Zãl in agony tore his white hair and cried, " Why did I not die for him, why was I not present fighting by his side ?" And never again did the land of Īrãn bear a chieftain like the gallant Rustem slain.

CHAPTER XIV.

SECOND PERIOD.

ANWĀRI—NIZĀMĪ—LAILĪ AND MAJNŪN—A FRIEND—
THE WEDDING — DELIVERANCE — THE MEETING IN
THE DESERT — DEATH OF THE LOVERS — THE VISION
OF ZYD.

THE second period of Persian poetry reaches from
the beginning to the end of the twelfth century,
and it may be termed the panegyric age, from the fact
that the poets of this period, nearly all of them, devoted their talents indiscriminately to the laudation
of the princes of their times. But we find also in
this age, the beginning of the mystic school which
was so fully developed in the thirteenth century. It
was during this period that Amig of Bukhara composed the Egyptian story of Yūsuf and Zulaikhā,
which was the original of many poetic versions. A
few good satires also belong to the twelfth century,
but the greatest panegyric poet of this period was

ANWĀRI.

There is but little known of this Poet Laureate
of Persia; he appears to have been born, however, in
the twelfth century at Bedeneh, a village in Khorasān. He was a poor student in the town of Tus, and
near the college grounds one day, he happened to
see the grand equipage of the Sultan, and observing

that one member of his suite was mounted upon a
more magnificent horse, and was more gorgeously
equipped than the others, he inquired who he was.
On being told that he was the court poet, the ambitious student aspired to the same position, and that
very night he prepared a poem in praise of the Sultan, which was presented at court the next day. The
royal vanity was so greatly pleased by this˙ offering,
that the young poet was offered a position at court,
which he promptly accepted. He attended the Sultan in all of his warlike expeditions until his death.[1]
He wrote a few long poems, and also some simple
lyrics that were worthy of preservation, but perhaps
the best of these productions was "The Tears of
Khorasān." Khorasān was overrun by a barbarous
tribe of Turkomans, who committed every species of
cruelty, and this poem was a plea to the Prince of
Samarcānd for relief. The following extract, which is
the opening stanza of his petition, will give a sufficient idea of his style :

"Waft, gentle gale, Oh, waft to Samarcānd,
 When next thou visitest that blissful land,
 The plaint of Khorosānia plunged in woe
 Bear to Tūrānia's king our piteous scroll
 Whose opening breathes forth all the anguished
. soul
 And this denotes whate'er the tortured know."

NIZĀMĪ.

The greatest poet of this period, however, was Nizāmī,[2] whose pathetic love songs are the best productions

1 About A. D. 1200.   2 Born A. D. 1141, and died A. D. 1203.

of the kind in the Persian tongue. He lived the greater part of his life at Ganja, and is therefore known as Nizāmī of Ganja. His first important work was called "The Storehouse of Mysteries." This was followed by the beautiful poem of "Koshrū and Shirīn," the theme of which was taken from ancient Persian history. In the latter part of the twelfth century he wrote his Diwau, a collection which was said to contain twenty thousand verses, but few of these, however, have come down to our own times. Soon afterward the great poet wrote his famous love story entitled "Lailī and Majnūn," which was followed by his Book of Alexander, an epic which was devoted to the glory of the Greek conqueror. His last work was the "Seven Fair Faces," and this was presented in the form of romantic fiction, and consisted merely of seven stories which were told to amuse the king by the seven wives of Būhram Gor. These five works are known as the "Five Treasures of Nizāmī." His eulogies were sung by the greatest Persian poets who lived after him.

It was of him that Sa'di wrote: "Gone is Nizāmī, our exquisite pearl, which Heaven in its kindness, formed of the purest dew, as the gem of the world."

His most popular work, and one of the best of the Persian classics, is the poem of Lailī and Majnūn, which, for tenderness, purity and pathos, has been seldom equaled. We give here a short prose version of the legend:

LAILĪ AND MAJNŪN.

Every nation has its favorite romance of love and chivalry. France and Italy have their Abelard and

Eloisa, their Petrarch and Laura, while Arabia and Persia have their Lailī and Majnūn, the record of whose sorrows is constantly referred to throughout the East as an example of the most devoted affection. This story, which has been versified by several Persian authors, is of Arabian origin, and hence it bears the impress of Arabic thought.

The poem contains the mystic lights and shadows of Bedawīn life—the fervid loves and passionate yearnings, the hopeless grief and stoical endurance, which belong to the sons of the desert.

Majnūn was the son of a haughty chief, while Lailī belonged to an humble Arab tribe, but her father carried in his veins the pride of his desert race, and the bitter hatreds of the Moslems. Lailī is described as being very beautiful, with the crimson of her cheek flashing through the dark olive shades of her face, and her heavy ringlets, "black as night," hanging in graceful profusion around her shapely neck.

> "When ringlets of a thousand curls
> And ruby lips and teeth of pearls,
> And dark eyes flashing quick and bright,
> Like lightning on the brow of night—
> When charms like these their power display
> And steal the wildered heart away—
> Can man, dissembling, coldly seem
> Unmoved as by an idle dream ?
> Kais[1] saw her beauty, and her grace
> The soft expression of her face ;

[1] Kais was the proper name of the lover, but he received the cognomen of Majnūn on account of his madness.

> And as he gazed and gazed again
> Distraction stung his burning brain ;
> No rest he found by day or night—
> She was forever in his sight."

But the wandering tribe to which the girl belonged
folded their tents and slipped away to the solitudes
of the mountains. They had left no trace of their
going—no hint of where they might be found, and the
luckless maid found herself far from her lover with no
possible means of communicating with him, while the
frantic boy was wandering through the wilds in the
almost hopeless search for his love.

> " He sought her in rosy bower and silent glade,
> Where the palm trees flung refreshing shade ;
> Through grove and frowning glen he lonely strayed,
> And with his griefs the rocks were vocal made."[1]

Alarmed by the condition of his son, the old chieftain gathered his men for an organized search, and at
last they found the mountain stronghold of the tribe
they sought.

They were challenged by a stern voice beyond the
rocky barriers, which demanded :

> "Come ye hither as friends or foes ?
> Whatever may your errand be,
> That errand must be told to me ;
> For none, unless a sanctioned friend,
> Can pass the line that I defend."

This challenge touched the chieftain's pride, and he
haughtily responded that he came in friendship, to

---

[1] Except the desert scene, the poetical extracts in this chapter are from
Atkinson's translation.

propose the marriage of his son to the Arab maiden to whom he had taken a silly fancy.

> "With shame,
> Possess'd of power, and wealth, and fame,
> I to his silly humor bend,
> And humbly seek his fate to blend
> With one inferior. Need I tell
> My own high lineage known so well?
> . If sympathy my heart incline,
> Or vengeance, still the means are mine.
> Treasure and arms can amply bear
> Me through the toils of desert war;
> But thou'rt the merchant pedler chief,
> And I the buyer; come, sell, be brief!
> If thou art wise, accept advice;
> Sell and receive a princely price!"

The haughty tone of the applicant was little calculated to call forth a favorable response, and the proud father replied:

> "Madness is neither sin nor crime, we know,
> But who'd be linked to madness or a foe?
> Thy son is mad—his senses first restore;
> In constant prayer the aid of heaven implore.
> But while portentous gloom pervades his brain
> Disturb me not with this vain suit again. .
> The jewel sense no purchaser can buy,
> Nor treachery the place of sense supply.
> Thou hast my reasons, and this parley o'er,
> Keep them in mind and trouble me no more."

The scorn of the father's reply had been, if possible, more bitter than the insulting demand, and Syd

Omri turned indignantly to his followers and ordered
the homeward march. The desert fates were stern, and

> " When Majnūn saw his hopes decay,
>   Their fairest blossoms fade away,
>   And friends and sire who might have been
>   Kind intercessors, rush between
>   Him and the only wish that shed
>   One ray of comfort round his head,
>   He beat his hands, his garments tore,
>   He cast his fetters on the floor
>   In broken fragments, and in wrath
>   Sought the dark wilderness's path,
>   And there he wept and sobbed aloud,
>   Unnoticed by the gazing crowd."

The kinsmen of Lailī brought to the encampment
the news that a youth, insane and wild, was haunting
the desert wastes below the mountain, and the fair
Lailī blushed when she heard the tidings, but dared
not venture forth to meet her maniac lover. The
Arab chief swore vengeance against the hapless youth,
and ordered his followers to slay him in the desert.
The father of Majnūn heard of the cruel decree and
sent his own followers into the wilderness to rescue
his son. . . Again and again he was carried to his
father's home, and as frequently he made his escape,
always wandering, with unerring instinct, near to his
beloved.

> " Lailī in beauty, softness, grace,
>   Surpassed the loveliest of her race.
>   The killing witchery that lies
>   In her soft, black. delicious eyes—

Her lashes speak a thousand blisses
Her lips of ruby ask for kisses;
Her cheeks, so beautiful and bright,
Have caught the moon's refulgent light;
Her form the Cypress tree expresses,
And full and plump, invites caresses.
With all these charms, the heart to win,
There was a ceaseless grief within,—
Yet none beheld her grief, or heard,
She droop'd like broken-winged bird.
Her secret thoughts, her love concealing,
But softly to the terrace stealing
From morn to eve, she gazed around
In hopes her Majnūn might be found."

An oasis with its cooling streams was near the
rocky fortress of the Bedawīn encampment, and here
the tall palms seemed to lean against the sky, while
the doves cooed in the thickets of foliage. Here the
gentle Lailī came day after day, hoping that her lover
might venture near. She gathered the lilies that
bloomed around her feet, as she wandered through the
fragrant grove, but her dark eyes were heavy with
unshed tears, when she reclined beneath a mournful
cypress tree and softly chanted her song of faithful-
ness:

" Oh, faithful friend and lover true,
Still distant from thy Lailī's view;
Still absent, still beyond her power,
To bring thee to her fragrant bower;
Oh noble youth! still thou art mine,
And Lailī, Lailī still is thine."

As she pensively sat one day beneath the cypress tree, a youth of kingly mien passed that way. His eyes rested a moment upon her crimson lips, and the flowing tresses which were dark as the plume of a raven's wing—he saw too the full form with its shapely curves and the beaming softness of the dark eyes, with their heavy lashes. Ibn Salâm was the honored name of this young prince, who with his suite had sought for a moment the cooling shades of the palm-tree grove, and he it was who hastened to her father with a plea for his daughter's hand. Dazzled by the gold and position of the suitor, the father of Lailî gave a cordial consent to the proposed union.

A FRIEND.

The chief of the domain where Majnûn wandered in his pitiful loneliness, looked with compassion upon him, for one day, while in pursuit of a bounding deer, he saw the wasted frame and wild look of the despairing lover. Dismounting from his splendid steed, Noufal, the Arab chief, came kindly to him and listened to the story so constantly told of love and suffering. With kindly words the chieftain soothed the restless spirit, and gently drawing the tortured mind away from its painful thought he offered nourishment to the sinking body. A change for the better came over him, and he took the proffered cup and drank, although he drank to Lailî's name. Refreshed by Noufal's kindly ministry and drawn by gentle urging, Majnûn went with his new friend to his home, and there received the best of care and hopeful cheer.

" An altered man, his mind at rest,
  In customary robes he dressed;
  A turban shades his forehead pale,
  No more is heard the lover's wail,
  His dungeon gloom exchanged for day,
  His cheeks a rosy tint display;
  He revels midst the garden sweets,
  And still his lip the goblet meets;
  But so intense his constant flame
  Each cup is quaffed in Laili's name."

The generous Nonfal was not content with the change so nearly wrought, but he gathered his bravest men in battle array, and marched at their head to the mountain fortress of the Bedawïn encampment. The troops of Arabian horsemen were halted and sword and helmet glittered in the sun, while Noufal sent his messenger forward with a demand for the hand of the coveted bride. His request was haughtily refused, and when the messenger was again sent forward with a threat of revenge if his wishes were not complied with, his power and vengeance were alike defied. Then the word of command rang along the glittering lines. There was a rattling of helmets and spears, a twanging of the bowstring and a gallant charge was made upon the foe that was so well entrenched in the mountain fastnesses. Amidst the clangor of brazen drums and trumpets, the fearful fight went on and

" Arrows, like birds, on either foeman stood,
  Drinking with open beak the vital flood;
  The shining daggers in the battle's heat
  Rolled many a head beneath the horse's feet;

And lightnings hurled by death's unsparing hand
Spread consternation through the weeping land."

There was no pause in the sound of the trumpets,
no stay in the wild flight of the arrows, as the dreadful work went on, and the dripping swords were
bathed with the crimson tide of shame.

The shades of night came down ere the fate of
the battle was decided, but the assaulting party had
suffered most, and in another hour of conflict the
friends of Majnūn had been undone. With the coming of the morning light the assault was renewed, and
the desert rang again with the sounds of war; all
along the long line glittered the sword and buckler,
the helmet and spear; swords clashed and the desert
sands were wet again with the blood of the fallen. At
last the tribe of Lailī's sire gave way, and Noufal won
the bitter fight, though many of his bravest men
lay bleeding on the burning sand.

" And now the elders of that tribe appear,
    And thus implore the victor. Chieftain, hear!
    The work of slaughter is complete;
    Thou seest our power destroyed; allow
    Us wretched suppliants at thy feet
    To humbly ask for mercy now.
    How many warriors press the plain?
    Khanjer and spear have laid them low;
    At peace, behold our kinsman slain,
    For thou art now without a foe.

    Then pardon what of wrong has been;
    Let us retire unharmed—unstay'd—

Far from this sanguinary scene,
And take thy prize—the Arab maid."

The aged father came forth with dust and ashes
upon his hoary head, and admitted that his tribe was
fully conquered, and offered the life of his daughter
for a peace offering, while still refusing to allow her
to wed with a maniac.

" My daughter shall be brought at thy command ;
The red flames may ascend from blazing brand
And slay their victim, crackling in the air,
And Laili dutiously shall perish there.
Or, if thou'dst rather see the maiden bleed,
This thirsty sword shall-do the dreadful deed ;
Dissever at one blow that lovely head,
Her sinless blood by her own father shed !
In all things thou shalt find me faithful, true,
Thy slave I am—what would'st thou have me do ?
But mark me ; I am not to be beguiled ;
I will not to a demon give my child ;
I will not to a madman's wild embrace
Consign the pride and honor of my race,
And wed her to contempt and foul disgrace."

The chivalry of the desert disdained to tear the
child from her father's arms, even though that father
was a conquered foe. The gallant Noufal, feeling that
he was himself defeated, and that in vain the blood
of his brave men had stained the desert sands, sadly
gave the order that the conquered tribe should be allowed to retire unmolested from the well fought field.

" And thou and thine may quit the field.
    Still armed with khanjer, sword and shield;

Both horse and rider. Thus in vain
Blood has bedewed this thirsty plain."

With a heavy heart the gallant chief pursued his homeward way with Majnūn, reckless and desperate, by his side. He tried again to calm the poignant pangs of hopeless love, and to bless, with gentleness and tender care, the wounded and despairing spirit.

"But vain his efforts ; mountain, wood and plain
Soon heard the maniac's piercing woes again ;
Escaped from listening ear and watchful eye,
Lonely again, in desert wild to lie."

In another part of the wild domain a cloud of dust on the horizon of the desert tells of the coming of a troop of horsemen, and soon a wearied and broken column is seen beneath the clouds of sand which obscure the blue of heaven. The women of the conquered tribe, who had been placed in safer quarters, come forth to meet the returning warriors. As the trampling steeds come nearer they hear the leader's angry word, as he breathes his curses, loud and deep, upon the victor in the fight, for he scarcely cares to survive the blow while burning with the disgrace of defeat. Poor Lailī listens sadly to the story of her fate, but no hope of aid can enter her crushed and broken heart. And still the story of her beauty is borne on every gale, and the neighboring tribes are wondering for whom her father is keeping the beauteous gem.

THE WEDDING.

At last, the lover comes with his magnificent offerings of embroidered robes, and carpets worked with

silk and gold; the rarest gems were brought to lay
at her feet, and a long line of camels, with their
tinkling bells, were laden with costly presents for the
bride of Ibn Salām.

Beautiful steeds were proudly stepping to the low
music of his march, for a long line of the purest
Arabian blood was coursing in their veins. But while
the nuptial pomp and nuptial rites engaged the chieftain's household, and every square was ringing with
the rattle of drums and the voice of pipe and cymbal,
the stricken bride was sitting sad and lone in her
retreat, mourning for her betrothed, and pleading that
she might be allowed to die rather than to wed the
man that she could never love. The joyous bridegroom
came with gorgeous litter and golden throne for the
chosen bride to occupy. He came in richest garb,
with happy smiles and costly jewels, into the presence
of his promised bride, but the Arabian maiden turned
with flashing eyes upon the intruder, and informed
him that the betrothal had been made by her father
without consulting her. She declared she would rather
die than become a wife unloving, for in her heart
she could find only hatred for the man who was willing to claim her under circumstances so revolting, and
then with the air of a queen she ordered him to leave
her alone. When Ibn Salām heard her frenzied words,
he turned away from the indignant girl and poured
his woes into her father's ear. The pitiful pleadings
of the girl were unheeded, and the fearful mockery of
marriage went on amidst the glare of trumpets and
sounding drum,— went on, with jewels and costly gifts
for the unwilling bride, and all the outward show of

happiness and joy. But though Lailī's plighted faith
to Majnūn seemed so sorely broken, she still cherished
his memory with tenderest thought, and

> "Deep in her heart a thousand woes
> Disturbed her days' and nights' repose
> A serpent at its very core
> Writhing and gnawing evermore ;
> And no relief—a prison room
> Being now the lonely sufferer's doom."

Amidst all the heartaches of humanity the slow
movement of sun and stars still goes on, and the
bare horizon of the desert is illumined by the lamps
of heaven. Night with her coolness and dews, comes
down upon the burning sands with the restful touch
of peace. Her primeval fountains of light have gathered for all time around the desert steppes, watching
their silent mysteries, and touching with glory the
far-away crowns of their palms.

Lailī sat in her prison tower, looking out upon the
peaceful beauty of the night, and its soft repose
crept into her troubled heart, bringing with it a message of hope. For days and years she had lived within that guarded tower, shut like a gem within its
stony bed, surrounded by the dragon watch which
her husband still supplied. But hark! there is an
unusual sound beneath her casement ; there are flick-
ering lamps and wailing cries; confused voices are
bearing messages to and fro; there is a death-note in
the wild chant which is ringing out upon the night.

> "Beneath her casement rings a wild lament,
> Death-notes disturb the night : the air is rent

With clamorous voices; every hope is fled,
He breathes no longer—Ibn Salām is dead ı
The fever's rage had nipp'd him in his bloom;
He sank unloved, unpitied, to the tomb."

Lailī looked up to the face of the moon, and thought of its chilling rays that fell upon the haggard form of her desert love. She gazed upon the flashing star that stood like a guardian above his restless sleep, and then she turned to receive the messengers who brought the formal tale that her jailor now was dead. And must she mourn for the man she loathed? Ah, yes; the Arab law must be obeyed, and she must assume the garments of woe! It was easy for her to weep,

"But all the burning tears she shed
Were for Majnūn, not the dead."

The days went by with weary feet, and the night still looked upon a lonely heart, for the Arab law maintained that years must pass before one breath of freedom could be given to the woman in the rockbound tower. But Lailī arose one morn with a new light in her dark eyes, and called her faithful Zyd, the boy who had long served his gentle lady, and to whom her word was the law supreme. To him she said :

"To-day is not the day of hope,
Which only gives to fancy scope;
It is the day our hopes completing,
It is the lover's day of meeting!
Rise up ! the world is full of joy;
Rise up ! and serve thy mistress, boy;

> Together, where the cypress grows,
> Place the red tulip and the rose;
> And let the long dissever'd meet—
> Two lovers, in communion sweet."

THE MEETING IN THE DESERT.

Then with her faithful attendant she went cautiously forth, and together they threaded their way over the desolate sand and through the grove of palms; but she stayed not to gather the lilies blooming around her feet—she waited not to catch the breath of the roses, or to drink of the tiny stream, whose life-giving waves had made this little oasis to bloom like a garden in the midst of the desert. But she hastened on her way, and the boy ran by her side wondering why she sped so quickly through the grove. On, beyond its cooling shade and over the barren steepes, she pressed with unfaltering feet until she saw the haggard form of her lover; then she stepped gently to his side and laid her hand upon his arm. "Ah! Majnūn, it is thy Lailī that has come;" his mind awoke with one glad cry, for the familiar voice with its caressing tones rang with the notes of peace and joy through the darkened chambers of his brain. For one glad moment he held her in his arms, and then, overcome with emotion, he fainted at her feet. She quickly knelt beside him, and then

> " His head which in the dust was laid
> Upon her lap she drew, and dried
> His tears with tender hand and pressed
> Him close and closer to her breast;

'Be here thy home beloved, adored,
Revive, be blest—oh ! Lailí's lord.'

At last he breathed, around he gazed,
As from her arms his head he raised—
'Art thou,' he faintly said, 'a friend
Who takes me to her gentle breast—
Dost thou in truth so fondly bend
Thine eyes upon a wretch distressed ?

Are these thy unveiled cheeks I see
Can bliss be yet in store for me ?
I thought it all a dream, so oft
Such dreams come in my madness now.
Is this thy hand so fair and soft ?
Is this in sooth my Lailí's brow ?

In sleep these transports I may share
But when I wake 'tis all despair !
Let me gaze on thee—e'en though it be
An empty shade alone I see ;
How shall I bear what once I bore
When thou shalt vanish as before ? '"

Then the beauteous vision rested within his arms,
with her dark ringlets flowing around her smooth
neck, and the sweet confession of her love beaming
in her tremulous eyes. He saw her chin of dimpled
sweetness, and the soft cheek with its crimson flush,
then her matchless voice came again to his ears with
its message of tenderness.

" To hope, dear wanderer, revive ;
    Lo Zemzems,[1] cool and bright,

---

[1] Zemzem is the sacred well enclosed by the temple at Mecca, and even a
stone dipped in its waters is thought to possess marvelous virtues.

Flow at thy feet—then drink and live
Seared heart ! be glad for bounteous heaven
At length our recompense hath given,
Beloved one, tell me all thy will
And know thy Lailī faithful still.

Here in this desert, join our hands,
Our souls were joined long, long before ;
And if our fate such doom demands,
Together wander evermore.
Oh Kais ! never let us part,
What is the world to thee and me ?
My universe is where thou art
And is not Lailī all to thee ? "

The tempted lover listened, with his soul in his
longing eyes, but he knew that he could not make her
his wife according to the Arab law—they could not
be legally wedded, and his love for her was too pure
and unselfish to accept the sacrifice that she proposed to make. To him, then, was given the hardest
task ever given into lover's hands—that of saving the
woman that he worshipped from his own embrace.
After the years of suffering that had been his, could
he push the tempting cup from his thirsting lip ?
Was the weakened frame strong enough to carry out
the dictates of his will ? Nay, did God require such
a sacrifice after all these years of loyalty and truth ?
Were they not already wedded in his pure sight ?
Had she not always been his own in the eyes of
heaven ? These questions surged through his throbbing
brain as he held the woman he loved in his close embrace.   One sweet taste of heaven, surely the Lord

had given, in the desert of his wasted life—one moment of bliss wherein he might taste the lips he had
hungered for, so long. But should he therefore out-
rage his own conscience, and sacrifice the woman he
loved, for the temporary enjoyment of the present
life? His manhood and his conscience answered,
never. He clasped her closer to his aching heart—
he kissed again the tempting lips—his eyes lingered
with one long sad look upon the lovely face, and then
he slowly answered:

" How well, how fatally I love,
My madness and my misery prove;
All earthly hopes I could resign—
Nay, life itself, to call thee mine.
But shall I make thy spotless name—
That sacred spell—a word of shame?

Shall selfish Majnūn's heart be blest
And Lailī prove the Arab's jest?
The city's gates though we may close
We cannot still our conscience's throes.
No—we have met,—a moment's bliss
Has dawned upon my gloom in vain
Life yields no more a joy like this,
And all to come can be but pain.

Thou, thou, adored! might be mine own
A thousand deaths let Majnūn die
Ere but a breath by slander blown
Should sully Lailī's purity!
Go, then—and to thy tribe return,
Fly from my arms that clasp thee yet;
I feel my brain with frenzy burn—
Oh, joy, could I but thus forget!"

With another kiss upon the silent lips—another close embrace, the manly lover tore himself away to another struggle between death and life ; still warring in the unequal strife with fate, he told to the desert wind, his piteous tale :

> " The fevered thoughts that on me prey
> Death's sea alone can sweep away.
> I found the bird of Paradise
> That long I sought with care ;
> Fate snatched it from my longing eyes—
> I held—despair.
> Wail, Lailī, wail our fortunes crossed,
> Weep, Majnūn, weep—forever lost."

DEATH OF THE LOVERS.

Time passed by on leaden feet, for he no longer carried in his hands the flowers of hope. No longer the bare horizon of the desert was illumined with the mirage of rivers and palms. Fate had done her worst, and Death, the great consoler, waited near to place his seal with the touch of peace upon the weary brow. The flower of the desert lay again in the tower where she had passed so many wasted years, and feeling that her life was going out with the glory of the setting sun, she called her mother to her side and pleaded that when she was gone Majnūn might be allowed to weep over her grave.

> " Again it was the task of faithful Zyd,
> Through far extending plain and forest wide,
> To seek the man of woes, and tell
> The fate of her, alas ! he loved so well.

With bleeding heart he found his lone abode,
Watering with tears the path he rode.

And beating his sad breast, Majnûn perceived
His friend approach, and asked him why he grieved?
'Alas!' he cried, 'the hail has crushed my bowers,
A sudden storm has blighted all my flowers;
Thy cypress tree o'erthrown, the leaves are scar;
The moon has fallen from her lucid sphere;
Lailî is dead.'"

His sad duty was done, and the bereaved lover lay
unconscious at his feet. With gentle ministry the
stricken man was roused from his swoon, and then he
started toward the loved one's grave.

"Now he threads
The mazes of the shadowy wood, which spreads
Perpetual gloom, and now emerges where
No bower nor grove obstructs the fiery air;
Climbs the mountain's brow, o'er hill and plain
Urged quicker onward by his burning brain,
Across the desert's arid boundary hies
Zyd, like a shadow, following where he flies.

And when the tomb of Lailî meets his view,
Prostrate he falls, the ground his tears bedew;
'Alas!' he cries, 'no more shall I behold
That angel face, that form of heavenly mould,
For thou hast quitted this contentious life,
This scene of endless treachery and strife;
And I, like thee, shall soon my fetters burst,
And quench, in draughts of heavenly love, my thirst.
There where angelic bliss can never cloy,
We soon shall meet in everlasting joy;

The taper of our souls, more clear and bright,
Will then be lustrous with immortal light.'"

The troubled day was closing fast in night, and
though he received the kindly ministry of his friends,
only a few more weeks had passed away, when the
stricken lover was found with his head resting lovingly upon her tomb, while upon his loyal brow there
rested the peaceful touch of death. His weary heart
had found rest at last, rest beyond the fevered dream
of life, with all its anxious hopes and fears. Reverent
hands opened Laili's tomb. and they laid the stilled
heart beside her own.

" One promise bound their faithful hearts—one bed
Of cold, cold earth united them when dead.
Severed in life, how cruel was their doom!
Ne'er to be joined but in the silent tomb!"

THE VISION OF ZYD.

No heart more loyal was left behind than that of
the faithful page who so long had done the lady's
bidding. He often pondered on the faith and devotion of the lovers, and one night he slept alone beneath
the desert sky, when the canopy of heaven seemed to
roll away. A new morning seemed to dawn in glory
upon the waiting earth, and touch the distant mountain peaks with crowns of light. Beneath the radiance
of its coming, the secrets of the earth, which had been
written in the roll-call of the ages, were read by the
waiting millions, for the age of recompense had come.
The desert sands gave way to vistas of golden fruit
and blooming roses; the white lilies gleamed amidst
the green verdure, and the almond blossoms waved in

silvery sprays upon the passing breeze. The nightingale sang in fadeless bowers, and the low, sweet voices of the ring-doves were heard among the feathery plumes of the palms. The desert voices gave way to the rich melodies from harp and shell. The fronded palms pressed upward, and a royal throne, with gems and gold, stood beneath their protecting shade.

> " Upon that throne, in blissful state,
> The long divided lovers sate,
> Resplendent with seraphic light,
> They held a cup with diamonds bright."

This cup was filled with the nectar of immortality, and, quaffing its rich contents, they wandered away, hand in hand, through the long aisles of unfading flowers.

> " The dreamer who this vision saw,
> Demanded with becoming awe,
> What sacred names the happy pair
> In Irem-bowers were wont to bear.
> A voice replied : 'That sparkling moon
> Is Lailí still—her friend Majnún ;
> Deprived in your frail world of bliss,
> They reap their great reward in this !' "

Zyd wakened from his wondrous dream, and, rejoicing, told the story of his glad vision. The sons of the desert took up the mystic theme, and still repeat the promise that pure and loyal love can never fail of its final reward.

> " Saki ! Nizámí's song is sung ;
> The Persian poet's pearls are strung ;

Then fill again the goblet high !
Thou wouldst not ask the reveler why
Fill to the love that changes never !
Fill to the love that lives forever !
That purified by earthly woes,
At last with bliss seraphic glows."

CHAPTER XV.

THIRD PERIOD.

GENGHIS KHĀN—JALAL-UDDIN RŪMI—SĀ'DĪ—WORKS OF SĀ'DĪ — THE BŪSTĀN — THE PEARL — KINDNESS TO THE UNWORTHY — SILENCE THE SAFETY OF IGNORANCE — DARIUS AND HIS HORSE-KEEPER — STORIES FROM THE GŪLISTĀN — THE WISE WRESTLER — DANGERS OF PROSPERITY — BORES.

THE third period of Persian poetry, which may be called the mystic and moral age, is assigned to the thirteenth century.

It was at this time that Genghis Khān, the Tartar chief, swept like a mountain torrent over the East. His first attack was upon the countries beyond the Oxus, where the devotees of science had taken refuge during the invasion of Persia by the Arabs. Bokhāra and Samarcānd were then the homes of scholars and the centres of civilization. Their colleges and libraries were celebrated throughout the Orient, but during the great Tartar invasion these cities were both destroyed, being stormed and burned by the Tartar horde, while more than two hundred thousand lives were sacrificed to the cruelty of the invading host. Bagdad was also devastated, the colleges destroyed and the most valuable books in the libraries were thrown into the Tigris.

During these stormy times the courts of the descendants of the Selucidæ were sought by scholars as places of refuge, some of their princes being literary men. A prince of this dynasty, by the name of Alladin Kaikūbad, became somewhat celebrated in the world of letters, and during his reign Iconium became the refuge of scholars from the Asiatic nations, who felt that on the western frontiers of the continent they were more secure from the attacks of the barbarians. The brightest ornament of this court was the mystic poet and philosopher,

JALAL-UDDIN RŪMI.[1]

His father was the founder of a college at Iconium in Syria, but after his father's death Jalal-uddin went to Aleppo and Damascus to continue his studies, and finally succeeded to the direction of the college. His literary fame rests upon his Mesnevi, a work in six volumes, which is a series of stories with moral maxims. Some portions of this work may be compared to the Hitapodeśa, while other parts appear to be an imitation of the Book of Proverbs or Ecclesiastes. He was, however, the author of several lyrics that are worthy of preservation: of these the following is, perhaps, the best:

THE FAIREST LAND.

" Tell me, gentle traveler, thou
Who hast wandered far and wide—
Seen the sweetest roses blow,
And the brightest rivers glide;
Say, of all thine eyes have seen,
Which the fairest land has been?"

[1] Born at Balkha, A. D. 1297.

"Lady, shall I tell thee where
Nature seems most blest and fair,
Far above all climes beside?
'Tis where those we love abide,
And that little spot is best
Which the loved one's foot hath pressed.
Though it be a fairy space,
Wide and spreading is the place;
Though 'twere but a barren mound,
'Twould become enchanted ground;
With thee, yon sandy waste would seem
The margin of Al-Cawthar's stream;
And thou canst make a dungeon's gloom
A bower where new-born roses bloom."

The most important bard of this period was

SĀ'DĪ.

Shaikh Sā'dī, as he is called, was born at Shīrāz,[1] while his country was under Turkish rule. He was educated at a college in Bagdad, where he lived until he was sixty-four years of age, when he had obtained an enviable reputation as a poet and orator. In later years, when the Tartar Chief Halāku Khān had over-run the adjacent territory and captured Bagdad, Sā'dī, with many others, was obliged to flee. He visited different parts of Europe, Africa, and even Asia as far as India.

The poet was twice married, but his caustic criticisms upon womankind would indicate that both of these ventures were unfortunate; the last was especially so. He had been living at Damascus, but becoming

[1] A. D. 1176.

tired of the society that he found there, he wandered
into the desert of Palestine. Here he was captured
by the Crusaders, and forced to work in the mud
with the Jewish captives, upon the fortifications at
Tripoli. A chief belonging to Aleppo found him
there, and recognizing him, he paid ten pieces of silver as the poet's ransom, and carried him to his own
home in Aleppo. It appears that the chief had a
beautiful daughter, with a temper like a vixen ; she
had a dower, however, of an hundred pieces of silver,
and by a little careful management of her temper and
an artful exhibition of her beauty she finally succeeded
in marrying Sä'dī. Of course his home was far from
being a paradise, and her beauty soon lost its charms
for her husband. Upon one occasion she tauntingly
asked him, " Are you not the fellow that my father
bought for ten pieces of silver ? " " Yes," retorted the
poet, "and he sold me to you for an hundred pieces."

Sä'dī had a son and a daughter, who were the children of his first wife ; the son, to whom he was de-
votedly attached, died in infancy, but the daughter
lived to become the wife of the celebrated poet Hāfiz.
Sä'dī closed his long life at Shīrāz, where it began,
having lived more than a hundred years.[1] He is honored as a saint by the Mohammedans, and his tomb
called Sädiya, near Shīrāz, is visited by many pilgrims,
and is also a resort for European travelers.

THE WORKS OF SÄ'DĪ.

This author was an accomplished linguist, and M.
De Tassy[2] claims that he was the first poet who

[1] Some authorities say that he died at the age of one hundred years,
while others claim that he lived to be one hundred and sixteen.
[2] Journal Asiatique, Jan., 1843.

wrote verse in the Hindūstānī dialect. He also wrote freely in Arabic as well as Persian. His style is vigorous and unusually simple for a Persian poet, but like all the others, he sometimes indulges in fulsome flattery, and florid description. His largest work is the Diwān, which is a collection of lyric poetry, but it is not so much admired as some of his smaller works. Indeed his lyric poems do not possess the graceful ease of Hāfiz's songs, but they are full of pathos, and like his other works, they show a fearless love of truth, and a tone of pure morality. Although he was the author of many works, the most popular among European scholars are the Būstān, or Fruit Garden, and the Gūlistān, or Rose Garden, both of which are dedicated to the reigning king.

THE BŪSTĀN.

This is a work consisting of ten chapters of didactic verse, and it teaches lessons of morality and prudence in the form of poetic fable. It has been published in Calcutta, Lahore and Cawnpore, as well as in the capitals of Europe. It has been translated into German, French, English and other tongues, always retaining more or less of the popularity which it still enjoys in its native idiom.

The following[1] are the best specimens of this peculiar verse:

THE PEARL.

" From the cloud there descended a droplet of rain ;
'Twas ashamed when it saw the expanse of the main,

[1] From Davies' version.

Saying, 'Who may I be, where the sea has its run ?
If the sea has existence, I, truly, have none !'
Since in its own eyes the drop humble appeared,
In its bosom, a shell with its life the drop reared ;
The sky brought the work with success to a close,
And a famed royal pearl from the rain-drop arose.
Because it was humble it excellence gained ;
Patiently waiting till success was obtained."

KINDNESS TO THE UNWORTHY.

" I have heard that a man some home sorrow en-
    dured,
For bees in his roof had their dwelling secured
He asked for a big butcher's knife from his dame—
To demolish the nest of the bees was his aim.

His wife said, 'Oh, do not effect your design !
For the poor bees, dispersed from their dwelling,
    will pine.'
The foolish man yielded and went his own way ;
His wife, with their stings was assaulted one ·day.

The man from his shop to his dwelling returned,
At his wife's stupid folly, with anger he burned.
The ignorant woman, from door, street and roof,
Was shouting complaints, while the man gave re-
    proof !

'Do not make your face sour in men's presence, oh
    wife !
Deprive not, you said, the poor bees of their life !
On behalf of the bad, why beneficence show ?
Forbear with the bad, and you make their sins
    grow.'

When the ruin of men, by flattery you note
With a two-edged sword, cut the flatterer's throat."

SILENCE THE SAFETY OF IGNORANCE.

" A good natured man who in tatters was dressed,
For a season in Egypt, strict silence professed.
Men of wisdom, from near and from far, at the
    sight,
Gathered round him like moths, seeking after the
    light.
One night he communed with himself in this way;
'Beneath the tongue's surface the man hidden lay;
If I carry my head for myself in this plan,
How can people discover in me a wise man?'

He spoke, and his friends, and his foes all could
    see,
That the greatest of blockheads in Egypt was he!
His admirers dispersed and his trade lost its note;
He journeyed and over a mosque's arch he wrote:
'Could I have myself in a looking-glass seen,
Not in ignorance would I have riven my screen.
So ugly, the veil from my features I drew,
For I thought that my face was most charming to
    view.'

Oh, sensible person! In silence serene
You have honor, and people unworthy, a screen.
If you've learning, you should not your dignity lose!
If you're ignorant, tear not the curtain you use!
The beasts are all dumb, and man's tongue is re-
    leased;
A nonsensical talker is worse than a beast!

A speaker should talk in a sensible strain ;
If he can't ; like the brutes, he should silence main-
    tain."

DARIUS AND HIS HORSE-KEEPER.

I have heard that Darius of fortunate race
Got detached from his suite, on the day of the chase.
Before him came running a horse-tending lout ;
The king from his quiver an arrow pulled out,—
In the desert 'tis well to show terror of foes,
For at home not a thorn will appear on the rose ;
The terrified horse-keeper uttered a cry,
Saying :—" Do not destroy me ! no foeman am I.
I am he who takes care of the steeds of the king ;
In this meadow, with zeal to my duty I cling."
The king's startled heart found composure again ;
He smiled and exclaimed :—" Oh most foolish of men !
Some fortunate angel has succored you here ;
Else the string of my bow, I'd have brought to my
    ear."

The guard of the pasturage smiled and replied :—
" Admonition from friends it becomes not to hide.
The arrangements are bad and the counsels unwise,
When the king can't a friend from a foe recognize.
The condition of living in greatness is so,
That every dependant you have you should know.
You often have seen me when present at court,
And inquired about horses and pastures and sport,
And now that in love I have met you again,
Me you cannot distinguish from rancorous men.
As for me, I am able, oh name-bearing king !
Any horse out of one hundred thousand to bring.

With wisdom and judgment as herdsman I serve ;
Do you in like manner your own flock preserve !"
In that capital anarchy causes distress,
Where the plans of the king than the herdsman's are
    less.

STORIES FROM THE GŪLISTĀN,

The Gūlistān is the best of Sā'dī's works, and one
of the most popular of the Persian classics. It has
been translated into the dialects of India, as well as
the languages of Europe, and the Latin version of
Gentius has long been popular with European scholars.

It has acquired a greater popularity, both in the
East and the West, than any other work by the same
author, on account of the graceful style of its composition, and the varied character of its contents. It
is a collection of short stories, each of which is intended to illustrate some cardinal principle. There
are one hundred and eighty-eight of these sketches,
while the final chapter is devoted to "Rules for the
Conduct of Life." Many of these rules, like the
Dhammapada of Buddha, appear to have been founded
upon the proverbs of Solomon. Of the sketches, the
following [1] are the best.

THE WISE WRESTLER.

A celebrated athlete taught the art of wrestling to
Persian youths, and so great was his dexterity that
his pupils learned hundreds of different methods
whereby an antagonist could be thrown. Indeed, it

---

[1] From Gladwin's Translation.

was said that the teacher understood three hundred
and sixty capital sleights in this art, and every day
exhibited some new feat to his pupils.   He had one
favorite pupil, whose fine proportions and manly
bearing were the admiration of the master, and he
taught him three hundred and fifty-nine of these
sleights. The young man became very proficient, and
at length very boastful.   He gloried in his youth
and fine physical development, as well as his proficiency in the art, and after a time he boasted,
even in the presence of the Sultan, that no one
was able to cope with him—that he merely allowed
his master to maintain a superiority over him in
deference to his years, and also in consideration of the
fact, that he had been his tutor.

The Sultan was disgusted with the conceit of the
young wrestler, and commanded him to make a trial
of his skill in the royal presence, choosing his former
tutor as his opponent.   The ministers of state and
many officials of the court were in attendance, and
the young champion entered the field with all the
confidence and insolence of his nature—indeed it is
said that "he entered with a percussion that would
have removed a mountain of iron." The old master
stood calmly awaiting the fiery youth, whose strength
he well knew far excelled his own, but when he came
up to him, the tutor made the attack with the sleight
the knowledge of which he had kept to himself.

The young boaster was taken at a disadvantage,
and was helpless in the hands of the master, who
took him up from the ground, and threw him over
his head, leaving him prostrate upon the earth.

The wildest cheers of delight rang through the assembled multitudes, and the Sultan commanded that a rich reward be given to the tutor. The discomfited youth complained to the royal donor that his master had not gained the victory over him through strength or skill, but had kept from him one little feint in the art of wrestling, and by this means had taken the advantage of him.

The master then observed, "I reserved it for an occasion like this; the sages have taught us not to put oneself so much in the power of a supposed friend that, should he become an enemy, he may be able to injure you."

DANGERS OF PROSPERITY.

A certain king, who was dying without an heir to the throne, directed in the royal will that, on the morning after his death, the first person who came in through the gates of the city should receive the crown of royalty and the care of the kingdom. It happened that the first man who came in, was in the depths of poverty, and his life was a struggle with hardship and suffering. The ministers of state, however, placed the crown of royalty upon the head of the astonished man, and he was delighted with the wonderful change in his fortune. After a time, however, the nobles of his court rebelled against his rule, the surrounding kings formed hostile combinations against him, and he learned that no position in life is exempt from trials. His troops were thrown into confusion, the peasantry sympathized with the leaders of the revolt and he soon lost possession of the disputed territories.

In the midst of these political misfortunes and military defeats, an old friend, who had been the companion of the king in the days of his poverty, returned from a long trip, and called to congratulate him upon the radical change in his fortunes.

But the unfortunate monarch replied, "Oh, my brother! this is not a time for congratulations, but for condolence; when you last saw me I was anxious only to obtain my bread, but now I have all the cares of the world to encounter. There is, indeed, no calamity greater than worldly prosperity; if therefore you want riches, seek only for contentment, which is inestimable wealth. If a rich man should throw money into your lap, consider yourself under no obligations to him, for the kindness of a humble and genuine friend is better than the alms of the rich."

BORES.

A busy student complained to his teacher that his time was constantly taken up by visitors. People, whose time is of no value to them, do not consider that any one else may value theirs; they therefore present themselves continually and gossip of people or things, merely to pass away the time and waste the golden hours. "How can I be relieved of them?" pleaded the pupil. His tutor replied, "To such of them as are poor, lend money, and from those that are rich, ask favors; then you may rest assured that they will cease to trouble you. If a beggar were the leader of the Mohammedan army, the infidels would flee to China, through fear of his importunity."

CHAPTER XVI.

LATER PERIODS.

THE FOURTH PERIOD—LITERARY KINGS—HĀFIZ—PĪR-I-
SEBZ—SHĪRĀZ — THE FEAST OF SPRING—MY BIRD—
FIFTH PERIOD—JĀMI— THE WORKS OF JĀMI—RECEP-
TION—THE SIXTH PERIOD—THE SEVENTH PERIOD.

THE fourth period, which began at the close of the
thirteenth century and continued until the beginning of the fifteenth, represents the highest development of lyric poetry and rhetoric, although these were
stormy times in the political and literary world.

During this period Persia had many men of culture, and, indeed, she boasted of one literary king.

Sultān Ahmed Ilkhāni, who reigned over Bagdad,
Azerbaijān, and some parts of Asia Minor, conducted
his court with great pomp and splendor. He was one
of the most accomplished men of the age, being an
artist and illuminator as well as a musical composer.
His beautiful calligraphy, in various languages, was
highly celebrated, and his poetical productions, in both
the Persian and Turkish tongues, were considered very
meritorious. His moral character, however, presented
a sad contrast to his intellectual attainments, and his
remorseless cruelty made him an object of detestation
to his subjects. He was entirely merciless when intox-
icated with opium, and on these occasions he would

put people to death on the most trivial pretenses. His conduct provoked the enmity of the influential families of Bagdad, and at length the public sentiment against him became so strong that letters were written by the principal men, inviting Amir Timūr (Tamerlane) to the conquest of their country, and pledging him their assistance. The invitation was gladly accepted, and when the hostile intentions of the conqueror became known, the poetical Sultan sent him the following message :

" Why should we bare our neck on the block of misfortune ?
Why should we despond at every trifling attack of adversity ?
Like the Sīmūrgh, let us pass over seas and mountains
And thus bring the earth and water under our wings."

The sentiment was given in Persian verse, and Timūr soon found a poet who could write a suitable response, when the following answer was returned :

" Place thy neck on the block of adversity, and move not thy head.
Thou canst not consider trifling a most severe misfortune.
Like the Sīmūrgh, why shouldst thou attempt to climb the mountain, Qāf ?
Rather like the little sparrow, gather in thy wings and feathers and retire."

Soon afterward Timūr approached Bagdad,[1] and he

---

[1] A. D. 1388.

not only captured that city and province, but he proved
to be the veritable scourge of the Orient. The country had scarcely recovered from the ravages of Genghis
Khān when Timūr conquered the whole of ancient
Persia, and, flushed with success, he invaded India and
sacked Delhi, where he obtained the richest spoils of
his campaign. It was said that he erected towers of
human heads,[1] waded through streams of blood, and
marched over the ruins of burning cities, in order to
achieve his triumphs.

Such men are scarcely calculated to encourage the
science of letters, but it is claimed that he was friendly
to scholars, and it is certain that history was developed during this period.

HĀFIZ.

Not only history, but also poetry flourished under
the rule of the Mongol conqueror.[2] This was the
period which gave birth to the finest lyric poet of
Persia, and when the great Timūr conquered Fārs and
put Shah Mansūr to death, Hāfiz was in Shīrāz.

It was at this time that he was ordered into the
presence of the new ruler, and severely reproved for
writing such a line as the following:

"For the black mole on thy cheek, I would give the
    cities of Samarcānd and Bokhāra."

Timūr sternly said to the poet, "I have taken
and destroyed, with the keen edge of my sword, the
greatest kingdoms of the earth, to add splendor and
population to the royal cities of my native land,—

1 It is claimed that he used ninety thousand human heads in erecting
pyramids to illustrate his horrible triumph.
2 Timur was also of Mongol origin, and a descendant of Genghis Khan.

Samarcānd and Bokhāra; and yet you would dispose of them both at once for the black mole on the cheek of your beloved."

Instead of being daunted by the sternness of the reproof, Hāfiz calmly replied, "Yes, sire, and it is by such acts of generosity that I am reduced, as you see, to my present state of poverty."

Timūr smiled, and bestowed upon him some splendid marks of the royal favor.

The name of Hāfiz was a *nom de plume*, the poet's true name being Shemsuddin Muhammed; he was born in Shīrāz early in the fourteenth century, and it was here that he died at an advanced age. He was a student from his childhood, but his especial talent was the gift of song. His style is clear, his imagery harmonious, and his work had a certain fascination of its own to the poetry-loving Persians, who are still charmed with the peculiar accent of his musical rhythm, and the flights of his vivid imagination. He was invited to make his home with the reigning Sultan, but he preferred to live in retirement, enjoying the society of friends and scholars, to the splendor and insecurity of court life.

Hāfiz was also invited to the court of one of the Indian princes, at a time when many poets of Persia and Arabia found favor with a literary king, and this courtesy he intended to accept, as the monarch sent a liberal amount of money with the invitation to present himself at the royal abode. The poet gave a portion of the money to his creditors, and supplied the needs of his sister's children, before he started out upon his journey. When he had crossed the Indus and traveled as far as Lahore, he met a friend who was in great distress, having been robbed by banditti, and to him he gave all his means without considering his own needs. But fortunately he soon met two Persian merchants, who were returning from Hindūstān, and who proposed to pay his expenses for the pleasure of his company. They journeyed together to the Persian Gulf, and he even went with them on board the ship that was to bear them away, but before the anchor was weighed a terrible storm arose, and the poet turned his back upon his friends, and returned home.

Before leaving the shore, he sent on board the ship an apology to his friends, and this was couched in graceful verse, but it was to the effect that at first the horrors of the sea seemed light in consideration of the pearls which it contained, but the terror of the storm had taught him that "the infliction of one of its waves would not be compensated for by an hundred-weight of gold."

PĪR-I-SEBZ.

There is a legend connected with his youth which is supposed to explain his wondrous gift of poesy. Tradition claimed that the youth who should pass forty successive nights at Pīr-i-sebz without sleep, would become a great poet. Young Hāfiz therefore made a vow, that he would fulfill the conditions with the utmost exactness. For thirty-nine days he went faithfully to his post, walking every morning by the home of the girl he loved, and on the fortieth morning she called him in, but he re-

membered his vow and the evening found him again
at the place of his lonely vigil.

The uneventful night passed slowly away, and the
gray dawn began to tint the distant mountain tops,
but no other light was visible save the gleam of the
morning star, when the watcher saw in the distance
a figure approaching him. It was a venerable man
wearing a green mantle,[1] and his white beard flowed
down upon his garments like a cascade of silver. He
bore in his hand a cup, filled with the nectar of immortality, and the reverent youth bent low before the
genius of the mountain, and then drank eagerly of
the proffered cup; therefore he still lives in the
memory of man.

He was loyal to his native land, and the following
lines indicate his strong attachment to the city of his
birth.

SHÍRÁZ.

" May every blessing be the lot
    Of fair Shíráz, earth's loveliest spot.
    Oh Heaven! bid Time its beauties spare,
    Nor print his wasteful traces there.

Still be thou blest of him that gave
    Thy stream, sweet Ruknabad, whose wave
    Can every human ill assuage,
    And life prolong to Khizer's age.

And oh the gale that wings its way
    Twixt Jaffrabad and Mosalay;

---

1 Khizer was the prophet who, according to Oriental tradition, discovered and drank of the Fountain of Life, and it was he who bore the nectar
to the waiting poet.

How sweet a perfume does it bear!
How grateful is its amber air!

Ye who mysterious joys would taste,
Come to this sacred city—haste;
Its saints, its sages seek to know,
Whose breasts with heavenly rapture glow.

And say, sweet gale—for thou canst tell—
With lovely Lailī was it well,
When last you passed the maiden by,
Of wayward will and witching eye?

Why, Hāfiz, when you feared the day
That tore you from her arms away,
Oh why so thankless for the hours
You passed in Lailī's lovely bowers?"

In his youth Hāfiz sang freely of love and wine,
and his verse upon these themes too often betrayed a
coarse sentiment, for it seems impossible for some bards
to appreciate the perfect purity of honest affection. Of
his love songs the following is the best:

THE FEAST OF SPRING.

"My breast is filled with roses,
    My cup is crowned with wine,
And the veil her face discloses—
    The maid I hail as mine.
The monarch, wheresoe'er he be,
    Is but a slave compared to me.

Their glare no torches throwing,
    Shall in our bower be found—
Her eyes, like moonbeams glowing,
    Cast light enough around;

And other odors I can spare
  Who scent the perfume of her hair.

The honey-dew thy charm might borrow
  Thy lip alone to me is sweet;
When thou art absent, faint with sorrow
  I hide me in some lone retreat.
Why talk to me of power or fame?
  What are those idle toys to me?
Why ask the praises of my name,
  My joy, my triumph is in thee.

How blest am I! around me swelling
  The notes of melody arise!
I hold the cup with wine excelling,
  And gaze upon thy radiant eyes,

Oh Hāfiz—never waste thy hours
  Without the cup, the lute, and love
For 'tis the sweetest time of flowers
  And none these moments shall reprove.
The nightingales around thee sing
  It is the joyous feast of spring."

As Hāfiz grew older he became attached to the Sufi [1] philosophy, and his poetry contained so many figurative allusions that the Mussulmans called his productions "the language of mystery," others claim that even his most sensual poems are figurative and should be thus interpreted. Of his graver poems the following is the best:

[1] Most of the Asiatic poets are Sufis, and claim to prefer the meditations of mysticism to the pleasures of the world. Their fundamental tenets are that nothing exists, absolutely, except God, and that the human soul is an emanation from his essence, and will finally be restored to him.

MY BIRD.

" My soul is as a sacred bird, the highest heaven its
    nest,
Fretting within its body-bars, it finds on earth its
    nest ;
When rising from its dusty heap this bird of mine
    shall soar   .
'Twill find upon the lofty gate the nest it had be-
    fore.
The Sidrah,[1] shall receive my bird, when it has
    winged its way,
And on the Empyrean's top, my falcon's foot shall
    stay,
Over the ample field of earth is fortune's shadow
    cast,
Where upon wings and pennons borne this bird of
    mine has past.
No spot in the two worlds it owns, above the sphere
    its goal,
Its body from the quarry is, from " No Place " is
    its soul.
'Tis only in the glorious world my bird its splendor
    shows,
The rosy bowers of Paradise its daily food bestows."[2]

The poet's life had been such that the clergy refused
to read the burial service over his body when he died,
his friends, however, obviated the difficulty by stratagem, and it was decided that scattered couplets from
his odes should be placed in a bowl and drawn therefrom by a child, the disposition of the body to be

[1] Sidrah—Tree of Paradise.   [2] Bicknel's Trans.

settled by the sense of the couplet thus drawn out.
The child took out the following distich:

"Withhold not your step from the bier of Hāfiz,
   For, though sunk in sin, he goes to Paradise."

And upon the strength of the evidence thus received the body was given an honorable burial.

FIFTH PERIOD.

The fifth period of her literature, beginning with
the fourteenth century, and ending about the close of
the fifteenth, marks a stationary condition in the Persian world of letters.

The sons and grandsons of Timūr, although at
variance in their political interests, vied with each
other in the encouragement of scholars, and for a time
the literary world retained its brilliancy. Astronomy
as well as history flourished at this period, and great
mathematicians were also in favor with royalty.

JĀMI.

The most distinguished poet of this period was
Nuruddīn Abdurrahman, who very wisely chose the
briefer and more euphonious name of Jāmi. He was
a native of Jām, a small town near Herāt, the capital
of Khorasān, and it was from this circumstance that
he called himself Jāmi, which signifies a drinking
cup, as well as a native of Jām.

It is said that he began his career as a student of
science, and attained great proficiency in his chosen
field of investigation, but wishing to learn the mysteries of the philosophy of the Sufis, he became a pupil of the Shaikh al Islām Saaduddin, and remained

with him until he became a master of the mystic doctrine. On the death of the Shaikh, he succeeded to
his position, and filled it so well that kings and
princes came from distant lands to obtain his advice,
while his home was the resort of scholars, as well as
court officials.

He was not only the most celebrated poet of his
time, but, in the opinion of many, he was superior to
his predecessors, and being also a Doctor of the Mus-
selman law, he was honored by all the princes and
nobles of the age in which he lived.

He was the last great poet and mystic of Persia,
and he seemed to combine the moral tone of Sā'dī,
with the imagination of Jalal-uddin, the ease of
Hāfiz, and the pathos of Nizāmī.

He was a master of the Persian language and a
most prolific author ; Shir Khān Lūdi, in his "Mem-
oirs of the Poets," claims that he was the author of
ninety-nine different works, which continue to be admired in all parts of Īrān and Hindūstān.

The enormous expense which has been incurred
in the illumination of fine transcripts of his manuscripts, indicates the high position which his works
still occupy in the literature of the East.

A work entitled "Khorasān in Affliction" was
transcribed at Lahore for the Emperor of Hindūstān,
during the sixteenth century,[1] which represents an ex-
penditure of many thousand dollars. The calligraphy
is the work of a famous scribe, who, on account of his
beautiful penmanship, was called "The Pen of Gold."

Sixteen eminent artists were engaged in the embel-

1 Finished about A. D. 1575.

lishment of this manuscript of one hundred and thirty-four pages ; five were employed upon the illuminations and marginal arabesques; and five upon the finely colored illustrations; there were three engaged upon the hunting scenes and animals, while three others painted the faces in the vignettes and margins.

The leaves of the book are of soft silken Kashmīrian paper, tinted in the softest shades of various harmonious colors. The broad margins are illuminated with chaste designs painted with liquid gold, and no two pages are alike. Some of these designs represent mosaic work, others are in running patterns, and many of them are delineations of field sports, where the simple outlines of gold indicate, with marvelous accuracy, the various forms of animal life. This was placed in the library of Shāh Jehān,[1] with the emperor's autograph, as the gem of his collection, and underneath it is a second autograph of another of the royal descendants of Timūr.

This elaborate manuscript is not only indicative of the great popularity of Jāmi, but it also shows the liberal patronage which existed for all works of art under the princes of the house of Timūr. The grave of Jāmi is at Herāt, where he was laid[2] at the age of eighty-one years, and this illustrious name completes the list of the seven great poets of Persia who have been called "The Persian Pleiades."

THE WORKS OF JĀMI.

Although this author was a voluminous writer, still his most important works may be briefly summarized ;

---

[1] A. D. 1611. [2] A. D. 1430.

there is a book on ethics and education containing anecdotes and fables, written both in prose and verse, after the manner adopted by Sä'-di, and like the Gūlis-tän, it is divided into eight chapters.

One of his books, entitled "Irshad" or "Instruc. tions," was dedicated to a Turkish Sultan—Al Fäteh, "The Conqueror." "The Seven Thrones" is considered by an eminent native critic[1] to combine the most exquisite compositions in the Persian language, except the "Five Poems" of the celebrated Nizämi. The seven gems which are thus alluded to bear the following titles : (1) The Chain of Gold ; (2) Selmän and Absäl ; (3) The Present of the Just ; (4) The Rosary ; (5) The Loves of Laili and Majnūn ; (6) Yūsuf and Zulaikhä ; (7) The Book of Alexander the Great.

The character of Jämi's style may be represented by the following extract from Yūsuf and Zulaikhä, which is a description of the reception of a Persian bride at an Egyptian court :

RECEPTION.

With a drum of gold the bright firmament beat
At morn the signal for night's retreat.
The stars with the night at the coming of day
Broke up their assembly and passed away.
From that drum, gold-scattering, light was shed,
Like a peacock's glorious plumes outspread.

In princely garb the Vizier arrayed,
Placed in her litter the moon-bright maid.
In the van, in the rear, on every side,
He ordered his soldiers about the bride,

And golden umbrellas a soft shade threw
O'er the heads of Zulaikhā's retinue.

The singer's voices rang loud and high,
As the camels moved at the driver's cry,
And the heaven above and below the ground
Echoed afar with the mingled sound.
Glad were the maids of Zulaikhā's train
That their lady was free from sorrow and pain,
And the prince and people rejoiced that she
The idol and queen of his home should be.

THE SIXTH PERIOD.

The sixth period, beginning near the close of the fifteenth century, and extending to about the commencement of the seventeenth, marks a gradual decline in poetry, although history and other literature still attract much attention. The so-called poets of this age are unworthy of notice, but a few good Persian historians made their appearance.

India now began to vie with Persia in the production of great historical works, under the government of the Mongol emperors from Baber downwards. The pantheistic doctrines of the Sufis were doubtless brought into Persia from India, and both the Rāmā-yaṇa and the Mahā-bhārata were translated into Persian by the order of Akbar. This monarch was the most enlightened sovereign that ever reigned on the throne of India. He was the patron, not only of learning and art, but he also richly rewarded the calligraphers and other artists that he employed to copy and illustrate Persian manuscripts. This illustrious patron of Persian literature was a descendant of Timūr, and therefore belonged to the race of Mongol emperors, usually styled the "Great Moguls." The history of his own times was provided for by the appointment of forty-four historians, ten of whom were on duty each day to record every event as it occurred. By Akbar's order the "History of a Thousand Years" was composed, several authors being engaged upon it, each one having a certain number of years assigned to him. A society for literary composition had thus been organized in India about two hundred years before that of Guthrie and Grey had been established in England.

THE SEVENTH PERIOD.

The seventh period, beginning near the close of the sixteenth century and continuing until about the end of the eighteenth, shows a marked decline in Persian literature. With Shāh Akbar[1] and Shāh Abbas,[2] who occupied respectively the thrones of India and of Persia, the brilliancy of Persian literature, and especially of her poetry, entirely disappeared. During this period no poet has arisen above mediocrity, and no historian has appeared who could be compared with his predecessors. The successors of Akbar, it is true, left contributions to the history at their time, and a valuable dictionary of the Persian language was compiled from forty similar works, but in lieu of poetry and history, letter-writing began to flourish in both India and Persia. Elegant calligraphy was now carried to an extreme, and a vast amount of time and labor were expended upon private as well as official letters. The state secretaries vied with each

[1] A. D. 1556—1605.   [2] A. D. 1585—1628.

other in the production of elaborate credentials for their ambassadors, and generally men of education who were well read in the best Persian poets, and able to recite their best passages, when occasion permitted, were selected for ambassadors.

From the time of Nadīr Shāh up to the present, Persia has suffered many revolutions, wars and famines, and although they could not destroy the admiration still bestowed upon their great poets, the genius of the race appears to have become extinct. The poetry of the eighteenth century is of little value, and the dominant spirit of the nineteenth is pure mysticism, as embodied in the doctrines of the Sufis.

Nations, as well as individuals, have their periods of mental growth and decay, and when once fallen they seldom rise again. History, however, has some splendid exceptions to this rule, and Persia has had three successive periods of intellectual prosperity,— three times has the national spirit awakened as from a torpor, and for a season it has gleamed like a star in the Orient, but three times it has either died out, or been crushed beneath the storm of conquest.

Elated with their success under the brilliant leadership of Cyrus, a change which was almost fatal took place in Persian character, between his reign and that of Darius. Thus his own people proved the truth of the warning words of Cyrus, to the effect that "the effeminate clime produces effeminate inhabitants, nor can the same soil produce excellent fruits and men who are valiant in war."[1] Under the Sassanian kings, however, the national spirit revived,

1 Herodotus IX.

and the literature of Persia sprang to life, only to be trampled beneath the foot of the Arabian invader. Toward the close of the ninth century her world of letters again revived and flourished in various forms during the six periods which have been previously discussed.

Henceforth she has a national literature, with its own peculiar faults as well as beauties, even though her best works belong to her past. No poetry has ever been more peculiarly national than that of Persia, for three centuries her lyre has been virtually silent, and yet her people cherish with peculiar fondness the memory of her poets. The finest odes of Ḥāfiz and the most beautiful passages of her Shāh Nāmah still live, even in the memory of her peasants; and the sorrows of Lailī and Majnūn will be chanted by Persian and Arab as long as the sons of the desert are found amidst the roses of Īrān.

CHAPTER XVII.

MEHER AND MŪSHTERI.

PERSIAN ROMANCE—THE TWO COMRADES—THE SEP-
ARATION—THE QUEEN—THE DEPARTURE—THE AN-
NOUNCEMENT.

PERSIAN romance, as well as Persian poetry, is
burdened with florid description, and the redun-
dancy of style which is everywhere found in the
works of even their best authors makes them tedious
to the reader. In these books of Oriental romance,
it often happens that a new story is begun before
the first is finished, being introduced as a narrative
by one of the characters, and the second is in turn
interrupted by a third, when the author apparently
forgets to finish any one of his fables except the last.
Whole volumes are constructed in this way, legends
being repeated as often by a bird or an animal as
by men and women. Story-telling was esteemed a
great accomplishment in the East, and those who excelled in the art were favorites at court as well as in
other grades of society. It sometimes happened that
a victim who had been selected for capital punishment, either deservedly or otherwise, could save his
life if he could find an opportunity of telling a pleasing tale to some official, who would bear the news
of his ability to the king. Royalty considered this

an easy method of entertainment, and the members
of the harem as well as the princes of the courts
were often favored in this way. It sometimes happened that a favorite of the king owed her position
in the affection of his majesty to the fact that she
could entertain him for hours together with pleasing
myths of her own composition.

In the life of Bāhram Gor, the poet prince, his
seven wives are represented as competing with each
other for the royal favor by weaving various romances
for his amusement. But amidst all the literary rubbish
which is thus formulated for the public eye, there is
an occasional gem which is well worthy of preservation. One of these is an affecting story of fraternal
love which was written by Assar, an author of much
ability, although the Persian chronicles have preserved
but little concerning his life. The story of Meher and
Mūshteri is considered the masterpiece of Persian romance, and as it is deservedly a favorite with the
literati of the East, we give a brief outline of the story,
which in the original fills a superb manuscript of four
hundred and thirty-four pages. It is transcribed in
beautiful Nastaalik characters, within lines of red,
blue, and gold, on paper which is richly powdered with
gold. The double title page is also richly ornamented,
and the heads of the chapters are illuminated in four
colors, while the text is illustrated with miniature
paintings.[1] The plot, the characters and the incidents
are of Persian origin; the author has chosen, however,
to tell the story in simpler form and briefer phrase
than any Persian writer would present it.

1 Ousley, Biog. Pers. Poets, p. 202.

THE TWO COMRADES.

Far from the dangerous boundaries, which were repeatedly crossed and recrossed by invading kings, stood the beautiful city of Persepolis. Amidst the mountains of Persia, the foundations of her palaces were laid upon the solid rock, and the gray marble pillars reached upward to hold cornice and roof above the gilded galleries.

Within were tesselated floors, and fountains whose silvery spray was perfumed with the costly odors of the East.

The walls were hung with pictured annals of earlier thrones, and draped with the richest tapestries of Persian looms, while silver urns gleamed here and there, bearing fragrant fires fed with costly sandal wood, or the spicy rods from more distant lands.

Beside this marble city there flowed the river Pulwâr. Springing from the dark mountains in the distance, it came down to water the gardens of kings; the sunlight tinted its waves with gold, the blossoms opened their velvet hearts upon its banks, and rich odors were wafted from clusters of pink and purple.

The gray mountains stood like guardian kings above the capital city, wearing crowns of snow and the heavy forest grew around their feet.

Here were gathered the treasures of Persia, the crown jewels, and the imperial regalia, besides other wealth in goodly store; but the conquering troops of Alexander marched upon the mountain city, her store-houses were plundered, her palaces were destroyed, and her people massacred by the ruthless invader.

It was afterward rebuilt, and, under the name of Ístaker, it became the capital of Shapur, the Sassanian king, who reigned with justice over his great domain. He was blessed with a Vizīr, who was not only wise and just, but also most loyal to his king; there was no service that he would not gladly perform and by his wisdom and discretion he was enabled to greatly lighten the responsibilities of royalty.

For a long time neither the king nor his faithful Vizīr were blessed with children, but after a time a son was born to the royal house, and while the songs of joy and shouts of congratulation were still ringing through the land, a child was given to the grand Vizīr.

The young heir of the Persian throne was named Meher (the sun), while the son of the Vizīr was called Mūshteri, or Jupiter. So intimate were the relations between the monarch and his principal officer, that the two beautiful children were brought up almost together; they saw each other daily, even during their early chidhood, and when it was time to educate them they were taught by the same masters. They learned to ride, to bear arms, and a little later in life they entered upon the study of the sciences together. A strong attachment sprung up between them, and long before they reached the age of manhood, they were united to each other by a bond as strong as that of fraternal love; there was no feeling of superiority on the one hand, no shade of envy on the other, but hand in hand with each other, life seemed one long dream of happiness.

There was one official, however, of the king's house-

hold, who looked with disfavor upon this growing inti-
macy, for in time the young heir would wear the
crown of Persia, and then, unless their friendship
could be destroyed, the playmate of his childhood
would surely occupy the highest position within the
gift of the king. The politic father at last succeeded
in having his own son Behrâm appointed as the
attendant of the prince, and the son, who was fully
in sympathy with his father's evil designs, became a
spy upon the conduct of his master. The innocent
boys worked or played together in their happy friendship, all unconscious of the schemes of their enemies;
but at last the father of Behrâm succeeded in persuad-
ing the tutor of the boys, that Mūshteri was not a
proper associate for the heir of the throne. The tutor
was a kind and benevolent man, but he was somewhat
advanced in years, and the testimony of Behrâm was
so strong and so carefully prepared that he innocently
fell into the bold conspiracy, and when requested to
do so he informed the king that the son of the Grand
Vizīr was not a suitable companion for the prince.

THE SEPARATION.

The monarch was greatly excited by the advice of
the tutor, and the conspirators took good care that
other reports should be borne to his ears at the proper
time, so at last he sent for his faithful Vizīr and angrily commanded him to remove his son at once, and
to see that no further communication took place between the two youths.

The Vizīr took steps to enforce the unreasonable
decree, but he was sorely grieved, both by the evident

cruelty of the command and the unusual severity of the monarch, who for years had been, not only his king, but also his warm personal friend. The tutor was ordered to attend the prince in his own chambers, but the unhappy boy was in no mood for study, and the work that had given him pleasure when his friend was by his side became so irksome that the old tutor despaired of any success in his efforts.

Mūshteri bore up bravely for a time in his cruel banishment, but at last he drooped beneath his long suffering and fell seriously ill. He had a faithful attendant, a boy named Bader, who volunteered to bring to his master some tidings from his friend, and to this end he bribed the tutor to allow him to visit him while he was instructing the prince.

He thus obtained access to the apartments of Meher, but Behrūm, the ever watchful and envious attendant, was constantly on the alert, and for a long time there was no opportunity for Bader to communicate in any way with the prince. At last, however, Meher succeeded in writing to his friend, and confided the letter to the care of Bader; an occasional correspondence was thus carried on until Behrām obtained one of the letters, which he hastened to lay before the king.

Finding that his express commands were being disobeyed, the anger of the Shāh knew no bounds, and sending for Mūshteri and his faithful attendant he ordered them both to be executed in the royal presence. Meher was also brought into the presence of his indignant father, and after being bitterly reproached for his love for his friend, the command was given that he too should be executed. A thrill of horror

ran through the suite of attendants when they heard
this inhuman decree, and Behzâd, who was a nephew
of the king, threw himself at the feet of the monarch
and pleaded for mercy for the victims; his plea was
treated with scorn, and for a time it looked as if the
intercessor might share in the fate of the condemned.
But the brave boy was undaunted by the royal displeasure, and continued to plead, even while he was
answered by threats, until at last the king consented
to pardon Mûshteri and Bader upon condition that
they leave the kingdom at once and forever, while the
punishment of the prince was commuted to imprisonment. Still it was feared that the king might even
yet order the culprits beheaded, and Behzâd hastily
supplied them with wardrobes, money and horses, ad-
vising them to make all possible haste in leaving the
Shâh's dominions.

The Vizîr was tenderly attached to the prince, and
knowing that he was imprisoned and constantly in the
power of a father whose whole nature had been changed
by evil associations, he grieved as much for him as
for his own banished boy; he grieved, too, over the
estrangement which bad influences had been able to
effect in the heart of his royal friend towards himself,
and being advanced in years, his health gradually
failed beneath the weight of care and suffering.

One day the news was brought to the palace that
the faithful Vizîr was dead, but so completely was the
king in the power of his evil counsellors that he
scarcely seemed to care for a loss which would have
caused him the greatest pain when his mind was in
a normal condition. The faithful Behzâd was untir-

ing in his efforts for the release of the prince, and
the king found also that the mother of the captive
was very far from approving of the course of her
husband, even though she said very little upon the
subject, and after a time he was released. Finding
himself again at liberty, the prince paid no attention
to his royal father, but he went where his heart told
him that he should find a warm welcome—to the
apartments of his mother.

THE QUEEN.

The dark-eyed queen sat alone in her splendid
rooms, for she had sent her maids away. Around her
was all the beauty and luxury that art could furnish
or money could purchase; the ceilings of her apartments were wrought in the richest mosiacs, and the
walls sparkled with designs which seemed to be traced
with diamonds.[1]

The rooms were draped with the richest portiéres
of Kermän, and the pure white centres were surrounded with heavy borders, where the soft colors were
blended in floral design ; behind those Persian hangings were vases of silver and gold where burned the
costly gums from Thibet, filling the air with the fragrance of incense.

The great windows opened into gardens where the
citrons and rose-apples kept their bright blossoms and

[1] A very popular style of decoration in Persia is the kainah-karree ;
while the plaster is yet soft, the surface is inlaid with minute mirrors of
every conceivable shape. The amount of work and skill necessary to inlay
a room in this style is almost incalculable, and although the materials are
comparatively cheap, the immense amount of labor required make the
work very expensive. The effect, however, is one of bewildering splendor
as if the light were flashed from the polished facets of millions of gems.—
Benjamin, Persia and Persians, p. 279.

gleaming fruits, and the broad leaved bananas waved
their silken flags in the sunlight. There were fountains where jets of water, smooth and unbroken, gleamed
like silver in the sunshine, and in the marble basins
below them the birds dipped their wings in the cooling
wave, and the bulbul sang of mornings without clouds.

But amidst all the splendor which surrounded her,
the eyes of the queen were heavy with unshed tears;
there were no flowers in her dark hair, no jewels
upon her shapely neck, for her heart was with her
lonely boy in his prison cell, and all her womanhood
rebelled against the cruelty of the Shāh. He who
had been so kind, so just, so loving in his home, had
yielded himself so completely to the influence of his
evil advisers that his whole character seemed transformed. He was no longer gentle, patient and loving,
even to his wife ; he was selfish and irritable, being
possibly troubled with some pangs of conscience, although he was a man of such intense egotism that he
usually looked upon his own conduct with the utmost
complacency.

A gentle knock disturbed the sad reverie of the
queen, and in a moment more her boy was in her
arms ; in her splendid isolation she had not learned
of his release, and the welcome that she gave him
showed that he had not been mistaken in the unfailing strength of mother-love. Long they remained together, talking softly of the happy past and the future with its threatening clouds ; the boy dared not
stay within reach of the unreasonable father, who was
liable at any moment to throw him into prison, or
hasten him away to the executioner, and he was also

anxious for the fate of the loyal friend who had suffered banishment for his sake. He was determined
therefore to leave the Shāh's dominions, and he had
come to his mother for her consent and her blessing.

It was a sad trial to the queen, but true love is
ever self-sacrificing, and she could not ask him to stay
in constant danger, preferring rather that he should
risk the unknown perils of a strange land.

Another difficulty, however, presented itself. Meher
had no money, his allowance having been cut off at
the beginning of the trouble with his father, and the
queen was no better supplied, for the women of the
East were not supposed to have judgment enough to
handle anything more than the very small amounts
required for the purchase of a few trinkets which
were comparatively worthless.

At length, however, the queen arose and went to
a casket of jewels, where rubies and amethysts reflected their color in the light of diamonds whose
purity seemed to mock the sunlight. Taking up in
her shapely hands the glittering mass of stones, she
carried them to her son and begged him to take them
all ; he refused to do so, saying that a very small portion of these radiant gems would amply satisfy his
modest needs. The mother, however, pressed upon him
a goodly share of them, for they would be current in
any clime, and being small in bulk they were easily
carried. Hours were passed in this last interview, for
the mother felt that she might never look into his
loved face again, and she clung to him with a devotion that would not be denied.

At last, however, he was compelled to bid her

adieu, and make his preparations for departure; his own magnificent Arabian steed was standing in the royal stables, besides several other horses which were rightfully his, though they were usually mounted by his attendants. There were also among his friends, three young men whose loyalty he knew that he could depend upon, and to them he hastily communicated his wishes; these Persian youths were not averse to adventure, and an opportunity to see the great world around them, in the company of the prince, was a temptation which they could not resist.

THE DEPARTURE.

Softly the night came over the Persian city, and the moon swung high above the eastern peaks, as the cool air floated down from the mountains and caught the fragrant breath of the night-flowers in the valley. There was the cautious tread of trained horses, for so sensitive were the high-bred steeds that they caught the spirit of their riders as the little cavalcade moved slowly out of the massive gateway. The moonlight touched the river with silver, and all the sleeping land lay hushed in fragrance, while the prince and his three faithful attendants rode slowly down beside the stream and took the road leading to Hindûstân. Thus they journeyed onward in easy stages until they reached the seaside, where merchant-ships were trimming their white sails for long voyages; here they were compelled to sell their horses, and the prince stood long beside his petted steed, stroking the shapely head and arching neck, while the magnificent animal pushed his face closely to that of his

master, and received the caresses with sadness, as if
he too knew that a long separation was coming. The
dark eyes of Meher were heavy with tears as he
bade his faithful horse good bye, and stepped upon
the ship that was to bear him far away from his
home, and far away from the loving mother who wept
alone in her splendid apartments.

THE ANNOUNCEMENT.

In the rich audience room of the Persian palace
the Shāh was seated upon the massive throne, and
robed in royal raiment; he was holding a council
with his high officials, when a messenger was announced who bore news of the greatest importance
to the king. Then he learned that the heir of his
throne had deserted his domain, and was perhaps
even now beyond the reach of pursuit. The anger
of the monarch was so uncontrolled that his court
officials were paralyzed with fear, knowing that any
one of them who spoke an unfortunate word might
be hurried away to the executioner. But his rage
soon gave way to the most heart-rending grief, and
he demanded that he be carried at once to the apartments of his wife. Half fainting and wholly helpless, he was taken through the luxurious halls and
fragrant gardens to the rooms of the queen. Here
he was laid upon the soft couch, rich with its costly
cushions and embroidered hangings; the anger of the
indignant woman was softened by his evident suffering, and she ministered gently to his needs, and listened to his wailings for his only child. His pride
was broken and his vindictiveness conquered, for he

could see only a cruel death for the unfortunate fugitive, who knew so little how to care for himself among the barbarous tribes whither he had doubtless gone.

For many hours he lay thus, and when he returned the next day to the duties of his court, it was only to be approached by the hypocritical Behrām, who was ever on the watch for an opportunity to promote his own interests at the expense of others.

He came into the royal presence affecting the greatest grief for the loss of his young master, and pleaded with the Shāh for an expensive outfit, that he might follow him and bring him back.

"Give me," said he, "a caravan, in order that I may pass for a merchant, and thus travel without suspicion through the country, and I will find my young master or lose my life in the attempt."

"My ever faithful servant," replied the king, "I will give thee camels and money and goods and slaves, and thou shalt follow him even to the far countries beyond my realm; if he is alive thou wilt bring him back, for I know that I can depend upon thy loyalty to thy young master."

Only a few days elapsed before a costly caravan was equipped, and Behrām passed through the gates of the city with a long line of camels laden with rich merchandise, and twenty slaves to do his bidding. He went exulting on his mission, for if he found and returned the fugitive he was sure of a rich reward, while if he failed he had wealth enough in his caravan to enable him to live in affluence in other lands far beyond the power of the Shāh.

CHAPTER XVIII.

MEHER AND MŪSHTERI—CONTINUED.

THE EXILES—THE DESERT—A SHIPWRECK—THE RESCUE
—THE CAPTURE.

MŪSHTERI and his solitary companion passed out of the city by the light of the morning sun on the day after their release, for except a few faithful friends there were none who cared whither the victims of the Shāh's displeasure might go, as long as they obeyed the royal edict.

The sorrowful exiles rode slowly onward, all unmindful of the beauty of the morning, which was gilding with glory the crowns of the palm-trees. They were leaving behind them all that they held most dear, and going forth into the world with no provision for the future, save the little sum that the generous Behzād had been able to provide.

Merely to gratify the unreasonable whim of a royal autocrat, they were thus banished from home and friends, and with hearts full of bitterness they scarcely cared whither they went.

They had taken the road to Isfahān, but before they reached the city they saw in the distance an old gray castle which looked as if it had withstood the storms of centuries, and with half a mind to test the hospitality of the occupants, they reined their horses toward it. The castle gates were opened as if some kindly eye had noted their coming, but a little band of horsemen issued therefrom, and, fearing some unfriendly act, the travelers turned away. Their caution came too late, for in a moment more they were attacked and overpowered by the banditti, and being bound they were carried captive to the castle where they had hoped for a kindly reception.

Here they were robbed of every article of value upon their persons, and an order was issued for their execution ; but behind the Persian hangings of the castle hall there were white hands moving nervously amidst the rich colors of silken embroidery, and a woman's heart listened breathlessly to the cruel death sentence.

Then the beautiful wife of the chief went to her room, and sent a messenger into the council of the banditti with an urgent summons for the presence of her lord.

"How canst thou be so cruel ?" she demanded with flashing eyes, "hast thou not robbed these ill-fated youths of every jewel upon their persons—nay hast thou not even taken the most costly articles from their wardrobes ? Why shouldst thou add to thy guilt the crime of murder ?" Half ashamed of his cruel decree, and wholly afraid of forfeiting the respect of his wife, the chieftain promised to commute their punishment, and hastily returning to the castle hall he demanded that the captives be taken to the desert and abandoned without food amidst its pitiless sands.

THE DESERT.

And thus it happened that Mûshteri and his faithful Bader found themselves alone and destitute in a desert where no caravans might pass for many months —where no palm-tree lifted its plumes in the distance, to tell of the spring in the oasis beneath its feet. The evening was cool and restful, even in the desert, and the exiles slept, for their lives were spared, and though their chance was small, it was surely better than certain death.

But the sun arose as if in anger, and as it climbed higher and higher the air became hot as that crimson haze, by which the prostrate caravan is often buried in the red desert, when the simoon is abroad on its mission of death. They wandered hopelessly, looking in vain for some sign of an oasis, until overpowered by the intense heat, Mûshteri, still weak from recent illness, fell upon the burning sand. Then Bader bent above him, trying to shield him from the pitiless sun as far as possible, by the shelter of his own body, and thus they remained until night came down again with its cooling shadows. They passed day after day in terrible suffering, until all hope of relief had fled, and they awaited the coming of death with hope rather than fear.

The faithful Bader was no longer able to shield his master with his own body, but lay helpless by his side, when the sun again came forth from the chambers of the east and began to beat upon them with apparently redoubled fury; but the boy raised his head to search once more the fiery horizon, and in the distance he seemed to see the figure of a camel. He

wondered if the delirium of death was cheating him
with a hope of deliverance, and he gazed until another seemed to appear behind the first; then he
aroused Mŭshteri by telling him of his great hope,
and together they watched what seemed to be the
slow coming of a caravan. After a time a long line
of camels could be seen moving patiently and wear-
ily over the heated sands, but they were not coming
directly toward the exiles, and unless they could
change their position considerably, the caravan must
pass them far to the southward. With an effort they
struggled to their feet, and Bader, who was still the
stronger, partially supported Mŭshteri, while they
slowly and painfully traveled toward the line of the
caravan's march. They could now see that the camels were laden, apparently with goods, and it was
probably some merchant's expedition returning from
a long journey.

They tried to call attention by waving their hands,
but their efforts remained unnoticed, and Mŭshteri
sank once more with exhaustion. Bader could now
see no hope of deliverance, but the master insisted
that his attendant should push onward, leaving him
to be rescued when the caravan had been reached;
reluctantly he did so, and Mŭshteri anxiously watched
his friend as he slowly approached the line of march,
trying with frantic gesture to attract their attention.
Would he succeed, or must they die within the very
sight of aid? At last the foremost camel turned his
head, and courage revived the efforts of the man who
was struggling toward him, while hope lighted the
heart of the faint watcher upon the desert sands; but

the camel turned away again and with long swinging step resumed his way to the southward—nay, he seemed to lengthen and quicken his pace, while his head pointed straight towards the horizon as if the wide nostrils were drinking in the welcome smell of water. A cloud had been gathering in the west, and when it floated over the blazing sun the soft shades of gray brought relief to the strained eye and a passing shelter from the fierceness of the heat. It seemed to give new life to Bader, and he struggled on with renewed hope, passing slowly over the long reaches of sand which were sometimes smooth as the beaten beach, and again were heaped together in long ridges like the drifted snow of a northern clime.

At last a driver turned his head, and fancied that he saw a dark object upon the pathless tract; he looked again, thinking there were signs of life, then he called to his companion, and the two drivers gazed until they were sure it was a man upon the desert waste; a halt was called, and then the course of the caravan was slightly changed, and the line bore down toward Bader. He was sure it was coming, and the reaction was so strong upon his exhausted frame that he fainted before it reached him, but onward came the great camels careening like ships on the sea of sand, swinging forward with long elastic tread; noiselessly they came, keeping the line so exactly that they all seemed to step in the very tracks of the leader. The exhausted man was taken up and a gurglet of skin containing water was brought from their stores, when the kindly leader sponged the face and hands of the exile; a little of the precious water was forced down his throat and then nature caught eagerly at the great restorative and he drank of the life-giving fluid.

The owner of the caravan was Mohiär, a Persian merchant, and he quickly ordered food for the sufferer; out of the strange baskets, closely woven from the fibers of the palm, they took dates and Syrian pomegranates, wine in gurglets of skin, and meats which were dried and smoked, but Bader, being unable to eat or to speak, was placed in a cot suspended by the side of a camel, and the caravan made ready to depart.

They had traveled a little way before the agonized man was enabled to tell them that his friend lay dying on the desert sands; then the line was turned again, and soon Müshteri heard the tinkling bells fastened to the brazen chains of the camels; soon he saw their long slender necks and the scarlet fringe upon the bridle across their foreheads; he saw them, but in a dazed, indifferent way, as if it mattered little to him whence they came or whither they went. But in a moment more he was raised in strong arms, and water, life-giving water, passed over his face and was poured down his swollen throat. They were soon able to taste of refreshing fruits, and then the caravan moved on its course, carrying the exiles upon restful cushions, while above them was stretched a kindly shade. That night they rested beside a cool spring and beneath the trees of an oasis; the generous Mohiär ordered a stay of a few days at the feet of the cooling palms that his own men, and especially the weakened exiles, might become refreshed.

They were then taken beyond the desert boundaries and generously entertained at the city of their host.

A SHIPWRECK.

Although in the care of hospitable friends they were still in the dominions of the Shāh, and liable at any moment to be apprehended and punished; therefore as soon as they were strong enough their host provided them with a little money, and with his own horses carried them down to the shores of the Caspian Sea, where a ship was standing in port, ready to start on a trading voyage to other lands.

Fearful of losing this opportunity they had traveled all the latter part of the night, and they stepped upon the deck of the merchant-ship in the early morning. After they had bidden their friends farewell, Mūshteri turned thoughtfully toward the soft green waves beyond him and said to his friend: "Surely here is a welcome change from the desert waste; the cooling breath of the water has a caressing touch, and the morning light is strewing the sea with opals."

"Ah, yes!" replied Bader, "the sea hath no perils like the desert heat,—better the cooling wave, even though it wraps our dying limbs than the hot breath of the simoon, and a terrible death amidst the bleaching bones of perished caravans."

Soon the order was given to raise the anchor, and with a merry shout the sailors sprang to their task; the ship drifted outward, slowly at first, and then as her sails caught the welcome breeze she sped over the waves like a thing of life.

The exiles felt that they were at last beyond the reach of the unreasonable monarch, beyond the reach of the Persian banditti, and far from the torrents of burning sand rolling before the desert winds, and they looked into each other's eyes with renewed hope and gratitude. Day after day passed by in restful calm, but the water itself was an ever-changing picture to the loving eye of Mūshteri; the early morning found him always on the deck watching the waves and listening to the changing voices of the sea.

One night he sat alone at his favorite post, even the faithful Bader had grown weary and gone to his nightly rest, but Mūshteri was watching the evening star, that seemed to lie cool and dim in the moving water; the young moon was swinging high in the heavens, while her faint light touched the waves with silver and gleamed on the white wings of the night-birds. But a quick wind caught the sail and a cloud swept over the face of the moon, the sailors sprang to their posts and orders were hastily given. A storm was gathering in the eastern sky and soon the sails were reefed and the good ship was placed in readiness to ride out as best she could the coming peril,

The Persian youth had no thought now of leaving his post; if the sea had been beautiful in her peaceful sleep, how much grander was the picture when the storm-spirit swept her waves into a fury,—when the wind smote the rigging like the edge of a hissing spear and the breakers dashed angrily against the hull. As the danger grew more imminent he went below and aroused Bader, but even while they were coming on the deck he perceived that the storm was increasing in fury and the gale was driving the help-less ship before it.

They were at the mercy of the blast, and soon a fearful shock told the story of the good ship's doom: she had struck a rocky coast and rapidly her timbers parted. The two exiles were thrown together into the water, but after a few minutes of struggling and swimming, Mūshteri caught a floating beam and at last succeeded in getting himself and Bader to this position of temporary safety. The storm still raged, but they clung to this their only hope of life, while the greater part of the passengers and crew were drowned around them.

At last the tempest had exhausted its fury; the winds moaned over the angry billows and the sorrowing sea-birds wept; the morning star gleamed behind the passing clouds, but it looked upon a scene of desolation. After striking the coast the ship had floated back in fragments, while here and there a human being clung to a portion of the wreck, but they were now too far from the shore to be able to reach it, and there was little hope that they would be seen and rescued. All day they tossed upon the waves—all day they looked anxiously for aid, but night came down without hope, and another morning found them still at the mercy of the waters. A beautiful land covered with stately trees lay like a mirage in the distance, but no friendly wave carried them to the shore.

THE RESCUE.

The king of Derbend was hunting on the coast, and the wild gor that he was pursuing ran close to

the water's edge, where he received the fatal arrow
before the king's suite had overtaken the royal rider.
While the monarch waited the coming of his attendants he rested beneath a tree and looked out upon
the waste of waters; there he saw fragments of the
wreck, and looking more closely he fancied there
were human beings beyond. When his suite came up
he ordered a boat to be manned, and soon the victims of the storm were gathered upon his hospitable
shore; they were chilled, exhausted, and some of
them died even there beneath the friendly hands that
strove to bring the life-tide back.

Mūshteri and his friend were among the survivors
and they became the guests of the generous king,
who soon learned their story and took them to his
palace home not far from the shore.

Their way lay through the low lands, where the
tall bamboos bristled like spears in the battle ranks,
but afterward the road was shaded with green-plumed
dates and bel-trees, gorgeous with their crimson blossoms. The palace itself was placed in gardens where
the blossoms hung in silvery sprays on the mango-
trees, and the many colored fountains played like
broken rainbows in marble basins. Within those
royal courts it was a maze of light and loveliness;
music from pipe and lute was borne through the cool
casement, and beautiful dancing girls seemed to float
through the soft measures. In the whirl of these
graceful motions one could see rings and pearls and
emeralds shining everywhere, while round the white
necks of the dancers hung necklaces of diamonds that
glowed like fire in the light of many lamps.

Such was the scene that greeted the eyes of the exiles when, after being provided with food and raiment, they were ushered into the home of their newly-found friend, and the air of rest and luxury was most grateful to the exhausted travelers.

Long they tarried· as the guests of their royal host, but the heart of Mūshteri was never at rest; he grieved for his lost friend, and not even the luxuries of a court could in any way atone for his absence. Grateful for the kindness of the king, he was still wasting away in very grief for the companion of his childhood; Bader sought in vain to cheer him, to divert his thoughts with the luxury everywhere around him, but Mūshteri was ever haunted by a conviction that somewhere, at sometime, the happy companionship would be renewed, and he seemed to live only in this great hope.

Persian traders were sometimes found even in the dominions of the king of Derbend, and when the news came to the court that the heir of the Persian throne had deserted his inheritance, Mūshteri determined to either find his friend or lose his life in the attempt.

No offer of the kindly king could tempt him to remain longer in idle luxury, and, still accompanied by the faithful Bader, he set out to cross the great mountain range that seemed to separate him from the rest of the world. Day after day they toiled over the rugged heights, and night after night they slept beside the sheltering rock; at last they had passed the summit, but the descent on the other side was scarcely less difficult and dangerous.

After a time however, they reached the beautiful valley lying at the foot of the range, and then it seemed that their toil was abundantly rewarded, for here were trees laden with fruit, and vines, which were burdened with clusters of gold and purple. Here were mango-trees and orange blossoms, while the river that flowed beside them seemed fragrant with the breath of her newly blown lilies.

Wearied with their long and tiresome journey, they made their simple couch in the shade of a great tree, and lay down to find refreshing slumber.

THE CAPTURE.

When the cool and malicious Behrâm left the dominions of the Persian king, not only supplied with money but also in possession of a rich caravan, he cared very little whether or not he ever found the fugitive prince; but he determined to find a safe retreat for himself, where he could enjoy his ill-gotten gains, far from the hope of successful pursuit by the agents of the Shâh. He therefore pursued his way by a safe route and easy stages to a distant province.

His caravan encamped for the night a few miles out of the city of Khârizm; the heavy loads of merchandise were removed from the backs of the camels, and food was taken from the baskets of palm leaves, but finding the water of the river near them was somewhat foul, Behrâm sent two slaves nearer to the fountain head of the stream for a supply. They walked slowly toward the foot of the mountain, where the stream gushed in a silvery torrent from the rocks, and soon they were in the beautiful valley of

fruits and flowers, where Mūshteri and his faithful
attendant had found repose. They gazed for a few
moments upon the lovely scene, and quickly decided
that if their master would consent to remove the
camp, this would be a more desirable locality, as
there was not only an abundance of pure water but
also a bountiful supply of fruits. As they were turning however to go back, after having filled their
leathern gurglets with water, one of them saw two
men under a tree apparently asleep ; fearing that they
might be in the vicinity of a powerful foe, they approached cautiously to learn at least the nationality
of their new neighbors. The wearied sleepers remained
unconscious of their careful approach and after a time
they came nearer ; they had already discovered the men
were Persians, and a closer scrutiny convinced them
that the faces which they looked upon were none
other than those of Mūshteri and Bader.

Hastening back to their master with this information, their message was received with incredulity, but
nevertheless, Behrām made haste to go into the valley with eight of his strongest slaves, while the others
remained with the camels and merchandise. When
he saw that Mūshteri and Bader were really lying before him, his malignant eyes flashed with triumphant
malice, and quickly giving a whispered order, the
young exiles were partially bound, even before they
wakened.

Being aroused by the handling of their captors,
they found themselves utterly helpless in the power of
their most dreaded foe, but even in this condition
they scorned to ask for mercy which they knew would

be denied them.   Behrâm ordered a slave to go back
to the old encampment with the message that the
camels and goods should be brought to the newly
chosen ground, and when the campfires were lighted,
the camels fed, and the wants of both master and
slaves provided for, the beautiful valley witnessed a
cruel scene.

CHAPTER XIX.

MEHER AND MŪSHTERI—CONTINUED.

THE FUGITIVES—ROYAL INTERVIEWS—THE CONFLICT—
A GARDEN SCENE—AFTERWARDS—THE DECISION.

IT was a ship belonging to a distant province
that carried the Persian prince beyond the reach
of the angry Shāh, and after a long trading voyage,
during which they battled with angry seas and perilous
rocks, they landed upon the friendly coast.

The commander was also a merchant, and he bore
the name of Sherf; he had become greatly attached
to the prince during the weeks they had spent
together, even though he knew not of his royal rank,
for Meher had given strict orders to his attendants
that no hint of his identity should be given; he was
known, therefore, simply as a Persian youth, who,
with his companions, had chosen to seek his fortune
in travel.

On his arrival in port the merchant sold his ship,
and fitting out a large caravan he made ready for the
journey to his native city. He warmly urged the
prince and his friends to join his party, and Meher
consented to do so, not only because of the greater
safety thus afforded, but also because he disliked to be
separated from his newly found friend.

The known wealth of the merchant caravan, however, was a source of danger, as the country was

infested with banditti, and they were only three days'
journey from the coast when a night attack was made
upon the encampment; the men were hastily awakened
by the guard; but in the confusion of the darkness
the well-planned assault proved only too successful, and
with one daring raid much valuable merchandise was
seized, and several men left in a wounded and dying
condition. Meher sprang to his horse, and calling to
his attendants to follow, he rode away in bold pursuit
of the banditti, who were only a few minutes ahead
of him; his horse was in good condition, and the rider
well trained, but the banditti knew every inch of the
ground which was new to their pursuers, and they
were thus enabled to pursue a circuitous path which,
for a time, baffled them.

After a long chase in the darkness, however, they
were overtaken, and a desperate struggle ensued.
Meher had been followed, not only by his own attendants, but a few of the more daring among the servants
of Sherf had also answered to his call. The banditti
were armed only with arrows and spears, while the
prince and his attendants carried the best Persian fire-
arms, and the men of the caravan were also well
equipped, or would have been, but for the suddenness
of the attack.

The banditti were overpowered, for they had de-
pended largely upon the panic they caused for an opportunity to make their escape in the darkness, and
their quivers were only partially filled with arrows.
The prince had been carefully trained in the use of
his weapons, and his quick and repeated firing brought
man after man to the ground, and though several of

his own party had fallen, he soon had the robbers in his power. He then demanded the stolen property, which was surrendered ; but not satisfied with this, he determined that they should pay more dearly for their baseness, and he required the stolen jewels which he knew must be hidden upon their persons, and also their finest horses. They protested that they had no jewels, but the argument which demanded their treasures or their lives was inexorable, and the pursuers bore away more than double the wealth which had been stolen. The morning dawned before they reached the encampment, and then the prince divided the booty among the servants of Sherf, who had bravely followed him in the hour of peril. The wounded men were carried to the camp, and they received a double share of the spoils.

The owner of the caravan was more than grateful, for he knew that he could never have recovered the property but for the bravery of the gallant strangers.

His admiration for Meher knew no bounds, and when order was again restored and the line of march resumed, he declared that only one woman in the world was worthy to be his wife, and that was the beautiful princess Nahīd, the daughter of the king of Khārizm.

Meher answered that his whole anxiety at present was to find a dearly loved friend, and when that was accomplished perhaps he might think of marriage.

On their arrival at the city, Sherf insisted that Meher and his friends should take up their abode in his own spacious home, and for the time being they consented to do so.

The next day the prince visited the public bath, and his splendid physique won the admiration of all beholders, greatly to the satisfaction of his friend. The merchant, on his return from his long journey, went to the court of King Keiwan, and laid costly gifts at his feet, as was the custom on the completion of a successful expedition. The king was anxious to hear the adventures of the traveler, and listened long to the story of his voyage and wonderful escapes.

The merchant was glad of an opportunity to thus communicate with the king, and always loyal to Meher he related at length the story of the night attack, and the daring pursuit of the Persian youth, who succeeded not only in restoring the property of his host, but also in gaining from the banditti a rich reward for the servants who so bravely responded to his call.

ROYAL INTERVIEWS.

The king was greatly interested in the gallant stranger, and he immediately sent a chamberlain to request his presence at court.

Meher stepped with easy grace into the royal presence and saluted with due courtesy, but there was no fear in his manner, no awkwardness in the salute, and the keen-eyed monarch saw at once that he was accustomed to the presence of royalty, and suspected that he carried noble blood in his veins.

He was most graciously received, and after a long conversation the king presented him with a beautiful horse; delighted with the gift, Meher sprang to the saddle, and rode away like the prince that he was, while the king looked admiringly on.

The next morning he received another invitation to visit the palace, and on this occasion he presented a poem which he had written in honor of the king, when the eloquence of his diction, the music of his rhythm, and the historical knowledge betrayed by his allusions to the past, made his production an object of admiration to the literati of the court. It was customary for those who were presented to make an offering to royalty, and after apologizing for the humble character of his gift, Meher ordered one of his attendants to present to his majesty a little casket which he carried in his hand. With a feeling of curiosity, mingled with a desire to extend an especial favor, Keiwan received the gift in his own hands, and upon opening the casket he was astonished to find richer jewels than any that gleamed in his own treasury. There was one ruby in that little collection, which, on being placed in water, radiated a light which colored the water like the blood of the grape, and the diamonds flashed back the green and purple fire of the emerald and amethyst beside them.

Here was another factor in the problem which was agitating the mind of Keiwan, for unless this youth was of royal birth he must surely belong to some band of robbers who had successfully raided a king's treasury. But with true Oriental reticence he forbore to express his surprise, determined to wait until he could solve the mystery without questions.

Again Meher was summoned to the court and challenged to a game of drafts with a skillful opponent; being successful in this, he was invited to a contest in chess with the best player of the kingdom. The king looked on and saw his young friend checkmate the veteran with six moves. Afterward the monarch sent him a letter requiring an immediate reply at a time when his secretary was known to be absent. The messenger waited a few minutes, and then carried to his royal master a letter which was a model in its literary style as well as in its mechanical execution. Every triumph of this kind raised the Persian youth more highly in the estimation of the king, but he was not yet satisfied, and after a time he was invited to a trial of strength and agility; the contest took place in front of the palace, while the queen and the princess Nahíd looked upon the combatants from behind a screen. Meher rode into the arena upon his white Arabian steed, and never royal rider mounted a more magnificent animal, or rode with more grace and ease; as the horse circled proudly around the arena, his young master shot his arrows through the distant target until the quiver by his side was empty, then he threw the javelin, and in a later contest with spears, he carried off the prize.

Safely hidden behind her costly screen, the beautiful princess watched the contest, and the victor won not only the plaudits of the multitude, but also the heart of Nahíd; the prince rode quietly away, but the princess went to her rooms, with her cheeks flushed and her heart beating with terror. Already offers had been received from foreign courts for her hand, and her father had hesitated only to find a more powerful ally. Full well she knew that, according to the custom of the East, she was liable to be bargained away at any time, without even a question in relation to her own preference, for the Eastern woman is supposed to give her affection wherever policy decides that her hand shall go. At last she went to her faithful nurse, and told the story of her love for the stranger, told her how impossible it would be for her to love any other than the gallant youth who now held her heart in his hands, and declared that she would take her own life if she were compelled to marry another.

The nurse was frightened by her strong emotion, and hastened to the queen with the information; the mother received the message with great agitation, and soon afterward she sought the presence of the king. Long and carefully the subject was considered, for they were both favorably impressed with the stranger, but an alliance of the royal house could not be lightly made, and whatever might be the accomplishments of Meher they were obliged to content themselves with his own representations, for surely there could be no good reason why a man of royal birth should deny his parentage.

No decision was made, but it must be confessed that Meher stood still nearer to their hearts on account of the love which their only daughter bore him. Although a confessed favorite at court, and living in the enjoyment of luxury, the heart of the prince was oppressed with grief and loneliness, for he constantly mourned the absence of his friend, and the fearful uncertainty which hung over his fate.

THE CONFLICT.

A messenger from the king of Samarcănd bore to the court of Keiwan an offer for the hand of the princess, for the fame of her wondrous loveliness had spread through all the neighboring kingdoms. The ambassador came laden with the costliest jewels and the richest brocades of the East as presents for the bride, for there was no thought in the heart of King Kāra Khān that his offer might be refused.

Keiwan had long considered the fading rose on the cheek of his beloved daughter, and more than once he had asked himself if her happiness was not worth as much as an alliance with some neighboring monarch, who was liable to betray his trust whenever it might be considered profitable to do so.

There was a shade of superiority, too, in the manner of the ambassador—an evident feeling that his master was bestowing a high honor that stung the proud spirit of King Keiwan, and he returned an unqualified refusal to the proposition.

This decision was made in opposition to the advice of the Grand Vizir, who dreaded to insult so powerful a prince, but the king refused to reconsider his action, and the ambassador went away in anger.

King Kāra Khān received the message of refusal, first with incredulity, and afterwards with rage; having never seen the girl, he cared nothing for her personally, but his indignation knew no bounds when he learned that his expressed wish had been disregarded.

As the Vizir had feared, the return of the disappointed ambassador was promptly followed by a declaration of war, and soon the Tartar horde was marching directly upon Khārizm.

King Keiwan was almost overcome with dismay

when the news of the invasion was brought to him, for the Tartar chief was not a foe to be despised; the court was in more or less confusion on account of the suddenness of the attack, and in the midst of the general terror, the nurse of Nahīd went to Meher and told him the story of the great love that the princess bore for him, and informed him that it was in deference to this feeling that the king had refused to give his daughter to the king of Samarcānd.

Feeling that he was the unfortunate cause of the attack upon his royal friend, the prince went to the king and offered to withstand the foe with five hundred chosen men. Although the offer was refused, being looked upon as a useless sacrifice, Meher and his friends insisted that they should be allowed the privilege of joining the army which marched out to repulse the attack of the Tartars.

Soon the wild horde of mountaineers bore down upon the Khārizmians, and it could be seen that the attacking force greatly outnumbered them, but the troops of Keiwan stood bravely at their post and sent their death-dealing arrows into the ranks of the foe.

The Tartar chief clad in black armor was leading his troops in person, and he looked a very fiend as his bloody falchion made great vistas in the ranks that opposed his progress. The heads of horsemen rolled beneath his splendid charger, and it seemed that only another Rustem could withstand the fury of his attack. The black banners were spread upon the air, and the wild music of gong and tymbalous cheered his reckless hordes in their fatal work.

There was the clash of spears, the ringing of

armor, and the shouts of the chieftains, mingled with the trampling of horses and the cries of dying men; still onward came the Tartar chief, cleaving his path through the opposing forces, even while blade for blade sprang up to meet him. The Khârizmians were falling back before the irresistible fury of the onset, and victory was surely perching upon the black banner above the fatal field. Confusion already reigned amidst the flying troops, when a warrior youth with a broidered vestment rode out of the retreating ranks and called upon the men to follow him.

It was a voice of imperial command, the order of a man who rode fearlessly into the ranks of the foe, and the troops of Keiwan quickly rallied, the officers reformed their lines, and followed the new leader into the very jaws of death.

Kâra Khân laughed mockingly as he saw the stripling, who had turned the retreating lines, riding towards him, but in another moment the boy was by his side, and before he could draw his sword a quick motion had thrown him from his horse; the cry went through the Tartar ranks that the king was slain, and, in the momentary panic caused by the false alarm, he was captured by the dauntless youth, who hurried him back within the Khârizmian lines.

Leaving his prisoner in the hands of his own attendants the prince again turned his horse to the front, and again he led the troops of Keiwan, this time to an easy victory; the fate of the day being turned by the capture of the Tartar king, the hordes of the invader either fled from the field or surrendered to the new leader.

When the royal prisoner was brought before the victorious king, the order was issued according to the barbaric custom, that he should be beheaded; but Meher interfered, with the plea that it were far better to send him back to his own dominions pledged to make an annual tribute to Keiwan. This would not only increase the royal revenue, but it would hold the Tartar host in subjection, and also preserve the peace; whereas, upon the execution of their king his successor would declare perpetual war against the Khārizmians.

After a time Meher succeeded in convincing the king of the wisdom of a humane policy, and the captive was allowed to depart in peace, having taken a solemn pledge to send a rich tribute to the conqueror every year on the anniversary of his attack.

Keiwan acknowledged that the victory had been secured by Meher, and he was escorted back to the palace by a portion of the royal guard, while the honors bestowed upon the prince were second only to those received by the king himself.

A GARDEN SCENE.

The enameled cupola of the palace, rich with its arabesques of gold, was partially hidden by the boughs of the tall trees that stood like sentries around it; at their feet were fountains that poured their silvery streams into marble tanks, where the gold-fish glided through the waves, and white lotus blossoms rose above them, filling all the air with their fragrant breath. There were aloes with their spikes of silvery blossoms, and pink oleander sprays were reflected back

in the water of the lilied tanks. The bulbul sang in
the thickets of roses, and the sunbirds fluttered
through the taller trees, where their eggs of mottled
gray were safely hidden.

As the triumphant warriors returned to the palace
the low sun dappled the green with creeping shadows,
and rays of golden light tinted the trees with
splendor. The prince was exhausted with the strong
excitement of the last few days, and especially wearied
by the bitter conflict which he had just passed
through : the voices even of victory seemed to jar
upon his ears and he sought in the cool shades of the
garden the rest which he could not hope to find
within the palace walls. Here, upon a bank of verdure, he laid his weary form, and soon fell asleep
amidst the flowers.

On the other side of the tall trees, the princess
Nahíd was walking with her nurse, and they were
talking in low tones of the great victory, the news of
which had reached even the apartments of the
women. The princess stood beneath an orange tree,
and the tints of rose were blushing through the soft
olive shades of her face, while the dark eyes were
beaming with a wondrous light, for she had heard the
name of her beloved in connection with the deeds of
valor upon that well fought field. Her love-lighted
eyes were curtained with long sweeping lashes, and
the mouth of rose and pearl was curved with a smile
divine, as they walked through the green aisles and
spoke in joyous whispers of this new triumph, which
could not fail to bring Meher nearer to the heart of
the king. Nahíd was walking slowly in advance of

her attendant when she came to a little opening in
the trees, and there upon the bank lay the man she
loved, still held in the restful arms of sleep. She
checked the exclamation of surprise that sprang to her
lips, and, cautiously advancing, she bent above the
silent figure and looked long and lovingly upon the
face she knew so well

The sleeping prince felt her presence, and through
his mind there passed a vision of loveliness; he
dreamed that a beautiful woman bent above his couch
holding a pomegranate blossom—the flower of faith.
Upon her dark hair there rested a little cap sewn
thick with beaded pearls, and something whispered in
his dream that this was the princess who had scorned
a Tartar king for his sake.

And still the prince dreamed on, and still the
bright face bent above him, all unheeding the frantic
gestures of the attendant who would call the imprudent Nahīd away. But the bulbul in the rose-tree
had bolder grown, and his voice rose higher in a joyous song,—the sleeping prince awoke, and lo! the
vision of his dream was bending o'er him; with one
quick movement, all unheeding Eastern law, he caught
her in his arms, and, as she lay blushing and trembling
there, he told her the sweet old story, which is ever
new to the listening heart.

In vain the attendant pleaded that he had no right
to even look upon her unveiled face—in vain she
warned them that if this meeting came to the ears of
the king, the life of Meher must pay the penalty of
the forbidden kiss; long he held her there in his
warm embrace, and then a Huma bird floated slowly

above them and the attendant thought that a future
king and his queen were before her; for never doth
this bird of happy omen fly around a human head
but it will sometime wear a crown. The sun had
rolled away behind the crimson curtains of the west
before the princess stole to her room, but not to
sleep, for if a treacherous eye had seen her with
Meher, she might be called with the dawn to witness
his execution.

AFTERWARDS.

The prince went to his chambers with his heart
filled with conflicting emotions; on the one hand was
the beautiful princess, who had confided her love to
him, and on the other was the humiliating knowledge
that he had betrayed the trust of his royal friend,
the king, who had taken an unknown youth into his
heart and home. Full well he knew that he had no
right to even look into the unveiled face of the
princess, no right to touch the soft hands which were
henna stained upon the palms, and yet he had vio-
lated the most sacred law of hospitality by holding
her in his arms—nay, he had even pressed her crimson
lips with his own; in that hour of strong self-con-
demnation he did not dread the righteous anger of
the king, he felt rather, that it devolved upon him
to go into the court, and make a full confession of
his base act and bravely receive the deserved punishment.

Another bitter thought added not a little to his
self-reproach, for was he not also a traitor to the
sacred trust of friendship? His chosen friend was in

constant peril, he knew not where, and he was living
in ease and luxury without trying to find him; he
thought he could go to the king, and, by proving his
royal birth and his claim to the Persian throne, he
could hopefully ask for the hand of the princess, but
this would be a virtual desertion of the cause of his
friend, and he could not consent to thus sacrifice the
sacred claims of fraternal love for his own pleasure
and happiness. Long he tossed upon his sleepless
couch and still the matter was far from settled; at
last he fell into a feverish slumber which was haunted
by a fair face, with dark, loving eyes, but there were
also visions of a loyal friend who was suffering on account of his unyielding devotion to the prince—
even the vindictive face of Behrām passed before his
mind, and the morning found him still weary and
disturbed. He decided, however, to pursue his search
for Mūshteri, even at the risk of losing Nahīd, for
was not this his first and most sacred obligation?

Having resolved to follow what seemed the path
of duty, at whatever cost, his tempest-torn heart was
at rest. Surely the sacrifice and renunciation were
better than the gratification of self-love, and when
he had found his friend he would present to the
king a formal request for the hand of Nahīd. While
yet he pondered, a messenger was announced from
the king with an order for his immediate presence in
the council chamber of the palace.

THE DECISION.

The imperative nature of the summons bore with
it an air of danger; it was not the kindly invitation

which he had been wont to receive, or at least the
messenger did not deliver it as such, and the scene
in the garden with all its possible consequences,
flashed before the mind of the prince. He dismissed
the chamberlain with the reply that the call would be
promptly obeyed, and then sat down to collect his
thoughts in order to be prepared for whatever ordeal
might await him.

He could not avoid the conviction that he must
now pay the penalty for his betrayal of the king's
trust, and he thought of the broken-hearted mother
who was grieving her life away over the uncertain
fate of her child; he had no hope that he could even
send her a message, for Oriental monarchs were not
in the habit of granting such privileges to men who
were condemned to execution.

But he had little time for sad reflections, and soon
he was on his way to obey the imperial summons.
He was ushered into the royal presence and was
received with the usual courtesies, but the king
ordered the Vizir to leave the room, and then Meher
knew that he should soon learn his fate.

The monarch slowly recounted the principal incidents of their acquaintance, and after giving an account of the battle and the victory which Meher had
snatched from the very hands of defeat, he said: "I
have consulted with my principal counselors, and we
have decided that the only suitable reward which we
can confer upon the unknown Persian youth is to give
him the Princess Nahíd in marriage."

Meher fell upon his knees in an ecstacy of gratitude, and it was some time before he could even

thank the king for his great kindness; but he could
not prove himself further unworthy of this great trust,
and after expressing, as best he could, his appreciation of the priceless gift, he proceeded with true manliness, to tell his whole story to King Keiwan. He
told of his parentage, his claims to the crown of Persia, his unchanging friendship with Müshteri, who
was exiled for his sake, of his determination to find
his friend, and his great appreciation of the kindness
of his royal host.

Nothing was hidden in this manly confession; the
scene in the garden was given with unfaltering truth-
fulness, even while the narrator watched the dark
frown that was gathering upon the brow of Keiwan.
The angry king listened in dismay, though he could
but admire the moral courage of the prince, who,
when he had finished, threw himself upon the clem-
ency of Keiwan.

There was a silence that seemed to bode little
good to Meher, and then the king said: "I have
seen how thou could'st forgive, even a foe; I have
seen thee plead for Kára Khán, who would gladly
have taken thy life, if it were in his power; a king
cannot afford to be less magnanimous than thyself—
arise and receive my forgiveness." But the grateful
prince remained at his feet and there expressed his
devout thankfulness.

In this long and candid interview he also told
Keiwan that while he held in his heart a great love
for the beautiful princess, and nothing in life could
give him greater joy than to call her his own, still he
dared not give up, even for her sake, his search for

the friend of his childhood, who might even now be
in jeopardy on account of his loyalty. Again he braved
the royal displeasure, by seeming to undervalue the
priceless gift, even while his own heart cried out for
his love. Again that ominous frown passed over the
brow of the king, and his words were followed by a
silence so profound that he could hear his own heart-
beats. After a time the king spoke, but only to chide
him for his ill-chosen friendship, only to tell him that
his hope was useless, and to urge him to give up the
fruitless search.

Meher replied that it was impossible—that he could
not be happy in heaven itself, if he had betrayed the
trust of his friend, and whatever might be the cost,
he must either find him or give his life to the unavailing search ; he was then dismissed from the king's
presence, and went away feeling that although he was
under the royal displeasure, he must still be true to
himself.

CHAPTER XX.

MEHER AND MŪSHTERI—CONTINUED.

THE CAPTIVES—ARREST AND TRIAL—ROYAL FAVOR—
THE SENTENCE.

A CARAVAN which was approaching Khārizm was observed to have in custody two prisoners, who had evidently been cruelly beaten. The report was carried to the city, and the king's officers were sent out to investigate the circumstances. They questioned the owner of the caravan in relation to the matter, and he informed them that these men were his slaves, who had escaped from his service and carried off with them large quantities of stolen goods; he had pursued them many days and at great expense, had finally captured them, but had succeeded in obtaining only a small portion of his merchandise, the rest having been sold and the proceeds expended in riotous living.

The man was evidently a Persian, and the captives seemed to be Persian also, therefore the story seemed probable, and the officers returned to the king with the statement that the matter had been fully investigated, and that the master of the caravan had evidently good reasons for whatever severity might have been used, and thus the matter was allowed to rest, while the strangers encamped in security just outside the city limits. A close guard was kept over the prisoners, and they were constantly told that if they varied from this story, in case they were questioned, that their lives should pay the forfeit of their imprudence. In view of the dreadful beating they had already received, they had good reason to believe that they would not only be murdered, but that, too, in the most barbarous manner, in case of exposure; Mushteri decided to tell the truth if he were questioned, whatever the result might be, but there was little prospect that such an opportunity might present itself, for they were not only closely guarded, but the indolent officers of the crown were glad to have the matter so easily disposed of.

After a few days of rest, therefore, in the suburbs, Behrām gave the order to proceed, and the men under his command slowly packed the camp utensils, and the caravan made its way into the city, where some of the merchant's goods were offered for sale. The rich Persian stuffs brought high prices, and the burdens of the pack animals were not only lightened but the master was rapidly changing his wealth into a more portable form. One of the attendants of Meher was attracted by the sale, for with his longing for home was mingled a desire to obtain some of the goods which had a familiar look in their fabric. He was merely looking on, however, at a short distance, for the crowd around the caravan was not easy to penetrate, and he wondered in an indolent way what portion of Persia he new comers were from, when he was startled by the sound of a familiar voice; the indifference in his manner quickly vanished, and he listened eagerly until he heard it again, for he could not at first recall the tone that seemed so strangely familiar. He pressed anxiously nearer, and at last caught sight of the face of Behrâm, who was so deeply engaged in the sale of his goods that he did not notice an eager look upon the face of one of the bystanders, and the man hurried away to carry the news to Meher. Feeling that he had possibly found a clue to the whereabouts of his friend, the prince applied for an interview with the king; but his cordial relations with royalty had been greatly interrupted by what the monarch chose to consider his indifference to the princess, and he refused to see him, sending out a message to the effect that he was too busy to be interrupted.

The prince sent his friend back to watch, unobserved, the movements of the caravan, and also to see if possibly he might not have been mistaken in the identity of Behrâm. This was all he could do at present, and he realized that even if it should prove to be his old attendant his discovery might not lead to any information concerning Mûshteri. The man returned, however, to Meher with the information that it was surely Behrâm, and he carried two captives, but they were so closely guarded that it was impossible to see who they were. In an agony of suspense the prince again applied for an audience with the king, but only to meet with a second refusal. In the morning he learned that, having sold all the goods which he wished at present to dispose of, Behrâm was preparing to leave the city.

ARREST AND TRIAL.

Meher would have been willing to follow and attack him with the aid only of his own attendants, but he knew that in case of an attack Behrâm's first act would be to slay his captives, whoever they might be; he therefore wrote a most piteous appeal to the king, saying that he knew the owner of the caravan to be a man of basest purpose, and beseeching that he might at least be arrested and more thoroughly examined.

Keiwan at last consented to this plan, but the caravan was already two days' journey from the city. The king's officers overtook them, and brought them back to appear before the tribunal in the council hall. Meher had succeeded in obtaining an audience with the king, who treated him with great formality. He consented, however, that the prince should be present at the forthcoming examination of the prisoners, and he chose to do so without being himself observed.

Behrâm and his slaves were brought into the hall and the prisoners were also compelled to appear, all the excuses of Behrâm having been unavailing with the officers, who had strict orders from Keiwan. Meher looked closely and anxiously at them from behind his screen, but they had been so completely changed by the barbarous treatment to which they had been subjected that he could not recognize them. Feeling grievously disappointed, he lost to a great extent his interest in the trial, for he cared little to have Behrâm punished merely as a matter of revenge.

The owner of the caravan was first plied with questions, and he told with great freedom the story which he had first given to the king's officers. He declared that both of his prisoners were his former slaves, and one of them being his treasurer had been intrusted with large sums of money; he had betrayed his trust, however, and with his companion had stolen a vast amount of money and jewels, taking them to a foreign land. The owner had pursued them at great expense of both time and money, and now having secured them he was taking them back to deliver them up to the proper officers. He then called his slaves to swear to the truth of his story, which they promptly did.

As the story proceeded, Meher was stirred with indignation, and with great difficulty succeeded in keeping his place behind the screen. He contented himself, however, with writing out questions to be asked the prisoner, and sending them by his attendant to the proper officer.

In this way he soon had the traitor involved in a mass of hopeless contradictions and lost in wonder at the ingenuity of a stranger who seemed to understand his entire history.

At last one of the captives was brought forward to testify in his own behalf, and Mūshteri took the stand. His head had been shaved and his face painted; his clothing was in fragments, and he was so weakened by the brutalities to which he had been subjected that he could hardly stand. His own mother would not have recognized him when he was led forward, but when the first question was put to him and he began to reply, the tones of his voice carried his identity to Meher, and, unable to conceal his emotions, the prince came quickly forward and caught him in his arms. The captive gave one glad cry of recognition, and then fainted at the feet of his friend. Keiwan was melted to tears by this scene of fraternal devotion, and, quickly giving an order to have Behrâm placed in irons, he called for restoratives to be applied to the victim of his cruelty. The face of Mushteri was bathed in rose water, and when he revived he was driven with Bader to the apartments of the prince.

Their wounds were carefully dressed, and the most delicate food placed before them; wardrobes were provided, and every luxury that art could devise or money could purchase, was placed at their disposal.

Long hours were spent in recounting to each other the history of the past, before Meher could consent to leave his friend, even to visit the palace.

ROYAL FAVOR.

When Meher again applied for an interview with the king, his request was not refused, for Keiwan could but honor the loyalty of a man who had so persistently followed his friend, and at last rescued him from the hands of a man who would soon have murdered him in the most barbarous manner but for the timely intercession of the prince.

After enjoying the cordial reception which the king vouchsafed to him, Meher said: "I have a right to speak to thee now, for no other duty intervenes. I come before thee as the heir of the Persian throne, and come to ask the hand of the beautiful princess in marriage. Having discharged the most sacred duties of friendship, I ask thee to give me also the blessings of love."

The king replied that the man who could be so loyal in his friendship could not be unworthy the hand of even the princess Nahîd, and their betrothal was formally sealed.

A message was sent to the apartments of Nahīd to inform the happy princess of her betrothal to the man she loved, and thus it happened that in an Eastern court a woman's heart was given with her hand. She was not allowed to see her lover, even the stolen interview in the garden being looked upon as criminal; but she told the story to the bulbul in the rose-tree, and the bulbul sang a sweet new tune as he looked down into the sheltered nest where three blue eggs were waiting the touch of life.

The princess told her story to the lotus blossoms, and they breathed a sweeter fragrance; she told the pomegranate tree that had witnessed their first betrothal, and the rich flowers grew more vivid and seemed to tremble with a new happiness; the sunbirds flew more joyously through the branches of the trees, and even the skies were of rose and pearl.

THE SENTENCE.

There came a day when Behrām was brought forth from his dark cell to receive his sentence, and there beside the throne stood Meher and Mūshteri, while Bader was only a little way in the background.

The face of the culprit was dark with shame and the poison of defeated malice, as he stood in the presence of those whose lives he had so nearly wrecked. There was a cloud even upon the face of the prince, for he remembered the suffering which this man had brought upon the friend of his boyhood, and, more than all, upon his gentle mother in her loneliness and grief.

The list of his crimes was formally read to the

prisoner, and then his sentence was pronounced by the king, and the executioner was ordered to lead him away.

Mūshteri looked upon the guilty wretch before him, and remembered the years of malice with which this man had followed him. He remembered the faithful father who but for him might still be living, and he felt that the sentence was just, but was not mercy the better part of valor? Could another death bring back the dead or aid in any way the living? Surely not; and stepping forward with the grace of one who was accustomed to the presence of royalty, he besought the king to forgive this relentless foe and let him go back in peace to his aged father. Keiwan looked in astonishment upon this gallant youth who could plead for so relentless a foe, almost as soon as he was released from his power, and he hesitated to grant the strange request.

Mūshteri then knelt before the king and continued his plea, while the officers of the court looked on in wonder. At last, however, the king yielded, and told Mūshteri that he might loosen the bonds of the prisoner. There was no reproach in the kind eyes of the victor as he came forward and unfastened with his own hands the fetters of Behrām. The prisoner looked amazed and humiliated; he had nerved himself to meet the executioner with a sullen courage; but freedom, and that, too, from the man whom he had so grievously and persistently wronged, he was unprepared for, and he broke down in a flood of tears.

Mūshteri led him to the door of the council chamber, and bade him go to his home and friends.

"Alas!" said he, "I have no home—I have no friends.
I have outraged the confidence of the Shāh, there is
no room for me in his dominions, and even the father
who taught me the lessons of hypocrisy is now ashamed
of his son. I have no home but the desert—no friend
but death."

He went away, but the disappointed malice, and the
hopeless future, had wrought a change in the strong
man that he was powerless to overcome; he returned
to his caravan which had been restored to him by the
intercession of Meher and Mūshteri, but in a few days
his lifeless body was found upon the plains, and his
servants claimed that he had died by his own hand.

CHAPTER XXI.

MEHER AND MŪSHTERI—CONCLUDED.

THE WEDDING — A COUNCIL — ROYAL CAVALCADE—THE MESSENGER—RECEPTION.

A PAVILION was built beneath the palm trees, and the fire-flies lit their signals afresh in the thickets of foliage, for it was amidst the shades of the garden that the singers were placed, whose sweetest notes were to be poured forth at the royal wedding. Within the palace, the courts were all ablaze with light and loveliness; lamps of graven silver were swinging from the fretted roof, suspended by long chains, and fed with the perfumed oils of distant lands. Their soft light fell on silken hangings and tapestries from Eastern looms, while crystal vases gleamed here and there, filled with branches of orange trees or sprays of magnolia blossoms. It was here that Meher received his royal bride, and when the ceremony was finished, the notes of music floated in through the casement, and mingled with the breath of the flowers. Still nearer seemed to come the dream-like harmonies, as the tones of pipe and lute were mingled with the voices of the singers and the musical ripple of the fountains.

Then the dancing girls floated into the bright halls, and swayed gracefully through the soft measures, and all was motion, light and jewels. Golden chains were woven in their dark hair, and silver bangles gleamed upon the shapely ankles, where little bells kept time with gliding feet. Each dancer held a dainty lute of gold and sandal wood, which answered to the swaying of her arms and the soft beat of graceful hands. And still the music from without floated through the lattice and mingled with the harmonies within. But in this festal scene Love was the honored guest. He came to rule the court and grove; his were the symphonies that breathed a richer note than all the garden singers; his were the harmonies that shaped the loyal lives, and led the happy feet along the aisles of time.

Bewildered with the beauty and love of his bride, Meher lived for weeks unheeding the lapse of time, for all the days were crowned with gold and radiant with the blossoms of love. But there came a morning when the picture of his grieving mother was forced upon his heart and mind with all its power, and he remembered that not alone to his lovely wife belonged his fealty.

They were sitting together beneath the sheltering branches of a great magnolia tree, whose creamy flowers were bursting from the green sheath of the bud, and the air was rich with fragrance. On the green bank beyond them, the peacocks drew their gorgeous trains, and birds sang in the tall trees in the distance.

The dark eyes of the prince had a look of sadness in them, and there was a cloud, the first that Nahïd had ever seen upon his handsome brow; she drew closer within the sheltering arm, and her soft, dark

eyes looked anxiously into his. His own heart read
her pleading question, even before her lips had framed
it, and then he told her of the loving mother who
was grieving her life away amidst the splendors of
another court—of the faithful heart that looked long-
ingly for his return and refused to be comforted, because he came not.

"But what can we do?" questioned the princess.
"Thou canst not leave the wife to go even to the
mother."

"No," answered the prince, "but can I not take
my bride with me? Can I not take my peerless pearl
to the royal court which is my rightful inheritance?
Can I not bear to her arms the beauteous daughter
that I have given her? Surely my wife should receive my mother's blessing! Let me take thee there
before the faithful mother-heart is cold in death."

"But my father," faltered Nahíd, "will he consent? Will he allow thee to bear me away to a
strange land to claim the lost inheritance?"

"The king should remember that not only filial
love demands my return, but I can never make my
bride the queen that she should be—I can never place
a royal crown upon her lovely brow unless I return
to the land of my fathers," answered the prince; and
then he told her, with loving thought, of the land
where the palms grew higher by striving toward the
sun, of the marble palaces of Istakhar, standing beside the river that came down from the heights rippling with low harmonies, as the waves dashed on
the sanded shores; told her, too, of the mountains
beyond the marble city, where the wild swans came

to their nesting places,—white voyagers on the seas of blue, calling, in soft notes, down the line, while love was leading them homeward, to the sheltered nooks beside the pools of the mountain stream.

Long they stayed in loving converse, and when they turned to the palace court, the prince had won from his bride a promise that she would see the king, and win, if possible, his consent to the long bridal trip, that she now looked forward to with pleasure.

ROYAL CAVALCADE.

The king listened patiently to the plea of Nahīd, for though he knew that the long journey would take her from him, perhaps forever, he also knew that the throne of Persia might be waiting for their coming, and at last he consented that the prince should bear his bride away to wear a crown in the halls of the proud Sassanian kings.

But she should not go dowerless to the home of her husband. Keiwan therefore gave orders for the fitting out of a magnificent cavalcade, comprising a thousand camels of the purest Syrian blood, a thousand splendid Arabian steeds and a thousand Indian slaves, besides a military escort composed of the finest troops in the service of the king.

The morning was radiant with golden sunlight when the splendid procession left the city of Khārizm; the streets were gorgeous with flags, and branches of flowering trees stood by every doorway, while the palace itself was covered with silken banners, lightly draped with wreaths of flowers. The excited horses, with their golden caparisons, tossed their heads in the air, and

pranced with joy as the strains of music rang out
from the balconies around them, and the camels gently
shook their light-toned bells in every passing breeze.
Hundreds of banners floated above the troops and waved
like the wings of birds in the sunlight; the gleaming swords of the warriors were pointed up to heaven,
and a thousand voices rang with joyous acclamation.
Keiwan and his queen rode in the imperial chariot
immediately behind the camels bearing the luxurious
cushions of the prince and his bride, for they traveled
a day's journey with them before bidding their children farewell, and then returned sorrowfully to their
lonely palace home.

The gorgeous cavalcade moved slowly onward, over
hill and plain, and through a forest where all the
branches laughed with songs of birds, and trusses of
scarlet pomegranate blossoms gleamed here and there
through the rich foliage. When night came down
upon the landscape an encampment was made beside
a river, and pavilions of scarlet and gold were furnished with costly cushions that invited repose.

THE MESSENGER.

The uneventful days passed slowly by, and still the
great cavalcade was far from its destination, when
Meher ordered his especial attendant to mount one of
the swiftest Arabian horses and carry a letter to his
father asking if he wished him to return.

The Persian monarch was sitting in the council hall
surrounded by his counselors, and they were considering an important affair of state when a messenger was
announced. He was ordered into an adjoining room

to wait until King Shapur was ready to receive him, and here he could look upon the once familiar form of his sovereign.

He was astonished to see how greatly the Shāh had changed with the passing years; only three times had the seasons made their cycles, and yet the stalwart form was bent as if with age, the dark hair was already silvered and the furrows upon the weary brow told that grief and remorse were leaving their impress upon his once serene countenance. At last the word was brought that the messenger could now approach the king, but he replied that his was a secret mission, he must see his majesty alone, and after a time he was ushered into the private audience room.

He then told the king that he brought him news from Behrām, who had obtained a magnificent caravan under the pretext of finding the prince. The king listened eagerly while the messenger gave a graphic description of the pursuit and capture of Mūshteri but his brow darkened with an ominous frown as the recital continued. He had been the prey of evil advisers who cared only to flatter him for their own gain, and in the years that had gone he sadly missed the faithful advice and unfailing loyalty of his old Vizir. He often reproached himself as the indirect cause of his death, and decreed in his heart that if the banished son could be found he should be recompensed, so far as lay in his power, for all sufferings of the past. When, therefore, he learned of the persistent brutality of Behrām his anger grew almost uncontrolable. He inquired anxiously for the prince. "You bring me bad news enough;" he cried, "can you give

me no knowledge of my son?" And he answered:
"Oh, king, great and mighty ruler of the wide realm,
I can bring thee news of the prince, for I have seen
him in a foreign court." "Where didst thou see him?
What is he doing, and why does he not return to the
land of his fathers?" he rapidly questioned. "He
has risen, oh, king, to great eminence at the court of
a foreign potentate, and he hath no need to return to
thee, but his heart yearns for his native land; he cares
much to spend his years near to the father whom he
still loves, and he longs to take his beloved mother
into his arms again. I have brought thee a letter from
him," and then he placed the document in the royal
hand. "A letter!" cried the Shah, "a letter from
my son!" and he ceased to be a king, for now he was
only a father, and the manly tears coursed down his
cheeks as he caught the precious missive and pressed
the hand of the messenger.

As soon as he could read the communication from
Meher he called for writing materials, and with his
own hand he penned a long and loving letter to his
son, telling him that not only his home but also the
Persian crown awaited his coming, urging him to
return and bring with him the faithful friend who had
suffered so much on account of his loyalty to the
prince. Then he hastened the messenger away, that he
might reach Meher at the earliest possible moment,
and he himself went to bear the glad tidings to the
sorrowful queen.

The next day a proclamation was issued that the
heir of the throne was coming to the capital city, and
orders were given to the Grand Vizir, to the chamber-

lains and other officers of the crown that suitable preparations be made to welcome the prince and his bride.

THE RECEPTION.

The announcement of his coming was a signal for general rejoicing ; even the children loved the young heir and knew the story of fraternal affection between him and Müshteri. The Shâh had been bitterly blamed in the hearts of his subjects, although such was the force of Oriental despotism that a man scarcely knew the thought of his neighbor. Never were the imperial orders more willingly obeyed than when the Shâh commanded a festal scene to be arranged for the reception of Meher, and never was the marble city fairer than when the coming of the royal cavalcade was announced. Silken banners waved in triumph from every wall and battlement, while strains of martial music floated through the air, and the streets were strewn with white lilies and the fragrant roses of Persia. Gilded barges on the river wore their festal flags, and bore the minstrels down the stream to the shore, where the voices of singers were mingled with the notes of lute and psaltery.

Without the city the Persian road of palms was festooned with arches of roses and strewn with the flowers of the valley, for all the way was glad with blossoms and vocal with the songs of welcome.

In the early morning a swiftly-mounted courier had been stationed on an eminence a few miles from the city, where he could see the approaching cavalcade far down the valley, and when he rode into the city with the message that the advance guard was already in sight there were loud acclamations of joy. For hours the finest horses in the royal stables had stood impatient, with tossing plumes and gorgeous trappings, waiting for the advance, and now the Shāh, with his chosen guard, rode out in royal state to meet the coming prince.

The white Arabian steeds, the costly armor of the troops and the rich raiment of the Shāh, made a gorgeous picture in the sunlight, when they swept down through the rose-covered arches and under the palms. As they rode onward a new strain of music saluted their ears, and a long line of camels came swinging slowly into view, their heads tufted with bright tassels, while their light-toned bells were shaking silvery notes upon the air, and their drivers were singing and playing on pipes. But lo! the lines were opened for a small troop of horsemen who galloped towards the Shāh, and Meher, swinging gracefully down from the saddle, came to his father's feet.

King Shapur quickly recognized the familiar face, and hastily dismounting, he caught his son in his arms. The hardy Persian soldiers turned away from the sacred scene with tears in their eyes, but after a time Mūshteri came forward, and humbly kneeling at the monarch's feet he craved forgiveness. The Shāh laid his hand upon the head of him who, in his childhood, had seemed almost as near as his own son, and freely gave the royal pardon; then the lines were reformed, Meher and Mūshteri riding on either side of the king, and the horses were turned toward Istakhar.

The sun was sinking behind the western mountains when the cavalcade approached the gates of the city, and the dark thickets by the roadside were vocal with the song of the nightingale; but his voice was soon hushed by the notes of martial music and the triumphant shouts of welcome that greeted their first appearance to the people who had been held back by the spears of the soldiery. Although the distant peaks still wore the crimson crowns of sunset, the side of the mountain was already dark with the gathering shades of twilight, and signal fires flashed from the gray depths of the forest or blazed upon the leafless slopes of granite beyond them. Within the city all was joyous tumult; but Meher had little heart for the general rejoicing, and scarcely waiting to be announced he hurried away to the apartments of his mother. A little later the Princess Nahîd was ushered into the rooms of the queen, and was folded closely to the warm, loving heart, so fully prepared to receive her. Little cared the mother for the wondrous beauty of the princess, but much she valued the loyal heart which had been given so fully into the keeping of her son, and from that day forth she was cherished as a loving daughter in the royal household.

The days flew by on joyous feet, but King Shapur was weary of the cares of state—weary of a life whose very pleasures were burdened with responsibility and embittered with the knowledge that treachery waited only for a favorable opportunity to show her cruel fangs. He therefore abdicated in favor of his son, and voluntarily invested Meher with the robes of sovereignty.

All the resources of the kingdom were taxed to provide for the splendors of the coronation ceremony.

Again the royal procession swept through the streets, and feasts were given where the richest wines of the East were poured in jeweled cups and the tables were laden with the choicest viands from many climes. There were plantains, golden and green, and grapes of gold; there were apples and pomegranates from Kabūl, apricots from the fairest gardens of Īrān, and the sunniest fruits in all the lands of the Orient.

Again the dark face of the mountain blazed forth at night with the signal-lights of victory, the river was covered with barges bearing illuminations, and the night rivaled the day in the splendor of its offerings at the feet of the new Shāh, and Mūshteri, his Grand Vizir.

CHAPTER XXII.

CONCLUSION.

SUMMARY—PRIESTLY RULE—RUSSIAN OPPRESSION.

W E have now passed in review the principal features of a great literature from its early mythology to the time when the rule of priestcraft,
combined with political tyranny, seems to have
quenched the fire of Persian genius.

The empire gathered to herself the culture of ancient
Nineveh and the poetic dreams of Chaldea, but, not
content with the heritage which she received from
more ancient kingdoms, she developed, from resources
peculiarly her own, a literature which is rich in all
that pertains to Oriental fancy. Her mythology, like
that of other Āryan races, is traceable to the system
of sensual idolatry which flourished in the valley of
the Euphrates; the origin of her myths was found ·in
the "sacred groves of Baal," and around the altars of
Ashtaroth.

Merodach and Nebo, Moloch and Chemosh reap-
peared in later times in other lands, and under different names, but still with the same characteristics
which they had in the land of their birth.

We have seen the gradual growth of her Zend-
Avesta with the inauguration of her system of worship, and noted the fact there was originally a close

connection between the Veda and the Zend-Avesta, although the Persian work was of later origin.

Some of the Hindū gods bear the same names in the Avesta that were applied to them in the Sanskṛit poems, although in the later books they may appear as evil spirits, and the same god is sometimes represented as an angel, and again as a fiend.

Indra, the storm-king of the Veda, was the god of war, for whom the Ṛishis made and drank the intoxicating Soma, while in the Vendīdad [1] he is expressly mentioned in the list of evil spirits, and · is second only to Ahriman, the arch-fiend of the Avesta. But another name for Indra in the Vedic songs is Vṛi-trahā, and this name is recognized as that of the angel Verethragna; hence it follows that under one name the god is cursed and feared as a fiend, while under another he is worshipped as an angel.

The name of Deva in the Vedas, and in all Brāhmanical literature, is applied to divine beings who are still worshipped by the Hindūs, while in the Avesta, from the earliest to the latest texts, and even in modern Persian literature, Deva is a name applied to a fiend. The word Asura, although used in a good sense in the early songs of the Ṛig-veda, becomes, in the later portions of that literature, as well as in the Brāhmaṇas and Purāṇas, a term which is applied only to evil spirits ; they are represented as the constant enemies of the Hindū gods, always making attacks upon the sacrifices offered by devotees. In the Avesta, Asura, in the form of Ahura, becomes a component part of Ahura Mazda, which is the name of God among the

Pārsīs, whose faith is called "the Ahura religion"[1] in order to distinctively indicate its opposition to the Deva religion.

The Vedic god, Vāyu (the wind), is readily recognized in the spirit Vāyu in the Avesta, who is supposed to be roaming everywhere.

Another instance of a deity who is scarcely changed in any way is Mithra, the Sanskrit form of which is Mitra. In the Ṛig-veda "Mitra calls men to their work; Mitra is preserving earth and heaven; Mitra looks upon the nations always without shutting his eyes." In the Avesta he is also the lord of the morning, the god of day, and the object of profound adoration.

These are but a few out of many similarities, and the careful student of the Veda and the Avesta will also notice the identity of many terms referring to priestly functions. The very name of "priest" in the Zend-Avesta is *atharva*, and it is merely another form of *atharvan*, which is the term applied to the priest of fire and Soma, in the Vedas.[2]

These and many other similarities do not necessarily prove that the Zend-Avesta was partially copied from the Veda, but they do prove that "the Veda and the Zend-Avesta are two rivers flowing from one fountain head; the stream of the Veda is the fuller and purer, and has remained truer to its original character; that of the Zend-Avesta has been in various ways polluted, has altered its course, and cannot, with certainty, be traced back to its source."[3] Nevertheless,

---

[1] Yasna, XII, 9, p. 174. [2] Dr. Haug, Essays, p. 2, 67
[3] Prof. Roth, Tubingen. Chips, p. 85.

their common origin must be assigned to the early Indo-Iraniān traditions.

Besides the official copy of the sacred books, which was burned by Alexander with the palace of the Persian king at Persepolis, there were other copies, or at least portions of them, and these the first Sassanian kings collected, and compiled from them, as far as possible, their sacred literature. For more than five centuries after Alexander, the empire of Persia suffered from foreign despotism and internal dissensions, but during this long period of political unrest, the Sassanian kings were able to collect a large proportion of the old writings, even though the literature which was thus restored consisted chiefly of fragments; it appears, however, that some portion of nearly every book was recovered by the zeal of these monarchs, and therefore the total disappearance of some of them must be assigned to more recent times.

A still greater disaster awaited the books of the Persians at the hand of the Moslem invader, when the Arabian horde swept over the hills and valleys of Persia like a simoon from the desert. Every tree and flower seemed to feel the withering touch of the barbarian, and the authority of the Korān was enforced with the logic of the sword. "Ye know your option, ye Christian dogs ; the Korān, tribute, or the sword," was the dictum of the conqueror wherever the Moslem flag was triumphant, and at last the Star and Crescent floated over the land of "the Lion and the Sun" —her nationality was humiliated and crushed, while her treasures of literature were again destroyed by a foreign foe. The kingdom of Persia now entered upon the long night of Mohammedan rule. Her sacred books were swept from the land, the Korân became the successor of the Zend-Avesta, and many of the Pârsîs went into voluntary exile, finding upon the shores of India that freedom which was denied them upon their native soil. Even the Persian tongue was placed under a ban, and Arabic became the legal language of court and council hall.

The Persians were conquered, but not subdued; the national spirit still lived in their hearts, and in more than one instance the conquest was repeated—for, in the defence of their nationality and their faith, they rebelled in different portions of the country and fought desperately against the hated Arab. They were subjugated at last, and, to a certain extent, accepted even the religion of the invader, but the vitality of the Persian character was not destroyed.

After a time, a few of the subordinate rulers, who were natives, rebelled against the tyranny of the Arabic tongue, and succeeded in establishing the Persian language to a great extent in its rightful domain. The national spirit again rallied, Persian poets were encouraged, traditions of the empire were once more collected, and the composition of a great national epic became possible. The Shâh Nâmah, which was written under royal patronage, has lived through the vicissitudes of more than eight hundred years, and is still the most popular Persian classic. Other centuries followed, bearing the names of distinguished poets and scholars, the cities of Bokhâra, Samarcând and Bagdad became great literary centers, their colleges and libraries being celebrated throughout the East.

But again the power of brute force was destined to sweep away the bulwarks of civilization, and Genghis Khân, the Tartar chief, came down like a mountain storm upon the fairest provinces of the Orient. The principal cities were pillaged and burned by the Tartar horde, colleges were destroyed, and the most valuable books in the libraries were thrown into the Tigris.

These were times which tried the hearts of men, for more than two hundred thousand lives were sacrificed to the cruelty of the invading host. Scholars were driven to various places of refuge, and the science of letters received an almost fatal blow.

There are, however, a few illustrious names upon the records of the Persian literati, even after the close of the thirteenth century, and such was the intellectual vitality of the people that lyric poetry and rhetoric were well developed during these stormy times in the political and military world, for the empire had still many men of culture, and also boasted of one literary king,

PRIESTLY RULE.

Nations, as well as individuals, have their periods of growth, prosperity and decay. It is seldom that they arise from an age of great prostration and regain their former strength and brilliancy.

History, however, furnishes bright exceptions to this general rule, and Persia has repeatedly recovered herself from the ravages of foreign conquest. Three times her territory has been invaded when the design of the conqueror has apparently been the extermination of the science of letters, and three times she has rallied bravely from the shock and rebuilded her institutions of learning, founding a new national literature upon the ruins of the old.

Her literature of to-day is profuse in quantity, consisting largely of the various forms of romance,[1] but the best works of Persian authors belong to the centuries past. Perhaps she might rally even the fourth time, and resume her old position in the world of letters, but she is held in a state of lethargy by the benumbing influence of a Mohammedan priesthood. Even the Shāh rules only by the permission of this power, being looked upon as the vicegerent of the prophet, and the laws of the nation are subject to the dictation of the priests.

They stand in the way of all progress, as even a railway cannot be laid without their permission, much less can institutions of learning be carried on outside of their control. Official corruption, which seems to threaten the very existence of some of the Eastern nations, gathers new power from the influence of these Mohammedan mollāhs, and a large share of the money which is appropriated for public improvement eventually finds its way into the coffers of the king's ministers.

There is little hope of intellectual growth under this baneful influence. At the beginning of the present century Īrānian poetry assumed a dramatic form,

[1] There are also many so-called historical works, which, although deficient in sound criticism, and to a greater or less extent unreliable, still furnish some curious and noteworthy data. They have translations of the Maha-bharata, the Ramayana and other standard works of Sanskrit literature, but the original fire of Persian genius appears to be hopelessly crushed.

but, like the Greek drama, and the "Mysteries" of
the Middle ages, it is the offspring of a religious ceremony, and the great attraction of the Persian stage
is a Moslem passion play,[1] even the drama of the
empire being under the control of her conquerors.

RUSSIAN OPPRESSION.

Not only is the nation firmly held in the chains
of priestly rule, but her political position is far from
enviable. Upon her northern border stands the most
unscrupulous power among the nations of the East.
The black eagles of the Czar are ever watching for
an opportunity to invade her dominions, ever looking
for some unusual sign of internal weakness which may
throw her completely into their power. Russia has
justly earned a reputation which, for political treachery, is unequaled among the children of men. She
makes treaties and signs the most solemn pledges of
national co-operation, apparently with the utmost sincerity, and then breaks them, without even a word of
apology, whenever she can gain a point or a province
by so doing.

For centuries Russia has coveted Constantinople as
the key of the East. For centuries she has looked

[1] The Tazieh is the outgrowth of a ceremony which, for centuries, the
Persians have annually performed in the holy month Moharrem. At this
time they celebrate the tragic death of Hossein, the grandson of the Prophet
who perished with all his house at the hands of a rival for the honors of a
caliphate. The month of mourning is largely occupied with the recitals
and ceremonies pertaining to the event; halls being especially constructed
for these rhapsodies, as after more than seven hundred years, the terrible
scenes of the tragedy were dramatized and placed upon the Persian stage.
In the royal Takieh, or theatre, the great drama is unfolded for ten successive days, during the month of mourning, while in all other portions of the
empire it is reproduced with more or less power, at the same time.

with envious eyes upon the wealth of India, and she has hesitated at no policy which might advance her interests by extending her boundary line.

Great Britain stands as the strongest bulwark in the world of nations against the insidious diplomacy of the Muscovite, which seems to be the enemy of all civilization, and therefore in every move that is made in the political world of either Europe or Asia, Russia is ever on the alert to defeat the plans of England, and the coming conflict in the Old World will doubtless be led by these two great powers. Intending some day to wrest India from the hand of Great Britain, she finds Persia standing in the way of her design, and it must therefore be conquered or absorbed. By the most unscrupulous methods known to nations, she has already acquired much of Persian territory, and the process of absorption is renewed whenever the opportunity offers.

She hesitates at no oppression, and has already ruined Persian commerce, as far as lay in her power, by permitting the transportation of goods across her territory, only under restrictions which are practically prohibitory. Flattering promises are carefully combined with threats in order to promote her designs, and the emissaries of Russia are abundant in Persia, and even in Northern India, where their mission is to educate a public sentiment by constantly instilling into the minds of the people false ideas of the magnificence and generosity of Russia. These men are not Russians, for they would attract attention and arouse public apprehension, but they are Asiatics, who are kept at work by Russian gold, making lavish promises of Muscovite benevolence when northern barbarism shall succeed English civilization.

While engaged in thus duping the Asiatic tribes, she is pushing her railway as rapidly as possible toward India, and preparing for war on a greater scale than ever before in her history.

The record of her political policy proves that she will fasten her iron hand upon the vitals of a nation, and crush out, as far as possible, every effort toward progress, until the crippled empire falls into her fatal embrace. Persia has little hope of escaping the Russian policy of oppression and absorption, unless either English or German troops are allied with her native forces against the common foe. There is no longer, therefore, a hope that Persian literature may be revived, and the intellectual resources of the empire again developed, unless the civilized nations of Europe come to her rescue. The yoke of Mohammedan rule must be broken, and the tyranny of the northern barbarian removed, before the Persian mind and heart can be stimulated to intellectual and moral activity.

INDEX.

A.

Abbas, Shah, 335.
Accad, 1, 2, 3, 4, 33, 51.
Accadian, 66.
Accadian Tongue, 6, 31, 55.
Achæmenes, n 46.
Achæmenian, 44, 46, 48.
Achæmenidæ, 50.
Adarbad, 114.
Adonis, 68, 77.
Adonis Phrygian, 42.
Afrasiyab, the Tartar Chief, 244, 245, 247.
Age, Babylonian, 7.
Agathokles, 10.
Agni, 66, 107.
Ahasuerus, 49.
Ahriman, 48, 54, 99, 106, 129.
Ahura Mazda, 86, 94, 99, 108, 128, 161.
Akbar, Shah, 334, 335.
Akhuni, 59.
Alborz, Mount, 91, 98, 103,
Alexander, 13, 14, 20, 21, 52, 112. 113, 406 ; book of, 333.
Allah-il-Allah, 23.
Al-Fateh, 333.
Almokaffa, 190.
Alp Arslan, 27.
Amicable Instruction, 189, 203.
Anâhid, 69.
Anat, 56.
Anderson, n 96.
Angra Mainyu, 127, 129.
Annatu, 70.
Antelope and Crow, 189, 205.
Anthon, 76.
Anu, 56, 69, 70.

Anwâri, 284.
Anwâr-i-Suhali, 189, 215 ; history of, 190 ; preface of, 192.
Apaosha, 101, 105.
Aphrodite, 76.
Apis Egyptian, 87.
Arabs, 166, 176, 183, 188.
Arabia, 7, 46, 48, 166.
Arabian Conquest, 1, 22, 25.
Arabian Nights, 28.
Arbela, 40,
Architecture of Persepolis, 18.
Ardvi Sura Anâhita, 93, 94.
Arjasp, 272 ; defeated by Isfendiyâr, 276.
Armenia, 15, 48, 69.
Arrianus, n 36.
Art, Asiatic, 17.
Art, Greek, 5.
Art, Persian, 1, 16, 17, 18.
Artaxerxes, 13, 30, 44, 49, 50.
Aryan, 23.
Arzang, the Demon Chief, 259.
Asia, 1, 8, 23, 39, 48.
Ashtaroth, 8, n 10, n 54, 67, 68, 77, 108.
Assur, 53, 58, 59.
Assur-banipal, 6, 36, n 37, 55, 69.
Assyria, 6, 15, 33, 34, 35, 39, 46, 48.
Assyriologists, 34.
Astarte, n 10, 68.
Asura, 404.
Asteria, 68, 70.
Atar, 86, 100.
Augustus, 7.
Aulâd, 252 ; capture of, 257.

Avesta, 23, 54, 104, 107, 114, 115, 116, 404.

B.

Baal, 8, 53, 66, 76, 107, 108.
Baal Moloch, 10.
Babylon, 1, 6, 7, 10, 17 ; fall of, 30, 36, 39, 41, 43.
Babylonia, 3, 6, 15, 33, 55, 61; North, 3, 40, 65.
Babylonians, 9, 41.
Bâhram Gor, 214.
Bagdad, 311, 321, 407.
Balder, 77.
Bardes, 47.
Bâzindah, 195 ; misfortunes of, 198 ; return of, 201.
Beer, 44.
Bees and their Habits, 189, 193.
Behistun Inscriptions, 17, 30, 45, 114.
Behistun Rock, n 20.
Bel, 10, 36, 40, 42, 52.
Bel Merodach, 56, 61, 62.
Bellona, 69.
Belshazzar, 35, 40, 42, 43.
Benfey, 44.
Berosus, 69.
Beth-anath, 56.
Bi-frost, (Rainbow Bridge), 103.
Birds, Mythical, 86, 95.
Bird, My, 321, 329.
Birs, Nimrud, 37.
Blackstone, Sir Wm., 156.
Blind Man and his Whip, 189, 201.
Bokhâra, 309, 323, 407.
Bombay, 161.
Bores, 309, 320.
Boscawen, W. St. Chad, 40, n 43.
Bosphorus, 13.
Bournouf, 31, 44, 116.
Brâhman and Ichneumon, 208.
Brockhaus, 116.
Buddha, 227.
Budge, E. A., n 5, n 37.
Bundehesh, 112.
Bustân, 25, 225, 309 ; extracts from, 313.

C.

Calligraphy, 19, 335,
Cambyses, 44, 45, 87.
Canaan, 63.
Canopus, lights of, 190.
Captives, The, 383.
Capua, John of, 190.
Capture, the, 351, 352, 362.
Cappadocia, 48, 69.
Carthage, 48.
Carthaginians, 10.
Caucasus, 7.
Cerberus, 102.
Chaldea, 4, 64, 65, 103.
Chaos, wife of Hea, 59, 60.
Chemosh, 53, 60, 63, 64, 65, 108.
Chinvat Bridge, 86, 103, 141, 153, 157, 158.
Chips from a German Workshop, n 109, n 126.
Christians persecuted, 104, 121.
Christianity, 125, 167.
Citagriva, 204.
Circe, 74,
Commentary, 127, 140.
Comrades, the two, 338, 340.
Conquest, Mohammedan, 165.
Constellations, King of, 67.
Coptic Girl, 174, 184, 185.
Creation, legend of, 54.
Cuneiform inscriptions, 3, 6, 30.
Curtius, n 36, n 113.
Cutha, 54, 61.
Cyprus, 6,
Cyrus, 12, 15, 20, 28, 30, 40, 44, 47, 52, 118 ; decree of, 20.

D.

Dagon, 63.
Daniel, n 36, 40, 41.
Damascus, 311.
Darius, 9, 13, 20, 29, 45, 47, 49, 50, 52 ; and his Horsekeeper, 309, 316.
Darmesteter, Prof., 20, n 110, n 150, n 156.
Dastur, 125.
Datilla, River of Death, 107.
Dead, Disposition of, 146, 153.
Delos, 68.
Devas, 105.

Demon, White, 248, 252, 257, 260 ; slain, 260.
Desert, the, 351, 353.
Diana, 75, 108.
Dihkans, 22.
Diodorus, 5, n 113.
Diocletian, 114.
Domitian, 50.
Dogs, importance of, 147, 152, 153, 156 ; of Yama, 153.
Druj, 152.
Dungi, 3.
Duza, 42.
Dynasty, Achæmenian, 25; Gaznevides, 24, 25; Sassanian, 20, 21, 22.

E.

Eastwick, Prof., xiii, 191.
Ecbatana, 20, n 43.
Ecclesiastes, book of, 310.
Egebi, 9.
Egypt, 6, 7, 15, 39, 46, 48, 49, 61.
Elam, 7, 11, 69.
Elamites, 3.
Elephant and Jackal, 189, 209.
England, 16, 411.
Epic, Persian, 24, 25, 214.
Ephesus, 76, 108.
Ephesians, 76.
Eridu, 56, 67.
Esar-haddon, 9, n 37.
Euphrates, 3, 5, 16, 35, 37.
Evil Spirits, seven, 56, 57.
Exiles, the, 351.
Exodus, 3.

F.

Features, physical, 1, 15.
Fimbul Eddic, 130.
Fire god, 56, 57, 66, 107, 124.
Fire, sacred, 100, 124, 154, 155.
Fire worshippers, 124.
Firdusi, 22, 25, 26, 118.
Firdusi, life of, 216; invective of, 214, 219; death of, 214, 223.
Flattery, wiles of, 206, 209, 210, 212.
Flood, 33.
Formulas, 140.
Fravishas, 140, 160.

France, 16.
Frey, 77.
Freyja, 76.
Fugitives, the, 365.

G.

Ganges, 92, 96, 107.
Garuda, 96.
Garden scene, 365, 377, 381.
Gâthas, 20, 111, 113, 119, 127, 130, 144.
Gâtha, Last, 135.
Gaznevides, dynasty of, 24, 25.
Genesis, 33.
Genghis Khân, 309, 323.
Gold, chain of, 333.
Gobyras, 43.
Greece, 4, 17, 27, 75.
Griffin of Chivalry, 96.
Grotofend, 31, 44.
Gulf, Persian, 3, 15, 51.
Gulistân, 25, 309; stories from. 317.
Gushtasp, 272, 277.
Gyöll, 93, 107.

H.

Hades, 78; queen of, 60.
Hâfiz, 26, 321, 323, 331, 337; songs of, 313, 326, 327.
Halicarnassus, 49.
Haoma. 142.
Hara Berezaita, 93, 99, 107, 158.
Haug, Dr., 116.
Hea, 53, 59, 60, 82,
Hea-bani, 53, 60, 61.
Heaven, 165, 180.
Hecate, 70, 74, 75.
Helbon, 14.
Hel, 77.
Hell, 165, 181.
Herodotus, 20, n 36, 45, n 87, 129.
Hercules, 63.
Hermöd, 77.
Hezekiah, King, 35.
Higrah, the, 165, 172.
Hindus, 9, 58, 65, 92, 95 ; mythology of, 89. 104.
Hincks, Dr., 32.
Hitopadesa, 22, 189, 191. 310 ; gems from, 189, 210.

Holtzman, 44.
Homer, 225; of Iran, 215.
Hyde, Dr., 118.

I.

Iliad, 97.
Ifing, 93.
Im, 53, 57; 66.
Incantations, 53, 65.
India, 4, 6, 15, 27, 48, 78.
India House, 62.
Indra, 66, 87, 95, 99, 404.
Indus, 15.
Inscriptions of Artaxerxes, 30, 49.
Inscriptions, Bavian, 36; Cunei-form, 3, 30; Darius, 17, 30, 45, 114; Western Asia, n 34, n 41. n 67; of Nebuchadnezzar, 30, 38; of Xerxes, 30, 49.
Invasion, Turānian, 228, 245.
Ionians, 48.
Irān, 1, 11, 52; laws of, 12.
Irānian romance, 27.
Isaiah, 21.
Isfendiyār, 228, 272, 274; conflict with Rustem, 276; death of, 272, 282.
Israel, prophets of, 39.
Israelites, 35.
Ishtar, 10, 42, 53, 60, 68, 69, 74, 75; of Arbela, 53, 69; of Erech, 53, 70; descent of, 53, 78.
Ishtar and Izdubar, 53, 71.
Isis, 95.
Ithaca, 74.
Iyar, month of, 50.
Ixion, wheel of, 77.

J.

Jalal-uddin Rumi, 309, 310, 331.
Jāmi, 26, 321, 330, 332; works of, 321, 332, 333 ; grave of, 332.
Jehān, Shāh, 332.
Jericho, 38.
Jeremiah, n 11, 39, n 41, n 62.
Jerusalem, 38, 42; siege of, 35.
Joel, Rabbi. 190.
Jones, Sir Wm., 191.
Joshua, book of, 56.

K.

Kaßbah, 173, 175, 184.
Kabul, 234, 245.
Kai-kaus, 248, 257, 258.
Karsipta (mythical bird), 97, 120, 151.
Khorassān, 216, 285, 331.
Kindness to the unworthy, 309, 314.
Kine, soul of, 141.
Kine, wail of, 127, 131.
Kings, Achæmenian, 20.
Kings, Assyrian, 5, 36, 58, 88.
Kings, book of, 67.
Kings, Babylonian, 88; of Judah; n 62; literary, 321; Moslem, 27; Persian, 35, 43, 54, 78; Saman-ian, 214; Sassanian, 23, 24, 189, 336.
Korān, 19, 23, 103, 165; arrange-ment of, 168; author of, 165, 168; extracts from, 180, 182, 183; literary style of, 165, 188; teaching of, 165, 178, 179, 185.
Krishna, 67.

L.

Lady of battles, 69 ; of kingdoms, 10, 41 ; of Tiggaba City, 80.
Laili, description of, 287; wed-ding of, 284, 296, 297; deliver-ance of, 299; death of, 304; and Majnun, 233, 284, 286.
Land, fairest, 310.
Lassen, 31, 44.
Layard, 31.
Law, Mosaic, 64, n 156.
Leopard, torn by dogs, 73, 75.
Leviticus, n 82.
Literature, Assyrian, 76; Baylo-nian, 4, 6; early, 1, 19; mod-ern Persian, 1, 24; of Nineveh, 1, 5; Persian, 1, 28, 54, 409; Oriental, 17.
Loftus, 44, 50.
Loki, 66.
Lydia, 6, 7, 15.

M.

Mahā-bhārata, 90, 106, 225, 334.
Majnun, 284, 286; temptation of,

302; victory of, 303; death of, 306.

Manuscripts, 1, 19, 35, 109, 115.

Manuscripts, Persian, 19, 20, 224, 331, 339.

Manuscript, Yasna, xvii, 117.

Marathon, 52, 121.

Marchesvan, month of, n 43.

Mardtmann, 44.

Marriage song, 127, 135.

Mazdeism, 118, 121, 129.

Mazinderân, 248, 251, 261.

Medea, 74.

Medes, 20, 40, n 43.

Media, 7, 11, 15, 48, 49.

Medians, 12, 47.

Meher and Mushteri, 338.

Merodach, 8, n 36, 53, 61.

Mesapotamia, 30.

Metamorphoses, Ovid's, n 75, 76.

Mir Amar, 19.

Moabite stone, 64.

Mobeds, 20.

Mohammed, 165; birth of, 168; family of, 168, 169, 171, 175, 184; death of, 165, 175.

Mohammedanism, see Koran.

Molech, 8, 10, 63, 64, 108.

Mountains, Alborz, 91, 103, 229; Ausindom, 28; Elvend, 18, 44, 49; Median, 13; Meru, 90, 107; mother of, 91; mythical, 86, 88; Nida, 90, 107; Nubian, 7; Oaf, 90, 180, 322; twin, 89; world, 107.

Müller, Prof. F. Max, xiii, 109, 117, 191.

Museum, British, n 5, 33, 35, 37, 49, 67, n 84.

Muhteshim, 214, 221.

Mythology, Asiatic, 108; Assyrian, 53, 55, 61, 65, 76; Chaldean, 54, 107; early, 1, 53; Greek, 5, 54, 63, 66, 68, 70, 75, 77; Hindu, 99, 128; Indo-European, 105; of Mazdeism, 105; Norse, 66, 76, 77, 90, 96, 103; Persian, 53, 54, 93, 98, 403; of tablets, 53.

N.

Nabonidas, 40, 41.

Nadir Shâh, 336.

Nawâzindah, 195.

Naram Sin, 33.

Nebo, 8, 36, 40, 52, 53, 62, 69.

Nebuchadnezzar, 7, 8, 9, 31, 36, 40, 62.

Neptune, 59, 63, 227.

Nergal, 53, 61.

Nile, 3, 92.

Nineveh, 5, 6, 14, 51, 54, 60, 76; arts of, 17, 18.

Ninip, 53, 60, 63.

Nin-ci-gal, 53, 60, 79, 82, 83.

Nimrod, n 2, 43.

Nisan, month of, 40.

Nizâmi, 25, 285, 307, 331.

Norris, 44, 45.

Noufal, 292.

Nushirvan, 22, 190.

O.

Odin, 77.

Odyssey, 74.

Olympus, 107, 108.

Olympians, 77.

Omar, 22, 216.

Omar Khayyâm, 215.

Oppert, Dr., 31, 32, 44, 49, 61, 66, 68, 114.

Oppression, priestly, 403, 410.

Ormazd, 12, 48, 106, 112, 121, 161; symbol of, 17.

Osirus, 77.

Ovid, 74.

Outline, Historic, 1.

P.

Pacorus, 50, 51.

Pahlavi, 22, 109, 112, 117.

Palestine, 7, 39.

Pancatantra, 22, 189.

Pârsis Early, 109, 121.

Pârsis Modern, 109, 123, 161; teachings of, 146, 161; laws of, 146; anglicized, 163.

Pearl, the, 309, 313,

Periods, Seven, 214.

Period, First, 214; second, 284; third, 309; fourth, 321; fifth,

321, 330; sixth, 321, 334; seventh, 321, 335; later, 321.
Persia, 1, 46, 49; government of, 14; modern, 15, 24; physical features of, 1, 15, 87.
Persian corruption, 14; magnificence, 14; romance, 1, 27, 338; scholars, 27, 191, 216, 284, 309, 323, 330, 334; texts, 44, 45.
Persians, 12, 14, 40, 50.
Persepolis, 13, 18, 20, 80, 44, 47, 49, 113, 340.
Pigeons, the two, 189, 195.
Pigeons and the Rat, 189, 204.
Pir-i-sebz, 321, 325.
Pinches, Theo. G., xiii, n 3.
Pleiades Persian, 332.
Pliny, n 36, n 69.
Pluto, 60, 102.
Polygamy, 165, 184.
Prophets, Hebrew, 11, 41, 163.
Proserpine, 60, 77.
Prosperity, dangers of, 309, 319.
Proverbs, Book of, 310.
Punishment, 146, 156.
Purification, laws of, 146, 154.
Pyramus and Thisbe, 76.

Q.

Qaf Mount, 90, 180, 332.
Queen, the, 338, 345.
Quaris, 170, 172.

R.

Rakush, 226, 252, 278.
Rāmayāna, 96, 225, 334.
Rassam, 31.
Rask, Dr., 116, 117.
Rawlinson, Sir Henry, 32, n 35, 44.
Records of the Past, n 34, n 38, n 84.
Rivers, mythical, 86, 91.
Rig Veda, 114.
Rule, priestly, 403, 408.
Rudabeh, 228, 234, 243, 244.
Russian influence, 16, 403, 410.
Rustem, birth of, 244; labors of, 226, 252, 254, 259; marriage of, 252, 262; conflict with Is-

fendiyār, 276; battle with his son, 269; death of, 283.

S.

Sacred Books of the East, n 20, n 115, n 150, n 156.
Sa'di, 25, 286, 311, 331; works of, 309; death of, 312.
Sag-did, 152, 153.
Samanians, dynasty of, 24.
Samarcānd, 309, 323, 371, 373, 407.
Sam Suwār, 228, 261, 279.
Sardanapalus, 6.
Sargon, 8, 33, 51, 60.
Sayce, Prof. A. H. xiii, 2, n 4, n 9, n 10, 31, n 34, 55, 64, n 95.
Sea, Ægean, 6, 107; Arabian, 15; Caspian, 15.
Sennacherib, 31, 34, 35, 36, n 37.
Serpent King, 235, 241.
Seven Eras, 214.
Shapur, 114, 121, 397, 400.
Shāh Mahmud, 216, 218, 222.
Shāh Nāmah, 19, 22, 25, 214, 228; extracts from, 228, 232, 234, 241, 287.
Shinar, 2, 4.
Shirāz, 11, 14, 311, 321, 326.
Sidon, 67, 108.
Silver, value of, n 9.
Silence the Safety of Ignorance, 309, 315.
Silence, towers of, 155.
Simurgh, 91, 200, 279, 322; nest of, 98, 228, 229.
Sin, the Moon God, 53, 60, 65, 76.
Siva, 67, 161.
Sleipner, 77, 227.
Society, Royal Asiatic, 32, 45.
Sohrab, 252, 266, 269.
Spiegel, 44, 110, 116, 117.
Spenta Armaita, n 150, 153, 155.
Storm Spirits, Seven, 56.
Styx, 107.
Sumer, 1, 2, 3.
Suez, 44, 49.
Susa, 44, 49, 50, 69.

T.

Tablets, 1, 3, 30, 53; historic, 5, 30, 33; Persian, 50.

Talbot Fox, 31, 32, 56, n 84.

Tamineh (wife of Rustem), 266; death of, 271.

Tammuz (the sun god), 42, 53, 63, 67, 68, 108; month of, 42, 43.

Tantalus, 77.

Tazieh, the (Persian Drama), n 410.

Tiamat, 55, 56.

Tigris, 5, 16, 40.

Tiglath-Pileser, 32, n 36, 67.

Timur, 322, 330, 332, 334.

Tistrya (storm god), 98, 100, 102.

Transactions Vic. Institute, n 87, n 40, n 43.

Tukulti-Ninip, n 36.

Tyre, 2, 38, 66.

U.

Ur of the Chaldees, 3, 40.

Ugbaru, n 43.

Ulysses, 74, 75.

V.

Valhal, 90.

Var or Vara of Yima, 97, 146, 147, 150, 151.

Vārengana (the raven), 97.

Varuna, 99, 128.

Vedas, 58, 110.

Vedic deities, 25.

Vedfolner (hawk), 96.

Vendidad, 95, 111, 126, 146, 151, 159.

Venus, 69, 76; Babylonian, 87.

Vishnu, 92, 96, 161.

Visparad, 111, 146, 158.

Vouru Kasha, 94, 95.

Vulcan, 63.

W.

Water, sacred, 154.

Water Dog, 157.

Westergaard, 44, 110, 116.

Williams, Sir M. Monier, xiii, 161, n 164.

Women, penalties upon, n 157.

Women, unprincipled, 123.

Wrestler, the Wise, 309, 317.

X.

Xerxes, 44, 52; inscriptions of, 30, 49.

Y.

Yasna, 111, 126, 127, 137, 142; concluding, 127, 144.

Yasts, 112, 119, 127, 142.

Yasna Haptang-haita, 127, 141.

Yast Sraosha, 127, 142.

Yazatas or Angels, 100, 112.

Yemen, 2, 23.

Yezdejird, 22, 215, 216, 225.

Ygdrasil, 96.

Yima, 86, 97, 98, 102, 148; Vara of, 146, 147, 150, 151.

Yusuf and Zulaikha, 26, 333.

Z.

Zal (the white-haired child), 18, 228, 234, 245, 261; banishment of, 229; sheltered in Simurgh's nest, 230; restoration of, 233.

Zedekiah, king, 38.

Zend, 110, 117.

Zend Avesta, 20, 109, 111; age of, 100, 113; divisions of, 109, 111; derivation and language of, 109; extracts from, 135, 140, 142, 148, 152, 159; teaching of, 127, 146.

Zoroaster, or Zarathustra, 100, 112, 118, 127, 141, 144, 148; life of, 118.

Zoroastrianism, 124, 162.

Zoroastrian Period, 25.

Zyd, vision of, 284, 306.

www.ingramcontent.com/pod-product-compliance
Lightning Source LLC
Chambersburg PA
CBHW030953110726
47900CB00004B/1249